CHANGING LANES

A CREEKWOOD NOVEL

A. MARIE

Published by Booktickets by AM

Editing: Sarah Plocher, All Encompassing Books
Proofreading: Julie Deaton, JD Proofs
Cover Design: Murphy Rae
Cover Photography: RplusMphoto.com
Cover Model: Quinn Biddle
Formatting: Champagne Book Design

PLAYLIST

Music plays a big role in my writing. You can find the full playlist link as well as bonus material and inspiration boards on my website at amarieauthor.com

Can You Hold Me—NF, Britt Nicole

Summer Days—Martin Garrix, Macklemore, Fall Out Boy

CPR—Summer Walker

Home—Machine Gun Kelly, X Ambassadors, Bebe Rexha

Woman—Kesha, The Dap-Kings Horns

Man or a Monster—Sam Tinnesz, Zayde Wølf

Unholy—Miley Cyrus

S.L.U.T.—Bea Miller

Play Nice—Jules LeBlanc

Girls Need Love—Summer Walker

Sick and Tired—iann dior, Machine Gun Kelly, Travis Barker

Wake Up—NF

Cruel—Glowie

Savior—Beth Crowley

Even If It Hurts—Clover the Girl

Hate Myself—NF

Under Water—NC Grey

Ocean Eyes—Billie Eilish, blackbear

Doomed—Rhys

Expectations—Lauren Jauregui

All I Think About Is You—Ansel Elgort

Home Alone—Ansel Elgort

Nightlight—ILLENIUM, Annika Wells

Tomboy—Destiny Rogers

Hooked—Why Don't We

Ride—Lolo Zouaï

Main Attraction—Jeremy Renner

Tired Of You—Foo Fighters

Lonely—Noah Cyrus

Woman Like Me—Little Mix, Nicki Minaj

Trampoline—SHAED, ZAYN

Wrecking Ball—Jasmine Thompson

Pony—Julian Perretta, Lil Baby

Goodbyes—Post Malone, Young Thug

Surrender—Natalie Taylor

For the ones who bleed punchlines and smile the bandages to cover them.

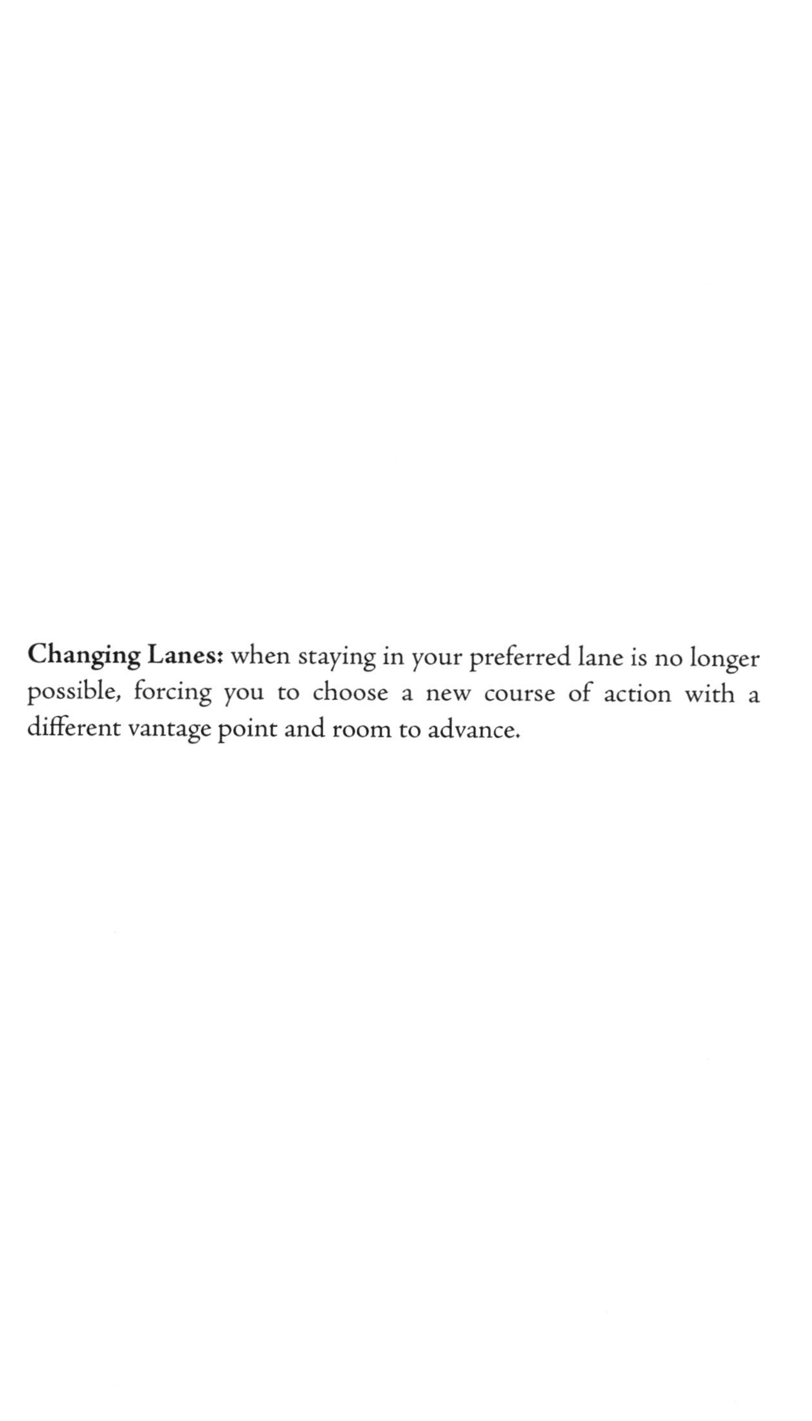

Changing Lanes: when staying in your preferred lane is no longer possible, forcing you to choose a new course of action with a different vantage point and room to advance.

PROLOGUE

Beckett

10 years old

"Mom!" I yell, bursting through our front door then freeze, listening.

My mom's always here when I get home from school. Lately though, she's been in her room, talking quietly on the phone, and when I try to get close enough to hear, she's usually laughing. And not the way she laughs with me and Dad either. It's deeper. Like she means it.

Like it's a secret.

"Mom? Where are you?"

Usually when she hears my voice, or the house creak under my big feet, she rushes to hang up, kinda like when I'm doing something bad and don't want my parents to see. But, why would she hide something from me? Why can't I know who she's talking to? I asked Dad once if it was him but he didn't answer me. He just got really quiet like he was trying to figure out a hard math problem or something. I understand though, I don't like math either.

I slow my steps, trying not to be too noisy, but her bedroom door is wide open and she's not on the bed this time. I check the bathroom too, just to be sure, but she's not there.

That's weird.

Walking back through the kitchen, I see a piece of paper on the counter and frown, looking around. My mom's never left me home alone before. She wouldn't do that.

I grab it, thinking it's just a note to say she's out back maybe. The weather is starting to cool off finally and she hates the hot summers here. My school even made us stay inside for recess all last week because it was over a hundred degrees every day.

As soon as I get to the bottom of the paper I can barely see anymore. There's too much water in my eyes. Reading it again, my stomach starts to hurt until I'm gripping it, wishing the pain would go away.

The letter drops from my hand and I let go of my stomach to wipe at my wet face. The tears keep falling even though I don't want them to. Boys at my school, boys I don't even like playing with, say it's weak to cry. That you're a baby if you do. But I can't help it, it hurts. Everywhere.

Whenever I get hurt, my mom is always here for me though. I'm so tall, it makes me clumsy, clumsier than most of the kids I know, so I get hurt a lot. Whether I need ice packs, bandages, medicine, or even just kisses, my mom's always here. This won't be any different. If I'm hurt bad enough, she'll have to help me.

So, even though I don't want to think about what I just read, I focus on it, repeating her words in my head, until my stomach aches so bad I throw up. I puke until the vomit turns pink with blood. I'm not scared of the color though. I'm sure this will do the trick. This will get her back. She would never ignore me when I'm sick, especially not for someone that's not even her family.

"I need you," I repeat it out loud, just in case she walks in.

"Come back, Mom." Over and over, until my lips grow numb and chapped, I beg her to come home. "Please."

I try to keep my eyes open—I really don't want to miss her—but the hard floor under my head is now warm from my body being on it for so long, and they stay closed longer every time I blink. With the stinky puke by my head starting to dry, I can almost pretend like it's not there. Like none of this is real.

Isn't she going to come home? To take care of me?

With my eyes fully shut, my mouth still mumbles out any promises I can. I promise to try harder at school even though I don't fit in there. They just laugh at me for being so big and awkward. Like I can't do anything right. I promise to clean my room more since she's always complaining about how messy I am. I promise I'll try not to grow as much so she doesn't have to keep buying me new clothes all the time. I promise to find something to keep me busy instead of bothering her at home every day. I'll do anything to see her again.

Just as my body starts to go all fuzzy, a door slamming shut startles me and I crack my puffy eyes open to see someone walking closer. Footsteps pound across the floor, then she's dropping beside me.

She's here.

I smile, flinching when my dry lips crack. I knew she'd come back for me.

Except when I lift my head, it's not my mom's worried eyes that are almost identical in color to mine I find. It's my dad's bloodshot ones.

No.

CHAPTER 1

Beckett

My face mashed to my pillow, I crack an eye, finding a hot pink bra next to me.

Thank fuck nobody's actually in it.

I shoot my head off the bed, glancing around my room, making sure there aren't any stowaways. Coming up empty—like usual—I close my eyes again and drop back down, hoping to get some more sleep.

Flipped onto my back, I throw an arm over my face, blocking out the faint morning sunlight streaming through my blinds.

Last night was epic. Our last hurrah with our boy Coty before the new roommate moves into his old room.

Before she comes in and ruins everything.

I still don't understand why Marc agreed to let that chick live with us. Having Angela, our first roommate's girlfriend, living in the apartment directly across the hall was close enough. Coty usually kept her pretty busy though, like rabbit-type busy, that I never had to worry. Well, except for that one time.

Luckily, Angie didn't make a big deal of it but I'll never forget the look on her face—confusion followed by understanding. At least it didn't hold any pity. Having her own demons, she knows it's useless feeling sorry for shit that's out of our hands. Shit our parents did to us.

She'd need to be there to have done something to you.

My eyes pop open and I run my hand down my stomach, releasing a puff of breath before climbing out of bed.

Not today, Satan.

Today's already its own kind of hell without bringing thoughts of her into the mix. I'll save that for a special kind of day—like the week after never.

After slipping on my favorite pair of shorts, I scoop up the abandoned bra and head out to the kitchen, pulling the busty garment through my fingers. Whoever had to do last night's walk of shame without her girls properly supported must've made for one hell of a scene. I think she was blonde. Maybe. I don't know.

A pink bra though, that must've been what caught my eye in the first place. Unfortunately, it ended there too, judging from the item still being in my hands with absolutely no memory whatsoever of the girl who wore it. I can't help but snort at the irony.

"Is this normal?"

I jerk at the feminine voice slicing through the still apartment, my gaze colliding with hers. Our new roommate. Paige.

Marc, my other roommate and best friend—before this whole lapse in judgment—speaks up from the breakfast bar, saying, "He usually only wears neutrals. He must be trying out a new look though."

I pin him with a scowl. *What?*

When his eyes narrow on my hands, my grip tightens on the bra.

"This color's all wrong on me," I half-joke. I wear pink. Not in bra form, obviously, but pink is badass and I have several shirts to prove it.

If this girl sticks around long enough, she'll see them.

She'll see everything.

A smirk pulled tight at my lips, I lift the stupid thing and say, "maybe it'll look better on you," then toss the bra across the room to her. She makes no move to catch it and the pink monstrosity ends up hitting her chest before falling to the floor with a thump.

Okay then.

Without so much as blinking, she cocks an eyebrow, sending a warm shot of *something* straight to my groin.

Ignoring her and the unwelcome heat below my waist, I yank

the fridge open and, seeing we're out of the coffee concentrate Angela keeps us stocked with, I grab the juice. With my back still to the room, I adjust myself through my mesh shorts before turning around and unscrewing the cap in silence. I tip the bottle to my lips, taking big gulps, never breaking eye contact with her.

Marc mutters "dick" under his breath but I ignore him, too. I never wanted her as a roommate. He made that dumbass decision alone. He can welcome her alone, too.

She finally cuts the connection but keeps her bright green eyes on me as they trail the rest of my body. I slow my swallows, taking her in as well. Skin-tight, black jeans cling to seriously long legs tucked into heavy combat-looking boots, a black V-neck tee with a white wing design on both sides hang loosely off a toned body—it must be tight to handle a motorcycle of her own—and dark, wavy hair with plum coloring frames a strikingly beautiful face. One that lures you in only to spit you back out begging for more. Her entire persona screams biker.

And *fuck me*.

Why does she have to live just past my bedroom door? Why couldn't we have had some fun together for one night before I forgot all about her like pink bra girl?

"Beige was it?" I poke.

Her eyes thin, coming back up to touch on my juice-coated lips before darting over to Marc, and I miss them immediately. I don't care if she's picking me apart like a lion consuming its last meal, I want her focused on me and only me. I don't know why, but I do.

"Cute. Beige and boring, that's me," she responds easily.

When she drags her gaze back to mine, there's a defiance in it that gets my blood pumping.

"And you're Beck, right? Is that short for something?"

"There's nothing short about me." *Duh.*

When the resulting silence stretches a beat too long, Marc supplies, "Beckett," for her.

I stand mesmerized as long, yet somehow still delicate, hands run down her shirt, smoothing the material.

"You remind me of a dog I had once."

"Was his name Beckett too?"

Meeting my stare head-on, she says, "No, he was just an asshole."

Cue a jaw drop accompanied by a cartoon-sized tongue rolling across the floor, ending at Paige's boot-covered feet. Honestly, I don't know if I should be offended or impressed. One thing's for sure though, what our new roommate lacks in a dick more than makes up for with a huge set of balls.

She nudges the forgotten bra at her feet. "Look, I'm sure it's hard-"

Not yet, but it's definitely getting there the more attitude she fires off.

"-having me here as your roommate when you'd prefer another guy but it really shouldn't be an issue. I work graveyard, so you shouldn't even notice me."

Too late, girl. Too fucking late.

"Thanks for giving me the opportunity."

Her eyes stay locked on my boy's as I narrow mine. "Why do you want to live with us anyway? The apartment across the hall should be available in the next couple weeks-"

"I couldn't wait that long," she says, cutting me off and pinning me with a no-bullshit look.

What's her deal? It doesn't make any sense why she'd rush to move in with the two of us when she could hold off and live by herself. Hell, Angie did it right up until Coty stole her away to the brand new house he had built for them.

She raises her chin and I grip the empty bottle in my hold.

"I've got plenty of experience living with the opposite sex, this is nothing new. I just need to save money and this was the soonest I could get in somewhere that didn't break the bank."

Although her emerald eyes didn't so much as flinch, the rest of her body stiffened at the end, giving her away.

Once upon a time another girl said something very similar but she was running. Always running.

Paige is hiding something.

Where I was mildly curious before, I'm all out suspicious now. And what the fuck does that mean she has plenty of experience living with men? Is she a bed hopper or some shit, always bouncing between different dudes' beds?

I shoot Marc a *what the hell?* gesture and he just shrugs. Of fucking course he shrugs. This guy, the one who's suspicious of a container of sour cream, chooses now to ignore the warning bells hanging over the girl's head as they blast at near-deafening levels. Unbelievable.

Unless.

Unless he's into her.

They have been sharing cryptic looks this entire time as if I'm not standing here, too. And he was quick to pick her instead of taking the time to interview other applicants first.

I eye him a little longer.

He hasn't laid a claim to Paige but that's not surprising. Dude's private as hell. He's like a damn onion with all his hidden layers.

Well, whatever's happening between these two will come to light at some point. Even if I'm the one lifting the goddamn cover, it'll come out. Creekwood isn't that big and secrets don't stay hidden for long around here. Our old neighbor girl found that out the hard way.

Dropping the juice bottle in recycling, I turn for the bathroom, pausing when she speaks again.

"It's Paige, by the way. But you knew that."

When I spin around, she's already gone, out the front door.

Marc's on me the next second. "Dude, what the fuck was that? She lives here now. Could you at least make an effort at being civil when she's around?"

"Oh, that's rich. You want me to get her a fruit basket while I'm at it, Mr. Welcoming Committee?"

He waves me off, moving to trail after her.

"I didn't even agree to her moving in, bro. I still think we should cancel the check and get someone else."

He stops short. "She didn't write a fucking check. What year do you think it is? She gave me cash."

"Then give it back." Neither of us are hurting for money and she can use it on another unit. Preferably away from Creekwood.

"She has a clean record, paid in full for the first month already, and rides. What more are you looking for? A dick? Too bad. Angela was basically living here for the past year and last I checked they both have the same parts."

Despite his shitty tone, I can't help but jerk my head, asking, "You checked?"

His face splits into a grin, shaking his head. "Coty would kill me."

We share a laugh but I don't miss the way he only acknowledged Angie in that statement, which leaves his interest in Paige a mystery still. A mystery I find very interesting—and not in a good way either.

I scrub my hands down my face. "I'll try, man, but you put me in a bad spot here."

My eyebrows lift with meaning and he simply nods, saying, "it'll be a'ight," before disappearing outside.

Worst famous last words ever.

CHAPTER 2

Paige

"HEY. HOW'S IT LOOKING IN THERE? ANY different from the last time you checked?" Cynthia asks from the nurses' station.

"Actually, no." I laugh, grabbing the chart at the top of the pile.

Cynthia and I completed the same nursing course fresh out of high school and we both got hired on fulltime here at Sunbrook Senior Living during our clinical rotation. We've been working together ever since and get along pretty well despite her taste in music. Seriously, techno just isn't for everyone. I get it. Working in an Alzheimer's care facility, we all need our outlets and raves are hers. The night shift hours alone can take a toll physically, not to mention the emotional strain that can happen as well.

"Is everything still set for tomorrow?" she asks.

"All the paperwork is completed and in with Rosie at this point, so everything should be good to go. I was thinking about coming in early to help out."

Cynthia's already shaking her head. "Remember, it's better to keep to the schedule. We have to create some sort of normalcy for the residents. All of them." She gives me an apologetic look. "I'm sure the day staff will do a great job."

"I know." I exhale loudly. "You're right."

We're not supposed to give any of the patients—or I'm sorry, 'residents' as management insists we call them—special treatment, even though every employee working here will admit to having favorites. We all do. It's hard not to. Working closely with others who depend on you to change their bedding, bathe them, sometimes even spoon feed them, it pulls at your heartstrings. It's natural to develop an affinity for those you care for. Whether they can remember you or not is irrelevant. They're still human beings and us human beings all want the same thing: to feel safe and loved.

Speaking of favorites, I flip open the chart to see how my main man Dennis is doing today. Dennis Gregory's been here longer than any of the other residents and he's got quite the reputation. When he's good, he's great. When he's struggling, we all do, too. He's one of the needier residents and has to be checked on often. According to the nurses on day shift, he can get aggressive but only occasionally and usually before I get here. Cynthia and I typically miss out on the sundowning phenomenon Alzheimer's patients can sometimes experience but we've definitely caught the aftereffects when showing up for our later shift. Dennis is what we call a waker, meaning he wakes frequently and wanders the halls looking for food, activities, even dates. Yep, Dennis is a regular Casanova even at eighty-two. I found him sweet talking a plant once and it's the only time I can honestly say I was jealous of a fern. He was probably a total player in his day.

From the notes jotted down in his chart, it looks like Dennis had a rough day already.

That makes two of us.

My mind flickers back to this morning at my new place, meeting the guys I'll be living with for the foreseeable future. One was nice, in a distant, unreadable kind of way, which only adds to his insane hotness. I can't wait to see him ride his bike—his custom red Ducati. Yeah, I checked it out. Bike first, man second. Always. A man's bike says a lot about him. Marc's Duc draws just enough attention for you to notice but not linger on. He likes to play under the radar, choosing when and where it's time to be seen. The maker of his own rules and the breaker of others'.

I bet he's a freak in the sheets. I wonder if I'll ever hear it living down the hall or if he handles his business in private. Time will tell, I guess.

The other was a complete shithead. Beckett's bike was showy

and obnoxious, just like him. A Ninja as colorful as his conquests, if the bra he was holding this morning is any indication. An absurdly handsome face that could make you fall to your knees in gratitude is wasted on someone as uptight as Beckett. A long, strong body that probably handles like my CBR—rough start with a smooth, easy finish. Too bad I'm not interested in either after his piss poor introduction today. A shame considering Marc described our roommate as having an over-the-top personality with a dirty sense of humor—a solid endorsement for a girl with more brothers than she knows what to do with—but all I've seen is a huge man-child throwing his weight around for shits and giggles. Unfortunately for him, I don't have an abundance of either these days. Avoidance, which shouldn't be too hard considering our opposite schedules, will work just fine with a character like Beckett.

"Have you seen Dennis yet?" I ask Cynthia whose eyes are lined with too much concern for my liking. It's been a long time since I've had a female caretaker and she comes nowhere near the original.

She shakes her head and, unable to say more, I leave to monitor the halls, triggering the sensored overhead lights as I go.

Rounding the corner, I spot movement in the cafeteria and push through the swinging door to find Dennis folding napkins in the dark. I flip the light switch and join him.

"Why, hello there. How's it going?"

Without looking up from the fabric, Dennis says, "Bend over and I'll show you."

I pause along the aisle, scanning him for anything he could use as a weapon. With a press of the talk button on my walkie-talkie, I let Cynthia know where we are before grabbing a handful of napkins of my own and taking a seat at the table opposite him. Distance and caution is always the best approach when one of the residents is in a mood. Not many, but some, can grow violent and with the notes in Dennis's chart already pointing toward aggression, I'm not taking any unnecessary risks.

"Dennis," I tsk firmly. "You couldn't sleep?"

My hands begin the familiar movements, folding, but my eyes stay trained on Dennis, ready to react should he try anything.

"Someone new is here," he spits in disgust.

My fingers still.

"Not yet. But you're right, someone new will be moving into room fourteen tomorrow. Is that okay with you? A new friend around here might be nice."

"She stole my goddamn magazine." His fingers freeze as he meets my eyes.

I shake my head, staying alert. "That's impossible. She's not even here yet. Do you want me to help you look for your magazine?"

There is no magazine. All the magazines are kept in the library and I've never seen Dennis bother with anything less than a full-length novel when he's in there. Late night reading is like a double-edged sword—it sounds relaxing until you fall into the right storyline preventing you from putting it down, no matter how tired you become—and Dennis is notorious for picking up a novel after waking in the middle of the night. But if it helps ease his mind, I'll walk around with him until he lets go of some of this hostility.

He picks up a perfectly folded napkin, shaking it at me. "Don't you tell me. I know she took it. Devil woman, she is. Coming in here with her thieving ways. I won't have it." With that, the cloth is lobbed directly at me, making me flinch back. Thankfully, it falls to the floor halfway to my table.

I've had enough of people throwing shit at me today. First that overgrown toddler and now this.

"Dennis, you cannot throw things at me. I'll have to report you to Rosie. I know you're upset but let's look at what you do have."

"I have nothing!" he bursts, his face red and sweaty. "She's going to take everything with her."

While it's not unheard of for some families to visit less and less due to the emotional toll it takes when their parent or spouse doesn't remember them, Dennis's wife died a few years back so he really doesn't have anyone anymore. There's always a possibility for a rare moment of lucidity and he may be having one now but as a memory flashback. It's hard to tell sometimes and you can't dismiss their feelings just because they won't remember come morning. Remaining positive and calm has always been my best technique and Dennis usually responds well to it. To me. That's why he's one of my favorites. I'm not sure what's setting him off tonight though.

"Hey, you have me. I'm here with you right now," I try to soothe.

He drops his eyes to the pile in front of him then resumes folding. So soft I almost miss it, he says, "She's going to steal you away and you don't even know it."

I focus on Dennis while he works, marveling at his steady hands folding the stiff fabric exactly the way the staff does it. This utterly useless skill has been engrained for retention but not his late wife's name. How can memories of your own family, the people you love most, be ripped from your clutches while meaningless tasks rest idle awaiting random use? The unfairness of Alzheimer's never ceases to piss me off.

My chest grows tight and I scoop up my abandoned pile before depositing it back to the bussing station.

"Would you like to go for a walk with me? Maybe you could help me find a cup of tea."

I wring my hands behind my back. A late-night stroll and a challenge—what man could refuse that? Hopefully not this one.

Dennis's hands still and I take a hesitant step back, unsure if his foul mood has passed or not.

"In this place? There's only one spot that comes to mind and lucky for you, I know just where to go."

Standing, he winks and reaches for my arm in a gentlemanly

gesture but I grab my radio, pretending to hear something. I shake my head at myself and we begin walking side-by-side toward his best kept secret, leaving this episode behind.

◆ ◆ ◆

"The lobby? Dennis, you sure know how to treat a girl," I say, smiling.

He blushes, fixing two mugs of hot water before I take over with the tea. Sleepy chamomile for him and two bags of tangy chai for me. I need all the help I can get and I don't drink coffee so doubling up will have to do.

After enjoying our drinks together, we sit for a while, silently gazing out the window at the moonlit back courtyard. He's much calmer and eventually lets me know he's ready for bed.

I escort Dennis to his room then make my rounds, leaving room fourteen for last.

Entering the room, I take it all in, not letting my bias sway me.

Sunbrook's a nice place with a well-stocked library, arts and crafts room, meticulously maintained grounds, and even weekly events like Bingo and movie nights. Although it's an assisted living facility, Sunbrook's focus is on people with Alzheimer's and dementia needing more outside assistance. And it actually smells good, which is not always the case.

Each room has its own bed and nightstand, a TV on the wall, a sitting chair with a small end table along with a private connected bathroom. They're meant to be apartment-like homes but with safety features aplenty. It really is like a little community.

I smooth my hand over the freshly-made bed. Cotton, not that synthetic crap most facilities provide. She'll like it. Or she would've before.

Before. A word not readily recognized within these walls but one I can't seem to purge from my vocabulary.

A tear forms in my eye and I blink it back before it can fall. *Before*.

I'm straightening the stack of magazines—not stolen—on the end table when an alarm sounds down the hall.

Cynthia's voice crackles over the radio but I'm already sprinting out the door.

Tonight's going to be a long one.

CHAPTER 3

Paige

I KEEP MY STEPS SLOW AND MEASURED EVEN THOUGH ALL I want to do is run. All day I've been on edge waiting for my shift. For this moment. Thankfully, both roommates were already off to their own jobs by the time I rolled in dead on my feet this morning. Last night being a full moon lived up to the hype. Every few minutes, it seemed, something went wrong, sending me and Cynthia into a frenzy of activity usually reserved for day shift.

I was originally hired on for nights only but over the past two years of working here, I've had to fill in several times already for nurses on days. Usually at the last minute for the moms with young kids that get sick. While it might be hard coming off a twelve-hour rotation when the sun's just coming up, there's no comparison to the exhaustion day nurses feel after a rowdy shift. After my last time covering someone's shift, I saw some ways the night nurses could help out more so I suggested them to my boss, Rosie, and we've slowly been implementing them. Things like putting out snacks and changing bedding for the residents who are already awake before we leave in the mornings. So far everything's gone over well.

Except with Vernon, that is.

He comes in every morning to go over the daily medications but more importantly, he's a huge pain in my ass. I swear he goes out of his way to be a prick. He typically saves his snide remarks for me, which I try to ignore, but I've seen him be gruff with a few residents before and that's just unacceptable. He's got a major superiority complex going, I guess because his position allows him to stay relatively hands off with residents, mainly dispensing medication throughout the day, and he gets paid better than most of the other nurses on staff. Living alone with only two cats, he has nobody else in his life to take care of, so he spoils himself regularly, making it clear to the rest of us where he stands—well above our peasant asses.

Realizing I'm clenching my fists, I shake out my arms, not wanting to walk in a bundle of nerves. At least not visibly.

After a quick knock on room fourteen's closed door, I announce myself then twist the doorknob, letting shaky legs carry me inside.

"Hello, Ms. Christensen. I'm Paige and I'm one of the regular night nurses here. I thought I'd check to see how you're settling in on your first day."

My stretched out smile slips as I get a good look at her.

I check her chart, immediately seeing she missed dinner. There's no reason listed so I make a mental note to look into it later. Asking her likely won't get me anywhere so I try a different approach, offering, "Would you like something to eat? Maybe some yogurt and granola?"

Favoritism be damned. Today of all days she needs to eat. Moving can be particularly stressful on people with Alzheimer's. Everybody knows that. How did they let this happen on such a tough day?

I walk around to face her as she gazes out the window and study her sitting in what looks like deep contemplation. She has yet to answer me, let alone acknowledge that I'm even here. *The parking lot isn't that interesting.* Something's bothering her.

My eyes flit around the room, checking for something, anything, to reveal what has her nearly catatonic. Finding nothing out of the ordinary, I glance down and that's when I see it. The picture. Not just any picture though.

My breath catches and I lower myself to her level. My eyes jump between hers, equally hoping she'll remember and that she won't. Some memories are better forgotten given the chance.

"Ms. Christensen, would you like me to put that somewhere for you?" I nod my head toward her lap where the picture rests.

She finally registers someone talking and meets my stare.

Please.

I don't even know what I'm begging for really. The same thing I always do, I guess. If not recognition, then just peace. That's all any of us can hope for. It's hard enough watching someone lose themselves along with their memories but it's worse when they turn into a different version they never even showed traces of before.

Slowly, she lifts her hand and, on reflex, I jerk back an inch. Her palm caresses my cheek, robbing all of my breath. After only a moment's hesitation, I lean into her touch, inhaling the once comforting smell mixed with a scent that now reminds me of the dozens of other residents I care for.

Tears cloud my vision and I squeeze my eyes shut. This is the last thing she needs but the only thing I want. I may be a well-trained nurse now but I've been a daughter my whole life.

"Mom?"

Her hand drops back to her lap and I open my watery eyes to see her focused on the parked cars once again.

Shit.

She was here, *right here*, but now she's gone. In an instant that feels more like a lifetime.

I sit back on my heels, wiping at my face, and let my gaze linger, just...watching her. Assessing her. Loving her.

Missing her.

She hasn't recognized me or any of her four other kids ever since she was moved to another care facility last year, but her momentary tenderness gave me that false hope that eats away at me faster than the disease consuming her memories.

Her eyes are vacant already as she stares at nothing.

Just like before today's move.

Knowing the picture isn't helping matters, I move to grab it but as soon as my fingers pinch it, my mother's hand slams down on mine, and the movement sends the picture fluttering to the floor. Our heads drop to watch but neither of us move otherwise.

"I miss him," she whispers, and my heart pinches. It aches. It bleeds. For her. For me.

Desperate to clear my throat, I choke out, "Who?"

"My David."

She states it like it's perfectly normal. Like she's not ripping my world apart with her frail hands sporting dusty-rose pink nail polish. One name, two words, and the room is closing in on me. The walls are pushing closer until the air begins to thin, forcing me to breathe deeply through my nose while waiting for the pressure to wane.

My David. She remembers him. My father who's been dead for well over a decade. That's the thing about this disease. It lies. It digs its deceitful talons into you, holding you hostage because you're so caught up in the false optimism that lying bitch Hope lures you into.

I angle my face to the side, sending up a silent "fuck you" to Hope and her torturous games.

"Is that him?" I ask, pointing to the picture. The picture of my entire family captured on a 4x6 rectangle. My parents—when my dad was still alive—my four brothers, and me. It's funny how whole generations can be immortalized on a piece of fucking paper, a pathetic excuse of a material, but completely erased from a person's brain, one of the most complex organs in the human body.

No matter what doctors say, I believe the heart is where these snippets are kept. Buried deep down away from the deceptions the brain notoriously plays on us. The fabrications we make ourselves believe during moments of intense heartbreak. Except it isn't our heart at all, it's our head telling us we hurt, warning us away from the danger. So, we hide those most precious memories where no amount of trickery can reach, where we feel without thinking, like breathing without trying—our hearts. While disease is busy rifling through the brain, searching for anything it can ruin and twist and manipulate, the heart protects each individual memory, only allowing clips to shine through for brief flashes before tucking them away again for safekeeping. I just hope my mom's heart is strong enough to store all of us in there. Big enough to fit our large, overbearing, crazy-as-hell family.

The problem is humans are inherently greedy, always wanting more of what we can't have. And I'm no exception, yearning for my mother's love again like a starving seagull scouring the beach for leftovers. I'll take whatever I can get but still want more. Always more. The shell of my mother who Alzheimer's has carelessly left behind will never fulfill me in the maternal way I crave but, just like the idiotic bird, I continue to wait, hovering in the crosswinds, eagerly hunting for any scrap of her past self, whether it's shown organically or I have to bear my own claws and fight for a glimmer.

That's one of the reasons why she's here now—with me. Between all my brothers, they were able to pay for her to live in a different place, but it wasn't good enough. Not even close. Working in the same field, I wanted her close so I had a better chance at catching those rare bits of my mother's old self, so I've been saving up for months and even gave up my beloved single-bedroom apartment.

I considered moving into my brother Jesse's spare room, but I couldn't do it. Seeing my own despair every day in the mirror is bad enough without adding his pain. We're all suffering without our mother but I can't step in as a cut-rate second-hand replacement. I won't. We've already been there, done that, got the butt-ugly t-shirts.

Having four older brothers and no father meant exactly what you'd think—overprotective assholes on power trips constantly watching my every move and not allowing me a life of my own. They thought they needed to band together to give me—the baby of the family—a father figure. As much as I love them for it, they also blurred the lines between sibling and parent which ultimately became confusing for everybody.

Once I graduated high school and moved out, my life finally began, and it was great experiencing all the things I'd been denied. Any spare minute I had outside of nursing school and the part-time job I somehow managed to stay awake for was filled with vices of my own—the three B's: booze, boys, and bikes. Unfortunately, it was all cut short with Mom's diagnosis, ending my dabble in debauchery quicker than it started.

I'd still prefer to live with Paul Bunyan and The Babe than those turds though. Nick is the worst. Only one year older than I am, he made it his personal mission to spoil any and all fun for me that he himself partook in greedily. We're the closest of the five siblings but we also fight the worst. Love hard, fight harder—that's Nicky and me. All of us really.

I meant what I told Marc and Beckett, living with them will be easy compared to growing up with four overbearing brothers. And if that blustering blue-eyed behemoth stays out of my way, I should still be able to splash around in the overflowing fountain of fun life has to offer a twenty-year-old looking to loosen the noose of misery constricting her throat.

Ignoring my question or maybe unable to answer, my mom just repeats quietly, "I miss him."

My name being called over the radio breaks the heavy silence and I retrieve the picture before placing it on her nightstand. Taking one last look at the smiling faces of an almost unrecognizable family, I rub my thumb over my smiling parents.

"Me, too," slips out before I can stop it.

◆ ◆ ◆

"Shit," I say, looking at my CBR sitting useless in the spot I parked her in last night.

Remembering Cynthia already took off for the day, I pull up

my oldest brother Jesse's name on my phone. He doesn't answer until the fourth call, gritting out, "This better be an emergency."

"I'm stranded on the side of the freeway. Can you please pick me up?"

A groggy rumble is the only response I get.

"Jesse! Wake up!" I scold. "It's not even that early. Come on, my bike won't start. I need a ride home."

"Call someone else," he mumbles, sounding like he's rolling back over to sneak some more z's.

Not on my smartwatch.

"You know what? Don't worry about it. I'll just stick my thumb up and see if I can hitch a ride. Serial killers are probably out of business now since Uber's so popular." I wait a bit, letting that sink in, then add, "Right?"

"Don't even think about it."

His sharp and very much awake tone has me chuckling.

"Where are you exactly?"

I ramble off the address, squinting even though he can't see me.

"Wait, isn't that Sunbrook's address?"

I don't answer. He knows it is.

"God, you're a bitch. I'll be there in twenty."

"Make it sooner and I'll buy you a coffee."

"That's already included in my fee."

"Maybe I should've called someone else," I mutter, then hang up before he can renege.

Even though I plan on hitting my bed as soon as I get home, a chai tea latte will help soothe my nerves after the long night I just endured; but really, I'd use any excuse to get the sweet, milky drink so it's a moot point. Or mute point, as my brother Nick used to say then arrogantly defend when we'd correct him. It kinda stuck and now we use the term as an inside joke.

Thirty minutes later, a grumpy but extremely pretty Jesse pulls up. With high cheekbones, light eyes, and a clear complexion partially hidden by a short beard, my oldest brother is definitely the prettiest in the family. After our gorgeous mother, of course. We used to joke that all the beauty was used up on the firstborn, leaving odds and ends to make up the rest of us. Caleb has a perfect nose, Tysen has well-defined muscles, and Nick has plump lips while I have the hair. Well, technically we all have the same hair color but I tint my long, mahogany waves with dark, berry-red undertones to make it my own.

I'm sitting at the curb with my elbows resting on my knees when his low-to-the-ground Toyota screeches to a halt in front of me. The window rolls down and he barks, "Get in."

Asshole. I love him.

Seeing my oldest brother is like taking my first breath after a long swim—it hurts but in a really, really good way. It's…been a while.

"Morning, sunshine."

He grunts something about dropping me off on a real freeway but I ignore the empty threat. I wouldn't have to lie if he'd just answer my calls.

Looking over my white nightmare as we pull away, he asks, "When are you going to stop driving that already? You need to get a car. A reliable car. One that you didn't buy off the internet from a fifteen-year-old child."

"First of all," I say, counting by putting my middle finger up instead of my pointer finger, "he was sixteen."

He releases a deep chuckle, lighting up his entire face along with mine. Jesse is such a stoic person that when you get him to crack, even if for a moment, it's addictive. You'll do anything to get him laughing again and when he finally does, it feels like winning the best kind of competition there is. I keep a mental tally every time I get him to break character.

He doesn't even realize the power he holds in his smile either. Most pretty people don't. Well, the good ones anyway. And Jesse, he's the best. But I can't tell him that. Sibling rivalry is alive and well in the Christensen family and I can't have him realizing how much in the lead he actually is over the rest of us. Plus, we haven't spoken lately, and I can't just vomit how much I love and miss and need him. I tried already and he just retreated even more from me, from us.

"Second," I put up my other middle finger, "he knew more about bikes than me. How was I supposed to know the thing had problems up the tailpipe?"

The snort he lets loose warms my chest straight through. It's close enough to a laugh I mark it down as a win, immediately looking forward to my next one.

"And third," I drop both hands to my lap, "you drive a car, you *ride* a bike. We all have our faults. She's mine."

"She?"

"Oh yeah, she's definitely a she. She's beautiful and moody and the baddest bitch on the block."

"She's a piece o.'"

"What's that?"

"A piece o' shit!" His loud laugh is so unexpected that while it fills me with pride, it also grates on my nerves that it's at my expense. I do not mark it as a win.

We grab drinks from the drive-thru of a little coffee stand called Latte Da. I've never heard of it but Jesse swears by their specials, specifically one they call the mocha-swirl latte but no longer serve for some reason. I stick to my tea drink before I direct him toward my new place at Creekwood Apartments.

Tysen, the quintessential middle child, was the brother I had help me move in the other day. He and my new roommate, Marc, both lifted the heavier items, whereas big, bad Beckett stayed behind his closed bedroom door, most likely pouting. He seems like a pouter. A very tall, very sexy pouter. I watched with wide eyes as Tysen and Marc did that bro handshake thing upon first meeting. Marc is a tough nut to crack but my brothers are expert ball-busters and Ty had him laughing about something within minutes. Ty has a higher laugh count in the Jesse department than me but he also gets decked when his idiocy reaches intolerable levels, so who's the real winner?

"Tell me about these guys you live with."

"No."

His head snaps to mine after he parks, asking, "Why not?"

"Because I don't need you to go all big brother on them, essentially making me look like an incompetent little girl who needs J-bone's constant protection."

"Don't call me that. That's the dumbest nickname I've ever heard."

I shrug my shoulders, keeping my comments to myself. We had four teenage boys in the same house at the same time, not to mention the insane amount of other teenage boys those four accumulated. We've all heard, and said, worse. Much worse.

"Regardless, I was barely able to get Mom in the door at Sunbrook, and in order to keep her there, I need money. Lots of it."

"What was wrong with where she was before? It was fine and didn't cost a fortune."

"It wasn't fine." At all. "You'd know that if you visited more often."

It's a low blow but it's true. Jesse filled the paternal role more than the others and took Mom's rapid decline the hardest. He's still recovering. Or self-punishing, I'm not sure. He's a fucking mess and rarely sees our mom anymore. Which is probably for the best, considering, but I still wish he'd try. With her and with me. By cutting her off, he cut me off too, and that hurts just as bad, if not worse.

"You're telling me this was the best solution you could come up with? Shacking up with two strange guys? Did you find them online or something? It all sounds suspect as fuck."

Shacking up? What a chauvinistic shit. Believe it or not, men and women can not only be friends but also cohabitate and not *shack up*. I spent my life around men, like a continuous conveyor belt of guys, and I never hooked up with any of my brothers' friends. Not even on my sixteenth birthday when a bunch of us were sleeping outside on a trampoline and I convinced one of Tysen's friends into being my first kiss. Or at my junior prom when I snuck Nick's BFF into the bathroom with me after pretending someone spilled punch on my dress and needed someone else to clean it up—with their mouth.

Actually, he might have a point. A tiny, inconsequential point that nobody, especially none of my brothers, needs to know about.

"Seriously? I cut my rent in thirds by moving in here. Probably even more because my first place was expensive."

He moves to follow me over to the stairs leading up to my second-floor unit.

"What are you doing?" I ask, packing on a healthy dose of attitude. He doesn't bother with seeing me for how long then insists on doing what exactly? A clean sweep of an already clean apartment? Intimidating my roommates?

Unfortunately, I already know the answer to both: yes. He plans on doing both. Thoroughly. Just like Tysen did in his underhanded *I'm not a threat until you make me one* type of way.

And when the next brother down the line comes to visit, he'll do the same, too. They're all the same.

"Don't worry about it."

"They're probably not even here, you know? They work."

"Where?"

My eyes roll on their own, I swear.

"Some new garage," I say, remembering my interview with them there. It was nice. Really nice. They both own it with their old roommate apparently. Everyone working there knew their shit when I scoped it out while waiting on the tallest one to finish a job. Honestly, they probably don't even price gouge their customers. Fraud tends to happen when the lips spewing it are as clueless as the ones devouring it and I doubt anyone within those walls is thirsting for lies, not when their skills speak for themselves.

I open the front door, dropping my backpack full of my scrubs and stethoscope on the floor.

Jesse whistles behind me and I spin to see him checking out the new digs.

"Right? Fully furnished. And they actually have decent taste, unlike the hooligans I grew up with."

He shoves me as I pass to the bathroom making me laugh, then I take my time washing my hands and face. The repurposed whiskey bottle used as a soap dispenser is my favorite thing in the blank canvas that is my new bathroom. Excuse me, shared bathroom. The thought of Beckett and I showering in the same space—separately, of course—sends tiny chills along my arms. His big, naked body lathering up where my naked body lathers up.

My eyes land on his body wash. The scent is faint, thankfully, but it's there. It's everywhere. A mix of wood and vanilla, earthy yet sweet, the notes tease my nose and I lose the battle, inhaling deeply. The moisture hanging thick in the air hints at his recent shower and my face heats at the images now flashing through my mind.

I find Jesse asleep on the worn brown leather couch when I return to the living room. Ah, the joys of being a man and not having any reservations about falling asleep in a strange place.

Why is he so tired though? He doesn't even work nights.

I watch him for a while, just staring at my big brother, and wondering what else I need to do to get our family back in order. When will we be normal again?

When were we ever?

Technically, we've never been normal with enough boys in the house to start a sports team but that didn't matter to me. I loved them. I love them. I love us as a family of differently cut pieces standing together as a whole.

Without our mom, the most important piece, we're sliding further and further apart. I can only hope we find our way back to each other. And soon.

Shaking my head, I lay a blanket over his sleeping form then head to my room to do the same.

CHAPTER 4

Paige

I TOSS THE LETTUCE, SMOTHERING IT WITH THE HOMEMADE Italian dressing before distributing it evenly between two plates. Jesse pretends to gag so I add more to his, piling it high. The brief smile I catch is worth the curse word that follows. At twenty-seven years old, you'd think he'd be out of his vegetable hating phase. He'll be fine eating one salad.

I think.

"Can you drop me back at work?" I ask, eyeing his fork as he pushes around his heavily-coated lettuce with it.

Waking up from a restless sleep filled with vanilla scented woods, I came out to find Jesse watching TV like he owned the joint. I made him help me with the box of DVDs I haven't had time to unpack yet before getting myself a shower and making us dinner.

We haven't spent this much time together in a long time and I don't want it to end.

"I can't. I have plans."

My lips dip as I rush to hide my face.

"You do? Like a date?"

Growing up, I knew Jesse had girlfriends but he never spoke about them or brought any around. The boys were relentless in giving him shit but he'd never waver. He was always putting Mom's needs first and often forgot to be a kid himself.

He stands so suddenly, he almost knocks over the barstool. "Yeah." He snaps like he just remembered. "A date. Where we eat. At a restaurant. So, eating this…would be rude. Sorry."

I narrow my eyes, treading behind his mad dash to the door.

There's practically skid marks on the tile. This idiot really hates veggies.

"Fine, scaredy cat. Wait until I tell Ty. He's gonna roast your ass for running from a salad."

He ducks his head back in, screwing his face up. "I don't give a shit. I can still beat Ty's ass."

This is undoubtedly true. Jesse pulls no punches—literally. But again, I can't tell him that.

I pretend to scoff, saying, "I don't know. I saw him lift my dresser without breaking a sweat. He's a beast. He probably eats his greens." The last part barely makes it past my lips without me cracking up.

"Good. Have him finish that pile of slop you're trying to force on me."

I follow him out to the hallway. It's open on both ends with two sets of concrete stairs on either end—one to the parking lot, one to the pool out back. It's not suffocatingly hot yet, but still, it's warm. Warmer with the air getting stuck in the concrete cage and no airflow.

"And he can take you to work, too."

"Whatever. Ungrateful ass. I'm just trying to keep you healthy." Something in me jerks to a stop, screaming to keep him here. To show him what he means to me. To make him understand. Without thought I wrap my arms around his middle from behind, pressing the side of my face into his back and whispering hoarsely, "I don't want anything to happen to you. You're too important."

He freezes, sighing, like he knew this would happen. Like he knew I'd never want to let him go.

He's right. I don't.

Like a good coach, I need all my boys, my team, lined up in front of me, following the carefully laid out plan—together. Not off scrambling with their own half-baked ideas—alone.

I need my family like plants need water. I'm not a fucking cactus. I *need* them. A person can go without water for three days but my throat's been aching from my mom's diagnosis two years ago and I'm still reeling. It triggered a drought I'll never be able to remedy. At least not by myself. I need the boys' support like they need mine, otherwise I'm scared we'll all dehydrate.

Jesse turns around slowly, his guarded eyes meeting mine, and we share a look that holds things neither of us want to say aloud. Things we don't even want to admit to ourselves.

I wrap my arms around his trim waist tighter, saying, "I love you."

He folds his over my back, letting them hang a little looser.

"I love you, too." It comes out chopped up worse than our abandoned salads. I never claimed they were good. Just healthy.

He pulls back, staring down at me and I can tell it's over. Over his head. Over this moment. Just over. "Now, how are you going to fix that bike?"

"What's wrong with your bike?"

Our heads turn to see Beckett's daunting figure taking up half the hallway. I didn't even hear him approach. With feet that big, it's quite the, well, feat.

Although the question was aimed at me, he hasn't taken his eyes off my brother still wrapped around me. Jesse stiffens, slipping into full brother mode as he pulls away, returning my roommate's merciless stare. I miss him immediately. Everything. I miss everything about him.

Except this domineering shit.

I clear my throat but neither one so much as notices and I roll my eyes hard enough to see the cobwebs swaying from the outdoor ceiling.

"I don't know. It wouldn't start this morning," I tell the unfriendly giant.

His eyes finally touch on mine but return almost instantly to my oldest brother. "Where is it now? I didn't see it in the lot."

There's an invisible wire holding each man in place but it's getting wound tighter the more words are flung through the air and they both start to shift toward the other. Jesse's not the bulkiest of my brothers but he's definitely the meanest, having basically raised three other boys himself. He's also incredibly smart using any weakness in his opponent to get the upper hand. He taught me that skill before I entered high school. It came in handy enough times for me to hone the skill into a fine point.

Looking Beckett over, I'd say his weakness is mental, not physical, but I don't know him well enough to know what that is just yet.

"What's it to you? Are you the roommate or something?"

"*The* roommate?" Beckett chuckles deeply, taking a step in our direction and I swear he doubles in size, enough to eclipse the sun at his back, casting a shadow over us all. "There's more where I come from, bro."

Jesse surges forward, practically spitting, "Same here, *bro*."

The wire whines from the taut pull now, and I place myself between the two men, giving it some slack before it snaps completely.

Before anyone snaps completely.

I put a hand on Jesse's chest, nudging him. Once he tears his heated glare away from Beckett's, I shake my head, silently telling him to back the hell down already. I don't need my brother, or my roommate, bloody before my shift even starts.

Is that full moon over yet?

"He's just a mechanic." My eyes widen, conveying his alpha male bullshit is unnecessary. "And you're gonna be late." For that date, right? At a place that obviously doesn't offer salads.

Jesse opens his mouth to argue but I lean up to kiss him on the cheek, stopping him in his blood-sniffing tracks. I used to kiss all my brothers on the mouth until I saw a clip online of a certain A-list actor make out with her brother on the red carpet. Now, I don't.

"Thanks for your help. I'll talk to you later." Hopefully. Hopefully he answers again, and not just because it's an emergency. Hopefully there are no more emergencies.

We can only take so much.

He pushes past Beckett then, bumping into his shoulder when the taller of the two refuses to move and more death glares are exchanged.

Really?

Once Jesse's out of sight, Beckett turns back to me, asking, "Do you work tonight?"

I throw up my hands, remembering I still don't have a ride, and stomp back inside to grab my phone, groaning when I see my forgotten dinner.

"I'll take that as a yes."

The deceptively deep voice behind me causes goose bumps to sprout like weeds in a neglected garden and I turn to watch Beckett drop his stuff on the counter next to Jesse's deserted dinner. He eyes it, disgust marring his handsome features.

"Uh, yeah. I was just calling my friend for a ride." Even though she's one of those crazy employees that arrives thirty minutes early for her shifts, I still might be able to catch Cynthia before she leaves.

"I'll take you. I can look at your bike while I'm there."

Beckett's eyes sharpen on mine.

The sincerity is there but he's working like hell to mask it. Why?

I work my bottom lip, letting the moment stretch, then say, "I don't want to put you out. I can find someone else."

"Who? Who else can take you to work and fix your bike?" At my silence, he continues, "I'll take you. Let me eat something and I'll run you over there."

He glares at the salad again before opening the fridge with more effort than necessary.

"Okay, thanks. You're welcome to this." I push Jesse's untouched plate across the breakfast bar.

His acidic gaze lands on the food before lifting to mine. "Nah, I don't do sloppy seconds."

What?

Jesse didn't even touch it.

With a shake of my head—I don't even know what to say—I take my dinner to my room then eat with the background noise of my roommate banging around the kitchen. Call me crazy but I've never heard of a recipe that called for every cabinet, drawer, and door to be opened and *slammed* closed.

What's his problem?

Is my brother stopping over really that big of a deal? If so, this living arrangement will go from mildly uncomfortable to downright unbearable quickly. My brothers may irritate the hell out of me sometimes and overstep boundaries I've been trying to set for years, but they're nonnegotiable. There is no me without them. That's what they still don't get. If they did, they wouldn't be treating me to radio silence over the decisions I made for our last remaining parent.

Losing our dad hurt. Slowly losing our mom is taking our legs out from under us, one by one. They're all I have left to lean on and when I get them within reach, I'm not letting go. Not even for some anti-green giant.

"Ready?" I ask after finishing my meager dinner. As it turns out, the salad wasn't that great.

Whatever. It's cheap and filling…kind of.

My eyes drift over the bare counters. Nothing. He made nothing. All that knocking around and not a single thing to show for it. I knew he was a pouter. I just don't understand what has his massive panties in a bunch now.

His underwear, regardless of what state they're in, are none of my business.

I clean the plates I used then grab my bag, stuffing it with a few granola bars and an applesauce pouch.

Beckett stalks past, out the front door, expecting me to follow. I do, but only after waiting a beat.

Seated in his hunter green Tahoe, he cranks the music the

second the engine roars to life, making small talk impossible. "Man or a Monster" pulses through the speakers, the after-market subwoofers sending tremors to all the right places.

I lower the volume, giving him directions to Sunbrook but Beckett's eyes stay glued to the road so I take the opportunity to check him out. A bit of his light hair is peeking out of a backward hat and his face still has a sheen of sweat on it. His simple shirt says *We Ride* but has a couple holes in it, reminding me of scratch marks. Beast mode comes to mind and I wonder what he's like in the sack, too. Probably growly and selfish. Most hot guys are. Like lazy house cats that do jack shit and still get fed by hand. Pants pulled tight against his thighs hint at a rather impressive package so at least he seems to be working with decent equipment. He's covered in grease stains but doesn't look filthy—at least not in a hygienic sort of way. He's giving off dirty, sexy vibes like only a hardworking man can. When I first met him and Marc at their shop, Pop The Hood, he was covered in sweat from a hot day under steaming hoods and the image has stayed with me ever since. Marc's leaner frame was smudged in dirt like maybe he works outside, but Beckett was all glistening muscle.

His long fingers spread wide, curl around the steering wheel like streams of hot lava igniting everything in their path. Visions of them on my body have me discreetly fanning my face and turning away.

Beckett's head finally twists my way and holds. Unable to resist, I turn to see him checking me out as well. His eyes lift to mine and he clears his throat.

"So, older men your thing?"

My eyebrows almost touch.

"Uh, not particularly?" Why that came out as a question I'll never know. I mean, most guys I've messed around with were older but by a year or two, nothing like a cradle robber or anything. I glance down at my chest, not seeing any signs encouraging sugar daddies to apply within taped to it. Beckett's eyes follow mine but when I catch him ogling my boobs he glares before facing the road again.

"Why do you say that?"

His grip tightens on the wheel. "Dude back there looked old, older than you."

My brain searches for the man he's referring to, landing on Jesse, and I fly forward, laughing.

"You thought? That-" I start then stop, unable to finish a single sentence while gripping my stomach as tears stream down my face.

Nobody has ever mistaken one of my brothers for my boyfriend before.

This must be that infamous sense of humor Marc told me about.

Wiping my eyes, I sit up to peek over at a frowning Beckett and, I can't help it, I start laughing all over again. My laughter fills the already hot space so I roll down my window, giving us some much-needed airflow. I regret it almost immediately as my loose hair starts blowing into my open mouth still cackling away. Nothing like a mouthful of hair to sober your sudden hysteria.

"So, that wasn't your boyfriend?"

I pull the majority of the strands out of my mouth before shaking my head. "No, and he's only twenty-seven. I wouldn't call that old." I eye him as my hair flies about chaotically. "How old are you?"

His shoulders visibly relax. "About to turn twenty-two. You?"

"I'm almost twenty-one. This month actually. I forgot it was coming up."

He glances over at me. "You forgot your own birthday?"

I shrug. I've had bigger things to worry about.

"Will your family throw you a party or anything?"

It sounds like he's fishing but I spot his bait a mile away so I keep to the shallow end, simply saying, "Doubt it."

My brothers don't typically throw parties. They attend them, they crash them, they bust them—well, mine anyway—but they don't really plan them. Plus, with Mom's new normal, nobody's pushed for anything that we'd have to exclude her from.

"What about yours?" Beckett's got that All-American party boy look. Throw in that tattoo I was happy to discover the other morning when he was shirtless along with his flashy bike and you've got a heartbreakingly beautiful bad boy. "Will your family throw you one?"

Ah, but the fisherman realizes he's now the one being reeled in and he goes quiet. There's a story there. A bad one, I'm guessing. His breathing has thinned and he's looking out the driver's side window, ignoring me and my question.

After a long pause, he surprises me by saying, "We're not big on family functions." He continues in a quiet, measured tone. "We, uh, never really felt like celebrating."

His pained eyes touch on mine for a split second, making a lump form in my throat.

"I get it." More than he could ever know.

And even though I feel like he just started talking to me, it's time to lighten the mood before I reveal too much, too soon.

"I'll probably go out to my favorite bar anyway."

Beckett's quirked eyebrow makes me laugh.

"What? I have an ID I've been using for a couple years."

"And you think suddenly showing up there with a real one on your real twenty-first birthday won't raise any flags?"

"Let me worry about that," I say, tipping one side of my mouth up.

The truth is I've got a couple bars I cycle through. Both have connections without *connections*. Well, except for the one with the bouncer I half-dated. I say half because while he insisted we were in a full-blown relationship, I was all about having a good time for a short time—a very short time. When he started watching me more than the door, I ended things completely; but he's still struggling to accept that fact a bit—meaning, he saw the subject line but he's avoiding reading the full memo. I don't know how else to say that we are never getting back together, but he lets me into the bar without too much hassle, so I suck it up for the sake of blowing off thick-as-pea-soup steam.

We listen to music the rest of the drive until he pulls up next to my bike.

"I'll have it running before you get off."

Our eyes slam together at his words and he chokes a little to cover a laugh.

"I mean, I'll fix your ride."

His snicker is not lost on me, neither is his love of double meanings, so I fire back with some innuendo of my own, saying, "Oh, don't worry about that, there's no complaints in that department." I wink at his now serious face. "But if you could take a look at my bike, I'd appreciate it."

Snatching my bag off the floor, I hop out of his SUV, throwing over my shoulder, "thanks for the *ride,*" as a bonus for him to chew on.

I don't look back. I don't need to. The guy can kiss my ass and the only way that's going to happen is if he sees it for himself, so I put a little more sway in my hips over to the employee entrance.

Unfortunately, the door swings open, cutting my exaggerated saunter short with a red-faced Vernon marching out and sticking his finger in my face.

"Whoa. What's this?" I say as I step back, trying to knock his hand away.

Unfazed, he pushes into my personal space but I match every step he takes with two of my own until suddenly, a large arm shoots between us, halting Vernon where he stands.

"Can I help you?" Beckett cocks his head to the side in a patronizing way and turns so his back is shielding me.

Yeah, fuck that.

I advance forward to Beckett's side to face off against Vernon… too? Why *is* Beckett here?

"Mind your business, boy. This has to do with her."

"Vernon, what the hell are you talking about now?"

His finger makes another appearance but before I can block it again Beckett is there pushing into Vernon's face. The shorter man sputters as the not-so-gentle giant presses on.

"She is my business." My scoff can be heard from space but the two men facing off in front of me don't seem to notice. "Keep that finger away from her unless you want me to break the fucking thing off for good."

Beckett's low voice raises the hairs on the back of my neck like spirits in a cemetery—awake with absolutely nothing to do besides make people uneasy.

This is getting out of control. Vernon is all talk and no walk. Him throwing fits is nothing new and I usually bat him away like the annoying gnat he is, but I do have to work with the guy.

I grab Beckett's tense bicep and pull, sneaking in a quick squeeze in the process, until he's facing me. He keeps his eyes locked on Vernon though, who looks like he's no longer breathing. Great, he probably gave him a heart attack.

"Hey," I soothe, gaining Beckett's attention. "I got this."

Growing up with four brothers plus their countless friends, breaking up fights became a pastime of sorts. I even had my second oldest brother, Caleb, put it on my resume—proficient in conflict de-escalation.

Understanding finally tinges his expression. Resigned understanding, but it's there.

"Can you get started on the bike and I'll join you in a few?"

His nod is the only answer he gives before walking away with a final glare aimed at my coworker.

I, however, round on the jerk, not really caring if he is in cardiac arrest. "What is your problem, Vernon? If you have something you need to say, say it already, but don't ever come at me like that again. Do you hear me? I have four brothers and every single one of them take my safety *very* seriously."

This finally rouses him as he jerks a thumb, sneering, "Is that one of them?"

I just grin like the cat that ate the dangerously outnumbered canary and say, "Nope."

Truthfully, I don't know what that was but there definitely wasn't anything brotherly about Beckett's outburst. His protectiveness bothered me in multiple ways and none of them familial.

"Thanks to your *ideas*, my daily shift is getting pushed back further and further. I have a very tight feeding schedule for my cats and now everything's thrown off with your new snack time." He all but spits the last words at me like they're the worst things to ever cross his lips. I have a pretty hard time keeping a straight face actually and I bite the inside of my cheek just to keep from laughing.

"Maybe it's time to find another job then. One where your kitties can have you at their beck and call. But the residents are doing better overall since they've begun eating first thing in the morning."

His hand twitches like he's getting ready to use it when a motorcycle, my motorcycle, revs loudly, making him freeze entirely.

"That's where you're wrong. Not everyone can take their medication on full stomachs. Some people must be given theirs on empty stomachs. But if they're all full when I get here, then I can't do my job properly and there's no point to me even being here!"

His screechy voice grates on my already tight nerves. I understand where he's coming from and it's true, his schedule has been altered to find the right time for everyone to receive their medication correctly. They're still working to find the perfect balance but his anger isn't helping anybody in the meantime.

I sigh, rubbing my forehead. "Talk to Rosie. Maybe she can suggest a better time that'll fit with your, uh, cats' schedule."

Wouldn't want the only pussies Vernon has ever seen to suffer any more than they already have just by living with the asshole.

In a deceptively soft voice, he leans in and warns, "She better. I'm not losing my job to a biker wannabe playing dress up."

Wannabe? Dress up?

I raise a single brow, knowing it'll irk the fuck out of him when really I'd love to show him exactly what I can do with my bike. *Here's a tip, stay the fuck out of my way when I'm on her.*

Vernon sidesteps me in a huff and I join Beckett as he sits on my bike, steadily twisting the throttle. I thought with his height he'd look like a bear on a tricycle but I was wrong. Dead wrong.

After watching Vernon drive off, Beckett's long, powerful body fills every crevice of my white and gray CBR 600 as he leans over to resume his inspection. And I continue mine. Strong arms grip my handlebars, toned legs straddle the seat while his hat covered head, bill now forward to block the sun, studies the body. Good. God. It's not even fair.

The sun is dropping toward the horizon, painting the sky an impressive orange ombré that reminds me of the creamsicles from the ice cream truck that used to circle our old neighborhood every weekend during the hot months.

"She purrs so pretty when she's actually running."

He looks me over and hums, the sound making me think of somewhere else I'd like him to hum.

"How often is it happening?"

I cough. "Excuse me?"

"You said 'when she's running.' How often does it break down?"

His eyebrows are drawn like the curtains on a recluse's home—keeping everything in while blocking everyone out.

"Oh, um, enough."

He nods thoughtfully before turning the key and dismounting.

"It should be good for now. If it happens again, call me."

He takes my phone to program his info in. As he passes it back, our fingers brush and a warmth spreads where they touch. It's not like accidentally touching a stranger where you panic and abort as soon as possible. It's comfortable and I don't pull away immediately. Beckett doesn't either and we stand with our hands both holding the phone between us, staring into the other's eyes.

Inside his car, his woodsy vanilla smell caressed my senses like a faint memory that hasn't happened yet. Now, the slight breeze mixes with the earthy sweetness to tease me like an unspoken promise.

Everything I've seen on him so far is long and his eyelashes are no exception. They blink once, ending the moment completely and he removes his hand, clearing his throat. "Dude was fired up. Does he always act like that?"

"Vernon?" I sense another line being tossed in my direction so I keep it short once again, telling him honestly, "He has his days."

"Well, if he gives you any more trouble, call me and I'll deal with him, too."

That's enough of that.

I step close to him, making sure my front brushes his. Feeling his sharp inhale instead of just hearing it, I crank my neck back to gaze up at him.

"I can take care of myself. I handle guys like him every day of the week and twice on Saturdays."

I spin on my heel, only pausing when he calls to my back, "Why Saturday?"

"It's my day off."

CHAPTER 5

Beckett

I'M WIPING MY HANDS OFF WHEN MY BOY AND BUSINESS partner, Coty, enters the now empty bay.

"How's it going with the new roommate? Can't be too bad if you're still alive. I figured she would've killed you in your sleep by now."

"Pssh, if it were that easy, neighbor girl would've taken me out first chance she got."

As if on cue, Angie—his better half—walks in, joining the conversation, saying, "Oh, boys. All Beckett has to do is make her one of his signature everything-but-the-kitchen-sink cocktails and she'll fall madly in love with him." She snickers proudly, tucking herself into Coty's side.

The two of them are sickening, not unlike my infamous drink concoctions Angie mentioned.

Although the jury's still out on motive, I get the feeling Paige could all out destroy with no remorse.

"I'm happy to report," I say, spreading my arms out wide, "she hasn't killed me in my sleep, yet." Mainly because she's not home when I'm asleep. *Thank fuck*. "And, there will be no falling in love. At least not on my end. She's more than welcome to fawn all over me. I could use a new president to head the Beck's The Best fan club now that you left." I give our old neighbor a wink, making Coty chuckle while Angie rolls her eyes.

Coty, Marc, and I grew up with different versions of dysfunctional families. One day at a local motocross track, we befriended one another over our love of dirt bikes but later became brothers out of necessity. We found something in each other that day that our real families weren't giving us, something we needed but couldn't begin to recognize at such a young age. Our hobby kicked off our lifelong friendships but our unwavering loyalty has kept us together, strengthening over the years until we moved into the apartment at Creekwood after high school, making us more—making us brothers. Years went by of the same old, same old and it's been great, but in a way that milk is great. Sure, it tastes good and not everyone can have it, making you feel a little smug that you get something so highly coveted by others. But, then you try chocolate milk and suddenly regular milk seems boring, less than, lacking overall. That's what Angie moving into the apartment next door was. The stubborn breath of fresh air moved across the hall but, more importantly, into our hearts, too. She stirred everything up, making us realize that what we were doing wasn't as great as we'd always assumed. That our triad was in need of another to balance us out.

Coty fell for her the moment he laid eyes on her, poor bastard never stood a chance really, and locked that shit up quick. She put him, and us, through the wringer, but looking at how we all came out the other side together, I'd say it was well worth it.

Last year, us roommates decided to go into business together, and six months ago we opened the only auto shop in town that fixes almost anything with an engine—my specialty—on one side, with a full-service car wash on the other. Angie runs the wash without much interference from us and has customers eating out of the palms of her more than capable hands. Having worked at a car wash once upon a time herself, we offered her the position and after some convincing, she accepted, proving us geniuses every day since. Coty may be the one that created the entire car wash addition specifically for her but I take as much of the credit as they let me get away with. Which isn't much usually. Our old neighbor girl is savage.

Coty happily fills the role as general manager while I work solely in the service department. If it drove at one time, I can get it running again, but faster. Marc mostly works off-site but gives a hand in any department needed. We work closely with his father's uber successful farm, so he's out there most days, working on vehicles that can't make the trip into town.

Due to our booming success and growing clientele, we're currently scouting sites for a second location and if all goes well, our team will be celebrating another grand opening by the end of the year.

"It wouldn't be the worst thing for you to finally fall for someone, you know?"

I clutch at my heart and stumble forward.

"How dare you say such horrible things to me. Coty, control your woman."

The happy couple just laugh, sending a shot of adrenaline straight to my veins.

"We both know that'll never happen." Angie stares into her man's eyes, daring him to argue, and I have to look away from the intensity.

"Never," Coty agrees before Angie turns triumphantly to leave, his eyes tracking her every move.

"Yes, please. Take your hate speech somewhere else," I call out while she's still in earshot, earning me a middle finger held high above her head.

"I like her unrestrained, man. You don't tame girls like her, you embrace the beauty in their wild and adapt." His gaze meets mine pointedly. "Or get eaten alive."

With a shrug of his shoulders, he spins to follow his girl.

"Sounds like great advice for your first satanic ritual. Did you find that on a greeting card?"

I'm rewarded with a second middle finger followed by a "goodnight."

Easy for him to say. He doesn't have to go back to Creekwood. It hasn't even been a full week yet but I'm already surrounded by her. Everywhere I go, Paige is there.

In the living room with her stupid DVD collection off to the side of the TV. What the fuck is *Final Girl* by the way? Shit looks weird as hell. One girl, four guys—sounds like a horror movie if I've ever heard one. Three guys and one girl though...that might be fun.

In the kitchen with her bulk snacks and tea. Almost twenty-one my ass, chick is on her way to sixty-one with the crap she likes. I hate even going near the bathroom anymore with her overwhelming scent invading the air—peaches with a hint of smoke from her constant riding. Smoky peaches? Who the fuck would've thought such a thing existed? Sounds like something Bobby Flay came up with—the brilliant bastard. It's the most erotic thing I've ever smelled and I've been walking around with a chubby all week.

The only place I find any reprieve is in my bedroom, except I don't. Not really. She's taken over every dream my sick head comes up with while I try to sleep off the constant state of arousal I've found myself in since Paige moved in. Even with all the reminders of our female roommate, I haven't seen her in the flesh going on four days now and yet I can't get her out of my mind.

And...thinking about her flesh has my dick growing hard all over again.

Jesus.

I knew a girl living with us would be a bad idea. I told Marc that but no, he didn't listen. Seeing her in that dumbshit's arms was...difficult. I don't expect her to be celibate while living under the same roof—hell, I know I won't be—but that guy's all wrong. For many, many reasons. Starting with how old he looked. I'm not even talking about his age either. Despite resembling a model fresh off the runway, dude looked like he's seen some shit and done even more. Like the weight of the world on his shoulders is winning and he's two seconds away from letting it. No wonder he was pawing at Paige. Any girl that rides her own motorcycle is hot, but Paige is more. She carries herself with a confidence that rivals any man's I've ever met. She's drop-dead gorgeous, prettier than I originally thought, with hair that demands your full attention no matter what you're doing. I had to work hard—so fucking hard—to keep from wrapping my hands in her wild locks in my truck as they flew around her face without a care in the world, completely unlike their owner. Paige has more going on than she shows. Her outside broadcasts carefree while inside she's twisted up with worries. She measures her words, only revealing what she wants you to know, almost like she's spinning an intricate web around you while you're too busy looking at how attractive she is. Problem is, I can't be captured by anyone, beautiful or not, let alone a woman that lives so close to where I sleep.

With that in mind, I send a text to a girl that brought her Lexus in last week, asking if she's down to chill tonight. Saturday. Paige's only night off. I need to get her out of my head and her first official night in the apartment is the perfect time to evict her from my thoughts entirely.

The chick, Carlson apparently, replies instantly, setting Operation Forget Paige in effect.

Let the fun begin.

◆ ◆ ◆

This shit sucks. I didn't know Marc had so many goddamn teeth but here he is, yucking it up with Paige with all his pearly whites on display. They've had their heads together laughing like a couple of hyenas while I've been saddled with this broad in snakeskin. I don't think it's real snakeskin but the god awful dress she's wearing is itchy as all hell. I'm pretty sure I've got a rash now. She's trying to keep my focus solely on her but...she's failing. Miserably. With the star of all my recent dreams sitting a few feet away looking like the posters on my wall come to life, how can I concentrate on anything else?

Paige's head is thrown back, exposing her throat, and my fingers itch to rub the length of it before grabbing a fistful of her merlot-colored hair and bringing her mouth to mine—if only just to shut her up. I've never been a fan of wine before but find myself craving a taste the longer I sit here watching. Watching her, with my boy. With my brother. She needs to be forcibly removed from my fantasies already. The best way to get over one woman is to be buried balls deep in another, right? I'm only guessing since I've never been hung up on anyone before. This feeling is new and incredibly unpleasant. I hate it. I hate her. Sort of.

Not really, but I wish I did. It'd make this whole thing a lot easier.

Time to kick this up a notch.

I stand, taking what's-her-name with me and she giggles. It's forced and I hate it, too. I hate it more. I'm tempted to drop her but snakes have a penchant for biting and I actually like all my body parts being puncture-free. Plus, I have plans for this viper.

Digging my fingers into her hips as I walk us out to the balcony, leaving Hee and Haw in the living room, only spurs the girl on and she begins moaning. Loudly.

I cover her mouth with mine, smothering the exaggerated sounds, and plant her ass on the banister. I don't have to look behind me to know Paige has tuned into the action. If the abrupt silence didn't give her away, the hole currently burning through my shirt from her stare would.

The kiss is lazy and boring, waiting for me to take control. Any other night I would, but tonight, I'm not feeling it. This poor girl has been spoiled her whole life, never having to work for what she has, including that shiny car she brought in for maintenance last week, and it shows.

Bubble gum—I've got a wad of bubble gum for a dick right now.

Her tongue flopping around inside my mouth like a beached fish has me choking back a gag but I forge on, not quite ready to quit this mission yet, even if it is starting to feel damn impossible. I need to get laid, yesterday. Judging from her lifeless mouth, I'll be putting in *all* the work tonight.

Beyond done with her joke of a performance, I drop my lips to her neck, pretending it's another's. The one I've been watching like Edward Cullen himself. Fucking Angie and her stupid vampire movies. That's the one thing I don't miss about our roommate and his girl—the cheesy movies we were forced to watch. Or more specifically, *I* was forced to watch since Marc always hides out in his room doing who knows what behind that closed door of his.

Actually, I saw once. More than once if I'm being bold which, since I speak in all-caps anyway, isn't too hard.

My lips quirk with the urgent need to yell out "that's what she said" at my own inner dialogue.

Wow. I really am bored.

I catch movement from below and pull back to see a thin, dark figure walking to Paige's Honda, recognizing her wavy mane before the helmet is yanked over it. *Where is she going?* This is her night off so I know she's not going to work. Her bike starts up without issue—*you're welcome*—and Paige is right, girl purrs like a cat in heat.

I feel my dick begin to stir for the first time all night. Carlson feels the change and starts pushing into me, chasing the hardness she's been expecting. Poor dude almost deflates from the contact.

Heavy revving brings my attention back to my new roommate and I spot Paige popping into a flawless wheelie with her knee on the seat before burning out of the lot. *Damn...*

And now my cock is sticking straight up like an eager explorer searching for his next great discovery.

Carlson releases another moan.

Not that one.

I lean back, looking at the girl currently trying to constrict me for easier consumption, and...I can't do it. Not with Medusa's long-lost cousin anyway.

I help her to her feet, smoothing her dull blonde hair and say, "It's not going to happen tonight." The words taste foreign and I lick my teeth, feeling them out.

Nope, just like I thought, I don't like 'em.

But I like Carlson even less.

Her face screws up in confusion. She's never been told no before and doesn't know what it means.

"You're really sweet-" like acid "-but I got shit to do." Like floss my teeth. Or organize my shoes—all three pairs of them. Anything but continuing this charade with Miss Priss.

Confusion morphs to anger a second before she snaps, "I thought you were different. I already told my friends about you!"

Oh, shit. Stage five clinger alert.

This bomb's about to explode in my face and I can't even remember how I got here. Oh, yeah, Operation Forget Paige. *Not all missions require you to hang off the side of an airborne plane, Tom. Some need a little more headwork.* Those movies make it look so easy though.

"Hey," I hush. Like seriously, pipe down. We have neighbors. Not that they care about the noise we make—not anymore thanks to Marc's…deal with Kary, the apartment manager—but if they did, she'd be bothering them. Hell, she's bothering me. "I never gave you any idea this was anything serious. The note you left for me basically said the same thing."

"It said 'call me'. That doesn't mean I want a one-night stand."

It doesn't?

"I misunderstood then. My apologies. You can just take off."

"What? You're just kicking me out?"

I shrug, not knowing what else to say. I mean, how many times do I have to tell her? I'm just not that interested.

"Well, you asked me here for something, right? Why can't we finish what you started?"

Her nails press into my wrists until it starts to bite and I fucking knew it. Chick is a serpent. I grow genuinely concerned her venom might infect my bloodstream if I don't extract myself quickly enough. Not that it's likely with my mind still stuck on a certain hot biker flying down the streets right now, making my blood practically boil as it runs hotter than it has in…ever?

I pull from her clutches, putting space between us.

"Sorry, I just can't."

"Why? Because I don't have leather pants and ride a motorcycle?" she snarls.

I snort. Like that would help her chances.

"You think I didn't see you eye fucking that skank all night?"

My heart starts racing.

"Are you talking about my roommate? She lives here. I was looking at her because I thought she was having a seizure in there." I jerk my thumb over my shoulder, glaring when I see Marc kicked back, grinning like a fucking douche. I flip him the bird and his lips spread even wider.

Carlson pushes past me, storming out the front door and I let her go before dropping to the couch, ignoring the triumphant grin my best friend aims my way. Dude's a regular comedian all of a sudden.

◆ ◆ ◆

My eyes snap open to a pitch black room and a crick in my neck. Looking around, I realize I fell asleep on the couch. A couch made for a normal person, not someone my size. At 6'6", most furniture is too small for me which is why I usually only sleep in my bed since it's the only thing that fits my tall ass. I must've passed out sometime during the night. I vaguely remember watching the front door before sleep took over.

Probably to make sure that snake in the grass didn't come back to bite me in the…anything.

A giggle followed by a thump out in the hallway has me up and across the room in a flash. Peering through the peephole, I see Paige slumped over some bulky dude and I rip the door open without hesitation.

My chest puffs as I step forward, my voice like ice, gaze just as hard. "What the fuck is this?"

Paige's head jerks immediately.

"Uh, oh. Fee-fi-fo-fum, looks like I poked the beast."

"That doesn't even make sense." I shake my head, thinking about our old neighbor who would mix up her fairy tales sometimes. No need to memorize them when you're living them—the Grimms' versions.

Paige's words come out slurred though and her lids are heavy, red lines distorting her green eyes.

"You're drunk?"

"Yep." She pops the p, bringing my gaze to her lips. They're swollen. From use.

I go to flip my hat but, remembering I'm not wearing one since it's the middle of the night and all, I rub my jaw instead.

"And what? You thought you'd bring home an easy layup?"

"I don't play ball, I break them." She laughs like she's proud of herself for coming up with such a good quip.

"That doesn't make sense either." *Denied.*

Underneath her leather jacket, her loose shirt's riding up the more gravity tries to claim her and thanks to her *helper's* hold on her, a nice little slice of skin peeks out, robbing almost all of my thoughts.

I finally tear my eyes away, pinning the loser attempting to hold her up with a glare so chilling I'm surprised he doesn't shiver. This motherfucker is wider than me, sure, but in a smokestack kind of way. Smokestacks fall, they break, they crumble to pieces given the right amount of pressure. And they probably cry like a little bitch while doing it.

Anticipation hangs in the air like smoke itself.

Paige sobers a bit, looking at the guy like she's just realizing he's there.

Jesus Christ.

"Where's my bike?" she demands and I'd laugh if I wasn't wondering the same thing myself.

Dude throws his hands up, the hands he was using to hold Paige up with, and I reach out to catch her before she replaces our welcome mat.

She groans from the transition but doesn't say anything, waiting for an answer.

"It's still at the bar. After we, uh-"

Dude glances at me and I swear to God I want to shove my fist down his throat just so I don't have to hear his next words.

"After we, you know," he says, beating around the bush—a bush I'm about to beat the shit out of myself, "you asked me to take you home. You were poured more than you should've been, so I drove you here myself."

I narrow my eyes, wondering what the hell 'you know' means, at the same time never wanting to find out.

"And who exactly are you?"

"Her," the hesitation nearly undoes me, "ex-boyfriend."

Paige snorts loudly, causing us both to look at her.

"Oh, shit. Did I do that out loud?"

I smother a laugh 'cause this isn't funny. Not really. She comes home smashed and brings a random, or supposedly not-so-random, guy with her. She could've been hurt, or worse.

Paige relaxes into me, her eyes fluttering to a close. I'm pretty sure she sniffs me but I'm too focused on how she feels in my arms to tell. This is the first time we've touched aside from our fingers grazing last week when I returned her phone. She's warm and soft, her hard edges lax and pliable in my hold. My arms slide under hers, bringing her flush against my body. She's tall, taller than other girls I've been with, and I like the way she fits. I always have to bend to fit everything—buildings, furniture, people. It's nice to have a tender body against mine that I don't have to adjust for.

A little moan escapes her lips and I stiffen.

"Dean, thanks for dropping me off."

Her meaning isn't lost on ol' Dean boy. He's being dismissed, a fact that disappoints him. Greatly.

When he makes eye contact with me, I nod, officially releasing him of his babysitting duties. I could be more gracious but he didn't have to share that detail about them doing whatever it is they did. She's my roommate and I don't want to hear that shit. Or see it. Her just-kissed lips have already been added to my overflowing spank bank material and now I have to work on erasing his ugly mug from the picture.

I wait until I hear his feet hit the bottom step, then I guide Paige inside, carrying most of her weight.

"I like the way you smell."

I glance down at her on the way to her room, smirking. I knew she was sniffing me.

"And how do I smell, girl?"

"Like home." Then, almost to herself, she murmurs sadly, "But not like than them."

My smile drops. *The fuck?*

"Who?"

She doesn't respond, staying silent but burrowing into my chest. A hollow chest that can't withstand the pressure she's threatening with such a simple gesture.

After depositing her to her bed, she reaches out, holding me in place. I'm hovering over her, only inches from her face but her eyes remain closed. Mine roam her beautiful face flushed from being over served. Her thin eyebrows furrow over delicate eyes. Long eyelashes drape across high cheekbones with a slender nose and full lips. Her chin has some powder on it, making my chest constrict.

Without thought, I swipe it with a finger and lick the substance. *Sugar.*

Paige's eyes open and zero in on the finger in my mouth. I release it slowly as her breathing hitches. Want flashes across her face like a stoplight at midnight and it's taking everything in me not to lean forward and kiss her with barely contained hunger of my own.

"Sweet," I mumble like the dumbass I am.

She moans again, arching up, and my mind goes blank. It's everything I thought it'd be. Paige's back is clear off the bed like she's being possessed yet somehow I feel like I'm the one in need of an exorcism.

I can't take my eyes off her. Wouldn't, even if I could.

God help me.

Perky tits strain through her thin shirt that's bunched at the bottom, showing more of that perfectly toned stomach of hers. My fists tighten with the need to slip underneath, my fingertips aching to feel her smooth looking skin. Her signature peach scent combines with her arousal and I want more. So. Much. More.

With labored, slow movements, I run my nose along her exposed neck, inhaling as I go. I'm hard as a fucking rock and when her leg lifts, brushing my dick, I damn near explode then and there, making a complete fool of myself. Her needy gasps echo off the walls as her nails clamp my biceps with an urgency I know all too well.

Right there with ya, girl.

"So, uh, that guy's your ex?" My staggered breath feathers over her sharp jaw. It's been bugging me since Dean said it. Not only his admission—*jerk off*—but her reaction to it. I'm still not convinced she and Marc aren't messing around either. He's been a different person around her and she seems all too happy being in his presence, giggling incessantly. She sure as hell doesn't act like that around me, which is insulting as fuck when you think about it, but the tension between us isn't my imagination running wild. Her actions tonight prove that. She's basically dripping for me and I haven't even properly readied the pipes yet.

Wonder if Marc gets that reaction out of her, too.

"Not really."

Not really? Either someone's your ex or they're not. *Right?*

Her fingernails skim up the backs of my arms, giving literally all of my skin goose bumps, even my fucking scalp. Holy shit.

"So," I work to clear my throat, "what was all that outside about then? I'm pretty sure Tree Stump thinks your hook-up tonight meant something." Enough to brag about it.

This dizzying laugh, similar to the one in my Tahoe the other day, floats past her lips, up above our heads, settling at the base of my skull.

"Our kiss tonight was…a mistake. But, it's still over between us. We want different things. The end. Are we done talking now?"

Paige's hands slide around my neck as she tries to close the distance but I don't budge. Too loyal to my boy, too afraid I won't be able to stop, too fucking wound up from it all, I lock my muscles in place, holding firm, inches away.

"What does he want?"

I bet I can guess.

"To fall in love."

I pull back to look in her hooded eyes. "And you don't?"

She squeezes her eyes shut, dropping her hands to the mattress with a bounce and swallows audibly. I twitch from the loss but don't move otherwise.

"I just can't right now. I don't have any room."

Can't?

My eyebrows slam together. I don't know what I was expecting but it wasn't that.

So, Dean caught feelings for a hard ass looking for a fling? Even though it's good to know where she stands, it still doesn't rule out her having a thing with Marc. I know for a fact that, like me, dude has no plans for settling down anytime soon.

They'd be perfect for each other really.

That thought fills me with something I'd rather not acknowledge so I focus on the latter part of her answer, asking thickly, "Room for what?"

Her light snore fills the silent bedroom.

Well, damn. Tonight's just full of firsts, isn't it?

CHAPTER 6

Paige

I'M NURSING WHAT I'VE STARTED CALLING THE HEADACHE. Not to be confused with a common household headache that all of us mere mortals suffer from occasionally. No, this is *The* Headache. The one that follows a night of complete and utter debauchery. The kind you bring upon yourself by ignoring any and all common sense garnered throughout your life by attempting to drink yourself into oblivion. The kind I've been bringing on myself too often lately.

I just hope I gave the bartender with no core values whatsoever a great tip for indulging my apparent death wish I had last night. That kind of customer service is hard to come by these days.

It's always strange waking up at the time I usually go to sleep but today it's even more off-putting since it's my first morning in my new apartment. I'm not sure if the guys have work today or not because it's still fairly quiet, save for the occasional heavy breath or two.

Feeling somewhat human again after a hot shower, I decide to make my roommates breakfast. If they're anything like my brothers who would wake up like a pack of ravenous wolves after a night of drinking, then they'll appreciate a home cooked meal when they do get up. Cooking will also give me something to focus on instead of my embarrassing effort at seducing Beckett last night. The guy probably had his fill from his scaly friend last night then was forced to deal with my Sloppy Jane impersonation.

What was I thinking?

My hand curls around the vanilla extract for pancakes and I remember. His smell. It does things to me. It makes me want things. Things I can't want right now.

Isn't that what he asked me? Why I couldn't fall in love? It's not that I don't want to, it's that I can't, at least for right now. Besides the fact that I absolutely do not have the time, I can't spare the mental realty for anyone extra. My brothers, and most importantly my mom, are it for me. They are my first, last, and middle priorities with only room for the sporadic stupid decision—or two. Last night easily fell into the latter category, what with Beckett ramming his tongue down his date's throat. No amount of Marc's motocross stories could distract me from that whole scene, even if they were mildly entertaining.

Dean wasn't much help either, peppering me with kisses that tasted like a cheap replacement for what I really wanted. For who I really wanted.

Dean. I should probably send him a text to thank him for taking me home but I'm dragging my sore feet. Beckett's nosey guess about him wasn't far off—Dean did take that kiss much more seriously than I did. Than I ever would. Kissing is like flirting—harmless fun that doesn't necessarily mean there's more to follow, despite what some men try to convince themselves.

But I do need my bike back and even though I have more men at my fingertips than most people, they all feel so goddamn out of reach still. The chair I ordered for Mom came in. Tysen has a truck. Maybe I'll try him. See if he actually answers this time. He may have helped me move but he hasn't responded to any of my texts since.

A door down the hall opens and I hold my breath, hearing a loud groan and then another door close with a click. *The bathroom*. The one I share with Beckett. I could've sworn I heard muttered voices—or maybe just one—coming from his room earlier.

I strain my ears, trying to make out any noises from…I don't know, like a guest or something, then cover my face with my hands before realizing my head is a no-go zone and drop them.

Pancakes. Those will help. Nothing like sugar-soaked carbs to drown out The Headache.

Beckett, freshly showered, appears as I'm setting out the last batch, avoiding me entirely as he goes straight for the coffee I brewed. I don't drink the stuff but Jesse and my mom always did so I can make a pot with my eyes closed.

He's wearing a blinding pink shirt that's just tight enough to hug some of his more prominent muscles. With the words *You'd be loud, too, if I was riding you* stretched across the chest, my mind wanders back to the noises I heard coming from behind his closed door. Is that what he thinks is loud? A few morning murmurs... huh. *Okay.*

Should be interesting when I finally do bring someone home. Then maybe I'll get myself a cheesy shirt, too, one that says *A better ride than your bike.* And he'll damn well know it from how loud *I* am.

Surreptitiously sneaking a glance down the hall, I say, "bad night?" hoping he was somehow drunker than I was. When I don't see anyone follow him, I prop my hip against the counter, facing him fully.

His eyes finally meet mine and I'm right back to last night being held in his impressive arms, the feeling of being wrapped up safe and secure piercing me like a stray bullet on a battlefield.

I press the heel of my palm into my chest, rubbing small, hard circles.

His sleep-drunk voice only rasps out, "I've had worse."

He's still holding my gaze but not in a hostile way like I expected. Maybe I'm making a bigger deal out of this. Last night obviously meant as much to him as it did to me—nothing.

"Sorry about last night." I drop my eyes to gather some condiments from the fridge. "I had a little too much to drink and I'm sorry it involved you at all. I didn't mean to wake you."

"What would've happened if you didn't?"

I turn to find him still locked on me like a predator to its prey—unblinking, unmoving, un-fucking-believably sexy—and scowl, which honestly hurts horribly.

"What do you mean?"

"What would've happened if I didn't wake up? Would you have invited *Dean* to come in? Dude was practically drooling after the bone he thought he was promised." His eyebrow cocks like maybe I won't understand the innuendo. *Oh, I get it.* How funny he thinks he must be.

I attempt to wave the thought away like smoke from a tire burnout.

"Dean knows where things stand." *Mostly.*

"But would you have invited him inside?"

I scan his face as he does mine, both looking for what's not being said. Searching for answers to questions neither of us is willing to come out and ask.

I flick another glance toward our bedrooms, saying, "No."

"Why?"

His question is quick like a cat on a mouse and I wonder if he's playing with me in the same way. Batting me around for his own amusement.

He'll have to get his kicks somewhere else though. The laugh that leaves my mouth next is humorless and pointed.

"Look, sorry again for disturbing you. I realize you had a date over." Another glimpse at the empty hall. "And I probably interrupted-"

"You didn't."

The look he gives me is full of arrogance, daring me to push the matter. See where it leads.

But I won't. I shouldn't care where it might take me even if a part of me—an itty, bitty part of me—is mentally already down the hall, throwing his door wide open just to see for myself.

"Well, regardless, it won't happen again."

"You could've called me, you know." He sips his coffee, never breaking eye contact. "To pick you up. You were in pretty bad shape."

Sticking by his innuendo-dipped tongue, his eyes caress my

entire body, starting at my toes. By the time he makes it to my suddenly parched throat, I lean toward him without meaning to. An arrogant smirk slashes across his mouth like a tally mark, righting me almost instantly.

Smug bastard.

"My shape is always on point, but thanks for keeping tabs." His eyes flare and now I'm the one smirking. "You sure your attention isn't better spent elsewhere though? Maybe on a certain princess in a Lexus?" My voice raises just enough for any eavesdroppers but I keep my gaze on his, not really interested in seeing her anymore. And she can't have my pancakes either.

Beckett pushes off the counter while I do the same, meeting him in the middle, less than a foot apart. I swear my refusal to be intimidated will be the death of me. That or The Headache.

"You sound jealous." My snicker is covered by him adding, "But don't worry, I have more than enough *attention* to go around. Let me know if you want on the roster. I'll see if I can fit you in."

The tall asshole grabs a handful of pancakes before walking around me, taking a huge bite as he leaves.

Forget the throb in my head, the only thing I can focus on now is the pulsing between my thighs and damn if I didn't just find the cure for The Headache.

Too bad it's at the oversized hands of my off-limits roommate.

◆ ◆ ◆

After a relatively quiet breakfast with Marc, I get him to drive me back to the bar I left my bike at. His BMW breathes sex like it was made for that very reason. The red and black seats are tailored for comfort and functionality for any position you might find yourself in. The sound system exhales deep beats of bass in a hypnotizing rhythm. The smell is leather and man—there's no other way to describe it. Marc is all man and his car is the testosterone-soaked cherry on top.

I slant a look at him, finding his flame tattooed arms flexed as one wrist rests overtop the steering wheel, the veins in his forearms pronounced enough to make a starring role in any phlebotomist's wet dream. His close to the scalp cut is partly covered with a baseball hat today and his caramel skin looks painfully smooth aside from some kind of brush burn just below his sharp jawline. His long black lashes rarely blink, allowing for his dark eyes to take in everything without interruption. His shirt's armpits are cut to his damn hip bones, showing off the tight muscles that make up his entire torso. Relaxed fit jeans with high tops complete the swagged-out look he rocks on the regular. He's even got a cut above his right eyebrow that looks fresh.

The man is hot in all the right ways and there's no doubt he'd make for a fantastic bed buddy—if I were interested. Fortunately, I'm not. First and foremost, he's my roommate and I can't ruin the sweet set-up I've got going living with him and his annoying bestie.

Which brings up reason number two—Beckett. While he's also my roommate, I can't deny he's got something over me. Something I can't quite put my finger on and it's not just his towering height. The guy drives me crazy, has from the second our eyes collided that first day, and I don't think about him the same way I think about his friend. I *like* to look at Marc. I can't stop looking at Beckett. At him, around him, behind him. What the hell is his deal?

Marc asks about last night, wondering how mad Beckett got.

I shrug, staring out the window. "Not too bad. If anything, I think he was more irritated he was pulled away from his date."

He surprises me with a low rumble resembling a laugh. When I turn my head his way, he says, "She left right after you did. That wasn't his problem."

That has me staying quiet the rest of the short trip.

I don't know what Beckett's issue was last night then. Was he really pissed at me for coming home drunk? And more importantly, why would he be? It's not like these guys don't drink themselves. The fridge at home has more beer than food, the freezer's even worse with hard alcohol, and don't even get me started on the cart in the living room dedicated solely to cocktails.

Before parting ways, Marc invites me to one of their Friday night family dinners sometime. I accept, knowing a meal with my new roommates and their close friends will be a step in the right direction. Since I work Friday nights, I won't be drinking and I can see if that changes Beckett's attitude toward me.

◆ ◆ ◆

Back on my white pony, I breeze through town with last night's events still on my mind. The details from the night before are like looking through a steamed-up window on a humid day, I can see everything but it's slightly blurred. As the stubborn mist wears off, I'm able to remember more and I'm beginning to wonder how the hell Beckett heard anything in the first place, especially if he wasn't up entertaining like I'd first assumed. Marc's room is the closest to the front door so it'd make more sense for him to be upset over my drunk and disorderly conduct, yet he acted like he didn't know about any of it.

Tysen meets me in the front of the furniture store with his pick-up and together we get Mom's recliner into the bed. My body continues to rid the toxins from last night in the form of rivers of sweat cascading down my face like spring waterfalls and I soak up as much of it as I can using the bottom of my gray tank. The growing puddles show on the light fabric but I can't bring myself to care. My newfound 6'6" remedy pushed from my mind has brought my hangover to the forefront once again and my head is absolutely swimming. The thought has me imagining the cold water of Creekwood's pool so I invite Ty to join me for a dip before we deliver the chair to Sunbrook all while crossing my fingers he doesn't see through my thinly veiled attempt to prolong our time together. I was lucky enough to get him out of the house today thanks to a promise to buy him dinner.

My brother and I race to the apartment, ignoring the car

horns honking as we weave through traffic. Tysen, being the middle child, is the glue that holds the family together. He's the chameleon of the family, too, a shapeshifter of sorts. He is whoever we need him to be to keep the peace. He doesn't like any discord and will go to any length to keep everyone happy. He blends with our grumpier, more serious, older siblings but can also keep pace with me and Nicky when we try to lighten things up.

"I think you dropped your exhaust pipe back there," I joke from my seat on the stairs when he finally pulls up. Riding a street bike has its advantages in traffic, like cutting through lanes like softened butter.

Tysen looks adoringly at his truck, rubbing the hood. I got my love of fast things from him. Unfortunately, I also got my love for junkers from him, too. The old Ford is dripping oil all over the two parking spaces it's taking up.

"Old Bessie's been needing to lose a few pounds. It was probably good for her."

He pretends to shine the rusty grill, making me snort.

"Bessie is the definition of a Ford—Found On Road Dead."

"Not as long as I can help it."

Ty spends more time fixing up the clunker than he does working, which is one of many reasons why I'm footing the bill for our mom's new place. I love the boy but he needs to pick a lane in life already, and not the one currently slicked in oil from his beloved whip.

We swim the afternoon away, lazily soaking in the sun while shooting the shit. Tysen is the easiest to be around because of his uncanny abilities but I often wonder what kind of a toll it takes on him to always be *on*. To always be who he thinks others want instead of being who he actually is. Even with Mom, I've watched as he slips into the role of charming stranger looking for a gossip buddy when a couple years ago he was seeking her approval at every turn, waiting for her to notice his good deeds and shower him with affection.

But like all families affected by Alzheimer's, we have a part to play.

I work to keep my emotions in check all day to ease some of his own. I'd take all of his worries on if he'd let me. I'd take on everyone's.

I am taking on everyone's.

Most people think being the oldest is the hardest, always having to lead by example, looking out for the others. But I've always thought the youngest has it the worst, seeing everyone's prior mistakes laid out for you like a mine field, each step you take measured and deliberated before you even set foot on the ground. Growing up the youngest means being shown what others want you to see, varied versions of the truth, forcing you to develop a sixth sense for sniffing out the hidden facts being kept from your presumed naïve mind. Some may choose to stay blind to the uncomfortable truths but not me. I've always dug around, searching for the real story, regardless how unpleasant the outcome. And studying Tysen now, I can tell something's weighing him down. His smiles are a little too tight, his laughs a little too loud. He thinks I need comic relief but all I really want is for my family to be okay. Nobody can hold another up while crumbling themselves.

That's also how I knew Mom needed to be moved out of the other facility while the boys were ignorantly paying for subpar care for the woman who raised us. Her sudden departure from any sort of reality should've been their first clue but none of them work in the health field so I let that one slide. The constant missed meals paired with the rapid weight loss was a dead giveaway though, so I stepped in and took over all medical concerns regarding our mother, moving her to Sunbrook as soon as I could swing enough money to get her in. It's still a sensitive issue between the five of us but I refuse to back down. I don't rub it in their faces that they chose a shitty home to put our mom in so they have nothing to complain about in my mind. If anything, I just put money back in their pockets while prolonging our only parent's life. Sure, she can't remember any of us but she raised us as best she could, mostly by herself, and while she's still alive it's our responsibility—our honor—to return the same, if not better care. I'd sell everything I have to ensure the rest of her days are lived out as comfortably as possible, memory loss or not. I don't want recognition; the ability to see my mother's face a little longer is the only incentive I need.

"How's Mom doing at the new place?" he asks as if reading my mind. "Is she getting along with everyone?"

My hands swirl in the water beside my raft, making ripples without even meaning to. There's a sign stating pool floaties are restricted and when the manager came out earlier to enforce it, all I had to do was drop my apartment number and she left me to float in peace. Maybe that's their hook-up? Marc told me before I moved in that we had certain…amenities others didn't. I'm still not sure what exactly that means, or how, but the woman was pretty young and attractive, so it's not that hard to imagine. I can't picture it being Marc since she lives like *right* there and maybe that's too close for someone like him? I don't know.

And in order to keep my lunch down, I definitely don't consider my other roommate sleeping with the landlady.

I know if I was her and only had a quiet complex to manage, I'd be spending my days at the pool any chance I got, except this was the first time I've ever seen her and she acted like she was too busy—no, not too busy, like she was *flustered*—to even come down those stairs she lives at the top of.

"She's okay. Not as responsive as I would've thought honestly. She sits alone in every setting, preferring to still be by herself instead of joining in with the others. She's eating but I'm not sure how much." We log everything from brushing teeth and bathing to meal consumption and bowel movements but ever since she arrived at Sunbrook, her chart's been missing information. I'm not there during the day to know whose fault it is or why it's incomplete at all, but I've brought it up to my boss already so hopefully it gets resolved soon. "She's had a couple…lapses since she's been there," I say, remembering that family photo sitting on her nightstand, "so maybe she is improving. You should visit soon. When are you and Clarise visiting her again?"

His eyes drop and mine narrow for the first time this afternoon.

Clarise and Ty are high school sweethearts and have been together ever since, even after graduating six years ago. They used to visit my mom at least a couple times a week before.

Before.

Before everyone in the Christensen family decided to go their own way.

"Maybe."

"Ty." I wait until he meets my eyes again. "You're the only one that visits her regularly besides me. If you're pissed at me for yanking her out of that shithole, please, please don't take it out on her. She needs us. We're all she has left even if she doesn't know it. Caleb's work schedule is crazy and he can't get away and Nicky is, well, Nicky. He's sensitive and takes it personally every time Mom doesn't remember him."

"When was the last time Jesse saw her?"

I shake my head softly. "I don't know, but it's been a while. He's having a rough time, too."

Ty mutters something about him not being the only one but the sound of a sliding door opening has us lifting our heads. Beckett stands at the banister of our back balcony. Creekwood is broken up into three sections forming a broken U shape with the pool in the middle. Our apartment is in the central hub and has two balconies—one facing the parking lot, one overlooking the pool area.

"Is that your other roommate or are gearheads your thing now?"

Unable to take my eyes off the arctic blue ones locked on mine, I just say, "Yeah." Maybe to both, maybe not. I don't know anymore but Tysen doesn't push further so I don't either.

Beckett's eyebrow lifts and I finally rip my eyes away only to find my brother missing. Suddenly, I'm airborne and landing face first in the deep end sans floatie.

Breaking the water, I yell out a watery, "Asshole!"

"What?" he asks innocently, totally not fooling anyone. "It looked like you needed to cool off." His gaze raises so mine follows. Finding the balcony empty doesn't surprise me. Big guy is probably off pouting again.

"Yeah, okay. Let's go drop that chair off. It's almost time for my shift anyway. What did you decide you want for dinner?"

He jiggles a sunburnt shoulder. "I hear the place down the street has good salads."

My jaw drops. "Jesse told you?"

"That you tried to poison him with your health food? He did."

I roll my eyes, busy climbing the ladder out of the pool.

"You guys are so immature."

Tysen joins me as I towel off, grabbing one for himself as well.

"I know you are but what am I?"

Giving him my best annoyed look, I ask, "seriously?" before turning to leave.

I hear a "yep" next to my ear a second before I'm pushed back into the cold water, towel and all.

Oh, it's on.

CHAPTER 7

Paige

I'M FINISHING UP WITH THE LAST OF MY CHARTS FOR THE night when Vernon appears in the nurses' station. His graying hair is slicked back and he's sporting a new watch—another new one. Nurses don't have glamorous jobs to begin with then you throw in our required uniform of basic scrubs every day and it can seriously stifle some people's sense of style. I've seen people try to mix things up with little details here and there as a way to still express themselves, and watches, which are a requirement for our line of work, are a popular way to do it. I always wear my smartwatch but Vernon would never bother with something so popular. I've seen him with no less than seven different watches since I started working here, each one fancier than the last. This one is so shiny I almost miss the storm forming across his pinched face.

Ever since Beckett's interference a couple weeks ago, Vernon's kept his distance, minus the nasty looks aimed my way I still catch when he thinks I'm not looking.

I grew up with four brothers—I'm *always* looking over my shoulder.

I ignore him altogether, standing to retrieve my bag.

Waiting until my feet cross the threshold, Vernon sneers, "Snitch."

The area is empty, save for the old grump and myself. I spin to face Vernon, whose eyes are now tiny slits of fury.

"Do you have something you'd like to say to me?" Keeping my voice clear but low for his ears only, I lean casually against the counter, acting like I'm not itching to get out of here. I figured my first Friday night dinner with my roommates' family would be a perfect excuse to get my family together, too. So far, I've gotten exactly zero replies from tonight's invite though, not even from Tysen who never turns down free food.

"I think you heard me just fine, snitch. You tattled to Rosie that 'I wasn't doing my job.'" He says this with wrinkled fingers shaped into quotation marks, like it's some far-fetched notion.

"No, I simply informed Rosie Ms. Christensen's chart has been lacking important information lately. If you're to blame for that as the floor nurse, then maybe you haven't been doing your job."

"Your *mommy* hasn't been eating her regular meals which means I can't give her the medication she needs. Hers must be taken on a full stomach but she hasn't had one of those since you forced her to switch facilities unnecessarily." The jab has me pinching the material at my hips between my thumb and middle finger. "It's not my job to feed the patients and I refuse to give special treatment to anybody, even if you don't."

I let his many snide and *unnecessary* remarks slide to hone in on the only one that actually matters.

"What do you mean she hasn't had a full meal since she's been here? You haven't given her any medication since when? Her first day?"

He cocks his head to the side like I'm an idiot. And maybe, just maybe I fucking am. Maybe I shouldn't have moved her after all. Was it solely for my mother or was it for my own selfish reasons like everyone seems to think?

"Vernon, why didn't you say anything? I need to know that!" I can't stop my voice from rising or the shake it unveils.

"Like I said, I don't give special treatment. If you really cared about your mom, you could've asked somebody instead of running to Rosie about something you clearly know nothing about."

But I do know. I do…know.

Right?

I've been checking in every shift. I've been watching her like nobody else ever would. I've...been busy looking at her from a daughter's point of view, forgetting to cover the nurse side, too.

Hands now balled at my sides, I say, "If you-"

Cynthia bounces around the corner then, completely oblivious to the tension between her coworkers coiling tighter and tighter, and says, "Hey, girl, ready to go?"

Vernon smirks, knowing I won't lay into him in front of anyone else. Keeping my eyes on his though, I nod to her silently.

Cynthia takes the hint, turning to leave. As soon as I know she's out of earshot, I say, "She needs her medicine. *That's* your job."

And I storm off, not really sure if I'm more upset about Vernon being an asshole or that he's right.

◆ ◆ ◆

Later that afternoon, I wake to a commotion from somewhere in the apartment. Just what I need today. *Visitors.*

Groggy and parched, I swing my bedroom door open to see a bikini-clad redhead—a real redhead, the kind where the carpet matches the drapes where my hardwood floors never did match my dye job—stumble out of the bathroom. And, I think the zoo called wanting its baby giraffe back. She's all arms and legs and can barely walk without bumping into something, the biggest obstacle being a shirtless Beckett who's just stepping out of his room to catch her effortlessly. He doesn't waste his time checking to make sure she's okay though. Not when he's too busy watching me, or more accurately studying me. I can only imagine what I look like after waking from a fitful sleep in...I don't even remember what.

Glancing down, I cringe. Yep, boxers and a raggedy white tank—both stolen from whoever I slept over with last. *Nick, I think.* Oh, and no bra.

I shoot into the now vacant bathroom. Before I can get the

door closed though, I catch sight of Beckett and am surprised by what I see—desire. His eyes are still locked on mine but don't hold disgust like I thought they would. Not even an ounce.

Which I find…amusing?

Something like that.

I decide to have a little fun with this. If Ginger can't light the guy up, I can at least enjoy knowing I can, so keeping the door open and my eyes glued to Beckett's, I grip the hem of my shirt, slowly dragging the material up. His gaze drops to follow, his tongue darting out to lick at his bottom lip. My stomach is tan from my daily pool sessions and is always toned from my job. Lifting grown adults can be a good workout even if it wrecks your back. Plus, my countless hours of riding help me stay fit. My girl doesn't just sound like a beast, she handles like one, too.

Beckett's hands grip the giggling mess in front of him but he doesn't so much as glance her way.

A heat so powerful, so dangerous, builds at my exposed belly, heading south to settle at my core. My lips part from the intensity and my fingers stutter to a halt, skimming just at the underside of my boob.

Beckett's gaze jumps to mine, a tortured expression overtaking his face.

This started out as a joke but there's nothing funny about finding myself in the same dilemma as him. I want, no, I *need* to satisfy this ache and yet, I know he won't be the one to do it. One red-haired disaster is enough without adding a burgundy-streaked one to the pile.

Luckily, Beckett sticks his Shaq-sized foot in his mouth, effectively ruining the moment when he says, "Cold water's to the right. Use as much as you want." He looks away, finally noticing the girl in front of him. "I won't be needing it."

After one look at his smug little smirk, I kick the door shut. On him. On us. On this whole fucked up situation.

With the temp cranked to hot, I take my time washing and

shaving everything since I already promised I'd attend their family dinner and the accompanying splash time even though I'll be flying solo.

Halfway through, I end up taking a little longer on certain parts with nobody the wiser. Especially not the giant entertaining his newest pet.

Exiting the apartment, I see an older woman climbing the stairs, her arms loaded with reusable bags with different food sticking out the tops. Her eyes light up in recognition when she finds me taking up the doorway. The only person I've heard of living up here though is some recluse named Gary. And the couple getting ready to move in across the hall, but I doubt she's visiting either.

"You must be Paige?" Her accented voice flows out like warmed honey and puts me at ease immediately.

"Guilty." As my eyes hit hers, I finally see the resemblance. "And you're Marc's mom?" Same charcoal eyes set in a thin golden face with wavy dark, almost black, hair. It's long and thick and makes me wonder if Marc's hair would be that luscious if he grew it out. Probably. I hate when boys are prettier than me, yet I'm constantly surrounded by ones that are.

I need to find a new crew, I think as her glowing face pulls my first genuine smile all week.

"I'm Esmerelda, but you can call me Esme. Or Mama."

A dagger, serrated and sharp, slices across my heart but I fight not to show it, saying tightly, "Esme it is." Glancing at the groceries again, I ask, "Can I help you with anything? This is all going inside? It looks like it could feed an army."

Esme transfers the bags to my arms and turns to leave. I stand here confused until she calls over her shoulder, "If you can take care of these ones, I'll get the rest."

The rest? As in *more?*

Shaking my head, I quickly unload everything onto the counter then hurry downstairs. And no, she wasn't kidding.

"Do you always buy their groceries?" I ask once we're in the kitchen, unpacking the massive food haul together.

"Groceries? This is for tonight's dinner." She clucks her tongue, making me laugh.

My mom and I would cook meals for our family, too, but it never even came close to this amount of food. She has sides for the sides.

"I didn't believe Marcos when he told me a girl was moving in." I place my hands on the counter behind me, watching as she floats around the kitchen, completely at ease in her surroundings. "These boys, they're tough. It's always been them against everyone else, even the ones that are supposed to love them most. *Especially* the ones supposed to love them most." I perk up at that but she pauses, staring at the floor. Is she talking about *all* the guys? "Anyway, it would do them some good to have a feminine touch around here. It might soften them up a little."

"I wouldn't count on it." Her eyebrows draw together, so I say, "I grew up with all boys," like that explains everything. When she still appears unconvinced, I shrug, moving away from her intense stare. "So, what can I do?"

Esme just shakes her head, shooing me out of the kitchen. "You go have fun. Marcos tells me you've done two things since you moved in—work and sleep. Today, you can play. You all have that in common, you know? Your work obsession. You need some balance though. That's what I try to always tell my Joaquin but he's as stubborn as an ass." She all but spits the last word and I smile softly at her.

That knife strikes again.

"I don't know. I think they have the playing part down just fine," I say, realizing I haven't been out to the races lately. I should go one of these Saturdays. Have some fun of my own while also finding someone to have fun *with*.

Esme cuts a hand in the air. "They're just practicing."

Now I'm the one that's confused.

"For?"

"For the real thing. For love," she states as if it's obvious. "They're, how do you say, throwing oats?"

"Sowing wild oats."

"Yes, sowing oats." She snaps her fingers. "They're making all their mistakes now so when they fall in love, they'll get it right."

"I'm not sure that's how it works," I mumble. It sounds like a lame excuse to sleep around. If you've got an itch, there's nothing wrong with having someone scratch it, but don't pretend like it's part of some bigger picture. I know I don't.

She leads me to the door, turning to face me with a seriousness I wasn't expecting.

"Trust me, when those boys settle down, it'll be for real and it'll be for life. Whoever can bring one of them to their knees is a lucky woman."

"Well, I can tell you it won't be me."

Although, the thought of Beckett on his knees is rather enticing and I'd like to revisit that image later, when I'm alone.

Her eyes search mine and I'm about to look away when she shrugs her shoulders, saying, "if you say so," before returning to the kitchen.

I descend the back stairs thinking over Esme's comment about being obsessed with work. I never realized I was obsessed with work. I don't think I even was until recently, now that I have very real, very large bills to cover.

My mother worked her ass off my entire childhood to pay for everything my brothers and I needed, and made sure to have health insurance on all of us kids. I never knew until her diagnosis that she'd been skimping on her own coverage to decrease the monthly payments. Had been for *years*. I'm not sure if the boys understand the repercussions of that but I connected the dots right away. Our mother wasn't going to regular doctor visits, let alone any specialists, squashing any chance of possibly catching the early onset symptoms sooner.

While it's true there's no cure, we would've had more time to figure out what to do with the time we had her at full capacity. I miss her easy smiles. I miss her light laughs. I would've counted each one like I do with Jesse's, saving them for days like today when I need them most. I would've started saving money earlier instead of wasting it on shit I no longer care about.

I would've, I would've, I would've.

God, the guilt is enough to choke the words from even bubbling out of my weak throat. The overwhelming urge to claw my neck has my hands trembling at my sides.

An unfamiliar voice—an unfamiliar *female* voice—catches me off guard, saying, "penny for your thoughts," as soon as I hit the bottom step.

Next to the outdoor staircase is a pretty brunette I've never seen before. Or maybe I have? Something about her seems familiar. Her long straight hair is pulled into a high pony and the words sun-kissed come to mind. If we lived near a beach, she'd be there. She's got a skater vibe to her but looks too dainty to actually skate. Athletic for sure though, if her clothes are any indication.

She smells like strawberries and sunshine.

Her eyes. As weird as it sounds I've seen her eyes before. For a brief flicker of time, maybe from another life, but I know I've seen them. They're not the kind a person forgets easily. Not only the distinct color—hazel—but the pain buried in them.

I tap my temple. "These ones cost a nickel."

She laughs lightly and I like it. I like her.

"I figured. This place breeds damaged goods."

Okay, maybe not.

"Excuse me?"

"Sorry. I didn't mean to say it like that." She squeezes those eyes closed, blowing out a breath, before reopening them. "I work and, well, I guess live with all men, so I say whatever I'm thinking. I'm not very good with my own gender."

Her sheepish expression along with her fidgety hands has me softening again.

"It's okay. I get it. I lived with four my whole life."

She nods her head, looking over my hair, like she's seeing me for the first time all over again.

"Wow, I didn't even think of that."

Um, what? *Have I met her before?*

"Living with two must be a piece of cake then," she rushes to add.

I glance over at Marc smoking a cigarette by himself then to Beckett sitting on a lounger chatting with a couple guys. After a moment, he looks up, giving me a once-over I can feel from across the pool area.

"Something like that."

"Anyway, I'm Angela. I'm with Coty, the old roommate."

She hooks a thumb over her shoulder at a dark prince. Dark brown hair sticking all different ways like someone just ran their hands through it and, judging from the heated look he's giving his girl, I'm willing to bet that Angela can't keep the guy off her for longer than a few minutes at a time. If she hadn't already told me he was hers, the head-over-heels vibes rolling off the guy would've given it away.

I quickly return the wave he throws me before averting my gaze. Some things are *that* off-limits. He's one of them.

"I lived across the hall for a while, so I know a little what you're going through. Also, I work with their sorry asses every day," she says loud enough to gain a few glares our way, then she leans over to whisper, "actually, they're all great, amazing even, in their own way, but it takes some time to see that and appreciate it. It's rough in the beginning but after you're in, you're *in*, and they'll never let you go."

I raise both eyebrows.

What is Creekwood really? A cult?

"I should probably be leaving now."

Laughing, she grabs my elbow when I twist at the waist, pretending to go.

"No, it's not bad. It's all good, I promise. But if you're not used to it, like me anyway, then it can be a lot to handle. At least in the beginning."

"Not used to what?"

She looks back at her man and he lifts his gaze as if sensing her. "Family."

I drop my stare to the ground, studying the cracks in the concrete. How they can start out so small, yet grow so fucking big, so fucking fast.

"Ah, the damaged goods part is starting to make sense now."

"Right?" She laughs again, motioning me forward. "Come on, let's go have some girl time or whatever the hell it's called."

Angela basically echoed what Esme just told me. What is it with these roommates of mine?

And why am I so interested in finding out when I already have more than enough to deal with, including my own screwed up family?

Putting everything I just heard aside, I join Angela and the pool party of misfits for some girl time or whatever the hell it's called.

CHAPTER 8

Paige

I DIVE OFF THE SIDE OF THE POOL INTO THE CRISP, COOL water, gliding to the bottom before kicking back up to the top. Swimming has always been a necessity living in this part of Washington where the summers last half the year with temperatures well into the nineties, if not worse. The shade offers almost no reprieve from the dry, desert-like air, so water's the only real defense at battling the unbearable heat.

We didn't have a pool growing up but we spent most afternoons at one of the three local rivers, cooling off. The boys would jump off anything with some height and thanks to my competitive nature, we'd end up diving off the highest cliffs we could find just to outdo each other.

We're lucky we're all still alive honestly.

"Someone can't take their eyes off you."

I twist to find Angela sitting on the edge a few feet away, soaking her legs. Her dark two-piece is stunning against her tan, thin frame. I'd expect every guy here to be hitting on her but Coty does a good job keeping them away with his ominous glare alone.

Needless to say, girl time has been uneventful.

"Who?"

She juts her jaw out and I follow her line of vision to see an imposing Beckett watching from his chair. Every time I look over there, he's watching. Waiting. For what though? What does he want from me? I haven't had a drink this whole time so I know that's not his problem.

Ignoring him and the feeling his gaze does, I dip my head back into the water, letting the water soak the long strands like

I used to during my nightly bath time. It was the only time I could actually get the bathroom to myself away from my brothers. Forget sculpting your eyebrows or doing your hair, the boys didn't give a shit about that stuff. They only wanted to pee and they didn't care who was in there to see it.

It was hard having girl friends as a child that didn't have siblings like I did. Hard because some of them would only use me to get to one of my brothers. Hard because I envied them so much sometimes it hurt to be around them. They had things I'd never had—new toys, makeup, privacy, freedom—and that somehow felt even worse. Hard, too, because they'd show a wicked sense of entitlement that I just couldn't relate to. At fucking all. With four older siblings, *nothing* is only ever yours.

When I lift my head again, I settle my gaze on a tatted rocker standing against the fence, telling Angela, "This guy hasn't stopped checking me out since I stepped through the gate." I look at her briefly. "I'm guessing Beckett is an only child?"

Angela's chest swells and my eyes narrow but she finally nods stiffly so I return my eyes to my own new pet.

"He's not used to sharing what he's deemed his," I say more to myself than Angela.

I should've known. Stupid men, always trying to mark territory they have no business claiming. Too bad for Beckett, I'm not his or anyone else's. I'm my own fucking woman and no matter who keeps my bed warm at night, I intend to keep it that way.

I jerk a nod at the Andy Black lookalike. He's not exactly my type, a little too grimy, but I feel like getting dirty and he looks willing as he happily saunters over with a smile carving his mouth up. He crouches down directly in front of me at the pool's edge, struggling a bit in skinny jeans tighter than the ones I own, and levels me with a simmering stare.

Now, we're getting somewhere.

"Hey, beautiful."

A loud whistle slicing through the courtyard cuts me and my eye roll off.

"Aye, River! Don't expect me to give you mouth-to-mouth when all that jewelry drags your ass straight to the bottom."

River's gaze leaves mine, giving a short nod but when he moves to stand, I say, "You could always lose the jewelry. And the clothes." I tip an eyebrow even though, really, his all-black outfit should've been shed hours ago. This is southeast Washington in July—the less clothing, the better.

"Don't be a twatsicle, dude, and just stay away from the deep end." Ahem, *my* end.

There's a bite to Beckett's playful warning but I don't bother checking behind me. Angela's hazel eyes tell me everything I need to know. So does the retreating back formally known as my next one-night stand. *Damn it.*

"That was…interesting." I keep my eyes locked on Angela's, watching as they round in thought. "I've never seen Beckett act like that before."

I finally break, chancing a look over my shoulder. Beckett's staring daggers at River, slashing him to absolute pieces, all while the redhead from upstairs wiggles on his lap, happy as a clam and oblivious as one, too.

Oh, the hypocrisy.

Now I let the eye roll fly.

"Act like what?"

"Like he actually gives a shit."

I eye her, wondering how much she's willing to reveal here.

"Are you two…?" She lets the question linger as I pull up on the side of the pool next to her.

"No."

Angela cocks her head and I almost laugh.

"We barely see each other."

And when we do, well, we're more likely to kill each other than fuck each other. I just don't know which one sounds better.

"Well, what he does see, he likes because he's never shown jealousy like that in the time I've known these knuckleheads. He may get protective over me sometimes but that's not what that was." Her finger swirls in the air.

I take a moment to observe the trio again. Marc, in a pair of red board shorts and matching red high tops, has his usual fuck-off attitude going strong, even as different people take turns attempting to pull him into the mix. With a hat sitting low over his face, you can't even read what he's thinking. I swear I see him wave his fingers to no one in particular though but I blink and his usual impassive self is back in place, the moment gone along with the...flirting? Who'd he wave at?

Coty, wearing black swim trunks and flip-flops, chats with a group of guys surrounding him like he holds the secret they've all been searching for. Like they know he did things the right way but now they want to know *how* he did it.

And Beckett's got a small audience riveted as he entertains them with some story or another. Every time one of his punchlines doesn't land the way he'd hoped though, his eyes strain a little and his gaze touches on his best friends like a reminder of who really matters. His colorful shorts are shorter than the others' but in a stylish way that makes him look ahead of the game. I wouldn't be surprised if he was. His whole persona is to throw others off and keep them guessing. People take him at face value, too shallow to dig deeper to what lies beneath, and he knows it.

And, yes, the redhead is still in his lap, looking like one of those partially inflated balloon people in front of car dealerships as she laughs hysterically at something the big guy is saying. Balloon goons, my brothers used to call them, because they were so creepy but funny to watch as they'd inflate to full height only to fall back down to half-mast then up again.

She just can't stand up on her own, can she?

Not with Beckett's strong, reassuring arms to hold her up when everybody else left her to struggle by herself.

Umm. Where'd that come from?

"Maybe he's just bored." Angela's voice brings me back from… wherever I just went. "Or he's just an asshole?"

At that we both crack up, letting our laughter settle over us like the sun's warm rays before it disappeared behind the building moments ago.

After a while, Angela finally pulls her legs out but, instead of getting up, turns to me with her face completely void of humor.

"He never lets his dates sleep over. It's his only rule and I can attest to him never, ever breaking it. He wouldn't admit why but I figured it out once." She darts a look over, making sure Beckett isn't paying attention. "On accident. I slept over with Coty as much as he was at my place and one time I was heading to the bathroom when I heard…"

Her eyes slam shut and I lean forward, holding my breath.

"What?"

She opens them with determination that I'm betting isn't in my favor.

"I'm sorry. I can't say. It's his secret to share, if he chooses to."

What?

She actually has the nerve to look apologetic after that epic lead up to nothing. Is this what it feels like to have blue balls? Because honestly, I understand the frustration.

The girl really had me going there.

She rests a hand on my exposed shoulder as she stands, saying, "I didn't think I'd like you. Not you specifically, but I didn't want to like the new roommate. I figured she'd come in and tear apart what they've worked so hard to build." She gazes across the pool before adding, "But you're different. You'll call them on their bullshit while dealing with your own. You're stronger than I expected and he needs that. Beckett needs someone that can handle the baggage he tries to act like isn't there."

I open my mouth to argue almost all of those points but she smiles down at me with a maniacal sort of look. Kind of like a pepped-up clown.

It's not pretty. It's intentional.

"I'm really happy you're here, Paige, just don't break him or I won't be anymore."

My jaw hangs off its hinges as I watch her stroll over to Coty whose arms are already open, waiting for her.

Did she just threaten me?

I let out an impressed laugh as I slide back down into the water. Truthfully, I didn't think she had it in her but there's more to Angela than meets the eye. There's more to all of them.

A band of beauties with broken pasts.

And I'm supposed to fit in here?

I relax my entire body, letting it float up to the surface, and I close my eyes. Not the smartest idea at a pool party but I need a minute. The last couple hours are catching up to me and the thoughts are swirling like a goddamn tornado. Marc's mom's revelations, Angela's semi-revelations, Beckett's...whatever that was—it's all given me a new look into the world I've found myself in. So many insights and yet no real details, like looking in a fogged-up mirror after a hot shower. Hints without facts.

Is Angela right about Beckett possibly being jealous? He doesn't act like that to me. He behaves like a brat most of the time except, of course, for the night he put me to bed. He was sweet, almost tender. The next morning, however, all traces of his kindness were gone, replaced with a cold front that could rival any chilly morning I've ever experienced.

How'd he end up like that? Who caused those coping mechanisms in the first place?

Esme mentioned the people that are *supposed* to love the guys the most. Who didn't give big, baby Beckett the love that they should've? And why?

Was it something he chose? Or did life take the choice from him entirely?

Hands latch onto my ankles then I'm yanked forward, causing my ass to sink and my head to spring up out of the water. The movement brings me face-to-face with the object of my thoughts as if my mind has the power to summon the devil himself. He's smirking down at me like one so I return the favor, except where his looks like he got the last laugh, mine says I'm just getting started.

"You met neighbor girl?"

My eyebrows nosedive until I remember Angela saying she lived across the hall for a while. I peeked inside last week when the cleaners were there and that place is *tiny*. No wonder she ventured next door.

"Angela? Yeah, she's cool. She said I should keep you in line."

The side of his mouth quirks and I notice he hasn't released me yet. His hands glide up to my knees, his thumbs rubbing the outsides of my legs and sending a trail of goose bumps up my body that even the cold water didn't cause.

"In line or in a gag?"

I pop a shoulder. *Whatever works.*

"And how would you do that?"

Tilting my head to the side, I place my feet on the bottom of the pool, slipping out of his grasp. With my chest in line with his face since he's in a deeper part, I look down at him and I get the feeling I might be the first to do such a thing. His eyes lift to mine and I swear they fucking sparkle like he gets off on it.

"I've got my ways."

I let the suggestion hang in the air between us like a volleyball net.

Ball's in your court.

He doesn't press further though. Instead we hold our standoff in silence, each letting the other wonder what's coming next.

Gesturing to Angela, I say, "You love her."

This response gets spiked without a second thought. "She's in love with Coty."

"That much is obvious. I meant as a friend. She's special to you."

I watch him closely as the words sail over to his side, landing at his feet.

Beckett only gives a lazy shrug, saying, "Angie comes from a broken home, too. She laughs through the heartache."

Too?

"Like you?"

His nostrils flare and I back up.

"You don't know me."

A humorless laugh glides across the water between us, reaching for something I've already tucked out of reach.

"I know you have a lot more going on than you show. I know your smile covers the cracks and your jokes stifle the pain. Whatever you're burying isn't completely dead and you know it but are too scared to face it. At least not without your trusty laugh track in place first."

"The fuck makes you think that?"

His face hardens to stone and I take a moment to look it over, recognizing the same fissures I see when I look in the mirror.

"Why don't you let anyone stay the night?"

"Easy. Just like you, I don't want a relationship."

"But you do."

"What?" he snaps, shooting those baby blues around.

Don't worry. They're still there.

"You do. You want a relationship so bad but you're terrified they'll hurt you. That you'll be the one to give them the power to destroy you, so you push women away with a smack on the ass and a smile on your face all while telling yourself that's what you want." I'd know. I've been doing the same thing for over a year now. It's easy to keep others out. The hard part is showing the mess hidden inside. "But you're already in a relationship with your boys and even if it's not a romantic one, it's a relationship just the same, proving your theory wrong and verifying what I thought all along—that you're just a coward with a pocket full of one-liners."

He stands to his full height and with one smooth motion, he

yanks my waist until it's flush against his, an embarrassing gasp falling from my lips from the contact.

"Here's a one-liner—fuck you."

Dropping me back on my feet, he stalks off, drawing notice from the entire party. When he joins his original plaything at the stairs, all eyes bounce between *that* and my stupid ass sitting in the middle of the pool.

I drag my hands down my face, catching movement by the gate.

My guy didn't leave.

Walking slowly past the tangle of limbs—someone really should teach the girl how to use her legs correctly—I climb the stairs, making sure to splash Beckett with every step I take on my way out. I'll need him for this next part.

Once I'm toe-to-toe with the rocker, I fist his unbuttoned shirt at his chest, pulling him to me gradually. My lips touch his and he finally catches on to what's happening. Opening his lips with my tongue, I slide in to massage the piercing there.

Smoke and metal, like a car crash waiting to happen.

Something feels wrong with this kiss and it's not just the taste of ash on his lips so I pull back slightly, taking his bottom lip with me. I'm still in it but I'm not *in* it.

His hands join in, dropping to just above my bikini bottoms with an eagerness I wish I could return. At least organically.

I hear a growl behind me and almost release the lip between my teeth from the smile sneaking out.

I draw the display out a little longer, pressing into him and earning a deep, loud rumble of a groan from him when my wet bottoms rub against the front of his skinny jeans. Those black-painted fingernails of his dig into my lower back to the point of pain and I almost slap the moron but hold off—barely—since it'd give the whole ruse away.

Happily releasing his lip with a juicy smack of my own, I roll my head over my shoulder, finding Beckett with the handrail in a death grip, watching the entire thing through glacial eyes. He's a twitchy bull in the ring with steam billowing from his nose, following the red cape of hair at my back.

With him still standing, I make sure to meet his gaze head-on, unsheathing my second sword, ready to make my final cut. Lifting my middle finger, I rasp out, "no, baby, fuck you," then leave the silenced party behind as I strut off, knowing I got the last laugh after all.

Nobody, not even a fuckboy on a power trip, determines what I can and can't do.

And would you look at that, I guess I did have a few more shits and giggles to spare.

◆ ◆ ◆

Back upstairs, after throwing on a cover-up, I find myself in the kitchen, diving into food prep with Esme. I'm still worked up from the scene outside and I'm not exactly sure what pulled me in here but Esme's massive dinner makes for the perfect distraction.

I should feel bad for leaving River with a raging hard-on but serves him right for wearing skinny jeans to a fucking pool party.

I refuse to even consider what Beckett's doing.

Esme and I chat about different topics ranging from farm life to zodiac signs. Both born in July, she's a Cancer while I'm a Leo. She's lived an incredible life but struggles with the constant unrest between her husband and their son. I guess things between the father-son duo have improved since Pop The Hood landed the farm as a major client but not as much as Esme would prefer. Her eyes light up anytime her kids' names are even spoken and when she describes her daughter like she's talking about a best friend, a jealousy like a deep cavern settles in my stomach, waiting to be filled with any inkling of affection in the vicinity.

I think I have that movie.

Cave dweller. I'm a cave dweller possessed by the ghosts of my family's present, not past. The feral creatures inside can't take me out. Their noxious parasites and bacteria won't harm me. But the love from my family being omitted will fucking annihilate me.

Fully immersed in chopping ingredients for the ceviche, I miss the door to the apartment opening followed by someone stepping up behind me until Marc's hand sneaks out to steal a red, slimy chunk with seeds stuck to it.

Seriously, how do you get them off?

He pops it into his mouth with an unapologetic smile then turns to his mom.

"You finally found someone to cut the tomatoes." To me, he explains, saying, "I hate that part."

She replies in Spanish, then the two continue in the language I always thought was sexy as hell but never learned a lick of. I chose German as my foreign language in high school. German. Ask me how many times I've used it in my life and I'll answer with the only word I actually remember—nein.

I find myself unable to turn away from their conversation, hanging off every detail, every roll of the R's—that shit's so impressive—every widening of eyes for emphasis, every laugh passed between mother and son. Esme's an animated talker while Marc speaks in low tones, getting his point across without needing theatrics. He's…intense.

When their gazes flick to mine, I resume my lackluster dicing.

Their easy banter makes me think of my mom's sense of humor. She was always funny but stern in her own quirky way. I guess raising four boys and one headstrong girl you'd need to find comedy where you could. Roll with the punches with a nasty jab of your own is the way I'd describe my mom's style of parenting. She put up with a lot from us kids, until she couldn't.

Moisture gathers at the corners of my eyes so I quickly switch out the tomato with an onion.

I get one half sliced when I catch Marc's hand reaching for something else but from Esme's pile this time. Before he can pull away though, a wooden spoon smacks down on his knuckles like a frog's tongue catching the arrogant fly. Marc hisses, rubbing at his knuckles, but the simple act cuts too close to home for me. Way too close. I've seen my own mom do that a hundred times.

The playful teasing crashes to a screeching halt when I drop the knife, watching it through blurry eyes as the shiny metal bounces off the cutting board onto the counter and I spin, keeping my head down, mumbling out, "I just remembered I work early tonight."

Without looking up, I tell Marc's mom, "It was great meeting you, Esme. Sorry I'm going to miss your food. It looks delicious." Already out of the kitchen, I say, "Marc, thanks for the invite and, uh, enjoy your night." *Because I'll probably never attend one of these again.*

The word vomit doesn't do me any favors in the credibility department and the hitch in my voice near the end is obvious, even to my own ears, but I'm halfway to my room before they can question me.

I tug my scrubs on over my wet face, hating that the tears won't fucking stop. The wind on my ride to work will dry them though. I don't need to go in early but I might as well. What's here for me?

Snatching my bag off the bed, I slip out my door and back into the hall. Low voices in the kitchen have me slowing my approach, wiping roughly under my eyes.

"What do you mean she's leaving? What'd you do?"

"I don't know. She was fine in here away from your bullshit." There's a shuffling sound. "Then she just fucking panicked and said she had to jet. What the fuck was I supposed to do? Paige is free to come and go as she pleases. You want to know about her, ask her your fucking self."

"Why would I fucking care? You're the one wedged up her ass."

A menacing chuckle settles over the apartment, coating everyone inside with discomfort. What are they even saying right now?

Taking a deep breath, I round the corner to find Beckett and Marc, heads together. Neither one notices me while Esme watches them through curious eyes, continuously stirring the sizzling meat in a pan.

I force an airy laugh that sounds fake at best but does the trick to separate the two friends. My eyes stay focused on my desired destination, saying, "Off to work again."

Work obsession, right?

I quicken my steps, reaching the front door in record time. As I go to close it though, a huge hand catches it easily.

Just let me be done for today.

Just let me be done.

"You're really going to work?"

Beckett pounds down the stairs, hot on my heels, but I ignore him. He heard what I said in there. I don't need to repeat myself. Whether he believes me or not is his problem.

I mount my bike, jerking my helmet on as quickly as my shaky fingers can manage before I say something I'll regret. My emotions are all over the place today and I don't trust myself to talk to him. I don't trust myself to be around him. Around any of them.

Angela was right—it's a lot. They are a lot.

Beckett yanks my key out of the ignition and it's then I notice one of his knuckles is split. He proceeds to fold his arms over his bare chest with the key still in his grasp.

Fuck this.

I'm off my bike the next instant, walking for the exit. I'll call one of my brothers to pick me up. Shit, I'll hitchhike from the side of the road, for real this time.

"Hey, where do you think you're going? After all that shit you just pulled?"

I bite my tongue, forcing my legs to take bigger strides, my breath pumping harder with each step.

"The fuck are you doing? I thought you had to work. You can't walk there."

Beckett catches up to me in no time, thanks to legs that are more like stilts and I rip my helmet off, knocking it into his stomach and scowling as he doubles over with a whoosh.

"Get off my fucking jock! I'm over your stupid games and I'm sure as hell not interested in having a heart-to-heart. So, get it through your thick head, I'm leaving for work and I'll get there however I see fit. It is none of your business. *I am none of your business.*"

Our chests are both heaving and sweat starts to gather. I'm wearing scrubs in ninety-degree weather under the blazing sun. It's fucking everywhere.

Before I can make my next move, Beckett spins and launches my keys across the lot. We watch as they sail over parked cars, landing with a metallic clang next to an old school Cadillac that looks like a hearse.

Without another word, he leaves, taking the stairs two at a time.

I can't tell if I'm in shock or awe but my tall roommate just rendered me completely speechless and I wait until he's gone to break from my spot. The last time I saw behavior that desperate was when we were kids and Caleb stole Nick's favorite train. He hid it for a week straight knowing it would upset him. Nicky, being so much younger, grew frustrated when he couldn't find it, so he cut off the head of a teddy bear given to Caleb by his first girlfriend. It was the saddest thing I've ever seen. Until now.

Retrieving my keys effortlessly, I release a steady stream of air, dropping the hand with my helmet to hang limp at my side. Helplessness is nothing new—not anymore—and if that's what Beckett's tantrum was all about, then maybe he's finally catching on to what I've been trying to tell him all along.

He's not in control here.

CHAPTER 9

Paige

I SLEEP THE NEXT DAY AWAY AFTER RUNNING SEVERAL errands straight from work. The attempt to ignore the shit pile my life has turned into until the last possible second somehow doesn't work though.

Nothing does.

After a rejected call to each of my two older siblings, I try Tysen again. He's keeping something from me that's also stopping him from spending time with Mom and I don't like it.

I don't like any of this.

When I only get his voice mail, I call Nick, too. He's been M.I.A. and today's no different it seems.

It's official. The Christensen men are dodging me like a deadbeat dad when child support comes around.

I'm *sick* of men right now. All of them. Vernon's giving me more attitude than ever. My roommates are egotistical jerks. Well, Marc's okay but Beckett's a shit. A sexy-as-sin shit, yes, but still a shit.

Seeing it's close to five, I quickly shower then dress, choosing a black lacy top tucked into a pair of high-waisted jeans. Once my leather jacket is thrown over top, I ride over to Sunbrook. It's technically my day off—my only day off—but I've got a date. I'm going to have dinner with my mom.

I put in a special request for tonight and purchased the fresh ingredients myself. As long as it's fresh and I didn't prepare it, the kitchen staff was willing to let me pitch in. I'm hoping her favorite food will entice her to finally eat.

Rosie approved another nurse to administer the correct dosage of my mother's medication should she actually eat a full meal.

Vernon can kiss my ass. If he wasn't so worried about his precious schedule he could've helped, too. And he would've been paid too, unlike me, who's technically paying to be here. Paying for the food itself and to consume the damn meal. The cooks are great at what they do though. Some visitors come in specifically at meal times just so they can eat while seeing their loved ones. They must pay like they would at a regular restaurant but it's worth it honestly. The food is delicious and the people make great company—just not Vernon.

Parked and hungry, I stride across the lot then wait to be buzzed in the front entrance. No employee entrance for me tonight. I can finally be my first and most important role again—doting daughter.

One of the front personnel lets me in and I head straight for room fourteen. When I find it empty, I search the hallway for that mahogany hair my entire family has. Not seeing her, I venture to the lobby, finding her frail body hunched over a cup of tea.

She's lost more weight at Sunbrook than she did at the other home and I can't help but rethink my decision to move her here—again. Maybe my brothers were right.

My mother glances up at me and even though there's not an ounce of recognition, all the good, all the precious comes right back up like she never really left.

Because she didn't. Not really. She *is* still here, with me, and that counts. It has to.

Transferring her wasn't a mistake. Good enough won't do. Not for my mother. If this place isn't right for her, then I'll find one that is. I'll get a second job if I have to. She made me who I am today and whether she remembers me or not, I'll never forget. I'll remember for the both of us.

"Good evening." I wait for her to acknowledge me before proceeding, saying, "I have reservations but my date cancelled at the last minute. Would you mind accompanying me for dinner? I hear this place is pretty good."

My mother scans my face and I hold my breath and that ever-fickle Hope makes another appearance despite me treating her like shit on a daily basis.

Expect the worst, hope for the best.

Hope can kiss my ass tonight, too. I'm taking over.

I hold out my hand, giving my mom a warm smile.

"Oh, honey, I'm sorry. My husband is meeting me for a cup of tea before bed and I'd hate to miss him. I've been waiting for so long."

What? No.

Her eyes scan the room, like he'll show any second, so I move to Plan B.

"That sounds nice." I lean in to mock whisper, "Chai is my favorite." Hers is too. She made it all my life and I can't think of anything I'd rather drink. Ever. "Do you happen to know where they serve the food maybe? I could use a guide."

Luckily, she stands and motions me forward but I hang back, waiting to walk alongside her. I walk as close as possible, brushing her hand with mine every few strides. If she notices, she doesn't say anything. I ache to hold her hand, to walk arm-in-arm, chatting like the mother-daughter duo we used to be, but we're not there yet. We may never be there again. I've worked here long enough to know that but the heart doesn't listen to common sense, or facts, only what it feels and wants. Sometimes they blur together until you can't decipher which is which though, and that's where you can get into trouble.

How can you tell the difference between what may be and what you wish was? Trial and error. Mistakes learned the hard way. Taking leaps of faith and seeing where you land. You only have to possess enough courage for the first step without knowing the result. The rest is out of your control.

Coming to the doorway, she lingers, and I shoot my last shot.

"Do you smell that?" I inhale loudly, waiting for her to do the same. "Butternut squash rigatoni," I sigh, holding my stomach. "I love butternut squash. Too bad I have to eat alone. You wouldn't be interested in eating some with me, would you?"

"It does smell nice. I appreciate the invite but I don't eat pasta. Have a good night."

Not yet.

Please.

My knees quake beneath me.

"Are you sure? I have it on good authority the butternut squash was bought fresh today." From out in the middle of nowhere to be exact. Everywhere else only carried frozen cubes, so I made the trek out to Marc's family's farm. I didn't see him anywhere but his mom was more than accommodating. "Could you just sit with me for a little while? Keep me company before your," I swallow the lump in my throat, "husband joins you?"

Her dark eyebrows meet as she looks at me again, like she's seeing me for the first time. Hope—the insistent bitch—shows up yet again.

Come on, Mom. It's me.

She shakes her head and my confidence all at once, saying, "I can't miss him. Not this time. Sorry."

With that, she leaves me standing here with a broken heart and an empty stomach.

◆ ◆ ◆

"This one. Or maybe that one."

I squint through my already strained eyes. Is the bright light coming from the dashboard really necessary? Why is it there anyway?

"I don't know," I throw my hands up, not really feeling them as much as I should, "they all look the same. Park wherever you want."

Ivan—or Ethan?—swings into a space, parking his car. Some sort of hybrid as unmemorable as the guy driving it.

Perfect.

Apparently, Ethan/Ivan lives with his parents—shocker—and

isn't allowed to bring dates over. I argued that this isn't exactly a date but he didn't find it funny. He's not much for laughs.

Ethan seemed excited to nail a chick that rides a motorcycle though and jumped at the chance to take me home from the bar. Guys see a strong female as a challenge, a wild animal they have the urge to break into submission. I am neither a challenge nor can I be tamed but I'll let E-Money here think whatever he wants.

Ivan doesn't bother opening my door, even drivers from those apps open the fucking door these days, and I stumble out on my own, unscathed. The door handle, however, does not make it out intact and I'll probably have to buy him a whole new car now. Add the ugly hatchback—whatever it is—to the mountain of shit I can't afford but will work until I die to pay off.

"You think my car's ugly?"

Oh, shit. Did I say that out loud?

I inspect the vehicle in question.

"No." I make my way over to him, draping my arms around his neck to soften the impending blow. "I think it's fucking hideous."

My chest shakes with laughter but he's not amused. Like at all.

Buzz Kill Ethan at it again.

He says, "my name's Evan," making me flinch.

"Nice, Paige. Didn't even catch this one's name first?"

Evan's head jerks upward while I casually lean mine back as well. I'd recognize that voice anywhere and I'm not going to give myself whiplash just because he's decided to cock block for the fifty-seventh time since I moved in. He should really find a hobby or something.

"Hello, Beckett."

Both his elbows rest on the banister as he stares down at us unworthy commoners from his cherished Creekwood throne, with the words *Just Ride It* in black on his chest a stark contrast to his tan tee with the sleeves rolled up, and black soft shorts he probably fell asleep in considering it's well past who gives a shit. His hair's deliciously mussed though. Like maybe he was in the middle of a really, really good dream before he decided to become my worst nightmare.

"Always a pleasure." And although Beckett's glowering expression from our front balcony is not one for pleasure, I'd still give him a shot at it.

I snicker at my own stupidity.

Evan looks back down at me and I sober, hoping my behemoth of a roommate didn't ruin this completely.

"Who's that?"

"Neighborhood Watch, I'm afraid. Except instead of looking for murderers, he's on the hunt for fornicators."

"Uh, what?" Evan stammers.

Unable to hold it in any longer, my head hits the top of his car as it's thrown back in another laugh causing Evan's arms to envelop me fully—not to protect me, I'm sure, but to keep me from damaging any more of his precious go-kart of a ride.

No sooner do his hands reach my back are they ripped away in a motion I am so not comfortable with. Wobbly as it is with my support suddenly disappearing, I crash forward into a brick wall. A never-ending brick wall I like to call Beckett. But only to his face.

"What do you call me behind my back?" He chuckles.

Fuck. "I have to stop doing that."

"Nah, I like you unfiltered."

He's undoubtedly wearing some obnoxious-as-shit expression I'd love to slap right off, but my face is cozy right where it is on ab number eight so I stay put. Beckett can move me if he so chooses.

"You don't like me at all," I mutter against my newfound pillow, sneaking inhales.

"Hey, uh, I think I should get her up to her apartment. She took a lot of shots."

Beckett's arms stiffen around me like a cage and I don't know if it's to lock me in or keep others out.

I sadly abandon his torso to look back at my chauffeur. I almost forgot about the boy. Beckett's scent has that effect on me.

Beckett's everything has that effect on me.

"That's right. Ivan, thank you for driving me home. Unfortunately, as Neighborhood Watch, Beckett takes his job very seriously in making sure nobody gets laid around here. So, unless you're up for breaking your parents' rule and sneaking me into your room, tonight just won't work."

"Jesus."

Ignoring my do-no-good roommate, I lean back, arching my spine to gaze into the small back window of Evan's clown car. In my descent, Beckett's hands move along my bent spine to accommodate the shift, practically bearing all my weight as I hang precariously, my hair only inches from the ground.

This also brings his face in line with my cleavage but I don't hear him complaining, save for a sharp inhale.

"Actually, I'm not a back seat kind of girl," not when the front is so much more fun, "but I might make an exception this once."

My head dangling between my shoulders is flipped upward abruptly, almost butting Beckett's head as our noses come less than an inch apart. He's now bowed over my body, yet I still feel completely at ease in his hold. The way he's got me, it's like I'll never have to worry about falling.

And if I did, he'd go down, too.

"Yeah, that's not happening." Beckett's sparkly blue gems bore into mine as he speaks to Evan, saying, "You can fuck off now. I got her from here."

I don't dare break eye contact to say, "I told you he was good at his job."

"I'm good at a lot of things."

Beckett's soft whisper is a promise carefully wrapped in a threat coaxing me to see what's inside. I'd happily start unwrapping if I could just figure out how to permanently shut that mouth of his. It ruins things more often than not and I can't risk that right now.

A forced cough next to us reminds me of my original plan

tonight. The plan to forget it all. To get lost in someone else for a few minutes instead of constantly obsessing about myself.

I am so tired of me.

But Beckett won't allow that. He thinks he can direct my life like a boy playing with matchbox cars—unconventional terrain, surprise routes, and collision after fucking collision.

Keeping my eyes locked on Beckett's, I sigh, "See ya around, Ethan."

With one last mutter about his name, he finally takes off, leaving me and my roommate alone in a parking lot full of dead dreams and unheard wishes.

We finally rise together, locked in the same embrace Beckett's strong arms were keeping us in, except our faces are now separated by several inches that feel more like miles. Unsurmountable miles.

Swallowing thickly, he says, "You're trouble, you know that?"

I nod slowly, mesmerized by his Adam's apple, finding that just like Eve I'm tempted to take a bite of the forbidden fruit.

Beckett's fingers brushing my back brings me to my senses and I croak, "I know exactly what I am. That's why you should stop trying to save me. If I wanted a savior, it wouldn't be you."

His light eyebrows furrow. "What's wrong with me?"

"You tell me," I shoot back.

Silence stretches with our gazes still connected, neither of us willing to relinquish the control each of us believe we have.

My palm grazes a rough patch of skin on his arm and he clears his throat to say, "I'm sorry for yesterday. I shouldn't have thrown your keys."

I study him for a long moment.

"I'm sorry, too. I had a lot going on and I shouldn't have hit you. Or yelled. Or..."

Beckett's watchful eye takes in everything and I have the sudden urge to cover myself, feeling stripped to my core. I don't budge though, afraid I'll reveal even more in the process. Instead, I silently take inventory of my hero in bare feet. Did he really run down here without shoes? Wait, how *did* he get down here so fast? *Never mind.* His legs and what he does with them are none of my concern, even if they look like they'd make for a hell of a test drive. Miles and miles of strong muscle.

I could take Evan on my worst day—which today may very well have been—and although I didn't need Beckett coming to my rescue like he did, his outright bulldozing, landing me in his solid arms is no hardship. It beats where I was an hour ago—drunk and miserable at a bar, stirring up drama for the hell of it. At least Beckett has a sense of humor. Well, a rumored sense of humor anyway as I still have yet to see it for myself.

His lips tip into a small smile and I zero in on them, worried I spoke my thoughts aloud again.

"What are you thinking about?"

"Honestly?"

He nods and I decide today can't get any worse.

What the hell?

CHAPTER 10

Beckett

"Your lips," Paige breathes out like the confession physically pains her.

She's made it clear I wouldn't be her first choice—with both her words and her actions—for damn near anything, but I can't figure out why. Aside from the obvious of us being roommates, I don't know what her problem with me specifically is.

I haven't exactly been the most inviting but she started it. She brings guys around here like she's testing out paint samples. What does she expect? Dudes show up pawing all over her drunk ass and who knows what the fuck would happen without one of us around. Not that Marc has been much help.

And yeah, maybe Neighborhood Watch is my new gig but whatever. There's not much that goes on around Creekwood that I don't know about so it only makes sense that I'd look out for the newcomer, too. She's obviously never had a male figure in her life to teach her how stupid us men really are, and that's not even accounting for the dangerous ones. They're not just ghost stories you tell around the campfire; sick fucks are out there, lurking behind far too many corners. Hell, most are hidden in plain sight.

If anyone can understand her need to get laid though, it's me. Shit, I may not be the most discreet but at least all my hook-ups know the deal—one night of fun on tap is all I've ever promised anyone. And all I've ever delivered, too. Nothing less and sure as fuck nothing more.

Not everyone's as upfront about being so utterly hopeless, and those that are, can't always hold true to their word.

Holding her securely in my arms, pressed against almost every inch of my front, with my mouth on her mind, I can't think of the last time anything felt so good and I start to wonder if I'm one. One of the lurches picking off the weak.

No way.

No way is Paige weak. Her mind games alone are worthy of wartime tactics and if I wasn't on her radar, too, she wouldn't bother with trying to throw me off the trail. Not when she has *so* many other opportunities, circling her like formation aerobatics at a goddamn airshow.

My eyes drop to see her tongue sneak out, wetting her lip, and I stifle a groan. One minute she's got it shoved down another dude's throat, the next she's using it for kicks as I all but lose my fucking patience. Remembering her kiss with River fills my back with tension that spreads up my neck and out to my ears, turning them searing hot. Dude got one straight to the jaw for that little stunt.

Hope it was worth eating through a straw for a week.

From where I was standing, it looked like it was worth that... and more. Paige is the kind of woman you'd sell your soul to the devil for, without needing the deal fully inked.

Whatever the terms, no matter the consequences—done. Signed. Sealed. Delivered with a black bow and tinsel. Maybe even a glitter bomb for the grouchy old fuck. Take the whole fucking thing 'cause she's gotta be worth it.

If only I had one left to trade for.

My soul fled long ago, leaving behind armor that looks deceivingly like appealing packaging.

Whatever secrets Paige has hidden up her leather jacket sleeves, she deserves better than what I can offer her. *If* I was the offering type, which I'm not. So, even though she's looking at my lips like they're her next meal, I choose to provoke her in a way those other jokers wouldn't dare. As much as she loves to play games, I'm gonna enjoy bending the fucking rules, and her, to my every whim, then we'll see if she can really keep up or if she's just playing at being fast.

"My lips?" Bringing my mouth in close to hers, I sideswipe her face, nudging it to the side and placing them just below her ear. "Not my boy, River's?" He sure as shit isn't my boy anymore but I'm not telling her that.

Instead of tensing for a fight like I expect though, Paige just laughs. A throaty laugh that tickles my lips. They twitch to close over the sound, pleading to swallow the noise whole. I want that laugh all for myself.

She makes a disgusted sound in the back of her throat. "Definitely not his."

Her head returns to look me square in the eye and the look she pins me with nearly has me coming in my pants. Jesus Christ, she's a fucking force.

"Baby."

The nickname falls from her lips as effortlessly as my hands fall to her hips, lifting her off her feet. Without further prompting, her legs swing around to frame my waist, clenching like she's on that hot ass CBR. We crash into the side of the building next to the stairs and her jaw drops in a silent moan. I'm grinding into her the next second to keep those lips from closing any time soon. I have plans for that mouth and none of them involve it being closed.

And just.

Like.

That.

The plan to field her off snaps as quickly as it formed, like a poorly constructed tightwire over a waterfall of madness. I'm up to my neck now, about to go over completely.

"You owe me," she chokes out and I'm already nodding. Whatever she thinks I owe, I'm ready to settle up. Now. With any luck, my debt will run *deep*. "For scaring off tonight's distraction."

Is she talking about that guy Evan or whatever his name was?

I've eaten sandwiches meatier than him. What the hell kind of distraction could he provide?

"Distraction, huh?"

I knew she was hiding something. I just need to figure out what.

"And since you're supposed to be the life of the party or something like that..."

Something like that? *Please.*

"Girl, I put the fun in dysfunction."

Her white teeth flash in the shitty lamplight above our heads swarmed by moths repeatedly throwing themselves against the opaque barrier keeping them from what they want, despite the high cost.

"Perfect. I put the ass in disaster."

I bark out a thick laugh, growing even harder when I grip the ass in question, rubbing my erection against Paige's center and watching that cliff of insanity creep up with increasing speed as her nails dig into my shoulders with the same urgency vibrating through my entire body.

She's quicker than I gave her credit for.

"What do you need to be distracted from?"

On a sigh, the word "everything" leaves her mouth the way one might pray for rain in a serious drought.

I try to catch her eye but she blinks long and hard, hiding those emerald-colored eyes from me.

"Just...make it all disappear."

That I get. That I can do—incredibly fucking well.

Under her open jacket, her nipples strain through her black lacy top and my mouth goes dry at the sight, making me realize that I'm the one stuck in a drought. A seriously fucked drought with skylines full of the same mirage-like wavy lines everywhere.

But then, why does it feel like I was just handed keys to a kingdom I know I don't deserve? It feels like a set-up. A set-up to fail.

Fail who though? Her or me?

Her eyes pop open, staring me down with more clarity than she's shown all night, then she says, "I won't ask again."

I'd smirk if I had any feeling left in my face but I don't, not with all the blood in my body rushing south for, you know, warmth—hers, hopefully.

What can I say to that? No? I don't think so. I'm a people pleaser, it's what I do, and if my Tahoe wasn't across the fucking lot, she'd already be laid out across the hood like an all you can eat buffet.

Working with what I got, I press her into the outside wall, wondering if I can really pull this off. Hell, I'd dry hump the shit out of her if I thought I could last.

"Fuck, Paige. What are we doing?" I ground out, against the soft part of her neck. Her sweet peach smell luring me in like a helpless sap.

"What do you want to do?"

Are we talking specifics here? Because I've got a lot of ideas.

I rear back to see her face again. Her usual spark is alive and well with a raised eyebrow egging me on. But there's something else, too. Something I can't put my finger on.

Vulnerability?

Nah. She hasn't shown an ounce of that since she showed up to Creekwood. Except for yesterday and whatever it was that made her run out of here like a ghost was chasing her. A ghost of…somebody?

Which reminds me.

"Would you've asked that kid Evan the same thing?"

Her eyes flare as bright and obvious as if one were streaking across the midnight sky, signaling a problem.

Here we go.

"Meet me in my room in five."

She wiggles out of my arms and I reluctantly let go, setting her back on her feet. The space between our bodies immediately grows cold but before I can bring her back to erase what I just said from her thoughts, she takes off up the stairs.

Shit.

I run my fingers through my hair, gripping the ends and pulling them over my forehead.

Why did I say that?

My hands drop to hang at my sides as I rest the back of my head against the same wall Paige's body just was, not really sure what's happening. Her expression said a lot without giving anything away. Was she pissed? Or was she just turned on?

If I had to guess, I'd say a little of both.

On one hand, if I go up to her room, I'm not exactly sure where it will lead. Paige is impulsive. She made out with a random dude just to piss me off. Or make a statement. I don't even know because the red veil of rage clouded my vision and I missed her point entirely.

On the other hand, I like her brand of crazy. There's a method to her madness that only she knows. It's like what Coty said before, instead of trying to crush a woman's spirit, you embrace the beauty in her reckless ways. I'm not interested in making Paige something she's not but I can't deny the fact that I want to taunt the fuck out of the fierce creature she is.

I check the time on my phone. Two minutes. Fuck it, that's all I'm giving her.

Nerves firing on all cylinders, I stalk through the dark apartment, fully expecting Paige to have a leather whip or some other kinky shit. I roll my shoulders, cracking my neck, ready to tackle whatever I'm in for.

What am I in for?

Except, my hand gripping the handle to her bedroom feels more like an opening to something else, something I don't know the first thing about.

And so, I falter. I freeze. I completely choke like a virgin on prom night. Whatever this is, it could ruin everything.

Feeling reckless myself, I decide to take that chance by turning the knob. Unfortunately, that shit doesn't so much as shift.

I glance around the dark hallway, finding nothing out of the ordinary. In fact, it's dead silent until…

Hearing a soft moan, I press my ear to her door. The husky hum grows louder, mixing with a moan, and I shoot my eyes to Marc's door down the hall. *Is he in there right now?* Nobody else was here and there's no way someone slipped past me downstairs. Is this the set-up?

His door is closed but it always is. I consider checking to see if it's locked but then a buzzing sound kicks up and my feet stay rooted.

My ear flat against her door, I listen as Paige works herself over with a motherfucking vibrator. Like everything else with this girl, it both pisses me off and excites me. She runs her own show and I'm left to watch from the sidelines, exactly how she wants. Something about her keeps my eyes trained on the production though, not willing to walk away like I normally would.

Her moans are uninhibited now, quickly building up to an orgasm and after absolutely zero deliberation, I drop my hand to my dick. The buzzing gets muffled with every thrust and I stroke myself under my soft shorts in time with Paige, imagining her sweat-slicked body naked, stretched across her mattress, similar to the night I put her to bed. Lights on so every detail is on full display. Hair, untamed like her, splayed out around her flushed face while she pleasures herself.

My hips thrust forward picturing Paige readying her pussy. For me.

Sweat beads at my hairline, threatening to fall, so I push the hair back, wishing I had a hat on instead.

Fuck. I flip the bottom of my shirt up, giving my abs some air as they constrict with my movements.

A gasp filters through the door and the way it wraps around my shoulders, tight and needy, I know she's almost there. I'm following close behind with my own long, quick strokes. *So fucking close.*

Precum beads at my tip and I quickly roll my palm over the moisture using the natural lube to pump my swollen cock.

She releases her breath with a short, tortured whimper so I pick up the pace, not wanting to miss a thing.

Out of nowhere, she cries out, "Beckett," and the sick satisfaction of hearing my name has me coming *hard* in the next second. With a grunt of my own, ropes of jizz spill all over my hand and shorts and fuck if I don't care one bit. She said my name. Not River. Not Marc. None of the other assholes she's brought around.

Just mine.

My name rolled off her tongue in her rawest form and it was the hottest thing I've ever heard.

Breathless, I drop my other fist to the door as my forehead rocks against the thin wood, wondering where that devil is when you need him. If he appeared right now, I'd fake a soul just so I could barter with him. To see what Paige looked like in that moment. To know if the images I conjured up are even close to the real thing. If so, I want round two immediately, preferably with me on the other side of the door this time.

I wait for some kind of acknowledgement—it's pretty fucking obvious I'm here—but nothing happens. Not a damn thing.

Except for a drawer opening and closing, Paige doesn't make a single sound.

What the fuck was that then? I just jerked off outside her locked door while she fucked herself thinking about me. If that isn't the biggest mind fuck of all, I don't know what is.

With a shake of my head, I leave to clean myself up in the bathroom, then pass her silent room again, heading to my own. At least I'm not going to sleep with blue balls like I have every other night since she moved in.

◆ ◆ ◆

"Beck, buddy, good news. It's time to go home."

"My head hurts," I groan loudly, worried it's too loud. "I don't

think they checked it. They only did x-rays on my arm, Dad. Tell them to look. Please."

My dad's head drops to his hands and a pang of guilt hits but I shove it away. I don't care if he thinks I'm lying. I'm not going anywhere 'til they call her. It's a hospital, that's what they do. They take care of broken people and I haven't been whole since she left. The least they can do is call the person responsible. Give my mom the chance to fix me herself.

"Son, it's been four years. She-"

"Dad."

His head snaps up, determined, and I flinch.

"She's not coming back. Damn it, I wish she was. More than you think. More than I show. Trust me, I'd give anything to have her back, but it's not happening. She made her choice and we're not it."

His voice cracking at the end does me in and I release the tears I've been holding in since the accident on my dirt bike.

There's a tapping.

I look up from the hospital bed, searching. Is she here? I knew she'd come. As soon as I saw my bone bent the wrong way, I knew she'd have to return.

My dad is watching me through watery eyes of his own, his suit and hair still styled to perfection. How? How can he act like nothing is wrong?

That takes a lot of work. I know because I've been trying for four years now and I'm tired. I'm tired of pretending. I'm tired of hoping. Every birthday without a homemade cake found off the internet, every sleepover with those stupid boys from school that only invite me because their moms make them. Because their moms care. Because their moms are still around and mine isn't.

"Where is she?" I wail, giving up on the whole head thing. I don't care if he knows I lied. I just want her already.

But my dad just shakes his head, sick of this. Sick of me. Doesn't he want her to come home? It's been miserable without her. We've been miserable without her. I've been freaking miserable without her. She didn't take anything while leaving me with absolutely nothing. Her clothes, her makeup, her books, everything is still sitting exactly where she left it, waiting for her just like I am. I've been put through absolute crap waiting around for her but here I am still, biding my time until she grows tired of her new life with her new husband. With her new family.

Snot pours out of my nose and I wipe it angrily with my hand, forgetting there's a cast now.

Knocking starts up.

I ignore the noise, too focused on the fresh pain. Narrowing my gaze at the cast, I use it to swipe at my nose again. And again. I raise my hand a third time but my dad grabs my wrist, stopping me.

"Stop that. Goddamn it, Beck! You're bleeding."

Blood replaces the mucus dripping down my face.

"She has to come, Dad! She has to!" I yell through the warm liquid. I'm a caged animal and he's the bars keeping me from what I really want.

We're both heaving, both fighting to breathe like we actually can.

"Listen to me. She's not coming back. You have to move on. You need to." My dad shakes me, his hair finally falling forward, and a whimper escapes…one of us. I can't tell who.

The pounding is making it hard to concentrate but I try anyway.

"Beck, I'm trying my best. I really am. I can't take losing you, too, so please just stop. We'll get you cleaned up, then we need to leave. They're not going to call her. She doesn't want us to. Do you get that?"

"You. You mean she doesn't want you. She'll come back for me." She has to. I need her. He doesn't.

"If that were true, she would've taken you with her."

I rear back as if he slapped me. He might as well have. It would've hurt less. The look in his eyes haunts me. It's the same one I see when I look in the mirror and I drop my gaze to the cast still in his hold, wishing he'd let go like he let go of her.

"She will. She'll come for me," I whisper over a hiccup. Maybe not

this time. Maybe not this injury. There will be a time though where I'm hurt so bad that she'll have no choice but to come back and when she does I'll be waiting. Always waiting.

There's yelling and I furrow my brows, confused.

"Beckett! Open the door!"

Paige? Why is she here? How?

In a quieter voice I hear, "here goes nothing," then my door is kicked in. My bedroom door. The one in my apartment, not the hospital room from so many years ago.

I sit straight up in bed, realizing too late that I'm drenched.

"What the fuck?" I yell at her. She wasn't supposed to see this. She's not supposed to be here period.

Thank all my unlucky stars her door was locked last night. What a mistake that would've been. This is already too fucking close, just like I told Marc.

Paige's eyes are frantic as she sweeps the room. Landing back on me, they soften but only marginally. It's enough though. Goddamn it, it's enough.

I grit, "get out," but am thoroughly ignored as she comes further into the room. Like, what?

My clammy body, ready for flight, is covered only by a sheet until it's yanked out of my grasp by my nosey ass roommate.

How long will an eviction notice take to type up 'cause I'm *done.*

I drop my feet to the floor, ready to end Paige's interrogation before it can even start but she catches me off guard, saying, "You're bleeding. What the hell happened?"

I pause, noticing the red pool on the sheet in Paige's hands and scowl. Feeling my upper lip, my fingers come away covered in blood.

Shit. This hasn't happened in a long time.

"What happened? I heard-"

"Fuck if I know," I cut her off, afraid to hear her finish that sentence. "I was *sleeping.* You're the one that busted in here without permission. Now get the fuck out of my room. And you're paying to fix my door, too."

I'm blessed with an eye roll and Paige coming even closer, not leaving like I told her to. *This girl.*

Parting my knees with hers, she plugs my nose just above my nostrils. She thinks it's a simple nose bleed. She has no idea and I intend on keeping it that way.

"What are you doing?" My voice comes out nasally and not at all intimidating like I hoped. "I told you to leave."

Her face lowers until we're at eye level with each other and my heart slows. What is she going to say? What does she see?

"Since when do I listen to you?" she asks softly. It's meant to be rude but there's a pleasantness to her tone, like her melodic voice is meant to distract me from being led to slaughter.

"Since you sit outside my door like a fucking creep."

She laughs then straightens, rearranging her feet. My legs fall open to the sides to make room which brings her chest in my line of vision. She's wearing an oversized plain t-shirt that barely covers her ass which appears to only be concealed by a thin, black scrap of fabric trying to pass as underwear.

Are you kidding me? She really is trying to kill me.

"You're one to talk." Her arched eyebrow has mine raising in response.

Touché.

Yeah, she knew exactly what she was doing last night.

A towel is wrapped around her head like she just got out of the shower and I fight the urge to rip the stupid thing off to run my fingers through her hair. My senses are on overdrive having her in my space. Her smell, the light yet sure touch of her care, the rumble of her knowing laugh—it's all clashing together into one tantalizing spell.

Leaning into her touch, she approves, saying, "Good. Tilt forward so the blood will stop."

Blood?

Oh, yeah. The reason she's in here in the first place. Not to seduce me but because she heard me dreaming about my mother. The only woman that's been able to twist me up like a fucking pretzel.

Until Paige came along.

Whatever that shit last night was must've brought on the dream. Or more accurately, nightmare. Either way, I haven't had one for a while. A long while, thankfully. The guys have heard them, maybe even seen the results a time or two when I couldn't get to the bathroom to clean my face fast enough, but nobody's ever kicked down my fucking door during one. No, that honor goes to Paige. The pushy as shit, sexier than hell biker perched between my thighs. The reminder has my cock pulsing to life.

"Want to talk about it?"

And *that* reminder has the poor guy shriveling up into a damn near comatose state.

"I'm not interested in having a heart-to-heart," I snap, throwing her words back in her face.

With a shake of my head, her hand falls away as I push to standing. Our bodies slide along each other's in the process and Paige's shirt raises from the friction. She goes to fix it but I shoot out to stop her hand with mine.

Her gaze leaps to my face, watching me closely.

My finger grazes her flat stomach and I almost groan from the contact. Seeing it in the pool nearly undid me. Her black strap bikini was the ultimate temptation daring me to look without being able to touch. Feeling her skin now has me contemplating dropping to my knees to taste the goods.

"Why would you kick down my door with bare feet?" I ask quietly.

"I didn't have any shoes on." Such a hardass.

"You know what I mean."

Sighing, she says, "My brother Nick had night terrors when we were younger and they always scared the shit out of me. You could never tell if it was real or not. The crippling fear from an unknown source always made me anxious. I would watch him through every single one just to be sure nothing was actually terrorizing him." Her voice lowers. "It felt so real, that sometimes I thought it was."

She drops her head to watch my finger move back and forth,

back and forth and I do the same. An image of this stomach tightened in climax last night as she cried out my name beckons my dick out of his abrupt nap.

Jumping on the subject change, I ask, "You have a brother?"

After a snicker, Paige spins on her heel to walk back out of the room.

Girl never does what I expect. Never. It's what I like most and least about her.

Spark fully back in place, she throws out over her shoulder, "Glad you're not dead. Next time, keep your door unlocked so I don't end up breaking my foot."

I snort. There won't be a next time if I can help it.

"Or you could try minding your own fucking business," I call out in vain as I watch her lace covered ass sway out my splintered door, my eyes swinging like a pendulum to track each cheek. As glad as I am not to be dying either, it's not a bad way to go. I'm just sayin'.

The outstanding ass and body attached to it stop and I jerk my gaze up to see Paige peering at me through heavy lids.

"I will when you do." *Eh.* Fat chance. "Get yourself cleaned up. I need a ride to get my bike and Marc already left for work."

Hold up.

"You weren't walking around like that when he was here, were you?"

Chick has the nerve to smirk at me then disappears into the hall before yelling, "Let's go, roomie."

The lack of ass in my room brings everything back into focus. And this, not only what happened last night but also today, now, is bad. So bad. This is exactly what I was worried about.

Oh, I'll give her a fucking ride alright. I'll drive her past her breaking point until she's ready to move out of both the apartment and my life.

Roomie.

CHAPTER 11

Paige

"NO WAY," I SAY, GLARING AT HIS NINJA.

After our weird exchange this morning, Beckett and I spent the morning ignoring each other. Once I had some regular clothes on, I went to clean up the mess I made but he'd already taken care of it and I felt too awkward to knock on the door that I broke with this morning's dramatic entrance. I ate breakfast on the balcony overlooking the pool, stealing glances at him as he ate at the kitchen counter, with his back strategically turned to me.

Why, oh why, did I have to choose today to care if Beckett was being strangled by a demonic ghost? It may not have been a night terror like Nick used to have but Beckett is absolutely being haunted by something. Or someone, judging by what I heard.

I throw my free hand on my hip. My favorite gray riding jacket and a helmet he loaned me take up my other arm. Today's heat calls for shorts even though I hate riding in anything other than pants but you can't argue with hundred-degree dry heat. My loose white tank covers cut-off shorts and my signature black boots complete the ensemble.

"What?" Beckett bites out.

Lip sneered in disgust, I lay on the attitude—thick. "Do I look like a fucking backpack?" If he thinks I'm riding with my arms wrapped around him after that whole scene last night, he's got another thing coming. It was bad enough having his finger on me this morning without making a complete fool of myself by begging for more. And that was just his finger. It is a long finger but still, it shouldn't have that kind of effect on me. *He* shouldn't have that kind of effect on me. He's my roommate. And kind of a dickish one at that.

Beckett makes a show of inspecting my body and it's like last night all over again. His demanding hands and teasing mouth. He's so good at playing around, he forgets how serious things can get. A want so primal began as soon as he speared me against the building that I couldn't think straight. My body required one thing and one thing only, and that was Beckett. He consumed me in those moments and I was spiraling into a frenzy of need and want, lost to the feeling of his tantalizing touch. The hardness just beneath his silky shorts, the softness of his hands as they held me in place, the teasing in his voice as it slid over my face coaxing me closer.

I almost gave in.

The allure was unbearable to deny until his words turned cold, practically freezing my reaction to him. The hunger raged on, but the provider changed. I scratched the itch he caused and made sure he heard it.

"Never mind, I'll get someone else to take me."

That'll do it. He hates the thought of someone else coming to my rescue, as stupid as that is, and he'll back down.

Instead though, he says, "Don't be an asshole. I get it—you're big, you're bad, you ride your own bike. Nobody thinks you're a backpack. Now, get on, shut up, and let's go. I'm late for work."

See? Dickish.

I can guess what he'll say but I still try with, "Then let me drive. You can hold onto me."

He barks out a laugh. "And here I thought I was the funny one."

"You're not."

"Now *that's* funny. Come on already. You're out of your mind if you think I'm riding bitch on my own bike, girl."

Ignoring my deep frown, he mounts his green machine and starts it up. With narrowed eyes, I suggest taking his Tahoe but am met with ear-splitting revving.

But I'm the asshole, huh?

With my jacket in place, my helmet is tugged over my head in the next instant and I'm gripping his arm for leverage to climb on behind. I feel the rough patch of skin again and briefly wonder if there's a story there.

My face blazes and I'm grateful none of my friends from the races are around to see me perched on the pillion. I'd never live down riding as a passenger.

Even though he deserves it, I leave my jacket unzipped and open in the front so it won't rub him raw and lean as far forward as his back allows until his shirt and mine are fused together into one thin cloth between our hot bodies. Beckett's muscles tense when I slide my hands along his sides then I wrap my arms around his solid chest, squeezing hard. My thighs are spread as wide as they can go, just shy of painful, making me glad I wore shorts today.

Beckett quickly busies himself backing out so I rest my head against his shoulder blade. Typical male, he doesn't know where we're going and refuses to ask for help, instead just blundering ahead and hoping it'll all work out in the end.

I'm not stupid. I know why we're taking his bike today. He's worried I'll dig into what happened this morning, or in his past, but going off what I saw in his room, I don't think I want to know. The day I ask about his life is the day he'll ask about mine and I have no intention of letting Beckett anywhere near my personal business. I've already witnessed four grown men buckle from the pressure of my mother's disease, I won't put that on anyone else's shoulders—regardless of how sturdy they might've felt beneath my hands last night.

It's a heavy load and I'm bearing it the way everyone obviously expects—alone.

The exit approaches and it finally dawns on him that he has no idea which way to take.

Biting my lip, I stifle a snicker.

Beckett's head turns and I hear his muffled voice demanding

directions. It would be too easy to give him the address and I don't feel like going easy right now considering I didn't even want to ride back here to begin with. So, I run my right hand down his abs, relishing the way his muscles tighten as I go, until I reach his hip. His work pants are stretched over his thick thighs and I slip my hand over the bulging muscles there, too.

Beckett's breathing halts while mine picks up.

Once I find the inside of his thigh, I spread my palm flat and squeeze to signal which direction to turn. Beckett only sits there for another moment, not reacting whatsoever so I squeeze again and return my hand taking the same path back to his torso.

His head drops then, shaking slightly, before raising to make a right.

Good boy.

The rest of the ride continues with my silent directions and soon we arrive at the first bar my brothers ever let me visit, Xen's. Them being friends with the owner is the only reason I was allowed in then and still allowed in now at only twenty. Jesse and Dixon graduated together and he makes it a point of reminding everyone within ear shot whenever I stop in. Hence why I had Evan as my designated driver last night. He was the only one Dixon approved of, probably thinking I'd scare the poor boy off before he had a chance to get his pants unbuttoned. Turns out Beckett beat me to it with his concerned roommate act. It was probably for the best considering I came pretty damn hard all on my own. I doubt that guy even knows where the clit is, let alone how to work one. Luckily, my vibrator is phenomenal at doing just that.

Just ask Beckett.

I'm full on chuckling when he pulls up next to my baby girl. Unfortunately, Beckett's thunderous face ends my amusement once I'm back on the ground.

"What the hell was that? Are you trying to make me come in my pants like a fucking teenager?"

Oh. That.

I make the mistake of grinning and Beckett growls, like literally growls. Instead of scaring me like he intended though, I lose the fight trying to contain my laughter, sending me into near hysterics. My head is thrown back in the hardest laugh I've had since one of my friends, Shan, wrecked his bike on the first day of owning it. The guy scraped the entire left side of his Audi, essentially fucking up both rides at once and I almost peed myself laughing so hard that day. It was funny in a pathetic kind of way. Just like this.

A few thigh squeezes is all it takes to get Beckett off? I file that information away for later use. It seems like it could come in handy.

And…that sends me into another fit of laughter all over again.

"Sorry. I'm sorry." I throw my hands up, biting my cheek.

Beckett rolls his eyes as he stands to his full height, adjusting himself. Sometimes I forget how tall he is until moments like this when his close proximity reveals the mountain he truly is. One I was all too eager to scale last night thanks to my effort at forgetting my clusterfuck life.

He adjusts his dick unabashedly and even as he catches me looking, I don't shy away. He almost brought me to orgasm last night with that impressive package. I'll gawk as I see fit. And I. See. Fit.

"It's bad enough I had to jerk off like a fifteen-year-old all over again, I don't need to add shooting my load before penetration, too."

My eyebrows skim the clouds.

"Oh, you thought you were the only one getting off last night?"

I shrug noncommittally making Beckett scoff.

"Tell me what you were thinking about as you fucked yourself and I'll tell you what I pictured when I nutted outside your door."

Holy shit. This guy's mouth is as dirty as it is tempting.

My eyes raise to it all on their own to see his tongue drag along his bottom lip before biting the whole thing into his mouth.

My thighs clench and I wish I was on my bike so I could get the hell out of here already.

I wanted a distraction, right? Beckett checks that box with all the dependability of a number two pencil. He's been one constant, *long* distraction since I moved in but he shouldn't be. Not for me. He needs someone that has the time to open up whatever the hell he has tucked away from the general public.

"Come here."

A moody Beckett is hot as fuck, a demanding Beckett is beyond. Beyond thought. Beyond words. Beyond reason.

That's what I tell myself when my feet move before my head can even make the decision.

Within reach, he slips a hand up my neck and into my hair before gripping a handful. I hiss at the pain that hurts in the best way possible, his cloudy eyes locking on my mouth as the sound escapes.

"What were you thinking about?" His husky whisper travels over my face, hypnotizing me like a shady snake charmer in a back alley.

With his hold at the back of my head feeling like it's gripping more than just my hair, I work, I fight, I all out scrap for the smallest bit of control still, needing it more than the shoes on my feet atop scorching asphalt.

"You know," I goad quietly, not breaking eye contact for a second. To show dominance you must look your opponent in the eye without wavering and I do just that. Bossy is cute and all but that doesn't mean he's in charge and it'll do him well to remember that.

"Why are you fucking with me?" It comes out strangled and raw. Exposed.

I open my mouth to ask the same thing but a whimper comes out instead as the hand in my hair tightens, drawing me closer so my body is flush with his much like this morning in his room. That was next to his bed and yet this somehow feels more intimate. More dangerous.

I'm ready to throw in the towel and ride him instead of my motorcycle but that's what scares me. He's too tempting. His moods—the indifference half the time and the intense awareness the other half—they shouldn't appeal to me the way they do. My loved ones take precedence over everything else, whereas the rest of the world could burn to the ground and I wouldn't even notice. At some point Beckett stepped over that line and has been straddling the damn thing ever since.

Do I care about the guy or not?

The more important question is—should I?

Everything is going wrong and while it's tempting to feel something that may be right, I'm not naïve enough to believe being with Beckett is right in any way. The guy is a manwhore with a superiority complex. Taking him down a few pegs is all I should keep this as, not invite him to equal footing.

Last night was one peg and I'm willing to bet he could down go a couple more. Easily.

With shaky hands, I grip his thighs—overly sensitive thighs—and squeeze as I bring my face in close to his. He bends to meet me halfway, our noses bumping from the momentum. Lips hovering an inch apart, I swipe my tongue across his seam and, as expected, his eagerness gets the better of him as he ducks down for more. Remembering his hold in my hair, I'm forced to lean my head back in order to avoid losing chunks of my beloved locks. His mouth clashes with my chin but instead of discouraging the guy like I'd hoped, he uses it to his advantage. He gives my chin a sweet peck before trailing his tongue lower to my throat. I can barely make out greedy moans and frenzied kissing over my own labored breathing. The pain behind my head as he grips my strands vigorously mixes with the pleasure of his ravenous caresses on my neck and I curse my stupid plan to tease him.

I severely underestimated Beckett.

That thought, and any other, disappear as his other hand cups my face, tilting it to the side. My body, no longer following my orders but his, does as its told, complying effortlessly. Beckett's lips graze my sensitive skin, landing just below my ear, causing a ground shaking shiver. Fighting my own traitorous body is futile, so I accept the tremble for what it is. Who am I to deny my body what it wants and what Beckett clearly wants to give it? The guy knows what he's doing. I should just let him do it and be on my way, one orgasm happier.

"It was you, on your back, tits in the air, begging for me to taste their rosy tips."

The unexpected words have my eyes snapping open only to see movement across the lot. I chock it up to hallucinating from Beckett's swirling tongue on the shell of my ear and tune back in. Seriously, the guy is talented.

"Legs spread, pussy glistening, aching for me to fill it."

Said legs nearly buckle as I see a form approach that isn't a mirage at all.

"Your mouth, parted and gasping, *begging* me to fuck you."

My panties are drenched, most likely soaking my shorts by now.

"But the part that made me come harder than any other chick has ever been able to milk out of my cock was when I walked away, leaving you a fucking mess, wishing you could actually keep my attention for longer than the two minutes it took for you to make yourself come."

What?

All at once he releases his hold on my body, sending me a few feet back. With my mind hostage in a serious loop of what the fuck, I gape open mouthed at him. Where did that come from?

I can tell by the bulge in his pants that he's as affected as I am but his harsh words were delivered with lethal amounts of spite, not wanting.

"Paige?"

Hearing my name jolts me back to reality.

Parking lot. Dickish roommate. Brother's best friend.

Right.

Dixon is standing so close I can hear him grinding the molars I know are chockfull of fillings from never flossing. One time he was the first to fall asleep at our house—a huge mistake—and my brothers and I tied him to the bed with dental floss. We used every shred we could find and our house smelled like cinnamon burst for weeks afterward, but it didn't help. He still refused to floss after that.

I was just getting felt up—kind of—in front of his bar's parking lot, in broad daylight, by my hot/cold/but still super hot roommate. This should be fun.

"Hey, Dixon. How's it hangin'?" I joke, surreptitiously rubbing at my neck, trying to rid the feel of Beckett's lips.

"Don't even try it," he replies then asks, "who the hell is this?"

He jerks his chin at Beckett who's suddenly very interested in what keeps *my* attention. His helmet's now in place over his head but the visor is flipped open as he stares at Dixon like he's found a new opponent. He's stock-still, save for his hand. The one closest to me. It's shaking like a junkie coming down from a high and I have this sneaking suspicion it's to grab something. *Someone.*

Me? Dixon?

Dixon has the scary bit down pat from running a rowdy bar but he's like one of my brothers—minus the ignoring me part. He was there to talk some sense into Jesse every time the boys would try to enforce another idiotic rule in the house that magically only affected me.

This is awkward on a whole other level and I don't even know what to say or how to say it. Do I introduce Beckett as my roommate? My arch-nemesis? The guy I want to fuck into next week mainly because this week has had enough disappointment? I can only take rejection at the hands of a man so many times before the pain sticks. And spreads.

I point at Beckett, squinting. "It's Jake, right?"

Dixon recognizes the inside joke right away and bites his lips together, trying not to let me off the hook but I see it and I smile over at him. Beckett obviously doesn't understand the insurance commercial reference. That was our go-to greeting for the many bill collectors that would call the house. Everyone knows Jake. Except Beckett, I guess. He's scowling like he forgot to eat a meal and doesn't think he'll achieve his proper gains for the day.

Too bad.

Dixon's face finally softens, the tenderness reminding me of the affection I've been depraved of in recent months. What I've been craving but pushed aside for everyone else's benefit. The shit-storm I've been digging my way through has been a cold and lonely endeavor and Dixon's warm expression has me almost running to him. Almost, because my legs are still a little wobbly after Beckett's sweet and sour treatment. But I make it there anyway, falling into Dixon's open arms.

I hear Beckett huff, "Fuck this, I'm out."

Tiny pebbles from his back tire kick up as he peels out and a few pelt us as Dixon pulls away from me. A warm hand slides into mine while we watch Beckett fly out of the lot.

"That was odd. Who's the drama queen?"

I grimace. "My roommate. He hates me."

I'm not sure if it was at first sight or a gradual thing but the man can't stand me. If he's not scaring off possible hook-ups, he's being a massive asshole. A masshole, really.

"Hmm, I'm not sure I believe that. What I saw out here didn't look like hate. Although, I have found that hate sex is often the most passionate. So many feelings you don't know what to do with, so many emotions you can't voice, it all pours out into one intense," he clears his throat and I scowl, "uh, session."

I shove his arm, hiding my smirk. Session? So lame.

"So, roommate, huh? Did the Christensen gang meet him yet?"

"Not really." I shrug. "I don't spend a lot of time there and the boys, well, they haven't been around much lately either."

He grows serious as we turn for his bar. Xen's is a combination of the end of his first name and the end of our last name. He really is like a brother.

"What do you know that I don't, Dicky?"

Dixon tries to ruffle my hair but I knock him in the stomach, thwarting his attack. Some things never change.

"Keep it down. You'll ruin my street cred."

"You have no street cred."

"Ha! Are those fumes killing your brain cells?" He nods over to my bike.

So what if she smokes a little? Don't all true bad girls?

"I just know you're all going through a difficult time right now. It's hard seeing my second family suffer, especially from the outside. I'm not in the thick of it with you but it hurts just the same, I swear. I wish there was more I could do."

I exhale, long and low. "Jesse's pulling away because he feels powerless and can't fix the problem. Caleb is using work as a scapegoat because he doesn't know where he fits in, not with Jesse avoiding his usual role. He's second in command and always has been. Taking the lead is unfathomable to him so he doesn't even try. With any of us. He and Jesse aren't even speaking last I heard. Tysen has his own shit to take care of and he doesn't know how to spread himself around for everybody else, least of all Mom." *Or me,* I think selfishly. "Nick is inherently self-absorbed, which will never change. He can't separate Mom from her disease and gets pissed because of it." My nose stings as I finish.

"And you?" he asks, wiping a tear from my cheek. "You're acting out."

"What?" I burst.

"I didn't want to say anything but your drinking is...bad. It's getting worse. Last time you were here I had to pay someone to take you home just to get you to stop drinking and last night I had to break up two fights you were involved in. And still pay someone to take you home."

I narrow my eyes. "So, that's why he was so adamant on getting me to my door. It wasn't to sleep with me, it was because big brother Dixon paid him."

"You're welcome."

I wave him off. I appreciate the lift but I could've and would've taken care of myself.

"It was the safest way to make sure your drunk ass made it home okay. I couldn't take you myself since you threw a drink on one of my bussers."

"He was awful. You should fire him."

"I did. But you didn't need to do that."

"Yes, I did. I watched him untie a girl's halter top when she was dancing."

"What about the woman with her boyfriend?"

He pins me with a look that says *gotcha* while I pick something off my shoulder.

"She said I didn't belong," I mumble purposely.

"What was that?"

I throw my hands up. "She said I didn't belong, okay? She asked if I ate at the Y, then cackled to her friend that I should find a bar more fitting for 'my kind.' I simply offered her boyfriend tips on how to go down on his girlfriend since she was obviously asking random strangers for head. She's lucky I didn't beat her ass."

"That's it? So what? There's nothing wrong with eating pussy."

"Exactly. Some of my favorite people eat pussy." My grin splits my face in half, glad we're not using the term 'session' anymore.

"Then why does it matter if she said you did? I mean, you don't, do you?"

"No, I don't, but it's not what she said, it's how she said it. Like there was something wrong with me if I did. Who I choose to have sex with isn't up for judgment by anyone, least of all some regular at a dive bar."

"Hey."

"Sorry," I say, even though we both know I'm not far off. The place is two-thirds dive bar, one-third regular bar. More of an aspiring bar. "Still, she was a close-minded bitch."

"Well, that doesn't change the fact that they both had to be escorted out because of their fight that *you* caused. And since they were, in fact, regulars that means their business went with them."

"Good. Maybe now you can get some better clientele."

His face is that of a disapproving father to a petulant child. Talk about ungrateful.

My middle finger twitches.

"I get one night off a week. If I can't go out and blow a little steam, I'll explode. My job, the boys, my mom, it's all too much. I'm doing it all alone and now I have this colossal roommate who's in my face every time I'm home and I have nowhere else to go." My voice cracks at the end and I bury my face in my hands. "I have nobody. I'm constantly surrounded by people, yet it feels like I'm the loneliest person in the world."

"Don't say that. You're breaking my heart here, kid. You're not alone. Ever." Could've fooled me. "And you're always welcome to come stay with me. Have you tried talking to any of them?"

Them meaning my brothers. The ones that are currently treating me to radio silence. As the communicator of the family, it's the easiest way to isolate me and drive me insane one missed call at a time.

I shake my head, wiping at my nose.

"Well, you know I love you like my own sister."

Dixon wraps me in a bear hug and I snuggle in, desperate for real contact, not the kind Beckett and I exchange as punishment.

"You don't have a sister," I mumble against his chest.

"But if I did, I'd want her to be just like you. Except without a smart mouth, or a penchant for finding trouble, or a drinking problem." I pull back to glare at him. "A one day a week drinking problem," he clarifies and I allow it because he's not wrong per se. "Otherwise, yeah, just like you."

His words have the desired effect and I end up smirking despite myself. What a jerk.

I missed him.

"About this roommate...do you want anything done about that?"

Cranking my neck, I look him in the eye. "Like what? Did you join the mafia or something?"

"No, but I know people. Or one simple phone call and I know the Christensen boys would show up swinging."

"One call from you maybe."

He looks at me pointedly and I know what he's saying, but crying to my brothers would only cause more problems. They'd force me to move out and think they have a say over my life again. I have to find some sort of happy medium where all four brothers are in my life without them ruling my decisions.

As for Beckett, some space might be good for us. His spiel today was flat out vindictive but I've done my fair share of riling him up, too. I'm not innocent by any means. Being at each other's throats, literally, is wearing me down even if I'd never admit it to him. Living with four older brothers, you learn to concede only when it benefits you.

So, I take Dixon up on his offer to stay with him and for the rest of the day I help out at Xen's until my own shift at Sunbrook, pushing everything else from my mind.

Everything but that mouth of Beckett's. Whispered threats disguised as empty promises that'll stay with me for a very long time.

Which is one reason why I'm backing off for a while—I need a place I won't remember, not somewhere I'll never forget.

CHAPTER 12

Paige

"GET OUT OF HERE," I WHISPER HARSHLY. "NO, please. Please, don't touch me."

Remind me never to stay with Dixon again. The guy has ferrets. Plural. Basically two vermin that roam freely around the house, hiding in the couch cushions waiting to pop out as you walk by, and sneak your things right out from under you. They also love to rub against you like goddamn cats. I may not have had an allergy to ferrets when I first got here a few days ago but I damn well have one now. Every time the stretched out rats touch me, I itch the rest of the day.

I have work later though and I'm down to my last pair of scrubs so I'm extra wary of them touching me today. Dixon takes his laundry to his mom's house, no joke, for her to wash but I refuse to make another woman clean my underwear. Although Dixon's always been like family, I never saw him in his own element, and now that I have I'm starting to see him in a whole new light. A smelly, lazy light that flickers from underuse.

Gin rubs on my left leg while Tonic tries to sneak up the opening on my right pants leg. As soon as I feel her soft fur touch my leg I start itching.

"Damn you!" I grit, finally scaring the critters away.

"What happened?"

I'm sniffling and massaging my irritated eyes with the palms of my hands when Dixon comes into the kitchen, looking fresh as a daisy.

"Your pets got their allergens all over me. I can't go to work like this." I motion to my entire body.

"You look fine."

Typical.

How else are we supposed to say it? If we don't feel good, we don't look good. Period. Looking *fine* has nothing to do with it.

"How are you getting to work anyway?"

"What do you mean?"

"It's pouring outside. Just started up but it's supposed to rain all night. It should be a crazy one, too. We're hosting a storm party and serving Slippery Nipples and Dark & Stormies for half price."

Classy.

"I'm sorry to miss that."

I hide my eye roll, reaching down to scratch the shit out of my ankle.

"S'all good. Do you want to take my car? I can have one of my servers pick me up."

"If you're sure you don't need it?"

He assures me he doesn't, so after thanking him, I'm on my way in his Mazda Miata to pick up some new clothes before heading in for my shift. It's small but handles surprisingly well in the rain. Dixon isn't a big guy so it's great for him but it's a little snug for my five-nine frame. That's just one reason why I like my motorcycle so much—I don't feel contained in any way. The sky's the limit and there's nothing holding me back. There isn't anything to protect me either, but I like it that way. Having all possible dangers eliminated for me during my childhood only made me crave the risk that much more when I hit eighteen.

I lay on the gas, taking corners faster than I probably should. It's been so long since I've driven a car, I warm at the thrill of pushing it a little further past the line of reasonable driving. No puddle too big, no corner too tight, I drive with no real forethought, squealing excitedly anytime the car hydroplanes.

Rainstorms are grossly under-appreciated. Dixon had the right, although greedy, idea of celebrating this tonight. Being in a semi-arid climate, rain doesn't happen as often as the local farmers wish so when it does it's a big deal. Most people act up by forgetting how to drive altogether but I've always loved the rain. Not riding on my bike in it—that's not fun any way you slice it—but any other time I'm all about it.

Pulling into Creekwood is bittersweet. I haven't seen my apartment since picking up some of my things for my stay at Dixon's. As much as I hoped a break from all the tension would help, I found myself missing my space more. It's not all mine but it's still mine. I was just starting to get used to it. The smells, the random bits from the guys' previous day discarded on every surface, the open magazines lying around, the milk carton sitting on the counter when I walked in each morning. I finally solved that mystery when I saw Beckett forget to replace it in the fridge after dumping a generous amount in his coffee before I left.

Before he ran me out of here.

No. I chose to leave.

And now coming back reminds me of coming home. A place that hasn't felt the same since Mom's diagnosis but still brings out the best memories that I yearn for like a bowl of hot soup on a cold day.

The excitement from the drive wears off as I glance around the lot. I don't typically see my roommates before leaving for work but it's a habit of mine—always checking for their rides. Unfortunately, the windows are covered by sheets of water blocking my view, so I shrug it off and make a run for the stairs, spotting both bikes parked and drenched but the Tahoe and BMW missing.

Alone inside, I decide to take another shower to get the fur-touch off my skin. With my toiletries still at Dixon's, I use Beckett's body wash and shampoo but forgo shaving. There are some things you just can't share. My brother Nick would disagree wholeheartedly but only when sharing works in his favor, not the other way around. There were many times I'd find rogue hairs in my razor thanks to my most self-centered brother.

The reminder of Nick's narcissism has me thinking of Vernon. He continues to mutter crappy things to me any time he thinks he can get away with it. What's worse is ignoring it doesn't even throw him off. His malicious behavior increases with each incident. I don't want to run to Rosie like he's accused me of but something needs to be done. And soon.

While everyone wants to point the finger at me and my mom's move, I can't help but think it has something to do with the boys not visiting anymore. Even when Tysen helped deliver her chair, he took one look at her, teared up, and ran. And since he won't pick up his phone, I don't know what triggered it. I mean, I know but I don't *know*.

What else is going on with him?

My mother still hasn't eaten a full meal and is more withdrawn than ever. That chair I bought her is about the only silver lining since she spends so much time in it these days. It's the kind that lifts with her when she gets up so she doesn't strain anything. I just want her to be comfortable.

I just want her.

It could be a combination of everything or maybe it's her disease winning the battle I seem to be fighting solo the more time goes on. I check on her any chance I get but working the night shift can have its disadvantages in that sense. Plus, she's been sleeping more, too, reducing the opportunities I have to visit with her fully. I still have a job to do and can't ignore my other responsibilities even if all I want to do is curl up next to her and watch her sleep all night.

Cynthia helps out when she can by checking on my mom but she recently put in her two weeks' notice, choosing to work at a higher paying job in the emergency room at one of the local hospitals. Since Rosie hired on another night nurse to replace Cynthia, I've also been training her along with constantly placating Dennis.

He's been all out of sorts lately and more aggressive than ever.

Last night was the worst I've seen him and he actually swung on me. I dodged the blow for the most part, only nicking my bottom lip in the process, but it was such a shock that one of my favorites would turn on me. Theoretically, I know not to take it personally but it's much easier said than done. Everything feels personal these days.

I run my tongue over the scab already forming on my lip. Luckily, there was only a small cut and Cynthia treated it before our shift ended this morning. It should be healed in no time.

My stomach, however, that's a different story. It's been tight, twisted, and sore for days now.

Beckett's actions outside Xen's were the inedible icing on the mud pie I've been shoveling down my throat. His sexy admission about the night before started out great. I loved knowing he was losing his mind outside my door while I was doing the same thing just inside. But then, it all changed. He changed. His hot words turned icy and mean, leaving me hanging in a bitter wind with nowhere to go and no idea how I got there.

I just want to know why he even bothers. Why the sendoff? If he doesn't want me around, leave me to my fucked-up life and be done. Our schedules don't even match up so it *should* be easy to avoid each other entirely.

Except, it's not that simple for me anymore. Beckett has a way of being here even when he's not. His absence takes up as much space as his tall body and the apartment is filled with him. As I smooth his earthy body wash over my legs, I smirk knowing it'll lace my skin all night.

If only it worked both ways so I could torture him the same way.

"Who the fuck's in there?"

Beckett's bellow followed by pounding on the locked bathroom door cause me to drop the bottle I'd just been replacing on the tub insert and it twirls between my feet like an enthusiastic game of Spin-The-Bottle.

"Shit," I curse, reaching for it.

"Paige? Are you in there?"

My eyes roll so hard I fear they'll get stuck.

"Yeah, it's me." Who else would it be? Despite my roommate being a bear to live with, my hair isn't yellow and my name sure the hell isn't Goldilocks. "Can I finish my shower now?"

When I'm met with silence, I rinse off the rest of the soap with shaky hands before cutting the water and wrapping a towel around my body.

Just out of the door, I run smack dab into a very familiar, very annoying wall.

I pop both my hip and head to the side, asking, "Can I help you?"

"You were in there alone?" Beckett's eyes dart over my shoulder as he swallows noisily.

"What gave it away?" I ask, checking over my shoulder and seeing I left the lid on his body wash up.

Ah, shit.

Still looking past me, he says, "I didn't see your bike outside."

Satisfied with his own findings, he finally drops his gaze to look at me and dark clouds pass over his face that have nothing to do with the storm raging outside.

"What the hell happened to your face?"

Before I can get a word out, soft hands gingerly cup my cheeks as Beckett lifts my face for closer inspection. Gently tilting my head back, he leans down, getting a better look at my lip. The intensity in his eyes mixed with his light touch has me fidgeting in my towel.

"Do you mind? I'm naked."

His moody sky gaze flicks to mine briefly, almost in annoyance, before dropping to my mouth again.

Completely ignoring what I just said, he demands, "Who did this to you?"

I scoff, shaking off his hands. Strangely, I get the sensation I'm missing something.

Pushing past him, I make it to my door before his hand is gripping my elbow, stopping me in my tracks.

"Paige, who did that to you? You haven't been here for three days and you show up with a busted lip. What am I supposed to think?"

Beckett's quiet voice raises the hairs on the back of my neck as I fight a shiver, the sound like a warm bath after a long day I want to get lost in for hours. Or days. Maybe longer.

I manage to step away, if only to keep from going to him, and get a good look at him finally. Beneath a dark hoodie, disheveled hair sticks out at all angles, casting shadows over bloodshot eyes with bags just below. His muscles are poised for battle despite his soothing speech. And while his eyebrows pinch together, his jaw ticks along with the seconds, drawing this out that much longer.

An entire war wages in his every fiber as he stands before me but I'm not sure with who. He's as confusing as my own feelings.

What's going on here? This isn't the Beckett I left.

Just when I think he's going to stomp away, he closes the distance, slowly lifting his hands back to my face, and I flinch when his thumb traces over the cut. His sharp inhale pierces me to my spot.

"Who did this?" His whisper is a scream into the void I hold in my heart right now.

"I'm fine." I shake my head softly, lowering my voice as well. "It was an accident at work."

His eyes flit between mine. "Where have you been?"

He still hasn't released my face, or my lip, or my interest. Why is he so concerned all of a sudden?

"Honestly, I'm surprised you even noticed I was gone. I thought I wasn't worth your attention."

Gaze solely on my mouth again, he lowers his head and on instinct I flinch backward. Beckett's unpredictable on a good day, today he's out of his fucking mind. I wasn't cast aside by the beast himself just to fall back into his ruthless trap.

He hovers there, saying, "I notice everything about you." His eyes meet mine again, reminding me to breathe and he asks, "Why did you leave?"

Under his penetrating stare, I swallow thickly, huffing out, "I needed a break."

I *need* a break.

"I didn't like it."

Only child syndrome strikes again.

"That's not my problem." But also...what? This is about the complete opposite of what he was saying before I went to stay at Dixon's. I thought he wanted me gone. I thought he would've been celebrating my absence, not pouting again. Was he pouting over me?

"What about Marc?"

Finally releasing my lip, his eyes narrow, something unreadable passing them.

"What about him?"

"Doesn't he deserve to know where you were?"

That's the weirdest shit I've ever heard. Why the hell would Marc, of all people, need to know where I was? My rent is paid up and that's all either of these two *deserve to know*.

"I don't answer to Marc any more than I answer to the apartment manager. If it affects rent, then maybe, otherwise I don't see why it'd matter to him where I went." He said it himself that I'm free to come and go as I please.

He loosens his hold on my face, his fingertips now brushing my cheekbones like an artist painting a masterpiece with careful strokes and intense focus. The tingle against my skin reminds me of riding a motorcycle for the first time. With the wind teasing my face from the visor being left open, I relished feeling as much of the elements as possible. To be one with nature instead of being boxed up in a metal cage.

Beckett's touch is like being freed all over again. Being shown what I've been missing. What I suddenly crave more than my next ride.

"There's nothing going on between you two? At all?" He watches me carefully.

"Marc's easy on the eyes," my shoulders lift and fall in the same breath, "but that's it. I don't sleep with my roommates."

The declaration tastes foreign. Like a lie. A lie I'm trying to convince myself along with the beautiful boy standing in front of me.

Beckett's gaze drops again just as his lips meet mine.

Stunned, I freeze in place, my eyes still open and everything. He lazily closes his like he's cherishing what he sees first. Gentle and sweet, his mouth caresses mine with such care I melt. Melt into him.

I didn't think at his size he'd have a gentle bone in his body. I figured his affection would be like a bull in a china shop—clumsy and hurried. Yet, his kiss has a sensitivity I've never known. One I never even believed could exist.

The rawness almost overwhelming, I close my eyes, ready to ride the wave of crazy I must've been swept away in.

Beckett kisses and kisses and kisses, content in bathing my lips in careful touches, never once pushing for more.

Even as my mind warns of the danger in provoking Beckett—*mess with the bull, get the horns*—I grow downright impatient. How can pain scare me anymore? I'm fucking choking on it and I'm still pulling air in my lungs. It's grueling and burns my insides like inhaling salt water but it's there and it hasn't killed me yet.

Gripping my towel, I slip my tongue past my lips, tasting the surprise on his instantly.

His body stiffens and he pulls back, pinning me with dusky blue eyes. "You're sure? What about your lip?"

A smile falls over my face. Such an innocent question from a not so innocent man. On a very long list of troubles plaguing my every waking moment, my lip is the least of my worries. In fact, it doesn't even register at all, so I nod my head, giving him the permission he's asking for.

Ruin me, Beckett. See if I notice.

Dropping one hand to my ass, he cups and lifts, bringing me onto on my tiptoes in a move that screams greed.

His.

His.

His.

The towel overlapping at my waist flutters like the butterflies beneath the damp cotton.

As his lips descend again, they have the perfect sweet/salty combination I've only dreamt about. A satisfying blend of give and take, neither of us fighting for dominance like I expected. The men I've been with usually struggle to control the pace, rushing to the finish line, but Beckett's relaxed exploration proves he's not racing anywhere.

He tilts his head to get better access, tipping everything on its axis, and my mind swims to stay afloat. This place we've ended up, it's as dangerous as it is safe. In my room, on my terms, but still the most precarious position I could be in—with Beckett at the helm. And yet, my heart beats a steady rhythm, content in having Beckett steer for a while.

His muscles are flexed against mine in a delicious meeting of bodies when the kiss turns lethal, threatening to consume me in a sweet, sweet demise I'll enjoy every single minute of.

A text notification shatters the quiet of the room, of the moment, reminding me the rest of the world still exists. Beckett's like an eclipse. A syzygy made up of me, him, and everything else. He obscures it *all*.

We break apart, catching our breath. Both of us swathed in the same body wash, the smell of secret woodlands swirling around us.

Breadcrumbs. He sprinkles them in his wake without even meaning to and the more breadcrumbs Beckett leaves, the harder it is to resist following them back into the forest I desperately want to get lost in again.

"Shit." My forehead pressed to his, I say, "I gotta go."

He cranes his neck to look at me. "I'll pay you to stay here."

Ripping myself from his grasp, I skirt around him to grab my phone all the while clutching my rumpled towel to my important parts.

"Just what every woman wants to hear. That she can be bought."

I type out a quick reply to Cynthia's text asking if I need a ride.

"I didn't mean it like that. I just, I don't want you to leave yet. Every time you walk away it feels like you won't come back. I, um, I hate that feeling."

Huh? Our last encounter the guy practically stuffed me in a box with enough postage to ship international but now he doesn't like it when I leave? I can't catch up with him and I've never had an issue keeping speed before.

I finger my clean uniform in my top drawer, studying him.

"For everyone or just me?"

Beckett flips his hood back up that fell sometime during our kiss.

"Forget it. Do you need me to drop you off at work?"

Mask back in place, Beckett grimly walks to my doorway.

My neck aches from the whiplash as I bat his offer away. "I've got it covered." Dixon's car is as light as a feather and skims across the water like one, too. My nerves kick start with the promise of driving it some more in the rain. I need…something to look forward to. *Anything.*

Still hesitating at the threshold, Beckett asks, "Aye, if you were in trouble, would you tell me?"

"I am the trouble, remember?"

My wink is thrown in a dumpster and set on fire. He is literally no fun.

"That old fuckwad didn't do that to your lip, did he?"

"Vernon? No, he's not that stupid." Rude AF but not stupid.

His gaze runs the length of my doorjamb, rubbing the

smooth wood and I grimace, remembering how shattered his is in comparison.

"What's his problem with you anyway?"

Sighing, I slide on a pair of underwear under my towel, careful not to flash Beckett.

"Old dog, new tricks."

Those dusk-like eyes flash with stars streaking across them as they abandon the doorjamb to track my movements. He catches himself a moment too late and his eyebrows nosedive trying to hide it.

Hmm. The war rages on.

"And you're the trick?"

There it is. That infamous mouth of his. The one he wields as a weapon to torture me with both pleasure *and* pain.

"Wow. Two prostitute references in one night. I bet your mom must be proud."

Back to his bullish behavior, his nostrils flare.

What the hell does he have to be offended about? I didn't suggest he was a sex worker. Twice. And honestly, most of them work their asses off for reasons people like him would never understand. I've never had to sell my body for money—thankfully—but if it ever came down to that or someone I love going without basic needs, I'd pick the former. Without question. Have my body but leave my soul intact because nothing could ever hurt worse than watching a loved one suffer. Nothing.

For people to judge that kind of sacrifice floors me but Beckett's idea of going without is probably using condoms geared toward her pleasure. I imagine him with two loving parents, doting on him so well, he never had to think about that sort of thing. About choosing someone else's well-being over your own.

I'm still waiting for him to mash his teeth and stomp the ground when he spits, "I call it like I see it. You just had your lips glued to mine after kissing how many guys since moving in?"

Laughing, I shove my scrubs on under my towel. I can't have

this conversation pantless. I just can't. He's been all over the same number of girls, if not more, than me and yet I deserve judgment? I'm the problem here?

Just when Beckett was proving to be something different, something better in a world full of less, he goes and reveals his true colors, and they're ugly. Just like mine.

"I didn't hear you complaining a second ago." Far from it. "I guess you like sloppy seconds after all. Now, if you'll excuse me, I have a short list of fucks to give and none with your name so..."

With a flick of my wrist, I turn my back to him and drop my towel exposing my naked torso.

"What about you?" His sneer lashes my back, quick and unforgiving. "I doubt you're making Mommy swell with pride."

I wait until his footsteps disappear into the next room to answer, choking out, "I'd give anything to know."

CHAPTER 13

Paige

"DENNIS, PUT THE MUG DOWN." TECHNICALLY, IT'S just the handle but it's still sharp and could be used as a weapon. He already smashed the damn mug into the wall and is now brandishing it in front of his body to hold us off.

Cynthia and I exchange glances and I give a slight nod in the other direction. She gets the hint, moving to her left, effectively taking Dennis's focus with her.

Seeing my opening, I dive forward and wrench the broken piece out of his hand before he has time to process what happened. I slip it into my pocket then hold my hands up in front of me to block any retaliation he might try.

Luckily, Dennis just stares at his empty hand in confusion.

"What's going on out here?"

My head jerks to the side at the sound of my mother's voice.

Wrong move.

The next thing I know my hair is being yanked back by a strong grip. Not like Beckett's careful hair pulling either, this shit hurts. Bad. So bad I cry out, squeezing my eyes shut.

"Oh, no you don't. She's not going with you."

My mother ignores Dennis's ramblings, scolding, "Let her go! Right now, or I'll get the spoon."

Almost forgetting the man with my hair in a vice grip, I open my eyes to watch my mother approach. She used to say that all the time. That was her preferred threat when any of us kids got out of line. It was scary as hell when she got the wooden spoon out. The notorious spoon was rarely used on me but the few times it was were more memorable than any other punishment I've ever received. The fact that she just used it in protection of me like she's done countless times has my frenzied heart soaring.

And she's out of her room, walking, and talking. This is the most interaction I've seen from her.

If only it was under different circumstances.

"Stay there, Ms. Christensen," Cynthia orders.

My mom continues advancing, unaware Dennis is twisting my hair in his clutches in time with her steps. He swings us both around until my face is almost pressed to the spot on the wall where the mug was just broken.

Cynthia frantically calls the new night nurse over the radio for back-up.

Latching one hand over Dennis's to try to ease the strain, I throw up my other palm to my mom, gritting out as professionally as possible, "Please go back to your room, Ms. Christensen. We'll take care of it."

I can't allow anything to happen to my mom and Dennis is off the fucking rails right now. He's never behaved like this in all the time I've been here, night shift or otherwise. I can take a hit if I need to, my mother won't though. No other patient will. Not on my shift.

"You heard me, young man. Get your hands off her or so help me..."

I close my eyes against the tears leaking out. Another saying from my childhood. She's remembering things. More of her old self is showing through instead of the withdrawn version she's been recently.

"You can't have her! She's leaving and it's all your fault," Dennis rages, not caring one bit he's being threatened by a mother of five. Anyone else would know better.

She takes a determined step forward, more fire in her voice than I could've hoped to hear during these times.

"Mom, stay where you are," I rush out.

Shit.

It just slipped out.

My mother halts finally, staring up at me blankly. Hope chooses now of all times to show her fucking insatiable self, and I curse the day I let her into my life. Again.

Please. Please see me. See me, goddamn it!

But she is seeing me, isn't she? That's why she's out here in the first place. Something called to her. Something inside me maybe. A broken heart calling for help. A call any good mother would come running to answer no matter what…right?

"Dennis, release Paige now or I have to use this," the other nurse, Naomi, interrupts, holding a full syringe that she passes off to Cynthia.

My mother blinks, looking around like she doesn't know how she got here.

No. Just give me a little more time.

Behind me, I hear Cynthia ask, "Won't his other medication counteract it?"

"No, he hasn't received any today. I checked."

My stomach plummets. *What?* No wonder he's a mess. Dennis needs his medication every day. Without it, well, this happens. Today is a prime fucking example why people like Vernon get paid as much as they do. Because the medication is that important.

"Dennis, let go please."

My neck burns from working so hard to counter the pressure he's applying and noticing the mug shards still clinging to the wall, I push back that much harder to keep from exfoliating my face with the sharp pieces.

"We'll get this all cleaned up and get you to bed, okay? Don't you want to get some sleep? It's been a long night." Made longer without Dennis getting his proper treatment.

"Honey, you're not cleaning this up. He made the mess, he'll fix it."

Oh, for fuck's sake. Now is not the time for Mom to start regurgitating all her parenting rules.

"Ma'am, step back."

"I will do no such thing. Not until he releases this nice young lady."

Dennis tightens his grip so hard I'm gasping just as my mom's face contorts into a shared agony. The concern written there is blinding. That or my vision is being affected.

I blink a few times, not wanting to miss any scrap of her love but it's no use. Spots swim in front of me like sharks circling chum.

It's gotta be now.

I thrust my head forward then, grimacing when a healthy chunk of strands rips from my scalp. The sudden move does the job of catching Dennis off guard but it also slams my forehead directly into the wall as fragments of jagged clay bite into the skin just below my hairline.

Spinning on my heel, I catch both his hands in mine and pull down—hard. When he stumbles a bit, I shoot Cynthia a look and she hurries over to inject Dennis with the calming liquid while he's still unbalanced.

"That's right, Dennis. Nice and easy. Everything's okay."

Cynthia and I make eye contact over his head, breathing out identical sighs.

"Ms. Christensen, let's get you to bed," Naomi soothes, leading my mother away. She's wearing a vacant expression once again.

Together, Cynthia and I shuffle Dennis to his room. After tucking him in, I rush out to check on the mess in the hall finding Naomi, hands on her hips, already taking stock of the damage.

How can a place that smells like a tropical paradise turn into an absolute nightmare so quickly? This wasn't supposed to happen. Not to me.

She glances over at me, saying, "Rosie's on her way. I'll take care of this if you want to get cleaned up." She eyes my forehead pointedly.

I raise my eyebrows in thanks but end up hissing on a wince as the pain comes crashing back to me all at once. Not only from the physical assault but the emotional battering, too, and by the time I reach the bathroom up front my entire body is trembling.

Alone in the bathroom, I suck in a lungful of air, facing myself in the mirror. Who I see looking back is foreign. Completely unrecognizable. An alien from a planet I never, ever wanted to know existed.

How long has it been since I've seen myself? The real me, not this disoriented version. One that has no idea what the fuck she's even doing anymore.

Hair stringy and kinked from the air-dry from earlier, eyes wired but still thoroughly exhausted, skin ashy and now bleeding, split lip on the mend—I look a hot mess. Worse than a hot mess. A steaming pile of trash only the unluckiest of garbage men would take.

When did I become this? A strong case could be made for last year when my mother went to live in her first facility. Having that lifeline taken away did damage. Damage I don't think I'll ever come back from.

But even through the ache of missing my mom, I always had my brothers. The four of them helped fill the gigantic void our remaining parent left in her wake on her own journey for survival. I was still able to tread water in the shallows, navigating my way back toward dry land.

Without their support though, I've started to sink. Plummeting into the darkest chasm with no rescue crew in sight.

Splashing water on my face to clean the miscellaneous bits sticking to my skin—blood, clay, paint, and plaster—it all runs into the sink, swirling the drain in a continuous loop before disappearing altogether.

The first aid kit was just restocked making it easy to find the items I need; so I clean the wounds as best I can, then pat them dry with stiff paper towels.

Rosie will want to know exactly what happened after a staff member and resident made physical contact. Even though I've worked here for a while, I've never had an altercation with anyone. Aside from the weird crap Vernon keeps pulling anyway, but that's small potatoes compared to what happened tonight.

Maybe I was naïve in thinking I'd never have a resident get physical during my shift but it doesn't make the bitter pill any easier to swallow. Given how many people were in that hallway, me being the only injured party really is the best-case scenario.

Fixed up enough to face my superior, I take one last look in the mirror.

My eyes drop immediately.

She's still there. The lost girl. The one scrambling for some sort of floatation device before she drowns entirely. She just has a shiny forehead now.

◆ ◆ ◆

Rosie's office is small and quaint. Photos of smiling elderly models line the walls as advertisement. Her desk has a large bouquet of fresh wildflowers and my nose stings from the overpowering fragrance. The early morning sunlight just beginning to filter through the curtains reaches her chair as she swivels back and forth. Her hands are steepled in front of her and her gaze is unreadable as we listen to Cynthia's take on what happened.

"Paige's actions saved multiple people from a dangerous situation. Had she not responded quickly and effectively, I fear other residents could've been harmed as well."

As valuable as nurses are, residents are priceless. They're the ones paying the bills to keep this place open. Their families are the ones ensuring the staff's paychecks are signed every other week. Without them there would be no us.

And without Alzheimer's we'd all be better off. *Fuck you, dementia.*

Cynthia chose her words carefully and I'm grateful. While my decision might've been hasty, it ultimately only hurt me. A nurse getting injured is forgivable, but a resident being harmed—not so much.

"Thank you, Cynthia. You may return to your station."

Cynthia rises from her seat beside me, giving my shoulder a squeeze as she passes. Tomorrow's supposed to be her last day working here so in a way she gave me a hell of a parting gift, vouching for me like she did.

Rosie watches from across her oak desk, waiting until we're alone to continue. You'd never know she was just pulled from bed. Not a single hair is out of place and her business professional attire is immaculate. A woman in her late forties, she's turned this place around from the dump it once was. Some directors can become lazy and complacent in their role but Rosie's always striving for improvement and I really respect her.

"Per our policy, I have to put you on leave."

No, no, no.

"Rosie, I need the money. Dennis wasn't hurt. Nobody was hurt," I plead, leaning forward, ready to fall to my knees if necessary.

"You were hurt, Paige. That's enough for me." She raises an impeccable eyebrow, asking, "Is it for you though?"

I study the swirls in the wood of the desk in front of her, willing the tears filling my eyes to disappear.

Rosie sighs. "It'll be paid leave. You may return the beginning of next week. Take the time to rest. Recharge."

Clutching the arm rest, I meet her gaze again. "What about my mom?"

"That's another thing." My heart picks up, a loud staccato in my own ears. *Don't say it.* "I'm afraid Ms. Christensen's presence has impacted your ability to maintain a professional approach while on duty."

"That's not true. Aside from tonight, I haven't had a single slip-up. I've managed to keep my connection to her confidential for the most part. Very few people here even know we're related." Although, I don't know how anyone could miss the similarities. It's the same for all us Christensens—once we're in one room, the resemblance is unmistakable. "I've only been able to visit once on my day off and I left as soon as it became clear she wasn't receptive. She hasn't been herself and I'm worried about her as any daughter, or nurse for that matter, would be but I haven't given her any special treatment. Just," I stop, swallowing, "give us a little more time to adjust to the new situation. Please."

My fingers twist in my lap. Sweat against sweat, they writhe like my composure.

Rosie looks me over. Can she tell I'm going under? Does anyone notice my lungs are filling with something other than oxygen?

Better yet, does anybody care?

She leans forward to rest her elbows on her desk, meeting my eye. "Okay. You're one of the best nurses I've got or I wouldn't consider it. I'll see you back here after the weekend and we'll see how things go from there."

I push to my feet before she can change her mind.

"Thank you. I won't let you down."

"I know you won't," she says, rising to see me out.

Coming face-to-face with a smug Vernon reminds me what got this whole knotted ball rolling in the first place and I turn around in the doorway, blocking his path.

"Before I go, I recommend Dennis's chart be inspected. It seems Mr. Gregory, along with Ms. Christensen, haven't been receiving their medication as prescribed and I'm wondering how many other residents are missing their necessary treatments. Vern, maybe you could provide some insight into that." My eyes lock on Vernon, watching as his widen in alarm.

Snitches get stitches, right? Well, if I'm nailing the last part of that, I might as well live up to the first part, too.

CHAPTER 14

Beckett

Waking this morning to find Paige's bike parked in its usual spot was surprising. Finding her bedroom door locked was not.

Her absence stirred up a shitastrophy of emotions I didn't even know I was capable of anymore. I didn't *want* to be capable of.

As much as I hated the idea of having her here in the beginning, sharing my living space with the woman became nice. Normal. My fucking usual without me even realizing it. I tried, I fucking *tried* shutting her out after she literally knocked down my door, planting her ass too close to personal business I've been managing alone for years. But the disappearing act she pulled as a result backfired. Big time. The words I spewed to her, that felt like coughing up my own intestines, turned into verbal darts piercing my already perforated façade the more I replayed them until I was ready to grovel at her feet. And I don't bow to anyone. Never had to before and I sure as fuck didn't plan on doing it now.

Yet...that's what I was willing to do for Paige. For her to come back, to come home.

Home.

Marc hasn't spoken to me outside of work since Paige took off, blaming me—rightfully so—for her taking off.

I thought it would feel better. I hoped it would settle the constant jumbled mess inside my head. She wakes things in me that have long been dormant.

Instead it exploded in my face. Not having her scent sneaking along my skin and into my veins was like coming down from a high and noticing you're all out of your favorite drug. Panic swirled like a waterspout over a tense sea, making my insides prickle, and I woke up bloody every day Paige was missing. I thought it was my body's reaction to her irresistible pull but the hole she left from her sudden withdrawal was more than physical longing. It was all fucking consuming, to the point that nobody at Pop The Hood dared approach me for fear of losing a limb. Or their life. *Whatever.*

Her toiletries sitting next to mine again placates a piece of me still rioting for her reappearance. Still demanding her return—to me.

Even though I regret letting them out, I meant the words I told her last night. Paige's existence feels like a temporary fixture in my life and where I'd usually relish that knowledge, I now detest the notion. The idea of this girl leaving with a part of me that's finally sprung to life scares me more than the fact that she's responsible for resuscitating it to begin with.

Every time we get close though, one of us tramples all over the moment with our egos. I thought I had a biting tongue until I met Paige. Girl can draw blood with a single sentence. Hearing her talk about my mom hit hard. She nailed a target I doubt she was even aiming for and I did the foolish thing by firing right back. Shame settled like a weight in my stomach after our war with words. The truth is she's in a league of her own but I tried to make her feel worthless. Again.

What the fuck is my problem?

Showered, I throw on one of my new tees I just got in. This one says *Ride More, Work Less* and I think it's pretty spot on. It's been a while since I rode for fun and Coty asked if we could ride together after work, so I take my Ninja to the shop. Even though Paige's homecoming has me breathing easier, I could still use some open air. Work's been great as far as my bank account is concerned but it's been a fun-sponge for hobbies.

Although, teasing Paige could give any extracurricular activity a run for its money any day.

Angie corners me as soon as I step foot in the bay. Girl puts in more hours than the rest of us and isn't even a full partner—yet. Coty's working on something big for our old neighbor girl. Nailing down a girl like Angela takes time but luckily that's exactly what Coty's willing to put in. And lots of it. Dude would wait 'til he's gray and balding for her to be ready for the next step in their relationship.

He pushes her in other ways though—like the bedroom. Goddamn, I'm glad they got their own place. The sounds that came from that room when Coty still lived with us will be etched in my memories forever.

I can only hope the same can't be said for what Angie, and now Paige, heard coming from mine.

"Morning," I greet, giving her a quick once-over. She's in her typical polo shirt half tucked into black pants and aviator glasses hanging off the few undone buttons at the neck. She somehow manages to bring a down to earth vibe to her otherwise professional look. Business casual with a hint of beach chick attitude. The patrons eat it up as does every other person that meets our boy's girlfriend. She's enchanting in a sea witch kind of way. Beautiful and charming until she swallows you whole for disrespecting her or her rules. Basically the perfect manager for our car wash. She attracts customers by the hordes but still maintains order with her no bullshit attitude.

"I'm so glad I hired you, neighbor girl."

She rolls her eyes, sticking her hands in her pockets. "You didn't. And why do you still call me that? I don't even live next to you anymore."

"So? You'll always be neighbor girl to me. Now, what can I do for you?"

"Paige."

My eyebrows skyrocket and I sputter like an Oldsmobile. "I said what, not who, Angie. Don't tell me you and Coty turned into swingers since you two moved out." I hang my head, shaking it. "You can take the freaks out of Creekwood, but..."

"You're an idiot."

I cover my heart, blinking my eyes at her and deadpanning, "You continue to wound me when I specifically asked you not to."

She ignores me, shooting her gaze over to Marc. "A little birdy told me it's Paige's birthday this weekend."

A frown erases all my humor. Like all of it. How the fuck did he know that information and I didn't?

"Coty and I want to throw her a party."

I'm already shaking my head. "I don't think that's a good idea. I get the feeling she's not close with her family."

Angela's doubtful expression has me questioning that now, too.

"Okay…well, we can keep it small then. A barbecue maybe. We'll call it a housewarming party or some crap." She waves her hand, still unfamiliar with domesticated life.

"What do you need from me?"

Simply, *too* simply, she says, "To get her there."

I curb my scoff.

"What makes you think she'd listen to me?"

After maintaining a staring contest that borders on uncomfortable, she shrugs and turns away, muttering, "I'll get Marc to do it."

Like fuck she will.

"Fine." Little rat. "What time do you want her there?"

Angie spins with a pleased grin plastered to her pretty face. Coty is one lucky dude even if his girl gives me as much shit as I give her. I wouldn't have it any other way though. Only the strongest survive around here. And the toughest thrive. Like those two.

She gives me the rest of her orders—I mean, instructions—then disappears back to the wash side.

Marc and I make eye contact after she's gone and he shakes his head.

"What?"

"She's back, huh?"

I shrug tightly, squirting some liquid dish soap into my palm.

"Looks that way to me," I say, rubbing the soap over the skin on my hands until it's dry. It makes cleaning my hands afterward a fucking dream. No mechanic hands for me. Fuck that. I like my shit smooth and moisturized.

Dude just nods thoughtfully.

"You know something I don't?" Like her fucking birthday that he didn't bother sharing. I remember her talking about it being this month but she never specified what day. We are starting to run out of days in July so it makes sense it's coming up. But still…he could've said something.

"I already told you, ask her yourself. Quit being a fucking pussy."

I thought I did. About what I really wanted to know anyway. I came right out and asked Paige if she was hooking up with my boy. And she finally gave me what I was looking for. What I'd been wondering since the day she moved in. The answer to the question I'd been dreading asking but ultimately did for the sake of my mental stability from not knowing. I'd resisted putting my mouth on her long enough. I was done waiting. And goddamn, the kiss was worth the awkwardness of asking at all.

"You heading out to Vega's?"

"Yeah."

"To work?"

He gives me a cryptic look then without another word, he jumps in his red BMW and takes off. July being one of their busiest months, his dad's farm has needed him onsite almost daily and it just so happens that's where we keep our dirt bikes, too. Can't say I blame him for taking full advantage from time to time. When we were younger, the three of us used to get lost for hours in his father's orchards, riding until the sun went down. Just three dejected kids trying to find their happy in life.

The landscape might've changed in the past few years but the quest for happiness sure hasn't. Not for me at least. Watching Marc leave, I'd be willing to bet dude's still searching, too. He never wants to end up trapped like his dad is to his farm but I don't know what he actually does want.

Coty's the only one I can look at and say he's undeniably happy. Yeah, he wants marriage and kids one day but Angela will give that to him and more. She just makes him prove his worth every chance she gets because she still questions hers.

Fucking bad parents.

There should be a special kind of hell for people that fuck up their kids with their own issues. One with planes full of crying babies and floors covered with LEGO blocks. My dad used to bitch about both. Angie's mom would make the perfect candidate if it did exist. The damage she caused her youngest daughter will take years, if not longer, to reverse. She's made great progress so far but once a parent grabs hold with their vile beliefs and toxic ways, it's hard to shake free from the decay they've triggered.

Or maybe that's just my experience.

Shit, mine's probably there already, sipping on her favorite white wine, having a grand ol' time. Anything but be with her son, right? Hell itself holds more appeal to a woman that self-centered than her own family. The one she started, then abandoned.

I shake off the disturbing thoughts bubbling to the surface. Luckily, they disperse as quickly as they formed and I move over to the Sportster still in pieces inside my station from last night. Unable to focus on anything other than Paige and where she might've been, I left early.

With the knot now missing from the pit of my stomach, I dig in for a full day's work with more energy than I've had all week.

◆ ◆ ◆

"I needed this," I say as I scan the canyon below. It's crazy. You wouldn't even know an entire storm rolled through last night. The wind kicked up after lunch and there's a thick haze that settled over the trees from the loose dust blowing around. Everything seems… calm.

But isn't that usually *before* the storm?

After a gnarly ass ride on some winding back roads, followed by a ripper of a curve, Coty led us to this piece of land near his, just a little higher up on the mountain overlooking the entire area. It's a cherry spot for anyone who's into that kind of thing, like a starter family or something.

Coty had this dream of me and Marc buying the properties surrounding his so we could all live close to each other. Unfortunately, some big shot snatched up all the lots but the one Coty brought me to today. Pretty sure that's why we're here now. Dude's relentless. But if that's really the plan, then Marc will get first pick, not because he's ready to settle down, but because I'd never be the greedy one to split us up.

Let that shit hang over his head for the rest of his life.

Plus, fun Uncle Beckett could couch surf like nobody's business. Marc's way too good of a person to make sleep on a couch which is exactly why he deserves the property over me.

Although, if Coty got his wish, this location would be perfect for me. I could look out over my boys and their lives and know that all is well. That everyone is exactly where they're supposed to be.

I like that idea.

I like it too much.

"How's married life by the way?" I nod at the newly finished house in the distance, the one we had to keep from Angie for almost a year while Coty had it built in secret. Worst year ever. I hate keeping secrets. Well, good ones anyway. "Ready to move back yet?"

Coty, atop his matte black R6, adjusts his gloves, chuckling. "As much as I miss living with you guys, I never want to be without Angela again." *Sucker.*

Even though I give him a hard time, Coty's one of the best people out there. Period. He's worked his ass off to be the opposite of what he was shown growing up. His dad is what I refer to as a shitbag. He sleeps with his students—college age students—while he's…wait for it…married.

Yeah, guy's a total douchebag and I pretty much hate him. We all do. We took a vote and everything. That's one thing we all agree on, hands down, no matter what, set in stone with a layer of shiny epoxy over the top. Once you're taken, like for real taken, it's fucking end game.

Basically, thou shall not commit fuckery. Ever.

And Coty's dad is a wasteland of fuckery. A wasteland with only one remaining resident who refuses to leave—Coty's mom.

Sometimes I wonder if my dad knew about my own mom's affair before she took off and just did the same thing Coty's mom did. Just stuck it out.

I hope not.

"I didn't really think my old room was up for grabs anyway." His eyes widen with emphasis. "She show up yet?"

I bob my head. "Yeah, she's back. Don't know for how long but she was there today when I left."

Which is kinda weird in itself since I never see her before I leave for work. She gets out later, once I'm already at the shop. What's that about?

"Marc said she works crazy hours. What does she do again?"

"She hasn't really said but I dropped her off at an old folks' home or some shit once."

"Have you asked her?"

What the fuck? He's the second person today to give me shit about asking Paige personal questions. Won't the girl just tell me when she feels like it? Why do I have to go around digging into her business?

Obnoxious laughter, complete with snorting like a hopped up pig, has me side-eyeing my best friend.

"You don't know how to pursue a girl, do you? Like 'can I hold your hand, I want to date you' pursue her."

The fuck? "Who said I wanted to hold her hand and date her?"

The girl has made her place at the apartment—I guess—and yeah, she's taken up residence in my mind. Hell, she's even made an impression on my body that just won't quit but that's it. I mean, I missed Paige but not enough to *date* her.

I just like knowing she's safe. And not in some other joker's arms. But that's my gentlemanly nature shining through. I deserve a fucking medal, not a relationship.

"If I remember correctly, you weren't exactly Mr. Chatterbox when neighbor girl showed up." In fact, he barely spoke at all—to any of us. He was wound tighter than a steering wheel running low on steering fluid.

"Are we talking soul mates now?"

"Soul mate, huh? Does Angie know that?"

Coty sobers, pinning me with a look to say flatly, "She knows."

Yeah, but…knowing it and admitting are not the same and I'd bet good money Angela wouldn't come out and say some simp ass shit like that. Only my pussy whipped friend would.

He covers his mass of dark hair with his matching black helmet before lifting the visor to say, "Marc was right. You've got your head so far up your own ass, you don't know which way is up. Here's some advice though, wherever she is, that's up."

I raise my hand like I'm back in school. "Uh, for clarification purposes, who's the she in this far-fetched, totally unbelievable scenario? Like which one exactly? Imma need you to clarify."

It gets real quiet after that, neither of us talking, then just when I think he's not going to answer, he says, "The one that makes you want to be better. Even if you have to reveal the worst version of yourself just so you have a shot at being the best version. For her."

"Bro," I shake my head, putting my own helmet on and making sure to open the visor as well even though this conversation officially drags, "you lost me at 'the,' okay?"

Thank fuck we have technicians trained in customer relations because Coty would make a shit salesperson. Whatever my man's selling, I definitely ain't buying. That sounds exhausting and not enjoyable in any way. People willingly sign up for that?

Hard pass.

"All I'm saying is make sure you're ready, man, because when it happens, you'll be in for the climb of your fucking life."

Dude starts his bike, revving the engine a few times and I follow suit, wanting to be done already.

"What if I like where I am?"

His eyes meet mine over the roar of our machines.

"Do you?"

My stare moves to the land below one last time. Sounds simple enough. Do I like where I am? Theoretically? Yes. Sure. I have a job I've dreamed about since I mounted my first dirt bike, financial stability most people my age wish they had, friends that I trust, family I chose, a dope apartment I share with one of my brothers and a smoking hot roommate.

Realistically though? I don't know. Lately it feels like I'm missing something. But what if that something was never really there for me to miss in the first place? What if I'm not set up for more? What if I'm not equipped to climb, as Coty put it? By no means am I afraid of hard work, but I've never had to exert myself for anyone else. I've always thought that by staying put, never moving forward or backward, the right person would find me when the time came. *If they were looking.*

We bump knuckles, saying our usual motto of "ride it" before pulling back onto the main road out of here. *Ride life, don't let it ride you.* Is that what I've really been doing?

He pulls off toward his house shortly after, jerking a nod in my direction, then I head for the apartment.

With the sun at my back, the sky before me looks like a painting with purple giving way to pink as it blends into orange and Coty's words stay with me no matter how hard I lay on the gas. What a load of shit suggesting I gotta climb. Climb where? If anything, women flock to me. He should know. He's seen the evidence himself. Everyone has. That's how I've always been. It's simple logic, really. If I stay in one place, I'm easier to find.

But isn't that what I've been doing with my mom all these years? Waiting for *her* to put in the work. Scared of what I'll find should I actually put myself out there.

That's not something you just get over. Especially not for that *one* person, whoever that may be.

Back at Creekwood, I notice Paige's CBR still in the same spot it was this morning so I park as quickly as I can just in case it shit the bed again. She might be waiting for a ride to work and I can intercept—if needed. Judging from the losers she insists on bringing around, it'll definitely be needed.

What I don't expect to find is Paige asleep on the couch when I open the door however. Her hair is piled on top of her head in some sort of crazy mess and a throw blanket is pulled up around her shoulders. Bare feet and jean-covered legs are peeking out the bottom as she lies on her side.

I contemplate waking her since she's clearly not ready for work but Marc comes out, stopping me as he motions me over.

"Should we wake her?" I ask quietly, joining him in the kitchen.

His head shakes as he grabs a Gatorade from the fridge. "We ate dinner." My teeth clench so tight I think a filling pops out. "Then she passed out watching a movie. She said something about having some time off so I covered her up and let her sleep." What a perfect gentleman. *Dick.* "There's some leftovers if you're hungry. She made kabobs and rice."

My eyebrows lift as he disappears back into his room, taking a bag of cookies with him.

Resting my elbows against the island, I watch Paige sleep. She's facing the back of the couch, hiding her face from the world—from me—and not for the first time, I wonder what else she's hiding.

Her back is hanging over the edge, just barely, and I have the urge to catch her before she falls. That thought alone should make me retreat to my room. Let her ass hit the floor. It'd be good for her, dropping without a safety net in place, learning she's not infallible. Maybe take her down a few notches.

Just then Paige shifts and I'm there instantly with my hands out and ready. Instead of tumbling to the floor though, she rolls to the other side exposing her face and I'm the one that almost collapses.

What in the actual fuck?

My knees actually do buckle and my fingers ghost across her forehead, too scared to touch the wounds. What happened to her? She explained away the split lip as an accident, but this? This is more. This is something else entirely. This is fucked.

My hands shake as they hover over her puckered eyebrows. What if she is in trouble? What if someone did this to her and I've just been talking shit to her this whole time adding to the stress she's dealing with? I thought I made it known that if someone hurt her, I'd handle it, handle *them*—the piece of shit—but what if our banter pushed her too far the other way?

Regardless, she has to know I'd take care of my roommate.

My roommate.

Marc's door bounces off the wall in the next instant as I throw it open, then I do something I've never done, ever—step up to my brother.

"What the fuck? We done with knocking?"

Marc sits up and I smack the open bag out of his hands. I try not to use my height advantage over my friends, always try to slump a little lower, sit a little sloppier so they won't feel intimidated, but not this time. This time I stand to my fullest height and let him bathe in my shadow. Make him feel the weight my presence actually carries. Let him fold from the pressure alone.

He pushes off the bed though, not backing down, but I don't care. I've had enough.

"Her face. Talk. Now."

"Ask. Her. Your. Self," he grits out each syllable, even breaking 'yourself' into two words but, uh, fuck you. It's one.

"I'm asking you. You sat across the fucking table from her, eating fucking rice and tiny pieces of meat-"

"Vegetables."

"What?"

"There wasn't any meat. It was all vegetables."

I blink twice in rapid succession. What the hell? Don't tell me the girl's a vegan, too.

"What-the-fuck-ever," I say, getting us back on track. One crisis at a time. "You sat there looking at her and you're telling me you didn't notice her fucking face? It's mangled to shit!" I press, my chest as twisted as a pretzel. "What happened?"

"Chill the fuck out." Dude shakes his head before bending to pick up the now empty bag. "She wouldn't say exactly," he sighs. "And I did ask, so fuck you. I'd never let that shit go and you know it." His hand thumps my heaving stomach and I fight not to rip the goddamn thing off his arm. He is my brother but there's only so much I can take. "She said it was work related but wouldn't go into any real detail. I couldn't tell if she was lying or not. Growing up the way she did though, she can take care of herself, so whatever did happen, I bet she already handled it."

My eyebrows collide. "What do you mean by that? How'd she grow up?"

"Fuck, you're stupid sometimes. Pay attention to someone other than yourself for once. Please."

"Like how you've been going over to Kary's more often? You want me paying attention to that?"

He just levels me with a look that I'd give anything to bottle just so I could unleash it on unsuspecting victims. Under any other circumstance, it'd be funny as shit. Right now though, he can fuck off with that look. Like all the way off, with a saddlebag stuffed full of his bullshit. I'll even pack it for him.

Instead of picking up the cookies scattered across his bed, he folds the entire comforter inward, catching everything in the middle, before tossing it over his shoulder and walking out of the room like a ripped, tattooed Santa Claus that smokes like the chimney he's supposed to go down.

He passes by a ton of maps, making them flutter. They're from literally everywhere and they cover an entire wall of his room, all decorated with differently colored pins. I know some of them are places he's been, most are places he wants to go, and the others...I have no clue. There are several colors up there but only Marc knows what they mean.

I trail him out to the living room and ask the question I can't seem to find the right answer to. "What am I supposed to do?"

Marc pauses at the front door, glancing at Paige. "What do you want to do?"

I follow his gaze. Another good fucking question. *What* do *I want to do?*

I know what I don't want to do. I don't want to be *that* guy. The one that steamrolls over everyone and everything in his path without stopping to consider what others might be going through, too.

I know I don't want to be the reason why Paige feels like she has to leave. Not anymore.

"Sorry about that." I jerk my thumb over my shoulder, feeling some of my earlier fight leave me.

He nods slowly, working his jaw. "I should've warned you. You two have your own shit going on. I didn't know what to think."

Wait...

"You didn't think I did that to her face, did you?"

A humorless laugh fills the room. "If I did, you'd be dead," he says straight-faced, before closing the door behind him.

Well, ho, ho, fucking ho.

I let the threat go and stare at the cracked doll fast asleep on the brown leather couch. I know what he means. I would slay for what was done to her. I was ready to kill a relationship with my best friend without hesitation.

That realization hits me like a Mack truck. It also reminds me of how Coty used to be when Angela first moved in across the hall. Dude got pissed if we even breathed near her. He was wound up all the time and broody as all hell whenever she'd duck him. It was like living with a pissed off Rottweiler for a while there.

This isn't the same though. Coty was *in love* with Angela. He was sick with jealousy. This is different. This is just being a concerned roommate. Marc said it himself—he'd kill me if he thought I hurt her. He has a mother and a sister he loves. It's only natural he'd want to protect Paige.

But, if that's true, what's my excuse? I have neither and yet I feel more protective over Paige than I do my own boys. *Why is that?*

Paige moans softly then covers her face, making me lurch forward. She winces, dropping her hand but otherwise remains asleep, so I shove my hands in my pockets, rocking from side to side.

"Who did this to you, girl?" I whisper, watching her.

One of the bigger scratches starts bleeding through the goop on her forehead.

"Shit," I mutter and sprint into her room in search of more ointment. I'm careful not to disturb too much of her stuff but honestly her room is pretty bare. I've been in her room before, of course, but my eyes were only for her. I didn't bother looking around when she was all I saw anyway. There are no decorations, no pictures of family or friends, nothing to explain who she is or where she came from other than her work clothes and moto-gear.

Marc mentioned her childhood and the way she grew up but I'm not seeing any of that. Not here at least.

What am I missing?

Coming up empty, I check the bathroom with the same results. *Nothing.* Isn't she some kind of nurse? She should have something, anything, damn it.

In that moment I know exactly what I want to do.

CHAPTER 15

Paige

The first thing I see when I open my eyes is a new nightlight plugged into the wall on the opposite side of the living room. I may not spend many nights here but I do know that light wasn't there before. It reflects off the metal bat next to the alcohol cart which I never really got the story about.

The second thing I notice is an entire pharmacy laid out across the coffee table. *Someone went a little crazy at the drug store.* My mind jumps to Beckett and I suppress a grin.

Sitting next to a year's supply worth of gauze is a glass of ice water and a bottle of pain reliever.

I squint in the newly lit room.

Two bottles. One of each kind.

The smile shoves its way through this time.

I slowly sit up on the couch I passed out on, killing the smile almost instantly. *Damn, that hurts.* Note to self: do not ram your head into a wall. Seems like solid life advice for everybody. Maybe I should write a book. Go on tour. Make a cool mil.

I snort. *So stupid.*

I guzzle the water, thankful for the cold snap to wake me up, and pop a couple of capsules. Whoever bought all of this put in a lot of thought. Again, my mind conjures up an image of Beckett. I try to wave it away because it's Beckett. The guy wouldn't go through this much trouble for anyone let alone me, his...enemy?

On the other hand, I can't see Marc doing it either. He was concerned during our friendly dinner together but in an impersonal *let me know if you need anything* way.

Not like Beckett who insists on being in my personal life any chance he gets. *Shithead.*

My sleep-filled eyes browse the supplies in front of me as I reach up to touch my forehead. Expecting to come away with dry fingers, I'm surprised to find a fresh coat of medicated gel covering the area.

He took care of me. While I was asleep. There's no way it was Marc. I just know. He would've made a bigger deal if he cared that much. Cared enough to not only buy all this stuff but to apply the ointment himself without waking me. No, I can't see Marc doing that.

But the thought of big, bad Beckett leaning over me, gingerly spreading medicine across my face fills me with a deep longing. A yearning to be seen, to be fawned over, to matter.

Fuck.

Another glance at the nightlight across the room and my gaze gets stuck there until my vision blurs all over again.

Grabbing a bottle of Jack Daniel's from the drink cart—I've had a craving since the first time I washed my hands here—I rip the front door open and walk outside, bare feet and all.

The pool is empty, as it should be in the middle of the night, so I cop a squat at the edge, not bothering with discretion. The cap is unscrewed and tossed over my shoulder in the next breath. The burn is swift. The flavor is shit. *What was I thinking?* Jack is never a good idea. I learned that the hard way on my eighteenth birthday.

I take another pull off the bottle, barely managing it without needing to plug my nose. It's nasty, but a couple more swigs and I can't even taste it anymore.

Unfolding my legs, I dip my feet into the water. First the toes, followed by the soles, then both feet. My jeans skim the surface and I watch, mesmerized, as the water climbs up the material. The rapid progression is almost overwhelming. How does one drop spread so quickly in such a short amount of time? And so blindly, too? There's nothing the water won't reach once it has an opening.

Another gulp of Jack and I dunk my ankles. The wetness climbs higher and higher as my legs sag lower and lower. Soon the water will swallow me whole.

Soon the water will swallow me whole.

Mouth on the bottle, scooting to the lip of the pool, I drop my calves into the biting water. The balmy night air isn't enough to stave off the cold sensation and my soon-to-be saturated jeans aren't helping either. Luckily, the alcohol makes everything warm so I tip the bottle to my lips again, dropping my head between my shoulders to get a good amount down my throat in one go.

An outdoor lamp flickers above my head and I can't help but think it might be its last night in this world, struggling to shine at half power. In fact, it could blink out right now. The bulb could just fade into darkness, never to be seen again, and how many people would care? How long until someone would even *notice*? Until they realize it was struggling to continue on this whole time? That it tried its best to glow bright for everybody else until it just couldn't anymore?

I place the bottle beside me and close my eyes against the sudden rush of tears.

It wouldn't even matter. Not really. Things get taken for granted every day. People get taken for granted every day. In the end, it'd just be one more loss in an infinite sea of loss. *A single drop.*

Opening my eyes, I blow out a stream of air then press both hands on either side of me, lifting my ass off the concrete, but just as I prepare to slide into the water, a second light catches my eye. This one from my apartment.

It was pitch black when I left.

Except for that nightlight Beckett plugged in…for me.

I release myself back onto the concrete with a *humph* and feel for the bottle next to me, still gazing up at the sliding door of my back balcony.

Who's up? And what are they looking for?

Another nip from my illusive friend, Jack, before I slowly tug my legs up one-by-one. I haul both water-logged limbs out of the pool before attempting to stand. The first couple tries end in sloshing. Copious amounts of sloshing. Everywhere.

I finally get it and can stand somewhat straight—the pants really are heavy—while I eye the pool one last time before returning upstairs.

The stairs prove to be another challenge but the handrail helps. A lot. I probably won't even need a workout for at least two or three months after this.

By the time I reach the top, I've lost all feeling in them but I'm almost positive they look amazing—all veiny lumps of muscle.

Eww.

Standing in front of apartment B-26's door, I blow at a stray hair that escaped my messy bun, only remembering my lubricated forehead when the piece doesn't move.

Discovering the bottle in my hold is completely empty only worsens finding Marc's scowling face on the other side of the door once I push it open with more force than necessary.

See? Muscles.

"You're getting water everywhere," he points out matter-of-factly.

"What's you doing?" *That's not right.* "I mean, what are you doing?" *Better.*

His frown dips lower like the emoji and I cover my mouth to keep from laughing.

"What's wrong with you?"

He's so pretty it hurts, then he speaks and it hurts even worse.

I whisper, "everything," without meaning to but when his eyes narrow at my slip, I hurry to ask, "What's going on?"

He's standing outside his bedroom door with his shirt off and *hello abs.*

Oh, but he's angry. Why?

Then I hear it. I hear *him.*

"Another nightmare?"

Using my hands, I carefully try to squeeze out my pants legs onto the welcome mat. It's absorbent, right? Hopefully, because the water just keeps coming. Like ants at a goddamn picnic.

"What do you know about that?" Marc's tone is razor sharp, like a ruthless wolf.

"Enough." I shrug, then stumble reaching for the bottoms of my jeans. I manage to catch myself before I face-plant though. Now *that* would be bad.

"Christ. You're gonna get yourself killed."

It takes me a while before I can lift my eyes from the empty bottle by my feet.

"Last time he got a nosebleed," I say finally, breaking the quiet.

"No shit. He does that every time."

My head whips to him as I straighten, forgetting the pants entirely. "He does? How often is he having these…episodes?" The question comes naturally, like breathing. Once a nurse, always a nurse.

"Enough." He throws my answer back in my face and my fists ball at my sides. I'm pretty sure they do anyway. There's still not a lot of feeling in my limbs. It's all just fuzzy naiveté—like happiness.

"Whatever. I'm going back to bed. Try not to make a mess."

Bigger than I already have? The question sits on my tongue long after Marc disappears back into his room.

Since I didn't actually fix Beckett's door yet, I'm forced to position my ear near the wood without applying any real pressure while trying to hear inside. Deep breathing resonates through his room so I back away to my own.

"Please! Come back!"

One minute I'm almost to my door, the next I'm on the other side of his. Alcohol's fun like that. It just transports you without consulting with you first.

Hesitating, I watch Beckett through the dark, wondering what exactly I'm supposed to do. Then I see his hand angrily swipe at his face and I dive across the room and onto his bed without any thought at all. With his hand firmly clutched in mine, I try to lower it but he's strong—stronger than my alcohol-laden muscles—and makes another swipe at his face. After struggling, and failing, to stop his assault, I stretch my entire body across his arm, wanting to keep him from causing any more damage to himself. His nose looks angry but it's not bleeding—yet.

His arm finally goes still beneath my torso and I take full advantage of this new vantage point. My eyes roam his handsome face, taking in the blond hair that almost reaches his closed eyes. Long lashes are draped across his sharp cheekbones as his breathing begins to slow.

My breath, however, hitches.

Full lips, that mine remember all too well, purse and I mash my own between my teeth as I continue my perusal.

What's haunting Beckett to the point of self-mutilation? What has him so worked up that he'd willingly hurt himself, even in his subconscious?

A voice in the back of my mind nags at me but now that all movement has stopped, my head starts to sway like a rowboat in a hurricane, losing sight of anything tangible as I fight to keep my stomach inside my body. It wants *out*.

I slam my eyes shut against the rocking.

For Caleb's twenty-first, Jesse booked the family a fishing trip and I got so seasick I almost fainted. The captain had me lie down on one of the bench seats and I accidentally dozed off sometime later. While it sucked missing out on the festivities, the relief my little nap provided was downright euphoric.

Falling asleep in Beckett's bed is not an option though, so I vow to stay like this only until he calms down, then I'll return to my own bed. If I don't move at all, it'll help even more.

◆ ◆ ◆

Wiggling. There's a wiggling in my side. It's not necessarily unpleasant but I don't know where it's coming from and that worries me. I couldn't feel my limbs and now some part of me is moving without my knowledge.

Something—warm and large—expands under my back causing my stomach to churn and acid burns at the back of my throat even as I swallow repeatedly.

Then, without warning, a groan thunders through my chest as I roll to the side in preparation for the impending purge.

"What the hell?"

My eyes pop open hearing a gruff, *male* voice behind me, and I spot Beckett's room in all its glory. *Ah, shit.* I fell asleep after all.

My groaning amplifies tenfold. This is not good.

Swift movement that shakes the entire mattress has me gripping my stomach.

"Hey, are you okay?" Beckett's hand gently smooths my hair away from my sticky face. "I'm right here. What do you need?"

"Space," I murmur, trying to push away from him.

Beckett rumbles with laughter. "Too late, girl. You should've thought of that before climbing in my bed."

"Ugh. I did not climb in your bed."

"Oh yeah? How'd you get in here then?"

My head dangles precariously off the edge as I consider my next words. Do I tell him the truth? About what Marc revealed last night? What I saw? Would he even want me to know what I do?

"Blame Jack Daniel's," I say shortly. "He obviously led me to the wrong room."

"You got drunk last night? Why didn't you wake me?"

My eyebrows pull together and I roll my neck, coming face-to-face with Beckett. His gaze roams my face, lingering on my scratched-up forehead before meeting my eyes.

A big, gentle hand cups my cheek as he gazes down at me and his voice drops dangerously low as he says, "I was worried about you."

"I couldn't tell."

I try to roll my eyes but the dark feels so good I leave them closed instead.

Beckett ignores my sarcasm, asking, "What happened? Can you tell me who did this to you?"

Opening them once again, I glare at him. "Why do you assume someone did it to me? Why couldn't I have done it to myself?"

His eyes study mine.

"Did you?"

Sighing, I roll to my back and bend my knees, placing my feet flat against the mattress. "It's complicated."

There are rules about these kinds of things. Laws. You can't just tell people about your patients. That's confidential with a capital C.

Honestly though, even if I could talk about it, I wouldn't. Because then I'd have to admit that maybe I'm the one that put my mom in more danger by moving her than Dennis did in that hallway and I'm not doing that. Not yet. Like I told Rosie, we're still in the adjustment phase. So we'll…adjust.

We'll get there. We have to.

"I'm serious, Paige."

His warm thumb rubs my temple and I lean into his touch before I realize what I'm doing.

"So am I," I whisper, drinking in his oceanic eyes.

The moment stretches as does the silence, neither of us willing to break the spell that's settled over us. The Headache picks now to come out from hiding but is promptly shoved aside as soon as Beckett leans forward, bringing his lips in close. Just before they reach mine, he veers north, laying gentle kisses above each eyebrow.

Both of my eyes close on a strangled moan.

"You need medicine."

What?

I'm just about to tell him exactly what kind of remedy he can provide when he asks, "Why is my bed soaking wet?"

Oh. *Oh.*

"I forgot to dry off after a late-night dip. Sorry." I cringe. "Are you mad?"

After a beat of awkward silence, he shrugs, saying, "It's not the first time a girl's been wet in my bed." He gingerly crawls over my body, pausing just long enough for my pulse to spike while taking care not to put any of his weight on me, then pushes up to standing as he walks to his dresser. "And it won't be the last."

Grabbing the first thing I can find, I lob it right at his head, missing by an inch as it—his wallet—sails into the wall beside him. I don't even know why I did that but it was out of my hand before I could fully contemplate the exact reasoning so I grit my teeth and roll with it as I climb out of bed.

"What the fuck was that for?" Beckett does a ridiculous double-take like he can't believe a girl can actually throw.

And for my next trick, I'll chew gum while walking.

"Your mouth is such a problem," I grumble as I storm past.

Unfortunately, he catches my elbow and cages me against the wall before I can get far. His gaze skims over my face again starting from the top and ending at my mouth. His breathing speeds up and I press myself into the wall so I don't rub on him like I want to. This is already embarrassing enough.

"You don't seem to mind it when my mouth is all over you."

"On me? No, I don't mind that at all. Off and running without proper supervision? That's where I take issue."

He stares into my eyes, the gears behind his turning in perfect synchronization. What's he thinking?

"Come to work with me."

"What?"

That's so not where I thought he was taking this.

"You're off today, right?" I nod slowly, watching him. "So, hang out with me for the day. I can doctor you."

"Pfft, you don't even know what you're doing."

"I got a crash course from the pharmacist yesterday. Then, later you can wear a nurse's outfit and we can role-play. It'll be fun."

"Are you talking about that stupid Halloween costume? You do know literally nobody wears that shit anymore, right?"

"Fine, you talked me out of it. You can be naked." I frown at him, not completely hating the idea but then he says, "And I'll show you my P.H.D. Pretty huge dick."

My knuckles tap his stomach, making a puff of laughter leave his lips before he grabs my hand, running his thumb along my fingers. It's such a sweet gesture. This whole morning has been like some alternate reality, one where Beckett and I are actual friends and can stand the sight of each other.

Admittedly, I've always liked Beckett's appearance—I've fallen victim to his all-American-on-growth-hormones good looks—it's the talking I could do without.

"Seriously though, I'm glad you stayed with me last night."

A look of horror crosses my face before I can school my features. *Please, make it stop.* Does he think he has to play up the nice guy role now? I don't need my hand held during the awkward morning after. I've got this shit down.

Besides, we didn't *do* anything. Not really. Spooning doesn't count unless there's penetration…of some kind.

"I told you that was an accident." One that won't happen again. "Thanks for getting all that stuff for me."

"I wanted to." His eyebrows dip with determination I don't fully understand. "And you're welcome. So, it's settled then? You'll be my assistant?" At my silence he urges, "What else do you have to do today?"

"Wash my hair?" It comes out as a joke but washing this mop is no laughing matter. That shit takes forever and is a real arm killer. I already feel a bone deep soreness from last night setting in.

Beckett's eyes spark with mischief as he leans down to rest his lips a breath from my ear, saying, "I can do that for you, too. Shower with me and I'll wash *everything*."

As usual, Beckett has to go and fuck things up. The guy just can't help but play around.

Twisting my head to the side so my lips mimic his just below his ear, I murmur, "We both know I'm more than capable of taking care of my own needs."

Large palms flatten against the wall next to my head.

"You can never give me an inch, can you?"

Scoffing, I push him back. "Not when you're constantly talking shit."

"Who says I'm talking shit?" He frowns, making me squint up at him.

Isn't he always? That's what Beckett does—he riles up my hormones before stirring the cauldron of bubbling estrogen, trying to piss me off.

But this morning, I can't deny he's being different. So far anyway. I just don't know how long it'll last.

"You can't bullshit a bullshitter, baby."

His scowl deepens as I shove past into the hall between our rooms and surprisingly he lets me go but not before calling to my back, "We leave in twenty."

"We'll see about that," I mumble as I shut the bathroom door.

And lock it.

CHAPTER 16

Paige

FORTY MINUTES LATER, BECKETT FINDS ME SITTING cross-legged on the counter in an oversized tee and my favorite pair of shredded shorts. Through fresh eyes I watch him approach as I lift a steaming mug of chai tea to my lips.

"We could save a ton of time if we start showering together, you know? Not to mention all the water we'd be saving. It's the green thing to do, really. We're being irresponsible when you think about it."

A smirk tips my lip as I set my tea down. "Uh huh, sure. And do you? Think about it?"

His eyes scan me and even though I'm fully dressed, I shift to cover what he can't even see. What I hope he never finds.

Somehow it feels like he already has though. Things are changing. There's been a shift. A weight's been lifted from the heavy strain between the two of us. It's lighter. He's lighter. *I'm* lighter—lighter than I've been in weeks, months, maybe longer.

More serious than I've ever seen him, he joins me at the counter. Standing against the smooth surface, Beckett grabs my legs, slowly unfolding them to fit on each side of his hips before bringing his hands up to my face and saying, "It's one of my favorite hobbies."

I shove his shoulder making him crack a smile. He doesn't bother removing his hands though and I grin against the pads of his thumbs.

"Let me put something on that and we'll head out." He nods to my forehead.

"You don't have to baby me. I already took care of it. And I'm not going. My face is jacked three ways from Sunday. I don't need anyone gawking at me."

Finally dropping his hands, he settles them on my thighs that are still spread around his and scoffs. "People gawk at you anyway. Your face is perfect, it's just a little banged up right now." My cheeks warm from his words. There is nothing perfect about me but it still feels good to hear him say it. "But if you don't want anyone staring at you, consider it done. I thought that was already established but if you need me to say it, fine, nobody but me will so much as look your way."

My eyes narrow. "Does everyone find your arrogance as annoying as I do?"

"God, I love it when you talk dirty to me," he growls. "Now come on, girl, let's go. We're already late because you had to wash your hair."

"I didn't wash my hair," I tell him seriously.

"What the hell took you so long then?"

I only quirk an eyebrow which causes both of his to shoot upward. Suddenly, I'm lifted off the counter and pressed against his rock-hard body. And I mean *everything* is rock-hard. The contact through my tattered shorts makes me gasp.

"Make another noise like that and we won't be leaving the house at all."

A devious laugh slides between us and the temptation follows us all the way out to his SUV.

◆ ◆ ◆

"Can you grab that-" Beckett's eyes widen at the lug wrench hovering over his shoulder and he jerks his gaze up to mine. "How'd you know what I needed?"

"I was helping my brother kick around the garage before I had my first bra." His eyes drop to my chest and I cock my head at him, asking, "Do you mind?"

Without missing a beat and still openly gaping at my breasts, he nods his head up and down dramatically while answering, "no."

I let out a breathy chuckle but only when I raise the tool in the air threatening to hit him with it, does he finally snap out of his trance.

"When you said you'd be the only one looking at me, I didn't know you meant in a sick, perverted way."

"You should always assume I'm looking at you in a sick, perverted way. My perversion knows no limits."

Shaking my head, I hop down from my perch on his work bench to help him with the tire he's trying to remove. We've been working together on various forms of transportation all day. It's amazing to watch him go from being under a standard sedan to the exotic three-wheeler that was just brought in. There's no question the guy knows his stuff and I bet Ty would love to pick his brain, if given the chance.

Beckett's knowledge and confidence is also sexy as hell. I find myself fantasizing about his sure fingers about every few minutes and it's becoming a bit of a problem the longer I'm here with him. He's both fast and effective but also pays special attention to the minor details most people would likely ignore.

Like now.

The trike was dropped off with a complaint about steering in tight turns so after taking it out in a few twisties of our own, we're back in the shop with it hoisted on the lift as Beckett adjusts the back wheel. Hands down it was the hottest thing I've ever witnessed and I'm still riding the high of watching him in his element. His strong arms laced with throbbing veins expertly maneuvering through the sharp curves…easily top five fantasy material.

"What's that look for?"

I look up to see Beckett boldly grinning at me and I shrug. "I like watching you work. It feels so familiar but different at the same time." Like most things with Beckett.

His eyebrows dip. "How so?"

Where do I begin? Tysen would spend hours in our old one-car garage, constantly tinkering around with whatever junker he could get his grease-caked hands on. Even in his teens, his hands had grease clinging to every crease. Beckett's aren't like that though. You'd never even know Beckett worked on cars for a living by looking at him. His hands are slightly calloused from obvious hard work but nothing like my brother's. And they're clean, too. Like obsessively clean. His entire workspace is actually. Which is the opposite of my experience with my middle brother.

The smell's the same though—a mixture of fuel, oil, and freshly laundered cheap cotton blend. Ty's pants were cheap, but I doubt Beckett's are. He's...particular, I've realized. About everything. For someone who laughs his way through life he sure does notice everything around him.

Grabbing my water from lunch, I say with a sigh, "Another life." One I miss with every ounce of my being.

My roommates' other friend, Coty, comes out of their office with his gaze focused on the ground. As soon as he notices me, or more specifically my face, his eyes narrow and he swings a glare up at Beckett. Beckett gives his head a subtle shake in response.

This has been happening all day. My forehead is starting to scab up already even through the half-inch of glossy medicine Beckett insists needs to be there. I don't have the heart to tell him that much isn't necessary but he's kept to his word that people wouldn't bother me so far. I'd say they're just scared of being slimed but Beckett's severe glower alone has been doing a pretty good job keeping everyone away from our little bubble.

"Paige, right? I don't think we've officially met. I'm Coty." We shake hands briefly. It feels weird touching him, like I might get zapped with a taser if our hands clasp longer than half a second. "How are you holding up over there? Everyone treatin' you alright?"

The pointed stare he gives Beckett is not lost on me. Or Beckett. The guy tosses his rag on his tool box, holding Coty's watchful gaze with one of his own.

"Actually, I was thinking about moving out already. My roommates are terrible slobs."

Coty's eyebrows shoot skyward and we both glance over at Beckett. His arms cross over his chest, the veins in his forearms pulsing like they're at one of Cynthia's raves, but he doesn't say anything.

"I'm just kidding. They're surprisingly clean."

My brothers were so messy that anytime we'd make bets, the loser would have to clean something in the house. It was the one thing everyone agreed on—the house was a pigsty and the boys were the pigs. Even our mom would try to get out of cleaning. That became a regular punishment in our teen years. I'm not sure if it did the trick though since they're still shitheads and not at all clean. *I miss them.*

"I met your girlfriend last time. Angela? She was really nice."

Beckett scoffs, finally breaking his silence. "Don't tell her that."

"Get fucked," Coty replies to Beckett in complete monotone that says they've been over this before. Many times.

"Is that an offer?" Beckett holds his hands in front of him like he's praying and I snicker under my breath.

Coty shakes his head, trying to hold back his own laugh and says to me, "We're having a little housewarming party at the new place. Why don't you come? Angela was just talking about needing more girls around."

The refusal is on the tip of my tongue before he finishes. "Thanks, but I'm not going anywhere like this." I point to the globby mess on my forehead. "Beckett's lucky he got me here today. If it wasn't for him dragging me-"

"Bullshit. You're just as much a motorhead as half the guys I got working here. Don't think I didn't notice the way you were eyeing that Scrambler 1200 that came in earlier."

The urge to wipe that smirk off his face has me rocking on the balls of my feet but I don't. The jerk's right and he knows it.

Coty makes a sound in his throat like a cough that has Beckett's eyes widening a fraction.

"If you come back tomorrow, I'll let you help me with it,"

he wiggles his eyebrows, "then we can ride together to Coty and Angie's afterward."

Coty nods like he's pleased with himself. *Did I miss something?*

I consider my options which honestly are slim. That bike was beyond gorgeous and I'd love to get my hands on it in any capacity possible. This might be my only chance at getting near a Triumph.

"Fine, but I'm taking my own ride so I don't end up being your third wheel when you try running game at the party."

Angela's words fill my head at full blast. *He never lets his dates sleep over.* While it's true I've never seen a girl sleep over—for either roommate—I was just in Beckett's bed last night and he didn't seem to mind the company this morning.

Maybe he's ready to try again but with someone else this time.

The plastic bottle in my hand makes a loud crack in the nearly empty garage and I look down to see my fingers wrapped around it in a death grip.

"No can-do, girl. You're mine." My eyes jump to Beckett's as he rushes to clarify, "I just mean you're not ready for a helmet yet. I'll drive us."

I'm still not convinced, considering he avoided the topic of picking up another date altogether.

"I can have a friend bring me," I try.

"No." His blue eyes turn arctic before he looks to his old roommate saying, "we'll be there," effectively ending the conversation.

Coty bids us goodbye just as Angela pulls up in a vintage Jeep to pick him up. She throws a wave over the top of the roll bar which I return before facing Beckett again.

"Hungry?" he asks, cleaning up the last bit of tools.

I meant what I said. His work station is by far the cleanest even though I know he works on more vehicles than the other mechanics.

I study him as he tidies up. How he puts everything just so. Most people would probably discount him as clumsy and careless.

I did at first. His uncaring façade has been nearly perfected, throwing everyone off.

Everyone but me.

I see how meticulous he really is. The care he uses when applying my ointment. He notices more than he lets on, too. It's in the way his tools are clean and organized. The way he refuses to let anyone else help me whether it be for a ride or treating my injury. He likes his things being right where he wants them, accessible at all times. I thought it was because he was an only child but now I'm starting to think there's another reason. Something that has to do with his nighttime issues.

My eyes slide along his tall frame, devouring every inch with my gluttonous gaze. He shakes out his sweaty blond hair, loosening several drops that fall to his Pop The Hood logo shirt. The material is then lifted to wipe his face, revealing his tight abs, and I follow the path between the muscles down to the well-defined V snaking below his pants. A fire ignites in my core as I imagine what that trail leads to.

Covering my view when he drops his shirt again, I meet Beckett's questioning eyes before answering honestly, saying, "Starving."

With shaky legs, I slip past him before I do something stupid. Like kiss the guy. I already made that mistake once. It was hard enough pumping the brakes on going any further with Beckett and that was when he was being an asshole. I don't want to test my strength when he's being sweet and attentive.

Before I'm out of ear shot, I hear him mumble something that sounds like "me, too" proving I made the right decision—today.

Tomorrow I'll have to exercise my restraint all over again.

So much for taking a break.

CHAPTER 17

Paige

We're just finishing some takeout on our balcony that overlooks the pool and some high school when Beckett eyes me suspiciously, asking, "So, you do eat meat?"

Marc watches through thick lashes as he pulls out a cigarette.

I take one final bite of my egg roll, my *pork* egg roll, and say, "Occasionally." Mainly when it's on sale.

I swear they both release a shared breath.

Okay…

Standing from the patio table, I stretch while also trying to ignore the way Beckett's gaze caresses my legs at the same time. It's difficult, to say the least.

I busy myself stacking the empty containers into a pile before grabbing the entire heap and turning for the sliding glass door. As Beckett rushes to open the door, our shoulders brush on my way inside, sending a thrill down my arm like I'm still in middle school and my crush just bumped into me in the hallway.

"You got it?"

I nod, grimacing.

We interacted with such ease this morning and all day at the shop when he'd find excuses to touch me and tease me but now it's awkward. Or maybe I'm the one that's awkward, I don't know. It just feels…different between us.

Roommates. We're roommates and that's how roommates are. They're comfortable around each other. They talk openly, laugh freely, and fantasize about ripping the other's clothes off with their teeth. Or…no? I don't think that's how these things work.

I definitely don't feel that way about Marc. Don't get me wrong, I would not kick that man out of bed—like ever—but I'm not actively picturing him there either. Not like Beckett.

No, nothing like Beckett. And I wouldn't exactly say I feel comfortable right now. More like I'm *un*comfortable not having his strong, skilled hands on me constantly.

Shit.

Marc stays behind to smoke outside while Beckett follows me into the kitchen, helping with the mess. Things only get worse from there. So much worse.

The sudden lack of conversation is louder than if we were screaming at one another. Instead of respectful and calm, the silence filling the kitchen is aggressive and charged. Charged with budding flowers of longing, desperately seeking nutrients to sustain them. Every grazed body part, every sharp inhale, they're all feeding the Franken-plant of need blooming between us.

Am I the only one feeling this?

After putting the last utensil in the dishwasher, I straighten to find myself caught between two rock hard biceps as Beckett cages me in against the counter, my back to him. Our spacious kitchen instantly feels microscopic and I step to the side to escape but he follows, keeping our bodies practically sealed together. I spin, my hands lifting to his chest and feeling his heartbeats pounding wildly beneath my fingertips. I freeze for a moment, enjoying the unsteady rhythm. My own heart performs a similar tune when he's pressed this close and I wonder if it's as noticeable.

I hope not.

Raising an eyebrow, I drag my eyes up to his. With the goo on my forehead now dry and making the skin around the area stiff, I probably look more like a pirate gazing into the horizon. *So not sexy.*

"What's going on?" *And why are you pressed against me like a magnet to a fridge?* Although, obviously he's the fridge in this scenario.

Beckett shrugs casually even as his heart continues its rowdy melody, saying, "Just wondering what you're up to tonight."

He's crowding me but in a good way—in the best way—and the longer we stand like this, like it's natural for us to touch and gaze and want, the harder it is to deny how much I like it. How much I like him.

"If you're worried about finding me in your room again, don't. Whatever I do from now on, it won't lead me there." At least that much is true. I cannot do that again.

Instead of pumping his fist in victory, an expression deceptively similar to disappointment crosses his face.

Hmm. I don't believe that. My private nurse is more the naughty variety than anything and he's probably just wanting to skip to the sponge bath portion of his self-imposed role already.

Needing some of that personal space I sacrificed by falling asleep in Beckett's bed, I slip under his arm, skirting around him as he follows my body stiffly.

I shouldn't even spend time alone with him anymore. We're like those religious nuts that require chaperones while they're courting. Except we're not courting. Or religious. We're just horny and stupid and bound to make a mistake neither of us can come back from. And so, we need supervision. At all times preferably.

But with my face in the shape it is, that's almost impossible. Usually on Fridays they have their old roommate over for family dinner along with a party to follow but tonight's been quiet. Something tells me they called off the company knowing I wasn't up for being on display. Or maybe they're going out later and don't want to tell me. Either way I appreciate not having an audience. Tickets to this downfall aren't free.

Going out.

I'd rather floss each one of my molars with my own hair than be around any more strangers today but maybe I can still visit with a friend. One that's already seen me in all my shredded face glory. One that'll provide me and Beckett that nice, *friendly* little buffer.

"Thanks for today. I really appreciate you keeping me busy."

Raising onto my tiptoes, I kiss his cheek gently and am treated to his labored exhale. Just as he begins pressing into my lips, I turn away and flee the kitchen while I still can.

His sigh barrels into my back just before I close my bedroom door and I lean against it once I'm on the other side.

I'm not the only one feeling it.

With that thought, I go in search of my phone. Last night was Cynthia's last shift at Sunbrook and I missed it. I wanted to show up with a cake and balloons and a bucket of tears because I'm going to miss my friend but I couldn't. Plans changed and now I'm forced to swallow my self-pity along with the rest of the shit life keeps shoveling down my throat. *Yum.*

Luckily, she answers on the first ring, immediately asking how I am.

"I'm fine. Trust me. My brothers left worse scratches than this."

Nick for sure had the worst habit of digging his nails into me during fights. I still have five full crescent-shaped scars on the back of my shoulder from him. I think I pulled out a solid handful of his hair during that round though. That was before he started getting girlfriends in high school and realized his energy was best used elsewhere. Suddenly picking fights with his little sister wasn't as appealing. Mocking me, cupping farts in my face, and generally being an ass, that was still in effect but not so much full-on wrestling matches. That's also around the time I started getting boobs and I think he was freaked out by that. They all were.

For men allegedly being so brave, they sure get scared of something as prevalent as change a lot.

"Are you sure you don't need anything? Gauze, rubbing alcohol, hard alcohol?"

We both laugh.

"Actually, yeah. I thought we could celebrate your last day together. Or at least the fact that you got a new job." Finally, something worth celebrating for a change. I'd almost forgotten what that was like.

"What do you have in mind?"

The floor outside my door creaks as I hear footsteps but I can't tell if they veer toward Beckett's side of the hall or not.

"Would you want to come over here? You can even stay the night."

She'll be my first official house guest and Beckett can't even object since neither of us has a cock to block.

"Ooh, yes. I want to meet those roommates of yours. You can't keep them all to yourself."

"Uh." I hesitate, not sure where to take this. I don't want to keep *them* to myself. "Marc's crazy hot."

There. My supportive, wing-womanly endorsement and it didn't even hurt. Not one tiny bit.

Maturity never felt so good.

"But he's definitely not mine to keep."

"And the other one?"

"Beckett?"

What do I say here? And how do I say it without giving her the wrong…impression. While Beckett isn't mine either that doesn't mean I want Cynthia trying to shoot her shot with him. Cynthia's gorgeous and smart and caring but she also measures in at a whopping five foot two and setting her up with someone Beckett's size would just be cruel. To her, of course. I'm only looking out for her here.

"He's okay, I guess," I mumble in a rush of words even I can barely make out.

Another creak from the hallway like someone's passing through from the bathroom maybe.

"Alright, I see how it is." She laughs like she doesn't quite believe that.

She will when she sees him though. He is so much more than okay. Beckett's like a hot air balloon festival—hypnotically beautiful, downright electrifying, and completely baffling. How does anyone control those things?

"But only if you put out some snacks," she says, knowing full well I'm stocked with plenty of small bites. All nurses are. I think it's a requirement.

"Hey, I *always* put out," I joke then frown, realizing it's been a while since I actually have. A long while.

As soon as my face heals, I swear I'm back out there on the hunt. This dry spell is ridiculous and being cooped up with my off-limits roommate is making it worse. His huge presence is both a blessing and a curse. He makes everything else seem to fade into sheer insignificance…except my sex drive. That he brings to the forefront like one of those telecommunication towers flashing its warning to airplanes in the dead of night—a steady pulse with no chance of blinking out anytime soon. Ugh.

We chat for a few more minutes before hanging up with a plan in place. She's going to bring all the ingredients to make peach margaritas while I provide the blender, chips, and homemade salsa Esme dropped off recently, and a movie. I even decide to include Marc and Beckett but when I go out to set everything up, I'm greeted by an empty apartment and a twinge in my chest. *Where did they go? Where did* he *go?*

I check both bedrooms and balconies before looking out at the parking lot only to find both bikes missing. He went out after all. No text, no medicine left out with overly detailed instructions—he swears I don't apply it correctly, as if my job doesn't consist of doing that very thing for others—nothing.

Beckett's disappearing act shouldn't surprise me. He's different from any other guy I've ever been around which, admittedly, is a lot. Some men bury their issues with a fucking excavator while others wear their problems like this season's newest trend. Beckett is a tricky combination of the two, where he does a damn good job distracting people from the shit haunting him from just over his shoulder, if you bother looking to see it—which I do. I know what skeletons look like no matter what state they're in and I bet Beckett's closet is full of them. His boys and everyone around him may accept him for who he is and maybe even know his story, but they don't share his pain. He works his fine ass off making sure they don't, that nobody does.

And it's not like I don't understand either. I've almost perfected giving the stiff arm to emotional connections with anyone other than my family and I fully expect that Heisman Trophy to show up at my front door any day now. Looks like Beckett's giving me some competition for it though.

I should be happy. He beat me to that five finger emotional punch, saving me the energy of having to do it first.

Why doesn't it feel better then?

◆ ◆ ◆

Oh, great.

He's in his bed thrashing again.

Cynthia and I collapsed in my bed after laughing our asses off watching an old comedy and filling ourselves to the brim. It felt good to just *be*. To be with somebody. Somebody who actually wanted to be around me, too.

When we left the living room, the guys still weren't back from wherever they fled to and after about an hour of tossing and turning, I finally heard them return but have been treated to complete silence ever since while I impatiently wait for sleep to descend.

I drank just enough margaritas to loosen my grip on reality but not enough to let go entirely, and now Beckett's furious tossing is blaring through the calm apartment, echoing all around me.

At least he's alone.

Right?

If the noises coming from his room are from him and someone else…

Nope, not going there.

I don't want to even think about Beckett entertaining for the night, much less hear it.

Hopefully it's just another nightmare. But that possibility doesn't sit well with me either.

With four siblings, I should be able to sleep through anything, but no. Not when someone I care about might be suffering.

Do I care about Beckett now?

I roll over to face Cynthia, wondering how she can sleep through all of this. He's hurting, literally, and nobody else even notices.

Beckett's mumbled voice increases with both volume and urgency before I hear a distinct smack of skin against skin. I'm out of bed the next instant and trudging across the hall.

A light knock to announce my presence goes unanswered and after a long breath, I push the broken door open to find Beckett—alone thankfully—in bed, having another night terror or whatever.

I catch his hand midair before he can make contact with his nose again and tuck it beneath my body as I climb onto the mattress next to his restless form. As I settle in though, his other arm swings over my body and relaxes across my middle, essentially trapping me. My tight white tank is on the short side and his warm arm sears my bare skin, almost like a branding, above my loose sleep shorts.

Last night I was able to blame the alcohol for my meddling, tonight he'll figure it out. I did drink but not *that* much. He'll know I saw a side of him not many people are privy to. And going off every other encounter I've had with Beckett…it's a complete mystery how he'll react. My money's on a blow-up. An epic blow-up followed by a substantial amount of pouting. Maybe a hate-filled make-out session in there somewhere.

I swallow a laugh. This isn't a romance novel.

Beckett groans and shifts to his side, pulling me closer in the process until we're spooning. I never thought of myself as a little spoon but it looks like I don't have a choice tonight. The big guy loves to act like he's in charge. Mostly in control of his emotions and how they're perceived. He's not afraid to throw his weight around to get his way either.

What happens when someone sees past the ruse though?

I peek at his serene face as his eyebrows pinch together in... what? What's haunting him?

And why is it getting worse?

CHAPTER 18

Beckett

FUCK.

Fuck.

Fuck.

There's a body snuggled against mine and I'm pretty damn sure it belongs to a female. Opening my eyes to see who it is seems almost as unbearable as the fact that I brought someone back to my place at all last night. There's usually nothing but groupies and girlfriends at the races and neither are my style.

Okay, fine, a groupie here and there is exactly my style. *Sue me.*

Even though I didn't drink anything stronger than water last night, my mind still scrambles to identify my guest but the only woman I can think of is Paige. She's been the only one occupying my head since she moved in and yesterday was no exception. Waking up to find her in my bed wasn't the kick to my junk I thought it'd be. Not like this.

There was a peace I've never known having her by my side the entire day. Even as we worked together, it was like coming home after a long trip abroad. You notice things you took for granted before, things you would've never noticed but now have a new respect for. Having Paige around reminds me of the little things, the stuff I've been too busy to appreciate—like laughs. Holy shit, her laughs are like magic. I make people laugh daily either for fun or for... other reasons, but getting Paige to laugh is the best head rush there is. I became outright addicted to the sound. Quick. Her throaty laughs are the best because you know damn well she means them. There's no pretense with her. What you see is what you get and I like what I see. Have since my eyes first collided with hers.

There's a sadness clinging to her lately though, and it seemed to lose some of its effect the longer she hung around yesterday. It wasn't gone completely last night at dinner but she was freer, more relaxed. That is until she pushed me away.

Hell, after hearing her invite who-the-fuck-knows over to *sleep* here, I was more than happy to push back. It's for the best anyway. As much as I like having her close, I have to rein in my reactions to her. She's seen enough as it is.

Which is why I can't believe I brought a chick home last night. Paige might've accidentally trampled over my only rule the night before with her drunken missteps but last night was all on me. I know better than to let someone sleep over, even if it probably had more to do with Paige's fuckbuddy than wanting my own.

I don't know what's going on with me but this shit has to stop. I'm not a kid anymore. Nobody should be able to affect me this way.

Even with that in mind, I touch my fingers to my nose to feel for any wetness while keeping my eyes tightly shut.

Dry.

Fuck yes.

Now I just need to get mystery girl out of here before Paige sees. I don't know why I care about her seeing someone else in my bed but I do. I should already be up to help with her medicine—girl does a shit job applying the stuff—but I need to take care of this, uh, situation first.

I've never had to do this in the light of day before but I decide to rip the bandage off as quickly as possible and get the awkwardness over with already.

Except when I open my eyes, I find a mass of burgundy waves fanned out on my pillow. And arm. And chest. And…yep, some of it's even in my mouth. Damn, Paige has a ton of hair. Good thing she never took me up on my offer to wash it. I'd be in there forever washing this mane.

My dick stirs.

On second thought, a long shower with Paige might not be so bad.

How did she end up in here again? Did she get drunk after we left? It wouldn't surprise me. Girl is going through enough, not that she's told me but she doesn't have to for me to know something's weighing her down. Sadness bears a heavy load and my back's been aching for years from the weight of my own.

A small moan passes her lips as she burrows deeper into my shoulder and I don't think I've seen anything sexier. That comfort. The ease of it.

My traitorous arm is slung across her stomach, her exposed stomach, and I consider pulling it away before she can wake to find me all over her, but her soft skin is like leather on a warm day—supple and inviting—and I can't seem to find the strength.

My fingers graze her spine instead, spreading out along her side. My dick strains against my boxer briefs, wanting to explore, too. I'd love to grip that waist and drag her on top of me, get her so close there's nowhere else for her to go. I want her all to myself but can't. I can't do that. Not to either of us.

Didn't she just have someone else warming her bed? Where is he?

Before I can move another muscle, her eyes open and meet mine with a wariness I wasn't expecting. She did come to me, right? Like, I didn't bring her in here. *Did I?*

Damn, I'm more fucked than I thought.

"Hi," she squeaks, which is so unlike her, the sound makes me smirk.

"Hey." My smile grows, despite all the emotions fighting for purchase. "Should we label our doors from now on? I thought the splinters sticking out of mine were a dead giveaway but maybe J.D. doesn't care about that sort of thing."

She frowns. "J.D.?"

"Jack Daniel's. Did he lead you to the wrong room again?"

Her eyes search mine before they're closed and she hums,

literally hums, as she exhales through her nose. My eyes gloss over her face, assessing her scratches. They're better but not by much. She needs more ointment but I'm not moving from here anytime soon. If heaven on earth was a thing, this moment right now might give it a run for its money.

"Jose."

"Excuse me?" Come fucking again.

She opens her eyes again, this time with humor lining them.

"Not Jack. Jose."

Ah.

That's why I always mix my liquor so blindly. The more players, the less likely you are to remember who exactly fucked you up.

Like I could ever forget.

"I thought maybe Jose was the nippledick you had over last night." No clue how big his dick is but if Paige left him to come in here for nothing more than a snuggle sesh, it's gotta be nipple-sized. Just sayin'.

The side of her lips quirks and she presses further into my shoulder, trying to hide it but I stop her with my hand on her exposed side, wanting to see. I want to see *everything* on her.

"That'd be Cynthia. My friend. A *woman*." She emphasizes the last word like that clears everything up. Like two women haven't hooked up before. And this is one of those oh so rare moments where I'm hoping they didn't.

Living in apartments makes it hard to tell whose car belongs to who around here but there was one parked outside last night when I got home that I've never seen before and I'd like to never see again, even if it does belong to a straight, platonic-as-all-hell, woman. Because it'll only remind me of what it felt like arriving home to see it there to begin with. Like I wasn't good enough. Like betrayal.

She notices my lack of relief and scrunches her eyebrows, asking, "When did you find out? Before or after?"

If I knew she was having someone over before or after I took off. *Fuck*. She's calling me on my bullshit and I don't have a good answer for her. How can I explain why I rushed out last night? I wanted to play with her a bit in the kitchen when she seemed off. Dinner was fucking fine, until it wasn't. She just changed all of a sudden, going from relaxed and talkative to uptight and quiet, and I didn't like it. I *hated* it. I thought we would tease each other like we'd been doing but then it all got away from me when she shut me down with absolutely fuck all reasoning then ran. I overheard her on the phone and assumed she was choosing to be around someone else.

I thought she chose them over me. Him. I thought she chose him over me.

And just like that, a wound I never bothered to treat like I've been treating hers opened up. I wrapped it with a half ass tourniquet of denial and left before she could see it bleed out.

I drop my voice, hoping it covers the obvious, to say, "I had a race."

"Before or after?"

She leans back now, furrowing her eyebrows over those blazing emerald beauties.

Her eyes never cease to amaze me. Their brilliant color alone stands out in a crowd but it's what's in them that slays me. Every fucking time. Paige holds so much in just a look and I wouldn't be surprised if lesser men crumble from the intensity. She could easily be a dream or a nightmare, but I already have plenty of the latter, so I try with the truth and see where it gets me.

"Before."

The truth is I would've done anything she asked last night. I would've touched her more than the few playful times I dared to in the shop, if she let me. Hell, I would've done a lot more than that. She has too much of the power that's slipping through my grasp every turn I take. I can't figure out how or why I react to her the way I do. Why she can be in my bed right now and my heart is as steady as it was before I woke up. How does she make me want things I've never wanted with anyone?

I wanted her last night. I wanted all of her. I *want* all of her. And that right there is why I ran like a fucking pussy.

If I want something, some*one*, and they don't choose me back, how am I supposed to handle that? I've been struggling with that very problem for more than half my life and I still don't know. I don't have a motherfucking clue.

So, I ran, too. I took off, ignoring the pain oozing from my every breath, and tried to busy myself with anything other than the truth. The problem is, there's nowhere to hide when you're running from yourself.

I came home with my hands covered in my own anguish and fell asleep across the hall from the person I didn't want there to begin with but now can't imagine her anywhere else. Anywhere further away anyway.

Then, in a twist I did not see coming, *she* came to *me*. And I don't know how it happened, or why, but I can't—absolutely can-fucking-not—find it in myself to question it. Some things are bigger than us and this feels like one of them.

Paige goes to roll away but my hand, still on her waist, catches her before she can escape. I overcorrect her movement and she ends up closer than before with our lips dangerously close and my hand burning where it grips her hip like my life fucking depends on her being here.

Of course, Paige—never one to be outdone—slips a leg over my hips and rolls me onto my back as she climbs on top.

I wish I could say I have a witty comment, or a sarcastic remark, or even a single fucking word to acknowledge this gorgeous woman mounting me but my brain malfunctions as all the blood rushes to my cock, leaving me completely speechless.

Holy. Fuck.

Paige broke my only rule, not once but twice now, handed me my own ass when I tried to lie, and is now straddling me without a concern in the world. Does she know how crazy this is? My self-control is dangling in the wind and one small gust from either direction is all it'll take for that shit to snap completely. She's playing a very dangerous game right now and looking up at her with that naughty ass little smirk, I'm pretty sure she knows it.

Her flimsy black shorts are pulled taut as her hips stretch across mine. The girl adjusts herself for the wide fit, rubbing her pussy against my solid erection and we both freeze from the contact. Our eyes connect and I can see the dare in hers. What will we do next?

I can also see the uncertainty. What should we do next?

"Last night I celebrated my *friend's* new job. One that isn't next to me every night anymore." Her voice is strained with a deeper meaning and I pause, taking her in.

"If you're upset about that, why would you celebrate it?"

It's written across her face how much she'll miss her friend.

"Because she's getting more money and she deserves that."

"Why don't you do the same thing? Didn't you say you need to save money? Then you can keep working together."

She shakes her head, exhaling. "Some things are worth more than money."

We sit with that for a minute, each of us lost in our own worlds full of priceless treasures we're not willing to share.

She stares down at me through heavy lids. "But I will have her or anyone else I want over whenever I want, and there's not a damn thing you can do about it. Tantrums included."

"I don't-" I don't like that. I don't want that.

I don't fucking think so.

Nice try.

Keeping our connection, I finger a stray wave along her neck and watch as her eyes close on a whisper. I can't make out what she said but her expression tells me everything I need to know. She wants this. She wants me. At least right now. And I can only give her this moment because that's all that's on my mind anyway. Not tomorrow. Hell, not even tonight at her little faux-surprise party. For now, I'm going to give her what she wants. What we both want.

She can talk her shit later.

Unlimited sleepovers with anyone she wants? We'll see about that.

We will definitely see about that.

Twisting the locks further around my knuckles, I grasp her collarbone for leverage at the same time as I push my hips up to collide with hers. Paige throws her head back with a moan falling from her parted lips. Her nails dig into my pecs almost to the point of pain but honestly, I wouldn't know. She's all I can see, hear, and feel, damn it, and she feels like heaven incarnate.

My other hand grips where her hip and pelvis meet and pulls down as I thrust upward again. Another moan is another shot straight to my bloodstream. Like a fucking drug addict, I do it again. And again. And again.

Lazily rolling her head forward, Paige leans down to capture my lips but my hand below her throat blocks her from descending fully. I've got a front row seat to the best show in town and there's no way I'm missing a second of it.

After. I'll kiss the shit out of her after. Right now she's mine to watch. Mine to play like a fiddle. She's just fucking mine.

Something unfamiliar sweeps through my chest but I ignore it and continue pumping as she finally meets my gaze again. She smirks, probably at me trying to take charge when she never, ever lets me otherwise.

Yeah, well, it's about fucking time, girl.

This game between us has finally reached its limit—as have I—and I'm doing things my way for a while. Fuck the rules.

Her smile falls away as my cock hits particularly close to her sweet spot making her eyebrows crease.

"Beckett," slips from her sexy mouth and that's when I lose all the patience I swear I was practicing before.

In one quick motion, I flip us so I'm hovering just above her. My thumb circles the hollow of her throat as my other hand lingers at her waistband. My eyes bore into hers, asking permission to take this one step further.

Shit, maybe ten steps, I don't know. Math sucks and I've lost count.

All I know is I need to give her something. Anything. It's like a deep-rooted need that I never had until this moment. One I barely even recognize but still know should be obeyed. If I don't touch her right now, all hell in my body will break loose. My heart, my mind—those I'll worry about later. She moaned my name for the second time now and I'll be damned if I can't coax it out of her again. And maybe again for good measure. I'm an overachiever like that.

Paige cocks her head at me, undoubtedly planning what she should do but I don't let her think too hard as I dip my lips to her stomach, tasting her exposed skin. Her torso is soft and warm until I push a little too far then I'm met with hard resistance from her toned abs.

"Let me in," I plead against her skin. In where exactly? I'm not sure yet but she seems to understand because she arches her back, allowing me to slide her shorts and panties down enough to reach where we both want me to be.

"Oh, fuck," I breathe, seeing her lower half come into view.

Paige is perfect when she's dressed like a badass on her bike or a tired nurse going in for a shift or in ratty ass men's clothing with horrendous bedhead, but naked Paige? Naked Paige is something else entirely. She's the type of dangerous all fathers should warn their sons about. She could *end* us if she wanted to. She could start a war in the blink of an eye because I'll tell you right now, I ain't blinking anytime soon for fear I might miss what's in front of me—her incredible naked body all ready for me and only me.

Fuck everything else.

Eager, or nervous maybe, Paige starts to squirm, but I can't. I just can't rush. Whatever I did in my life to deserve this beautiful woman in my bed today, I don't know, but I'll take my time showing my appreciation. I'd planned on working her with my long fingers, keeping it slightly impersonal—just in case—but with her pussy on display, plans have changed and goddamn, I need to taste her.

Fuck impersonal. Shit's about to get real personal, real quick.

She's completely bare below the waist without a hint of stubble like most chicks that shave, proving she gets waxed. Makes sense since she rides street bikes. I've heard it's uncomfortable for females if they don't keep up with their shit. At least I won't get rug burn on my face if she lets me take this spontaneous trip south of her border.

Kissing my way down to her hip bone, I glance up to see her watching me through thick dark lashes. Her nipples are poking through the white, almost see-through material and I make a note to circle back to those. Usually, I'd try to cover all my bases at once, but this time I want to focus on each individual spot. Doesn't mean I can't appreciate the view in the meantime though.

"Lose the top."

As fucking usual, Paige just shakes her head, driving me crazy.

She'll learn though.

Grabbing her hips with both hands, I flip us again so I'm flat on my back and she's straddling my face with both knees on the mattress on either side of my head. She shrieks and laughs, trying to move away, but my hands hold her in place with her pussy right above my jaw.

My eyes catch her widened ones. "Off. Now."

Still. Still she doesn't surrender.

Instead she sasses, "Say please."

"I'll say whatever the fuck you want me to, just take your damn top off so I can eat your pussy already. I'm fucking hungry and I want my breakfast in bed today."

She purses her lips, so I tack on a "please" at the end. Fuck if I care. I'm not above begging.

Her hands hit the bottom of the fabric, and as soon as her perfectly round tits are revealed, my eyes roam her sculpted body in my direct line of vision. I'd love to see all of it from every angle but her pussy hovering above my face is kinda stealing the spotlight at the moment and I'm happy to give it the respect Paige deserves.

After getting an eyeful, I finally dive in, licking and sucking and lapping up everything Paige will allow me. It's everything I thought it'd be, and more. Paige always smells like peaches and I'm happy to discover she tastes like one, too. I heard a local farm call their peaches Two-Napkin Peaches once but I'm thinking I might need three when I'm finished here. Chick is sweet and warm and has me fucking captivated.

A hand on each ass cheek, I position her wherever I need for me to hit each spot smoothly.

She's a panting, sweaty mess in no time and I'm loving every fucking second of it. I'm doing that to her. No one else.

But she's doing so much more to me. She's impulsive and resilient and makes me feel impulsive and resilient, and I've never felt so free. The highest jumps on my dirt bike never felt this good. The tightest turns on my street bike never got my blood pumping like Paige does. The girl stole damn near every thought in my head with no guarantee of returning them and damn if I don't care one bit.

Swirling my tongue around her clit, Paige jerks forward to grasp the headboard and I immediately break away to make sure she didn't hit her head again.

A knock on the broken door has both of us freezing in place.

Unable to stop myself, I sink my teeth into her thigh, loving the way she hisses down at me without actually stopping me. She's just as reckless as I am. Maybe more.

"Dude, you alright in there?" Marc asks from the other side.

Paige's eyes widen and I smile around the skin in my mouth before releasing it to lick my bottom lip.

"All's good, bro." He has no idea how good.

"There's some girl here," he pauses, probably giving Paige's friend that infamous stink-eye, "looking for Paige."

I move Paige's hips again to meet my mouth and smirk to myself when I catch her covering hers to stifle a moan. There's no way she's stopping this. She's a rider through and through.

"Hmm," I hum against her folds, pretending to think. "Did you check the bathroom?"

There's some chatter outside my partially open door but I block it out, not really wanting my boy's face, or anyone else's, to interfere with this real life fantasy I'm experiencing right now.

"Whatever. I'm taking off soon. You want a ride today or is Paige coming again?"

Jig's up. He knows she's in here. This Cynthia character may not be clued in yet, but my boy knows full well where our roommate is.

I murmur, "I was thinking both," then nudge her most sensitive spot with my nose, lapping her up real good.

She works to swallow another moan with no luck whatsoever.

"Beckett," Paige warns discreetly, trying to stay quiet but fuck that. When I'm done with her, Marc will need another one of his cigarettes.

She starts shaking and, knowing she's getting close, I grip her, bringing her down harder onto my tongue so I'm practically fucking her.

"Beckett," she hisses again, more breath than word.

Oh, yeah, this should be fun.

"Dude, is she coming or not?"

Turning my face to the side, I ignore Paige's needy protest to say, "Inquiring minds, Paige."

"Fuck," she grits, making me chuckle lightly before resuming my previous pace that was driving her up my wall. "Yes, I'm coming."

Her voice is shaky and not loud enough. Not nearly loud enough. Fuck Marc, I want the neighbors to need a cigarette when we're done.

I guide Paige's hips in an eight motion as her breathing grows louder and louder. *That's it.* I want her lost out of her fucking mind. Maybe she'll finally get a glimpse of how I've felt since she turned up in my life.

"Tell him," I demand, not breaking rhythm for a second. It comes out muffled but she understands just the same. Of course, she's gotta take her goddamn time giving it to me though.

Nothing's easy about Paige. Not a damn thing.

Her movements grow erratic and I know she's ready. She's fucking coming alright. I just need to hear her say it. I want to hear her yell that shit. Scream it if she can find the strength.

My own moan is what sets her off finally as the vibration rumbles over her soaked pussy.

"Shit, I'm coming." She cries out, "I'm...coming!" loud enough for Marc and maybe even old man Gary across the way to hear. *Just like I told her to.*

Spasms rock her entire body as her legs clamp up on both sides of me and my hips jerk clear off the mattress chasing some sort of release of my own. My boxer briefs are so wet with pre-cum, I bet I look like I came, too. I probably could've if we went any longer. And didn't have an audience.

Actually no, that was kinda hot.

"Shit," Paige repeats as she goes limp almost falling face first onto my pillows. Luckily I catch her with my forearm before she makes contact and guide her safely to the side instead.

Marc, still in the hall, mutters a "what the fuck?" before finally taking the hint and kicking rocks, hopefully taking Cynthia with him to get her ride out of here situated. If her car isn't gone by the time I leave this apartment, I'm calling our guy at the tow company we work with. Last night feels like its own bad dream and I don't want any reminders from it. Not after this.

I'll catch up with Marc later anyway. Or not. Dude can wallow in wonder.

Propped up on my side, I wipe my face on the sheet, then try not to laugh as I kiss Paige's trembling back up to her neck.

My lips flat to her ear, I say, "Thanks for the snack. Want to shower first or-"

She's already nodding, making me release the laugh I'd been holding in. Her head twists to the side with a tired sort of sigh and I see her cuts.

I smack her bare ass, giving it a strong kneading, then promise to take care of her forehead once she's all cleaned up. I offer to do that for her too, but she doesn't so much as bite before getting dressed.

I'll give Paige this, there's not an ounce of shame in her walk as she leaves to face her friend. If anything, she looks ready to do a victory lap as she strides past the door she broke.

And that right there makes me want her all over again.

How many hours are in a day again? I have a feeling I'm gonna need them all today.

◆ ◆ ◆

After getting properly dressed in a pair of shorts dark enough to cover any wet spots and meeting Cynthia with a giant smile plastered to my face—ain't no shame in my game either—we take turns showering, separately unfortunately, then meet back up in the living room to head out for the day.

With her friend long gone, I find Paige standing by the front door rocking a loose skull tee with the armpits cut clear out to the top of black shorts that barely cover her ass. Luckily, she has a strappy bra thing to cover the tits I was just ogling but the thin material leaves little to the imagination. Her hair has a braid on the top that looks like a faux-hawk pulled into a ponytail with her burgundy waves flowing down her back.

Chick looks like she's going to a rock concert, not a car garage with heavy machinery and dickwads galore.

"Yeah, no." She turns to me with a questioning look on her face. "It was hard enough keeping the guys' eyes off you yesterday. There's no fucking way I'll be able to fend them off today. You can't wear that."

A dazzling smile showing off almost every one of her straight white teeth is the only response I get before she opens the door and struts outside—still wearing the goddamn outfit.

Releasing a low growl, I switch my hat to face backward on my head then follow after her. And damn if a grin doesn't slip out in the process.

CHAPTER 19

Beckett

Paige and I arrive a little late to the party-that's-not-supposed-to-be-a-party. Even after spending the day with her, I wanted to prolong our time together by taking the long way out to Coty and Angela's new house. I even drove her by the property Coty showed me. I started to tell her about his big plans of wanting the three of us to live near each other someday but ended up stopping when she got tears in her eyes. Like what the hell? Sentimental much?

I don't know what that was about but then Angie whisked her away the second we stepped out of my Tahoe and I haven't been able to follow up with her about it. I just hope it wasn't something I said that upset her. Every time I'm around her I say something to screw things up. Except for today. Today's been pretty fantastic so far.

And now as she bounces through introductions, I don't dare take my eyes off her. She doesn't know many people here and I might need to rescue her from an awkward situation. Or beat up the guy that's currently eye-fucking the shit out of her. You know, friendly support or whatever.

Leaving Paige on her own, Angie joins the table, putting her hand on Coty's shoulder and asks me, "Why are you looking at Paige like you're about to devour her and go back for seconds?"

'Cause I already did.

Fed up with keeping my hands off her for the entire morning—I mean, *come on,* she looked like a fucking wet dream waltzing around my workspace—I sweet-talked Paige into the bathroom for a repeat of my breakfast but for lunch this time. She argued that it was brunch since it wasn't even afternoon and I told her I didn't give a shit what it was called as long as I got to taste her again. The debate ended the second my head dove between her thighs and let's just say I walked away a fully satisfied man.

"Who says I haven't?"

To be honest, watching her from across the yard is getting my dick hard again and these blue balls I've been sporting are about to become a real problem soon. Chick is turning me on without even meaning to and I might have to steal her away again before the end of the night. She hasn't even touched me yet, which is crazy because in the world of give and receive in sex, I'm definitely a receiver. Sure, I give enough in the heat of the moment—I'm not that much of an asshole—but make no mistake, I'm a receiver. With Paige though, it's not even about that. I actually want to make her feel good. I want to watch her come apart again and again without even considering my own needs.

"Please don't tell me you fucked the new roommate," Coty says.

"He did," Marc interrupts. "I heard it this morning. I had my suspicions but dude hit that for sure."

I scoff. "First of all, serves you right lurking outside my door." Dude just shrugs, completely unapologetic. Our entire apartment is overrun by lurkers, I swear—myself included. "Second, we technically haven't had sex yet, unless you count her fucking my face." I point at said face for reference. *Exhibit A, motherfuckers.*

"Oh…my god. I'm not supposed to be listening to this." Angela swats my arm and I feign pain. A little compassion goes a long way in my opinion. Unfortunately, she sees right through it so I drop the act. "What's wrong with you? You're such a pig talking like that."

"Sorry." *But, like not.* I've got nothing to be ashamed about going down on Paige. I probably wouldn't go around claiming that shit with anyone else but I don't mind the guys, and Angie, knowing I gave Paige oral. If anything, I'm proud I gave her multiple orgasms already without any reciprocation in sight. It's no small accomplishment, especially for me, and I kind of want to try again. Maybe I'll go for more next time. Us overachievers never rest.

"Are you sure you know what you're doing? What about-"

"It's fine," I say, cutting her off. I don't need the fact that I have nightmares shoved in my face. I'm all too aware, hence my original no sleepover rule. "It's not like we're dating or anything. I think she might've heard some of one already."

Coty rears back. "Really? What happened?"

A harsh chuckle escapes me. "Chick broke my fucking door down."

Angie widens her eyes and glances at Coty while Marc laughs his ass off.

"That's what happened to it?" I nod as he continues more seriously, "What did she say?"

Popping a shoulder, I tell them honestly, "Nothing really. She didn't *see* much." My gaze lingers on both my boys. They know what that means. More than Angie anyway. She may have heard one, too, a long time ago, but she didn't see the aftermath.

Coty nods in understanding but Marc, he looks away sharply. *What was that?*

"Is that why you two were late tonight?" Angie asks hesitantly and I smirk, shaking my head.

"I took her up there." I jerk my chin up to the property halfway up the canyon Coty specifically chose to plant his and his future family's roots.

"Are you considering buying it?"

The uncertainty on her face doesn't match the hopefulness on both my boys'.

"What are you so eager about? That's your property and you know it," I tell Marc.

He rubs his chin with his fingers and thumb. "The fuck it is. I left that one for you. I can't believe you haven't snatched it up yet."

My eyebrows sink. "What do you mean you left it for me?"

Confusion rolls off both Coty and Angie so I know they're as lost as I am.

"Who do you think bought the other lots?"

"That was you?" Coty asks him.

Marc just looks at us like we should know that he went behind our backs, making major moves without telling any of us. But, how was anyone supposed to know that? That's boss ass shit right there.

And here I thought he resented his family's good fortune. Maybe he's not allergic to spending some of that money after all.

Angie shakes her head, grinning at each of us. "I should've known I'd never get rid of you two."

Marc, Coty, and I all parrot back to her at the same time with "Never."

All around Coty's acreage is long grass, blowing gently from a breeze. With summer in full swing, it's starting to die off, turning brown like the dirt beneath it and the surrounding sagebrush. Swear there's more sagebrush here than Arizona. We went there once and felt right at home with the muted tones of neutral on neutral on neutral.

It's all I've ever known though and I've never even considered moving away. This part of Washington is a great place to start a family. Lots of open space to roam, low crime rates, extended summers for all the outdoor recreation you could ever want. A family of my own is like far, far on the horizon. So small I can barely even make it out in the distance. A mere blip on the radar really. But that blip, there's nowhere else I'd rather it happen than right here, next to my original starter family.

I'm fucking in.

"Well, it's settled, cupcake. You're getting your wish," I say to Coty. "Looks like I need to find myself a realtor now."

Marc lifts his fingers off the table and for a split second I swear I see a sliver of sparkly polish there, but...nah. Must be the sun. It's fucking brutal out here without any buildings or trees or structures of any kind to block that shit.

"Call mine. He's had it on lock for the last year anyway, waiting on your slow ass."

I laugh quietly. "Anytime you want that rematch, dude, I'm ready."

"For the master again?"

I raise one shoulder, leaning further back in my chair to put an arm over the backrest.

When we first moved into Creekwood, the three of us raced our bikes for the master bedroom. Marc managed to pull off a W and still has it in his head he's actually faster than me and Coty. If we were talking dirt bikes, that'd be a different story. But since everyone knows Coty's the looker of the three, and I'm obviously the entertainer, well, I'd like to think we kinda let Marc have that one to give him *something*. If he wants to hold that title above his head for all time, fine, but I'd just like to get one thing straight—I'm not slow. And if I *wanted* to take that master bedroom, I'd steal it right out from under him. Or die trying, which we almost did the first time around.

"Don't you think Paige and I are better off racing for it then?" His gaze lingers on the property he had set aside for me.

And what? I'm supposed to just move out, leaving Paige and Marc to live together in happily ever after bliss?

Something fills me to the absolute brim imagining that scenario. Something fucky.

Movement at that exact moment catches my eye and I turn to witness four dudes I don't know walking up the loose gravel driveway. Paige's back is to them but they're all walking right for her. One is holding a present for fuck's sake and after further inspection I realize it's the same one that I caught Paige in the hallway with her first week living with us. Dude was all over her and they were saying something that sounded like they were close. Too close.

What is going on here?

Rising out of my seat, Angela puts her hand up to stop me

and I swear I'm about to cuss my boy's girlfriend out when Paige's squealing has me swinging my gaze back to her and the intruders in time to see her launch herself into the shortest one's arms before he passes her off to the others. By the time she's put back on her feet she's full-on sobbing.

I start forward again but Marc stands up this time, blocking my path.

"The fuck, man?" There may even be spittle flying out of my mouth when I say it. It's been a long day and I'm in the dark right now—a place I've already spent too much time in. I'll come out swinging if I have to. Screw anyone in my way, family included. "Who are all these douchebags? And why are they here?"

I narrow my eyes on Angie but it's Marc that answers, saying, "I invited them."

"*You* did?"

Everyone turns to Paige who's looking at Marc in complete awe. Um, excuse me, but I brought this chick to orgasm at least twice today. *Twice.* And right now she's looking at Marc like the dude holds the goddamn moon or something.

Without warning, she throws herself into his arms and hugs him tight with the gloomy as fuck foursome waiting just behind her.

The muscular one jerks his chin at Marc over Paige's head and they tap knuckles.

And what in the unholy fuck is happening right now?

The one holding the gift glares at me and nods at the shortest one in the bunch making him turn his unfriendly stare on me, too.

I return both of their scowls with one of my own though. Fuck him. Fuck them all.

I take my eyes off her for two minutes and the vultures descend.

The fourth seems somewhat aloof and keeps checking his phone every few seconds between his gauging glances at Paige.

I stand a little taller which isn't hard since none of these assholes come close to my stature.

Paige finally releases Marc with a thank you then disappears into her newfound guy squad. *Seriously?*

My face is hot and I want to punch something. Or someone.

Make that multiple someones.

"Dude, chill."

"Fuck you," I spit back at Marc before checking around the group. Coty's watching the man-sandwich happening in his front lawn while Angie's eyes are leaking something that looks a hell of a lot like tears. *The fuck?*

"Am I missing something? Why would you invite them?" I jerk my thumb at the boyband littering the yard, taking turns fawning over Paige and her sliced up forehead, which is healing up nicely thanks to me—fuck you very much. *NBD.*

My back teeth grind together until I'm positive I'll be spitting dust when I leave.

"He doesn't know?" Angie asks Marc as if I'm not standing right here.

I almost yell. "What? What else don't I know?" You know, aside from the fact my life is being planned out without my fucking knowledge.

"Does anything look familiar about them?"

Familiar? Meaning we know these fuckers?

Facing Paige and her fans, I see that the tallest one with a beard and a little too long on top hair—the one I saw at Creekwood with her—has similar coloring in his eyes, almost like Paige's but lighter. The difference between the dark hair and the light eyes is so significant he should be a model, but he's got the same sadness about him Paige does.

Muscles has the group in stitches already and while his head is thrown back in a deep laugh of his own I notice it sounds vaguely familiar as well. Kind of like the laugh I had the pleasure of listening to for the last two days, yet different somehow, more masculine. He watches their little crew with wary eyes, waiting for his next joke to land but in an almost nervous way, like they mean more than even he realizes. Like his comic relief alone can make or break the entire group. He's lean but built and has a dirty air to him, not like a slob, but like his work is long and harsh. Some of our technicians at Pop The Hood have the same way about them.

Didn't Paige say she spent time in the garage with her brother? And isn't this guy who I saw her with at the pool once?

The one glued to his phone is dressed like he just came from work. His clean-cut look is different from the rest as he's cloaked in black dress pants with a long sleeve dress shirt even though it's almost a hundred degrees out here. Oh and also, he has a nose almost identical to Paige's. He seems like his mind wants to be here but it just isn't. He smiles every now and then when Paige focuses on him, otherwise he's back on his phone, typing away.

Paige frowns each time she catches him looking at the device and my fingers itch to rip the fucking thing out of his hands.

The shortest one has lips I'd recognize anywhere. It's almost disconcerting looking at the lips I've been dreaming about for weeks attached to a dude but there they are—Paige's mouth but in male form. He's lighting a cigarette with a tilt of those lips in Paige's direction. She says something to him making him bark out a laugh that dies out as she snatches the nicotine stick straight from his mouth. He shoves her shoulder a little too hard to be friendly and my fists clench before she pushes him right back, making him stumble a few steps much to the others' enjoyment. He's a cocky little shit and Paige putting him in his place doesn't sit well with him but it sure as fuck does with me.

Now that I'm really searching, all of them have the same thick ass chocolate colored hair. The only real distinction being Paige's with her merlot streaks mixed in which make her stand out amongst the pack of lookalikes.

"Are they related?" But that doesn't make sense. I thought she was *with* at least one of them before…or something.

"Those are her brothers, jackass. They surprised her today thanks to Marc."

"Brothers? Fuck." I adjust my hat, facing it forward. "Whenever she mentioned her brother, I thought she was talking about one. I had no idea she had four!" I crush my empty beer can and toss it in the pop-up bin a few feet away.

This whole time I assumed the worst about Paige and never gave her the chance to set the record straight. Not asking Paige about her life but expecting her to share details like her siblings was shitty. One more shitty thing I've done in a long list of shitty things Paige has experienced due to my stubbornness. I bullied my way past her defenses without stopping to see why they were there to begin with.

Goddamn it. I fucked up. I've fucked up a lot in my life but this time feels monumental. Like I need to fix it. Now.

Without another word, I trail after Paige's family to introduce myself with mine at my sides. I didn't know if they'd follow me but I'm glad they did. Even in my mistakes they're willing to stand by me.

I look each of her brothers in the eye as I shake their hands. I may have pleasured the ever-loving shit out of their sister today but I'm still not a bitch.

They return the favor of holding their ground which I respect now that I know they're not trying to get in Paige's pants and all goes relatively well until the youngest one, Nick, steps up with his unbuttoned shirt and fuck all attitude trying to intimidate me. It does about the same as a Chihuahua barking up an evergreen tree. Dude could never be on my level so I ignore his bullshit to focus on Paige. She's been smiling politely during introductions but is now refusing to meet my eye which pisses me off to no end.

Is she upset the cat's out of the bag? Well, too damn bad. Beside the fact that I may or may not be crushing on the girl, she's still our roommate and I think we need to know who she is.

A little voice in the back of my mind whispers that she deserves the same respect but I silence that shit real quick. Nobody needs that kind of negativity.

We all make our way over to a long table Coty brought from the garage and I follow Paige as she grabs a plate for food. She's got a bounce in her step that wasn't there when we arrived and my chest constricts knowing Marc had a hand in the reason for her sudden happiness.

I open my mouth a few times to speak to her without knowing what to say before just closing it altogether. Now isn't the time to rain on her parade even if I wish I was the Grand Marshal of the fucking thing.

After loading up a plate with the first actual food I've eaten all day—I don't care, Paige still tastes better than anything Angie ordered—I join the table Paige's family and mine are both occupying. Oddly, the mishmash works and conversation flows effortlessly with Paige's middle sibling, Tysen, leading the group with some amusing story he's retelling.

While everyone's eyes are on the newest entertainer, mine rest solely on Paige. She listens to her brother with both admiration and what looks like concern. The worry etched on her face only increases as her gaze touches on each of her other brothers.

Nick, sensing her, looks up, meeting her eyes and they have a silent conversation right here in the middle of a boisterous barbecue without even uttering a single word. A better man would give them some privacy. I, however, watch on with a desperate fascination. What's plaguing them? If they're even half as strong as Paige appears to be, then they're better off banding together as a unit rather than bearing the burden alone like single children like myself are often forced to do.

My answer comes at the end of Tysen's long winded story—I'm not gonna lie, I have no idea what the dude was talking about and I should probably give him some pointers after all this—when Nick breaks the staring contest to ask Paige about their mom. My ears, along with everyone else's at the table, perk up. She's never spoken about her parents before and I'm wondering why the fuck he'd be asking Paige. Wouldn't he know as much as her about their mother?

Paige's eyes drop to her lap as her hand reaches up tentatively touching her dry scratches.

Damn it. I need to treat those again soon.

Putting that on the back burner for now, my eyes eat up every detail as Paige fidgets in her seat. She's still breathtakingly beautiful in all her badassery which somehow makes this even harder to watch.

I glance up to Marc with a furrowed brow. He just shrugs a shoulder, looking around the table as I follow suit.

"You'd know if you bothered showing up," Paige says before meeting her brother's stare dead-on, all the good feelings from a moment ago now gone. "If you checked in on her, on me, you'd know, wouldn't you?"

Her eyes meet mine briefly before shifting to Tysen.

"And what the hell is your excuse? You were the one that visited her the most out of all of us, and now? Nothing?"

Dude looks ashamed but just shakes his head in silence.

"Caleb," she starts, then pauses, sighing, "you're too easy. You know exactly what choice you're making and you're going to regret it when she finally leaves us."

When he doesn't respond, she turns her attention to the oldest brother seated at the head of the table but he won't even meet her eyes, choosing to keep his head angled toward his plate instead. "She needs you, you know that? I need you." Paige's voice cracks at the end, making every bone in my body ache.

The plastic chair I'm sitting on creaks from the pressure of my hands tightening on the legs. My body is draped across the seat taking in the scene as if I'm an oblivious bystander but this shit's eating me up. The girl is breaking right here in front of all of us and there's nothing I can do about it. I have half a mind to shield her with everything I got but Jesse, her oldest brother, finally speaks up, startling the table.

"She doesn't even know me anymore." Face still aimed at his untouched food, his voice comes out as a pained murmur but with both families in utter silence we all hear him loud and clear. Jesse lifts his head, finding his sister's glare aimed directly at him—no holds barred whatsoever. "She doesn't know any of us and she never fucking will again. How we choose to deal with that is our business. We can't all walk around pretending to be a sympathetic nurse in our mother's life, now can we?"

My eyebrows shoot to my flat bill. One: I don't appreciate dude's scathing tone nor does Paige judging by her narrowed-to-slits eyes. Two: what, and I cannot stress this enough, the fuck?

Risking a quick glance around the table, I see a mix of reactions. Jesse is staring daggers back at Paige, which upon further consideration I might have to talk to him about because that shit just won't fly with me. Worker bee Caleb has a perma-scowl that I'm guessing is directed more at himself than anyone. Nick still looks like a little shit with a mug that I wouldn't mind slapping a time or two, while Tysen actually looks like he might be physically ill from the family conflict. He's got guilt for days and it's obvious he's not handling it well. None of them are, including Paige who stands so suddenly her drink goes flying across the table and into Angela's lap.

Without so much as flinching, Angie rights it in the next instant like it never even happened. It'll take a lot more than water to rattle her, girl works with it for a living after all, and I know this scene is nothing new to her either. Family drama runs deep with that one. She still looks a half second away from slapping a few faces herself though. Angela's all about women empowerment and anyone talking harshly to a female in her presence will face quite the wrath. I've been on the receiving end more than once and it sucks. Big time.

"Fuck you, Jesse. I did what I had to. I did what nobody else sitting here would even think of. I worked, no fuck that, I *work* my ass off to pay for *all* of Mom's bills. I gave up my own apartment that I loved more than you could ever know to live with two complete strangers which, if I'm being honest, is only a step above living with you domineering assholes."

Marc's scowl across the table meets mine as we listen on, both of us biting our tongues. *What did I do?*

"All so I could save more money to afford a better facility for Mom. I bought a piece of shit, as you called it," she sneers at Jesse, "used bike instead of a new one like I'd been saving for. I don't even buy new clothes because every dollar I spend on myself is a dollar that could make Mom's life a little bit more comfortable in her new warped reality."

She takes a deep breath like this next part might hurt.

"I eat fucking salads now. Since when have I ever liked going without meat? Huh? Since it was too fucking expensive, that's when."

The youngest brother, Nick, pushes to his feet and points across the table at her, shouting, "I knew it!" His gaze falls on their leader. "I told you something was wrong when she tried to feed you that salad. If there's one thing the Christensens don't do, it's eat that disgusting shit." Dude even shakes like a shiver is eating his spine one vertebrae at a time.

Look, I get it, going meatless is beyond comprehension, but read the fucking room. It's obvious Paige is unhappy about the sacrifice.

"Shut up, Nicky," she sighs like she's exhausted.

"You decide, on your own, to move Mom out of a place that *we* chose and then you want to complain to us about it? Because you can't afford the occasional steak anymore? Really? The way I hear it, you've been drinking plenty of calories to get you by." All eyes bounce between him and Paige like we're at a tennis match. "Yeah, Dixon called to let me know about *everything* you've been up to at Xen's."

Xen's is that bar I dropped her off at. With that fuckface that she hugged like a lifeline. With the way I'd treated her plus all of this family drama, maybe in that moment he was. *Shit.*

"Funny how you'll answer his calls but not your own sister's."

You can tell that betrayal cuts deeper than Jesse's accusation.

Which, what exactly is he accusing? That she spends too much on alcohol or that she's plain drinking too much? I don't think any of that is really his business, especially if he's not actively involved in her life, but I haven't noticed an issue on either front. The girl strolled home drunk a few times, yeah, but I was there to make sure she didn't do anything stupid and I'm the best voice of reason there is. I can vouch for what *not* to do like a champ.

"If you were truly worried, where have you been? You've seen where I live. You have my number. What's stopping you from doing *anything* about it? You want me to know you're pissed? You want to show me you're disappointed? Message received. I got it. Okay?"

Her near hysterical voice has other partygoers tuning into the show and I stand to reach for her elbow in what…I'm not sure. Support? Strength? Hell, I'll give her anything to help her in this moment.

The second my skin touches hers though all four of her brothers rise in unison, followed by both of mine immediately after. They drill glares into the side of my face as Marc and Coty stiffen, waiting for someone, anyone, to jump.

Before that can happen, Paige rips her arm from my grasp to continue. "The least, and I mean the *least* you could do is show up to see the woman that raised you. It's true, Mom can't remember you, but I sure the fuck do, and I'll never forget the way you abandoned your family when things went to shit."

She's straight seething as she meets each of her brother's conflicted gazes then says, "When she dies, you're better off digging two fucking holes because I'm halfway there already myself."

Shaking, she turns to leave while I stand here with my mouth hanging open.

Going off everyone else's blank expressions, I'm not the only one. That was…a lot. Once again, I had no idea what Paige was going through. I still don't really.

Facing Tysen, since he seems to be the only semi-rational one, I ask, "Is your mom a patient of Paige's?"

He swallows thickly, nodding. "Now she is. Paige works at a different Alzheimer's facility than the one we," he gestures to the others, "originally placed her in. We thought it was a good one but Paige thought otherwise so she moved her to the home she works in."

Alzheimer's.

"I did the research before we paid for the year in full and it was rated one of the best in the area," Caleb adds.

"All that time on your phone and you still got it wrong?" Nick, the punk, chimes in rather unhelpfully as he lights up another cigarette underneath the long, dark hair flopped over his forehead.

I'd give anything to see that shit catch on fire right now.

"At least I have an excuse for not checking on Mom. What about you? Couldn't handle Mommy not babying the golden child anymore?" Caleb retorts.

Nick flips Caleb the bird while plopping back in his seat like a disrespectful child.

"If I didn't have the pressure from work constantly hanging over my head, I'd have visited Mom, too. Some of us have paying jobs though. Obligations. Not that you'd know what those are." Caleb directs the last part at Tysen.

"Oh, fuck off already, Caleb," Tysen snaps as Nick reclines as far as the fold out chair allows, watching the two volley insults back and forth like it's his entertainment for the night. Dude's begging for one to the face, I swear.

Jesse's chest heaves as he stares off the way Paige left. Angie does the same but Coty's arm is around her waist in a protective manner, keeping her from getting involved. The gesture is almost laughable considering she's not the one that'll need protecting if she does.

The tense silence continues until Tysen speaks again. "Clarise and I just broke up. And she's pregnant. Baby's due this winter."

Every head snaps to him with only a murmur of "congrats" from my friends. The break-up sucks but a baby's a good thing, right? Better him than me, but still, why does it sound like he's miserable about the whole thing? People can make that co-parenting shit work if they want to.

Also, what's up with all the color draining from Jesse's face while the other two drop theirs into their hands? This family has problems.

"Does Paige know yet?" Angela pipes in. When dude shakes his head, she steps forward and lowers her voice. "You should be the one to tell her then."

Tysen takes her advice and heads in the direction we last saw Paige and I let him pass even though it takes everything in me to stay put and not be the one to approach her first.

Nick, still lounging with a cigarette dangling out of his mouth, mutters, "This is why we don't do celebrations anymore."

"Or communicate properly," Marc adds with a deep frown.

With a cocky smirk, dude wags his finger at us. "Glass houses, boys. Don't think we didn't notice the shock on your faces as our bitchy sister aired our dirty laundry."

I take a step forward which finally brings Jesse back to life and he matches mine, putting us toe-to-toe which is fine with me. I've been itching for a fight since they showed up.

"Your household isn't full of chatter either or you would've known more about Paigey-poo."

He's got a point but fuck if I'll tell him that.

"Bitchy?" Angie scoffs, while Coty, flexed next to her, gauges the smoking tool. "I know bitchy, I was born and raised by the biggest one there is, so trust me when I say the only bitch I see here is you." Pointing a finger in Nick's direction first, she moves it to the other brothers, ticking them off one-by-one and I smirk proudly. It feels so good not to be on the receiving end of Angie's anger for once. "And you. And maybe you. It sounds like your sister is breaking herself to care for your sick mother and you have the balls to talk shit to her for it?"

I drop the smile and instinctively tighten my fists at my sides.

Out of the corner of my eye, I catch Angie's old stepbrother, Drew, taking in the scene not too far away, ready to jump in if needed. Ginger-twerp's help isn't necessary but I appreciate the sentiment all the same, even if he does still dress like a prep.

Seriously, who the fuck forgot to send out the memo that it's summertime?

"What can I say? The Christensen crew is a mixed bag of tricks. We like to keep things interesting."

My gaze collides with Angie's and I know we're both thinking the same thing: *mixed bag of dicks*.

Instead of saying it aloud though, she says, "if by interesting you mean deserting your only sister, yeah, real fucking interesting," then aims a pointed look at each man, and Nick, at the table. "But a real family doesn't give up on each other. *My* crew taught me that."

And, I don't think I've ever been more proud. Pretty sure a tear forms in my eye and I go to wipe at it using my middle finger. It took her long enough but she got it. She finally understands that this family shit is real for us and we sure as fuck wouldn't give up on one of our own when they need support most.

A few minutes of heavy silence later, Caleb speaks as he walks past Nick, smacking the back of his head—I'm sad to report it's not as satisfying as I'd hoped. "She's right, it's our baby sister's twenty-first birthday. We came here for a reason. Let's remember that and fuck the rest. Today we celebrate Paige and smooth things over as best we can. We'll deal with everything else later."

Jesse glowers at me one last time before he joins the other two as I'm left watching from the goddamn sidelines yet again.

One thing I do know is whoever dropped the weather report also failed to inform me that today is her actual birthday.

Fuck.

◆ ◆ ◆

Coming out of the bathroom later that night, I catch Paige darting across the hall from her room into mine and I smile.

"Lost again?" I tease as she burrows into my covers without even bothering to look sorry.

Paige rejoined the party-that-definitely-wasn't-a-party with her brothers in tow and stayed tucked safely between them the rest of the night. Each brother took turns spending time with her and as much as I hated it, I also appreciated it...for her. She needs her brothers. If she hadn't already said it herself, you could tell just by watching them together. Which I did. All fucking night. I watched as she drank and laughed and loosened up, having a genuinely good time that I don't think even she knew she was capable of. It made for a shit time for me but it also allowed me to come up with a plan of action for a few ideas I've had swirling around in my head.

I was hoping she'd already be asleep so I could get away for a bit but with her sleeping next to me, I doubt I'll be able to slip out unnoticed.

"No, that's cool. Make yourself at home in *my* bed." I toss a pillow at her, making her chuckle. "I'm going to sleep on the couch though. My back's messed up from that four-wheeler today." That part's true at least. Shit fell off the ramp partway up the trailer and I had to jump in to help Marc lift the fucking thing the rest of the way.

If Paige notices the lie about the couch, she doesn't say anything, only frowns as I turn out the lights and leave the room. It takes a lot of effort but I know I need to now or I won't be able to.

Spread out on the cool leather couch, I think over the last week while I wait for her to pass out. My nightmares were increasing and I was waking up bloody more days than not until a couple days ago. Until Paige started showing up in my bed. She's like my own personal dream catcher. Thankfully she doesn't know the full extent of them. Although, Marc did act a little weird when the subject came up earlier. He wouldn't have told her though.

Maybe he knows something I don't.

I snort to myself.

He's known more than me this whole time. Motherfucker's been keeping plenty of shit close to the chest lately. Except for the tidbit about overhearing me and Paige this morning—oh, he was all too happy to share that information. Funny how that works. If I didn't love the guy so much, I'd hate him right about now.

"I'm sorry."

Paige interrupts my thoughts, damn near scaring the shit out of me in the process, before she straddles my stomach and looks down at me seriously.

Frozen from the contact, it takes me a minute to figure out what she said.

"Uh, for what?"

"I could've been more upfront about my family. At least about my brothers. They've just always been around so I never had to explain who they were to anyone. This year's been…different."

Guilt eats a hole through my stomach like a hungry caterpillar.

Using Paige's thighs, I push her down until her groin is in line with mine making things a bit more comfortable. She lies down across my chest and I drop my chin to her head. I can still smell the peaches from her shower this morning mixed with a tang from the alcohol she consumed, too. Not riding her motorcycle for several days has almost eliminated the usual smokiness and I realize I actually miss it. Without it her smell is just soft and sweet. Like how she tasted this morning but not exactly how I'd describe her overall. She's caring yet gritty. Tender but edgy. She's a tough exterior guarding a delicate heart.

"My mom left when I was ten." There's a roughness to my voice I wish I could rid but can't. "She wrote a note telling my dad that she was leaving one day and never returned. She ran away to be with another dude. So fucking cliché, right?"

Paige doesn't move a muscle, so pretending she's asleep, I continue. "I wanted her to come back more than anything. I hoped and prayed and wrote letters to her, to Santa, just begging for her return. I didn't even care if she stayed. I would've gone anywhere she wanted, been anyone she wanted, as long as I could see her again."

"Did she ever come back?"

Throat clogged, I shake my head.

"I'm sorry."

And there it is. The pity born from pure helplessness.

"Don't be," I bite out.

Paige lifts her head, staring into my eyes. "No, not for her. She doesn't deserve someone else apologizing away her actions. She owes that to you herself. For now, you don't need it."

I frown, not sure I'm following.

"You're a great guy and she's missing out, not the other way around. I'm sorry she lost the chance to watch you become the amazing human you are today."

Now I scoff. There's no way she means that unless the alcohol is talking for her.

"I mean it, Beckett. I've watched you the last couple days. You're funny with your friends, you're generous with your employees, you're fair to your customers, you're a genius in the garage—you almost put Tysen to shame."

It came out that Tysen being strapped for cash as a floating mechanic was the reason the Christensen brothers weren't as overjoyed about the baby news as they could've been. He struggles finding steady, reliable work.

"You're fiercely loyal and protective over Marc and Coty and even Angela. I see the way you follow her every move when she's around, making sure nobody messes with her. You've taken such good care of me ever since I bashed my own forehead into a wall."

Okay, now I know the booze is loosening her tongue. She's been dodging my questions about her injury all along, until now.

Running my fingers up her sides, as innocently as I can, I ask, "Why did you do that by the way?"

She returns the side of her face to my chest and sighs. "My job can be dangerous, too, big guy." That's news to me. I thought she just took blood pressure and made beds maybe. "I can't really talk about it but one of the residents had an episode and became aggressive. I did what I needed to in order to avoid anyone else getting hurt."

Her mom. I'd bet last month's paycheck her mom was at risk. You can tell she'd do anything for her mom, even bloody up her own face.

Where have I heard that before?

I squeeze my eyes shut on an exhale.

"Anyway, I understand where you're coming from. My mom's been missing for over a year and I'll never get her back fully."

My eyes pop open.

"At least your mom is within reach. I couldn't get to mine with the best GPS in the world."

"Within reach?" Paige releases a humorless laugh. "Have you ever tried to pick up sand and end up watching it slip through your fingers? That's what having a loved one with Alzheimer's is really like. The biggest tease of all. The mindfuck to top all mindfucks. You can see, touch, talk to, and even hear them but it's like doing it as a fucking ghost. They can't see you for you, they can't talk to you like they used to, their touch is cold and distant, they hear you without really listening. So, where GPS *could* find your mom, mine is hidden in plain sight where nothing and no one will ever get to her again."

"You're wrong."

"Excuse me?"

She jerks up to look at me again.

"You're wrong. At least about one thing. Your mom can feel you, maybe without knowing who you are but she can feel how good of a person you are. She can feel your love even if she doesn't know what kind it is or why it is. If you believe in one thing, believe that her love for you is stronger than any disease ever could be and return that back to her. Love her the only way you can because that means more than anything else on this planet. The love between a parent and child is the most important kind there is and when it's gone, that's it. It can never be replaced. Not by friends, not by anyone. You can choose your family, sure, but you never really recover from that kind of loss." I know I haven't. "It goes too deep to fix."

With a frown marring her otherwise serene face, she leans down to brush my lips with a quick, gentle kiss. It's the first real kiss we've shared since our first a few days ago and it wakes an insatiable hunger for more.

"You are loved, Beckett." Every muscle locks beneath hers. "Everyone around you loves you. I see it whenever you walk into a room. Everybody is drawn to you and your bigger than life energy. You're like a magnet, attracting everyone in the vicinity. Losing a parent's love is one of the worst feelings imaginable, we can both attest to that, but in your case your mom is the real loser. Don't let her take your happiness along with her."

My eyes search hers. What about her happiness? She's given up everything for her mom. How is that fair? How is she better off than me?

"Do you regret giving up your own place? I heard what you told your brothers. Do you like living here?"

Something flashes in her eyes that I can't make out before it's gone completely as she takes in the mostly dark room. Her gaze lingers on the new light I bought then she lowers her head, relaxing once again before promptly passing out on top of my ribs and pressing into my heart in more ways than one.

Nobody's ever said those things to me. Nobody's ever shown me another perspective to the problem I've been fixated on since I was a boy. I never thought of my mom as the one suffering from being without me, I was too focused on painting her as the villain. Even if what she did was wrong, she's still going to miss out on all the big moments in my life. The day I finally tie the knot, the day my children are born—hopefully all boys, although a little girl with dark waves surprisingly comes to mind, too—and everything in between. Also the shit I've never thought about mattering to anyone other than me, things like landing a jump on my dirt bike for the first time, or creating a job I've always wanted, or falling in love with the girl of my dreams…whenever that time may come.

Regardless of how perfect Paige feels in my arms, I still have errands to run. So after several minutes of letting the girl rest, I lift her up and carry her down the hall, hesitating between the two doorways.

To the right is my room, and to the left, Paige's.

I should put her in hers. Let her wake up in her own bed after such an emotional day. She only gets into mine after a few too many drinks but right now I'm sober and can do the right thing. I also don't know how much sleep I'll be getting tonight and don't want to bother her when I get back.

But then why can't I make myself go left?

Knowing I shouldn't like waking up next to her doesn't change the fact that I do. And she does help with the nightmares.

That's what I tell myself as my feet hook right.

CHAPTER 20

Paige

I HAVE TO STOP WAKING UP IN BECKETT'S BED. HE'S GOING to get the wrong idea soon. Though I will admit his room is much more comfortable than mine. Where his is lived-in and welcoming, mine is cold and blank, void of anything personal of my own. I don't mind because I don't spend much time in there, even less since I've started squatting in Beckett's, but I do miss my old place. My room was comfy and cozy and had my personality all over it with trinkets from each of my brothers over the years along with framed pictures from our many family escapades.

Last night would've been frame worthy. Well, the parts after the volatile dinner anyway. Family are the only people that can get under your skin like a bad rash but also soothe the irritation away like it was never there to begin with. I love those boys so much but they can push my buttons like no other. Each of them apologized and promised to try harder with Mom after being guilted into being better sons. *Jerks.*

Then, I was so excited to find out I'll be an aunt soon that I eased up on my emotionally immature brothers more than I probably should've, but it's hard. It's hard being the baby in a family of egotistical assholes while feeling like you're the only adult. Which, being an adult is its own shitty charade, by the way.

Beckett's still fast asleep next to me, so I look around one last time before I can slip back to my barren room. Posters cover almost every square inch of Beckett's walls, from concerts to barely-dressed models to sweet rides. A small, yet neat desk sits below the window with a laptop open to what looks like a Pinterest browser. I strain my eyes but can't make out what he was searching for from the bed. The bed I need to leave but don't want to part ways with just yet.

No matter how I ended up here last night, I can't keep letting myself into his room while he's sleeping. Which now that I think about it, how did I end up in Beckett's room? The last thing I remember is talking with him on the couch before passing out. Did he take me to my room then I came in here later? He wouldn't have brought me in here himself, would he?

Pulling the bulky striped comforter down, I scan Beckett's peaceful face. The same face that was buried between my legs not once but twice yesterday.

I groan, covering my eyes with an arm. How did I let that happen?

I know. With his stupid beautiful face and his stupid beautiful smile with the wicked delicious mouth that was dirtier and bossier than I anticipated.

I feel my cheeks heat and know it's time to leave before I do something stupid. Again.

The mattress shifts as I drop a leg over the edge, but Beckett's large arm circles my waist, catching me in one smooth motion.

"Where are you going?"

His sultry timbre glides across my skin as he pulls me in close, inhaling where my neck meets my shoulder. My entire scalp tingles.

"To my own room?"

Something about that ruses him and he releases me to jump from the bed the next second. I watch him through wide eyes as he runs his hands through his messy hair.

"Don't move," he stresses before leaving the room.

Okay.

A few minutes later, he returns with something small pinched between his fingers and his other hand behind his back.

"You're creeping me out. What the hell are you doing? And can I put my pants on first?"

One side of his mouth tips into a sexy smirk. "My answer to

that question will always be no. You should never wear pants again as far as I'm concerned."

His eyes scan my half-clothed body. Not only is Beckett's bedding thick as hell, but I don't like feeling restricted when I sleep. A girl needs some air.

"Here."

I catch what he tosses at me and inspect the item, turning it over in my hand and cocking my head.

"A brake pad?"

"I changed your rear brake. That's the old one." He nods at the heavily-worn pad I'm holding. "And I installed a new battery along with a manual CCT. Your bike is as good as new. Better than new actually."

My jaw drops making Beckett chuckle.

A cupcake with a single lit candle is presented to me next.

"Happy belated Birthday, although in my defense you didn't say a word about it being your actual birthday yesterday."

I can't even form a response as I look from the treat to Beckett. How did he do all this? Better yet, when did he do it? I've been with him for the last forty-eight hours and I would've known if he was fixing my bike. Or...baking?

He passes me the cupcake with a grin tugging at his lips.

Why did he do this?

His words 'good as new' hit me like a bucket of cold water. First, his friends threw me a quasi-surprise party for my birthday when we're not even, like, friends.

Wait, *are* we friends now?

Or does he think he and I are something more because of yesterday? What happened between us confused the hell out of me and once my family was added to the mix, I didn't even know how to react. So much more came out than I ever wanted either of my roommates to know, not to mention a guy that I...like?

Ugh. It's all so complicated now when that was the last thing I wanted.

Now he's fixing my motorcycle up after my embarrassing explosion yesterday. He knows more than any other guy I've hooked up with at this point, and I don't know how to feel about it. Should I cut and run now, saving myself from further humiliation? Should I wait and see how this all plays out? A part of me thinks I should move the hell out and in with one of my brothers. A bigger part of me abhors that idea.

I didn't answer his question last night because I couldn't. I didn't have the guts to admit to myself, let alone to Beckett, how living here really makes me feel. How he makes me feel. I keep guys at arm's length for a reason—several actually—and with the guy's impressive wingspan, I thought that would be easy, but the situation took a sharp turn when emotions suddenly appeared. As much as I've tried fighting it, my feelings for Beckett have morphed from barely being able to stand the guy to tolerating his company to craving more from him.

More is something I've been training myself to go without though and my first instinct is to automatically reject it. To avoid the craving altogether so it goes away quicker. But how can I deny a six-foot, six-inch man in his underwear handing me an overly-frosted cupcake?

"Make a wish," he urges.

Outwardly, I'm calm. Inwardly, it's a whole different story.

Closing my eyes, I try to think of what I really want. What would turn my life around from what it's become. What I haven't dared to dream about.

I wish…

My gaze finds his and he smiles down at me reminding me that this little happy bubble of ours won't last. I sleep during the day, working the nights that Beckett and I just spent getting cozy. That's my normal. The opposite of his schedule. What happens when I go back to work tomorrow night? What happens when reality bites us in the ass with its constant harsh expectations?

The last couple days might've been a dream in their own right but soon we'll have to wake up and face the decisions we've made. Will I regret mine? Will Beckett? I don't have the answers but right now feels too good to pass up.

Raising onto my knees, I take the cupcake and place it on the desk.

Beckett, watching through hooded eyes, quickly shuts his laptop then seizes my unsuspecting lips making me forget all about the cupcake and that mysterious Pin. With a groan, he lowers us to the bed, careful to keep most of his weight off me.

Gathering all the feelings that are better left unsaid, left unidentified at all, I direct them into our connection and give everything I can, letting Beckett know what his gesture means to me without speaking a single word. Unexpectedly, he matches my intensity with one of his own. He's revealing things I know he'll never admit, maybe not even to himself, and I accept his confession greedily, suddenly desperate for what's brewing between us.

Beckett repositions us further up the bed, only breaking contact for a second to rip my sleep shirt over my head, and begins kissing lower until I reach for him through his underwear ready to take things up a notch. He rears back out of my grasp so suddenly, I open my eyes, sure he's disappeared into thin air.

"Nuh uh," he scolds. "This is about you."

Breathless, I ask, "Didn't you already get enough?"

I'm not complaining about him going down on me twice in one day but a man like Beckett? I wouldn't expect him to give so freely without wanting something in return.

His instant response of "never" rocks the room like an earthquake followed by an awkward pause that neither of us knows what to do with. We sit with it, we dine with it, we take it out for fucking ice cream.

Never…as in not ever?

How do I respond to that?

My back begins to sweat as does my conscience. Are we talking a for-fucking-ever, eternal desire here? Or more like a chocolate craving? The kind you know is always a good idea regardless what form it's in. Like today Beckett's hankering for semi-sweet but tomorrow he might want milk chocolate. Is that what he means?

I don't get to find out though because Marc chooses that moment to knock on Beckett's door, interrupting the loud silence.

"Come in," Beckett calls out with more relief than annoyance while covering me back up before Marc can catch a glimpse of my exposed chest.

Beckett's erection though? That's not getting concealed no matter how big a pillow he tries to hide the monster with.

Marc's gaze takes in the room before landing on our position with a funny look.

My eyes flit to Beckett but he's not looking at me anymore.

"What's up?" he asks gruffly instead.

A frown creases Marc's already rigid expression. "Cruz just called. They're having a party down at the river. He said it was cool if we stopped by. You down?"

"I don't know, man. I got shit for sleep last night."

I watch as Beckett picks at his cuticle. He works with cars for a living. Engines. Grease upon oil upon who-the-hell-knows-what, but now's the time he's decided to take an interest in his nail beds?

"Paige? What about you? Cruz wouldn't shut up asking about you." His laugh that follows should be criminal. He's so attractive when he's just scowling and generally frowny but when he lights up, it's practically indecent.

Beckett's hands freeze but he still refuses to meet my eyes. I wait a beat, giving him time to come to his senses.

When he doesn't, I shrug a shoulder and stand from the bed facing my other roommate. "I don't have anything else to do."

We agree on a time frame that works for both of us and just as he's about to leave, he adds, "Wear a swimsuit. Cruz is taking his jet skis and you can show if you've got skills riding anything other than that Honda."

I laugh under my breath. "I thought I already proved my riding skills to Beckett but sure. I'm game."

The smile Marc flashes tells me he knows exactly what I'm referring to.

"Fuck it," Beckett bursts out, finally looking between the two of us. "I'm going."

Hiding a grin, I make my way over to my own room in search of an outfit. And a swimsuit.

◆ ◆ ◆

The park hosting the impromptu soiree is hidden away in a quiet riverside neighborhood I've never been to before. There's a tiny boat launch with a dilapidated dock that's proving to be quite the hot spot on this sweltering afternoon with several tweens taking turns jumping from the rough wood they'll undoubtedly get splinters from, if they haven't already. The nurse in me cringes while the daredevil in me cheers them on with great envy.

The hot air sits like crackly tissue paper all around us with no wind whatsoever to break up the itchy heat. Basketballs bouncing on the nearby court along with various watercraft engines skimming past on the water create a backdrop soundtrack to the otherwise sluggish summer day as hints of watermelon and flattened grass fill my nose.

With a plate of food, I make my way over to a picnic table, sitting next to Angela while keeping an eye on the preteens.

"They make it look so easy, don't they?" Angela nods at the squealing bunch.

With a tee tied at the midriff, cut off shorts, and a baseball hat paired with aviator glasses, she looks like she belongs in California. If I didn't know her better, I'd assume she was carefree, living the dream instead of troubled, having survived a nightmare that she thinks she'll never fully wake up from.

"Not a care in the world." I shake my head. "It must be nice."

We exchange a knowing look.

While most of the guys were caught up in a game of beer pong last night, we swapped childhood stories. Hers nearly broke me to hear, yet here she sits with an amazing boyfriend and a family of friends she blended into seamlessly.

"No salad today, Paige?"

Marc's question is greeted with crickets as he finds a seat at the end of the table.

Too soon. Too fucking soon.

"See? This is what happens when the broody one tries to make jokes." Beckett, dressed in colorful swim trunks and a light blue shirt that says *Remember To Twist Your Fist,* sits opposite me with a heaping plate of his own. "Don't go there, bro, that's my thing," he says to Marc before leaning in to lock eyes with me seriously. "If you or someone you know has been personally offended by one of Marc's dark jokes, you may be entitled to generous compensation."

"You're the most offensive one here," our roommate openly accuses.

Beckett throws his hands in the air, looking around wildly. "Did you not see the guy on the way in here? Dude was wearing a banana hammock while riding one of those wiggle scooters. Ba-na-na ham-mock. At a family park, wiggling his junk back and forth aggressively. *That's* offensive. I thought we were gonna have to pick Paige's eyes up off the concrete."

He's not wrong. There are some things you just can't unsee.

Still talking to Marc, he says, "just watch and learn," then pins me with his best smolder. "You craving sausage, baby? I got a pound right here."

His hand disappears under the table, most likely grabbing his own junk, and the table erupts in mixed reviews of groans and amused chuckles as Angela tsks "offensive" under her breath but loud enough for everyone to hear.

Coty joins the group with an extra plate full of lime wedges that he hands off to her.

I toss one of the gluten free chips we picked up on our way over—there's at least one person at every party with an intolerance these days—but Beckett catches it with a smile on his face and pops it into his mouth. Eyes dancing with humor that's been absent since our awkward hiccup this morning, he digs into his food without further delay only to stop short when my foot grazes his inner thigh.

"Hmm. Are you counting packaging because I'm only coming up with half a pound?"

I wink at him as the joke lands, better than both his and Marc's combined.

Beckett shakes his head while fighting a smile but snatches my foot in his hand, refusing to let go even as I attempt to wrestle it from his grip.

A silent war between us ensues before I catch sight of a little girl over his shoulder joining the crowded dock. Her head of tight curls sticking out of the littlest ponytail I've ever seen bounces as she sits down at the edge, watching the older kids play around her. I glance around for an adult but come up empty. She can't be older than five or six years old and doesn't even have a life jacket.

The fast-moving water has a reputation for being dangerous for even the strongest of swimmers around here. Drownings have actually become a top cause of death in recent years. I can only hope she's with an older sibling that'll keep an eye on her.

Normal conversation picks up around me but I'm too distracted to partake. Beckett notices and glances over his shoulder to see what caught my eye just as a bikini-clad—Brazilian bikini to be exact—woman steps up, blocking his view. I say woman because she stands out among the rest of the laidback crowd here. Easily. While everyone else is dressed in outfits meant for a day at a park, she's got breast implants practically bursting from her string top, and wedges on her feet. If I tried wearing wedges in this kind of terrain, I'd easily topple over but she floats through the barely maintained grass with a seasoned agility. While stunning, in a trying too hard kind of way, she also has a bit of a weathered look to her, like she's spent many, many days outside under the sun. The words *rode hard and put away wet* come to mind before I can shake away the disturbing image attached to it.

And wouldn't you know it, she plants herself right behind Beckett, digging her freshly painted nails into his bicep as she leans down to whisper in his ear.

With him distracted, I yank on my foot again but to no avail. If anything, he tightens his grip, making me huff out a breath of frustration.

His smile grows but it's hard to tell if it's at my expense or for the woman currently puffing her hot ass breath in his ear. *Gag me with a salad.*

Using my other foot, I kick his hand and the unexpected move gets him to finally release my imprisoned foot.

Still keeping an ear to his friend as she takes a seat beside him, Beckett shoots a frown at me but I ignore him. Everything about him. Even the way he casually shakes her hand off his arm. And the way he tells her "it's no problem" after she thanks him for the third time for something I can't quite make out due to my successful attempt to ignore them.

Their employee, or friend—or both maybe—Cruz, sits on my other side, stealing a strawberry off my plate. A strawberry I was *planning* to eat.

Beckett spots the new addition like he just found a pimple on his blemish-free face.

Seriously, what is he using for face wash? I use the same shower as him and all I've seen is a bottle of body wash and some kind of shampoo/conditioner mixture. Two things, that's it. Meanwhile I use an entire regime and I still have more break-outs than him. It reminds me of the time I caught Tysen using *only* a bar of soap for his entire body, even his hair. He swore it worked best at getting grease off but…his scalp, too?

Catching Cruz eating my food, Beckett places his elbows on

the table and clasps his hands together, resting his chin on his knuckles as he watches on unabashedly.

Really?

Cruz has been glued to my side since we arrived and even though he's been polite, until now, I'm struggling to find anything remarkable about him. The small reprieve from my new shadow while he loaded his jet skis into the water was actually kind of nice.

I refuse to meet Beckett's intense stare for the rest of lunch which proves to be quite difficult when that's all he's doing. Literally. He hasn't eaten a single thing as he just stays in the same position, locked on what Cruz and I are doing, like if he blinks for a second Cruz might finger me under the table or something.

Give me a break.

If Cruz notices the Great Wall of Beckett, he doesn't let on as he keeps up a steady stream of one-sided conversation while I continue stealing glances at the little girl on the dock. I just do it around Beckett's big head and even bigger attitude problem. Luckily she has yet to move from her spot.

Full of enough small talk to last me the next decade, I take a walk beside the rocky shoreline after I finish eating.

"So, how does it work living with two dudes?" Cruz asks, falling into step beside me.

"What part?"

"Dating."

"It just does, I guess." I shrug my shoulders and follow Cruz closer to the water's edge, listening in on the rambunctious kids splashing around.

The truth is none of us have really dated since I moved in. I've yet to see Marc with a guest, overnight or otherwise. He's about as inviting as a barbed wire fence wrapped around hot coals. He's actually really thoughtful when you get to know him but I don't know what kind of girl could skate past his daunting exterior to claim his heart. Hats off to any woman who tries and helmet off to the one who succeeds—she'll probably need it. He's...

intimidating. In an extremely sexy way. He looks like he fucks with every part of his body including those charcoal eyes. Like those eyes alone could undress a fully clothed woman in seconds if he wanted. *Seconds.*

Beckett, on the other hand, has entertained a few times but I never stuck around long enough to see how any of them unfolded. I'd rather put my head through another wall.

Then the only times I had visitors, Beckett scared them off before I could even try anything, so I'm not really sure how dating is supposed to work. The thought of bringing a guy home now, or worse, Beckett bringing a girl home, makes my chest tense.

"We all keep to ourselves." *Except when we don't.*

"What would they say if I asked you out?"

I bite out a laugh.

All my life decisions have gone through the men around me like a moat surrounding the locked-up princess. I'd hoped that I'd be passed that point but here we are—same shit, different army of bossy bastards. Can't the princess make her own decision of who gets to wait at the bottom while she rescues herself?

"They have no say over my choices. Any of them."

"Okay." Cruz nods as he watches the fast water. "Then what would you say if I asked you out?"

My first thought is no. I would say no. But is that because I really don't want to date Cruz or is it because someone else is still on my mind? Someone that was just pressed between my legs only hours ago.

At the end of the day, what does one date matter? Cruz is charming in an inexperienced kind of way and he doesn't know my brothers, which is a huge plus. Although, him hesitating about my roommates was a major turn-off, among other things like taking food off my plate without asking. And while he is cute, I find him to be lacking. There's nothing that stands out about him. His build, although he appears to be in good shape, is average. His clothes, stylish but void of any real personality, are average. And his height...his height is so incredibly average. What is he? Only six feet tall?

When did I start thinking of six feet as average?

Beckett appears out of nowhere, handing Cruz a couple of bills that look like hundreds then leans in to tell him something too quiet for my ears to pick up. What the hell?

Cruz nods slowly, looking slightly confused, as he studies the grassy area around his truck that was just covered in water toys and life jackets but is now cleaned up.

Beckett grabs my hand, saying, "Let's go."

I stay rooted to my spot, pulling with all my strength.

"Where?"

Over his shoulder, he points to one of the jet skis and says, "I'm hot," like it's obvious. His shirt is up and over his head in the next instant allowing me to soak up the well-defined abs I didn't get to fully worship this morning. *Take me to church...* "And you looked like you were about to fall asleep."

He shoots Cruz a nasty glare and I cock my head. So what if I was a little on the bored side? Beckett isn't always entertaining either.

Lie.

His eyes dare me to argue.

Glancing toward the little girl again, my stomach drops when she's not where I saw her last and I start forward in a panic, already scanning the water in front of the dock.

"Hey." Beckett wraps an arm around my waist. "Don't worry. It's taken care of."

I swing my frantic gaze to him. *What's taken care of?*

"Look." He points to the bit of water between the dock and the shore where the strong current is blocked. Marc's standing there, knee deep in the still water, fastening a life jacket on the little curly haired girl, his flame tattoos covering his forearms on full display as he works quickly to get her properly fitted. Some of the smaller kids are already in the water, floating around in life jackets that they most definitely didn't have before as they all watch someone in the middle of their little circle demonstrate how to doggy paddle.

I squint.

Not just someone. The woman who was just sitting next to Beckett, chatting him up.

I eye him again and he sighs, explaining as he pulls me along behind him, "Staci and I know each other from high school. She's one of the only people that didn't make fun of my…appearance, probably because she resented hers just as much."

Appearance? What the hell is he talking about? Beckett's gorgeous on a bad day and I have yet to see one of those. Maybe he means his height? It figures kids would tease him about that. Kids can be such assholes.

And the woman? Is that why she got plastic surgery? To change the way she felt about herself?

A sadness for the two young kids they used to be takes over and I feel terrible for judging her for just wanting better. Isn't that what we're all after?

"When her husband lost his job, she called to see if we were hiring." I didn't even think to look for a ring. *Oops.* "He's been with us for a few months now while she works at that new rec center," he stops and spins to look at me, not exactly meeting my eye, "as a swim instructor." He steps closer, dropping his voice and our eyes finally connect. "If something's bothering you, all you gotta do is say it. We got you now."

I suck in a short breath. Why does it hurt to hear that?

I already have a family. One that needs me. All of me. Beckett's a package deal, as am I, and neither of us is looking for that kind of commitment. I'm still working on fixing my own. I can't risk taking on anyone else's. Not right now.

I've been saying that all along and it's starting to feel like nobody's listening—not even me.

Ignoring his claim and how it makes me feel, I ask, "Did you really buy all that gear for those kids?"

And Marc? Since when is he kid-friendly? I'd assume kids would be scared of him, but that little girl looks almost smitten with my mysterious roommate as he tightens the strap around her back.

Beckett doesn't say anything at first as he guides one of the jet skis closer to the sand he left me standing on. With his strong back stretched tight, he shrugs, muttering, "They needed it anyway."

That's it? They needed it, so he provided it. He saw me upset about something and he took care of it. Just like my motorcycle.

Beckett grew up without the love of his original caretaker yet he's constantly trying to take care of those around him. When he doesn't even have to. When he probably shouldn't. What have I done to earn his consideration so far?

Once he's situated on top, he holds a hand out to me and it's like he's asking me for so much more than a ride on a jet ski.

I shake my head, trying in vain to get my heartbeat under control, then remove my clothes and toss them onto a nearby rock.

Down to my bikini, I pull myself on behind him, letting his hand fall away.

This is the most skin-to-skin contact we've had besides the brief interaction this morning and we both sit motionless for a minute, letting our bodies become acquainted again. It's then I realize how different today could've gone had our talking not gotten in the way. Beckett's mouth, as talented as it may be at times, is still the one thing that can ruin the mood like a stomach bug on a cruise ship—fast and without mercy. Except, I don't think that's what he meant for this morning in his bed.

It doesn't matter though. It's for the best. It has to be. Things were getting heavy between us, even if it felt like the exact opposite at the time.

"So, what do you think? Can I take you out or what?"

Cruz.

Again, Beckett made me forget about everything else.

"What's he talking about?" Beckett presses, looking over at Cruz approaching the shoreline.

"A date."

His entire body goes rigid as he cranks his head to face me. "You're not actually going to go out with him, are you?"

My eyes search his before dropping.

"Maybe." It comes out as a whisper but feels like a scream. A scream for help. What do I do?

Coty, oblivious to the tension, wades out to us, handing over life jackets.

Cruz is waiting for an answer but I can't make the words come out. I *know* I should just accept and get it out of the way. There's no risk of anything between Cruz and I turning serious, so why can't I just say yes? Now that it's out in the open it should be easier to take Cruz up on his offer but why does the thought of going through with it make me feel sick? That alone is enough to go out on the date. I need to break out of this bubble forming around me. The bubble that won't let anybody in or out, except for Beckett. Whether the bubble is my doing or his is irrelevant, it just needs to pop sooner rather than later.

Angela, watching Coty with a smile pulling at her lips, takes glances over at Marc still helping to get the kids situated. How has she adjusted to the protective cocoon those three have her in? From what I've seen she's made it work to her advantage, benefitting from the tight-knit family they offer, and flourishing into a complete boss babe in her own right despite her tragic upbringing. She, at least, was able to find love within the walls they reconstructed to include her.

But she helps them. She's a part of their group. An important part that makes them stronger. I'm just this. This disaster of a girl who has no idea where she's going or how the fuck she's getting there. My real family is in utter shambles, arguably at my own hands. Who's to say I won't do the exact same to theirs?

Closing my eyes tight, I ask, "Does Thursday work?"

If the friend zone had a designated day and time, it'd be Thursday afternoon. Nobody falls in love on a Thursday afternoon. Hopefully my forehead will be completely healed by then, too. I'm ready to get back to my regularly scheduled programming. To my reality full of dead ends and crushed dreams. Away from the false hope of what this weekend showed glimpses of.

This is all too much. They are all too much. Beckett is too much.

"Perfect."

Pop.

I open my eyes again to see Cruz beaming and I almost call it off. He's an innocent bystander in this attachment drive-by I'm preparing to commit and he doesn't deserve the stray bullet that's about to clip him.

"I just have to run it by my boss," he jokes, oblivious.

The ensuing silence is deafening.

Life jackets on board, Beckett makes a show of putting mine on first. Restless fingers, jerky movements, and a gruff expression lining his face don't match the gentle giant I've come to know the last few days. Once the vest is attached, his hands drop to my bare thighs and run the length of my legs with an intimacy anyone with half a working eye could see before twisting back around and securing his own.

To keep from checking the reactions at the water's edge, I pull some seaweed off my ankle, tossing it back into the water. There's no way Cruz didn't see Beckett's lame attempt at dominance. The entire park saw it.

"Yo, Bailer's coming into town later. Make sure you're ready!" Coty yells over the engine starting up.

Great. More men. Just what I need.

Beckett turns his scowl to Coty.

He repeats, "*Bailer*...remember him?"

My roommate only jerks his chin in response.

Why do I feel like they're talking in code?

He lays on the gas next causing me to grip his waist tightly, nervous laughter bubbling up.

Countless jumps in, a nasty wave encroaches as Beckett rips the jet ski hard to the side, sending us both sailing off and into the cold water.

Out of breath, I break the surface to find him already floating with barely contained laughter wracking his body.

"What?" I snap.

The water is fucking freezing and my swimsuit may or may not have survived impact. I'll have to check once we're on the jet ski and I regain feeling in my limbs because as it stands now, I'm struggling just to tread water.

"Bail-er. *Bail her.* Get it?"

Through chattering teeth, I attempt to scoff. Beckett pulls me to him as we paddle our way back to the watercraft together—him using one arm, me using exactly none. They might be flopping about but they're definitely not contributing in propelling us forward. Even if they are, I've lost my ability to tell at this point. Seriously, this water never warms up. Must be a side effect from all the rumored chemical waste a nearby nuclear plant allegedly dumps into it. Fuck with Mother Nature and see what she does. Hell hath no fury like a woman being mistreated.

"What was all that about back there?"

"I don't know what you're talking about."

"Sir Gropes-A-Lot, I think you do."

Beckett sneers. "Fuckface is lucky I didn't kick his teeth in."

I feel his hand graze my ass and I'm thankful to see my swimsuit did stay on through the fall.

"Take it easy, Chuck Norris. I'm going on a date with a respectable guy, not bringing him home from a bar after too many shots. There's nothing to worry about."

His only reply is a stiff head shake as he slows his one-armed stride.

Tomorrow I'm returning to work which means things will go back to how they were before my stupid injury. The sleepovers, the constant babying, him going down on me, it's all over. Although, truth be told that last one will be the hardest to say goodbye to. I'm not one to kick a gift horse in the mouth and Beckett's mouth is a gift—when it's used for something other than pissing me off.

Regardless, he had to know this little respite from real life would be short lived, right?

"I mean, Cruz works for you." If he's good enough for Beckett to employ, he's good enough for a platonic lunch date.

"Not for long he doesn't," he mumbles.

"You can't be serious."

Louder, he barks, "He knows the rules, Paige."

Reaching the jet ski, he helps heft my water-logged ass onto the back.

"What rules are those?"

"It's not rocket science. Dude is just trying to piss me off."

We work together to get him on board, too, before situating ourselves back on the seat but with me in the front this time.

"And why would that piss you off? Unless you don't let your employees date any of your roommates?"

My stomach churns as sensation returns to my body and I bend to look at Beckett. Eyebrows creased, he stares at a pontoon boat full of passengers flying past, ignoring my questioning stare.

With a huff, I face forward and start the jet ski up again.

My turn.

It's a while before either of us relaxes enough to actually enjoy ourselves but when we do, it's like nothing else even matters. Instead of focusing on the tension from the morning and Cruz's proposition, we choose to live in the moment, helpless to think about anything other than the here and now. After all, if we take our eyes off the present, we'll miss what's right in front of us—obstacles constantly threatening to break our progress.

We spend the rest of the day in the water, taking turns and switching out partners whenever we return to shore. Angela proves to be just as fearless as the boys and we spend the most time together, getting to know each other better between the monster waves we chase away from the guys' watchful eyes.

Cruz doesn't even try to ride with me, and for whatever reason, I'm thankful.

CHAPTER 21

Paige

Back at the apartment, soaked to the bone and drenched in river stink, I move straight for the bathroom but a hand shoots out just as I turn to close the door, stopping me.

"I thought I could wash your hair for you." His tone is calm while the pulsing vein in Beckett's throat is anything but. "So you don't get any chemicals in your scratches."

Chemicals? What kind of shampoo does he think I use?

I'm about to decline his seemingly altruistic offer when he says quietly, "Just…let me in."

My eyes study his and just like before when he uttered that same plea, I do. I open the door wider and let him in.

The bubble I thought I just popped hovers dangerously close in the peripheral. We won't be able to keep this up after tonight. He has to know that. I need to remember that.

Before I can change my mind, I busy myself testing the temperature then undress and climb in, facing the wall the entire time. I'm clenching and unclenching my fists as I hear him close the curtain after he gets in behind me.

"Get your hair wet." His husky voice warms the small space even more.

"I, uh-" Yep, that's my eloquent contribution before I plunge my head under the spray of water to save myself from further embarrassment.

Why did I agree to this?

All of a sudden I feel Beckett's hands on my scalp, dragging his fingers through my hair to get every strand wet, ratcheting the heat up another couple notches. This is such a bad idea.

Determining it's wet enough—*little does he know*—I turn around to watch as he squeezes my shampoo into his palm before coming at me with what can only be described as a Rapunzel-sized amount dripping from his hand.

I manage to block the gooey assault by capturing his hand in mine and wipe most of the heap into the running water.

"Just because you have big hands doesn't mean you have to fill them completely," I say, chuckling. At his blank stare, I explain, "You mainly use shampoo to clean the scalp. Conditioner is for the ends. You don't need a lot of either."

"Conditioner? Isn't this all in one?"

His wide eyes make me laugh again.

"No, that's for kids." I glance over to the shelf, remembering he uses a 2-in-1 combo. "And men, I guess."

"Shit, I didn't realize this was a whole process."

"Why do you think I don't wash my hair every day?"

Now we both laugh, splintering some of the tension.

"You don't have to finish. I can do it myself."

Reaching to swipe the rest of the dribbling puddle from his palm, he jerks it away with a frown. "I want to try. I've never done this before but I'll stay in here 'til I get it right, damn it. Now turn around."

During his mistake with the shampoo, we didn't even acknowledge the dick shaped elephant in the room but with his hand to the side, it comes into focus. And then some. Beckett totally lives up to that old saying of *big hands, big feet, big everything*. This morning with him in his underwear was as close as I've been to seeing him fully naked and that sight alone was enough to render me speechless. Now, words fail me entirely.

I'm half expecting it to poke my back when I finally turn back around but it never does and I don't know if I'm disappointed by that or not.

Cautiously, Beckett starts spreading the shampoo evenly then goes about massaging my head with the sudsy lather.

It. Is. Everything.

The fingertips circling the skin on my scalp might as well be circling my clit, it feels indistinguishable honestly, and I have to work to keep my moans locked deep inside where they're safe. Once they're out, he'll know. He'll know how much I want him. How much I crave him. And he'll have the upper hand because I'd give anything to let him satisfy the ache he's creating.

He grips my shoulders softly, turning me to him so he can get the front as well. His face darkens as he kneads my scalp with his fingers, deep in concentration. With his attention diverted, I soak in every detail of his naked body my curious eyes can reach. This is the most of his fit body I've seen and I'm using what's probably my only chance to stare openly to my advantage.

Keeping his eyes on his task, he works the shampoo in thoroughly until he pushes me gently under the cascading water to rinse it all out. He keeps a hand at my hairline above my forehead, making sure no 'chemicals' make it past. Once the water finally runs clear, his gaze drops to watch, too, blazing a scorching path along my entire body identical to the one I just left on his.

My thighs inch closer together.

Without so much as blinking, Beckett grabs the conditioner and squirts a good amount into his hand before sinking his teeth into his lip when I run my hands over the rest of my body to rinse off any remaining bubbles. It's not meant to be a tease—at least not for myself—but the fact that both our chests are heaving lets me know it is. It definitely is.

Even though I told him it doesn't go on the scalp, he applies the conditioner much like he did the shampoo. I don't dare complain though. In fact, I'm regretting not letting him use that half cup of shampoo he poured originally—we could've been here all night.

Swirls and swirls and swirls later, my eyes close on a moan I couldn't suppress if my life depended on it and Beckett's hands disappear from my hair instantly.

When I open them, he's staring at me with eyes so dark they look like a tsunami building in the distance. Impact is guaranteed, I just don't know how much longer until it hits.

"Rinse," is all he rasps, like even that's too much.

Keeping his hand as a dam again, our eyes lock onto each other's, and I lean back under the spray, blinking away any errant drops that land on my lashes.

Beckett drops his hand, sliding it around to my lower back, then he brings me forward until our fronts are mashed together with his impressive erection pressed between us against my stomach. Warm mist whirls around us as he looks down at me, wet hair clinging to his forehead.

"Can I touch you?"

In any other circumstance I might laugh—I mean, what parts aren't touching right now?—but seeing his serious expression combined with the longing he's battling awaiting my answer, all I can do is whisper back, "Where?"

"Everywhere."

My eyes shift between his and I nod, licking the clean water droplets off my lips.

Wrapping his arm further around my back, he lifts me straight off my feet and I wrap my legs around his torso as he turns to push me against the shower wall with the spray of water still hitting us from the side.

His mouth is on me in the next second, tasting every bit of skin he can reach, including my throat. My arms slip around his neck while he feasts on mine and all I can think about are the hickeys I'll be wearing on my first day back to work.

While I still can, I pant out, "Lower."

Beckett misunderstands and lowers my entire body just until the tip of his cock teases my opening. We both groan from the contact.

"Do you have any condoms in here?"

He pulls back, eyebrows furrowed, and shakes his head once. "They're in my room."

"We can go get them," I suggest even though the thought of interrupting this moment sounds like actual torture.

"Marc's home."

"So?" I grin. "You can cover yourself with a towel."

"So, I'm not fucking moving without keeping you on my dick and he might see *you* naked."

"I'm not on your dick."

My body is dropped an inch more directly onto Beckett's dick, officially making me a liar. I gasp from the slight intrusion, digging my heels into his ass to keep him from pulling back out.

"If you want me to stop, tell me now. Please." His forehead rests on mine as we both drop our gazes between us to watch our bodies start to adjust to each other's, like they know something we don't. "I've never done it like this, I swear, but if you don't want to, if you're worried, we don't have to."

The sincerity painted across his face says it all—he's telling the truth. He's been here with me, revealing his true self all along, it's just taken me a while to finally see it. How he was today, the sweet gestures, the proactive measures, that's Beckett. The one not everyone gets to see. The one he makes sure people don't see. But he's showing me now. He's trusting me just like I'm trusting him. I've never had sex without protection either, so this step feels big. Bigger than Beckett even.

"I'm not worried," I say, shaking my head. At least not in the way he's referring to. "I'm on birth control," I tell him since he seems like he'd freak about that.

Nudging between my folds, I receive him with all the fanfare one would imagine you'd welcome a giant with—a few curses of disbelief but overall a great appreciation for their company. I already knew he was big but seeing and believing really are two different things because until this moment I did not heed the warnings my brain was sending me.

I stop squirming to see him studying me.

"Are you ready?"

My head is already nodding as I grab his face, pulling his lips to mine. I've never been more ready.

Our bodies move together to fit him the rest of the way in but once he's fully sheathed, he freezes as do I. Fitting together like a perfectly matched lock and key buried deep in my core, it's like I can *feel* all the tumbler pins fall into place as he meets my inner walls, cementing the fact I've been trying desperately to ignore—this is different. He's different. *We're* fucking different.

After years of dealing with the wrong match again and again and again and ending in disappointment more times than not, being with Beckett is like running full speed at a semi-truck barreling toward you. The collision—imminent. Danger—inevitable. Carnage—every-fucking-where.

How are either of us supposed to survive this, let alone come out unscathed?

After getting our bearings, his hips thrust up into me while his arm on my back pulls me down and the contrast creates an aggressive sort of friction, kind of like hate-fucking, minus the hate. No, there's not an ounce of actual aggression in Beckett's movements. Just pure need. A need so strong, sparks ignite with every connection. Not bright sparks. Sparks you don't see until it's too late. The kind that burn entire countries to the ground before anyone even knows what happened.

We barely speak as our movements pick up speed but words aren't necessary. There are no directions when you're spinning out of control. And so, we fumble through whatever this is, both of us touching and kissing and groping and grinding on the other one until our movements grow messy, absolutely crazed for the other as we approach our final destination together.

Growling, Beckett rips his lips from mine so suddenly, my eyes jolt open.

"Swear to fuck, I'm about to lose it."

"What? Why?"

Everything in me tenses, including my pussy muscles clenched around Beckett still buried inside me.

"No, no, no. Don't do that yet. It's not you." His lips brush mine briefly. "It's this fucking thing." Twisting the top portion of his body, he uses his free hand to grab the shower curtain liner. "It's sticking to my ass." Then he yanks it, ripping the material clean off and sending some of the rings airborne as they fly off the rod broken. Only half of the actual shower curtain is still hanging in place with the plastic portion falling to the tub floor.

We both stare at the crumpled mess for a minute before meeting each other's eyes.

"You killed it."

"Nah, it's just-" he frowns, his bottom lip sticking out, "asleep."

Our laughs settle around us as thick as the humidity.

"You think that's funny?" he asks, getting ahold of himself first and pumping into me with long, slow strokes now that I'm relaxed again.

The laughter shrivels up into a tight ball of sensation and I nod, unable to speak from the unhurried pace. A piece of hair falls over my eyes and that same free hand he used to murder our shower curtain comes up to brush it away.

"There you are." His blue eyes hone in on mine. "I thought I lost you today. You hid."

I couldn't.

"You ran."

I wouldn't.

He pulls me tight to him so the base of his shaft hits my clit and I cry out sharply.

"This is what you want?"

His breath comes out in spurts while mine gets stuck in my throat. Beckett rotates his hips in circles, rubbing against my aching clit each time and I'm finally able to breathe again as it all rushes out at once.

"Yes," I moan. To his question. To the feeling building between my legs. To all of it.

I try to kiss him again, wanting to get fully lost in him, but he leans his mouth out of reach, still watching every expression cross my face. His continuous motion falters though and I see that moment of *oh shit* register. He's coming much sooner than he wanted. The short-lived self-satisfaction is quickly replaced by my own orgasm forming right behind his as my legs latched around his hips shake. With my toes curling almost painfully, my heels press him to me even harder.

Only a few more circular pumps and we both tumble across the finish line, clumsy and sweaty and loud. Very, very loud.

I slam my eyes shut against Beckett and the rest of the world. A little more time. I just need a little longer in this moment. With him. With us.

His forehead presses to mine, and he breathes, "Fuck."

I open my eyes again, watching Beckett's sharp jawline as he works to catch his breath.

Yes. Exactly. *Fuck.*

The water eventually runs cold so he lowers my legs to the floor as I reach to shut it off.

"Are you okay?"

"I'll be fine."

Even as the words that taste like a lie slip past my lips, I still hold on to that last bit of hope that I'm right. That this didn't just blow my plan to coast through life without being tied down wide open. Why the fuck did I think this would end in any way other than pain? Beckett and I have been drawn to each other since that first meeting with the magnetic pull only growing stronger with every encounter since.

But how can meaningless sex actually mean something? When did feelings enter the picture? And why did I let them?

Grabbing our respective towels, we dry off in silence. It's not exactly awkward but it's not *not* awkward either. My outside is quiet while my inside is anything but and I don't know how to reconcile the two. Not yet. Not now.

I need some time to process. Or avoid. Truthfully, either will work—I think.

He exits first, wrapping the towel around his trim waist, and takes a seat on the closed toilet lid as if he's settling in for the latest blockbuster. I follow after but keep my eyes on the task at hand, any task at hand, while Beckett's trail me like I'm the leading lady.

Wearing my own towel, I set about braiding my hair. Blow drying it will take forever and even though Beckett looks like he wouldn't mind the delay, my stomach is already full of butterflies on speed, so I braid it down the middle, hoping it'll at least make for some nice waves in the morning, and finish getting ready for bed.

Although I refuse to look at him, Beckett's gaze never wavers from me, taking in everything I'm doing from brushing my teeth to smoothing on lotion. He sits silently, just observing my mundane bedtime routine without so much as interrupting or falling asleep. I have no idea why he's doing it or why I like it so much.

Neither of us acknowledges the fact that he ruined both the shower curtain and me, and while I'll never be the same, the shower curtain can be replaced.

So can you, I think bitterly.

"Well, I'm off to bed," I say to the floor.

One foot out the door and Beckett is there instead, gripping me, steering me, tempting me. At his doorway, I finally turn to meet his eyes.

"Give me," he starts, then drops his hands smoothing them on his toweled waist, "give me this one night. That's all I can offer you. That's all I got."

"Beckett."

Leaning down to my eye level, he whispers, "Please?"

Tonight's the last night I'll be there to ward off his nightly ghosts, after that he's back on his own. A victim to whatever's plaguing him in his weakest state. He's a big boy though, he can fight his own battles.

But my body chooses for me by walking backward into his room, ready to take on Beckett's demons one last time.

"Hold that thought."

He returns to the bathroom, leaving me standing confused in my own towel until I hear the telltale sounds of him brushing his teeth.

With a shake of my head and a racing heart, I grab a shirt out of the first drawer I open and shove it over my head before peeling back his covers to climb in.

One night. All he wants is one night. All I want is one night. I can handle one night. He can handle one night. This is perfect. Absolutely perfect.

Isn't it?

CHAPTER 22

Paige

"SO, HAVE YOU HEARD FROM YOUR BROTHERS SINCE your birthday?" Cynthia asks over the phone.

Pulling into the parking lot of the guys' garage a few minutes before Cruz was ready—his boss wouldn't give him the time off after all—I called Cynthia to catch up. She just started her new job and filled me in on all the differences so far. She does well with the high stress situations often accompanying nursing positions so she should do amazing in the emergency room.

As far as I've seen in the days I've been back, Dennis, and the others, have been doing much better. Everyone except my mother. She's looking healthier from getting her medication regularly again, but she still doesn't seem quite herself. And maybe that part is just another piece of her slipping away to the disease. Another chunk of her DNA that makes her so uniquely her is just gone, forever lost to the turbulent sea of Alzheimer's. But that doesn't mean I have to like it. I refuse to accept this is the end and I never will.

My eyes flutter closed as I lean back on my bike, soaking in the sun. My face is almost back to normal and the rays of sunshine feel like forbidden kisses from a long-lost lover across my daylight deprived skin. It's taken the whole week to get adjusted to working nights and sleeping days again, that last one in particular has been especially hard. After Sunday night with Beckett, I returned to my room, to my bed, to my customary seclusion—to loneliness.

Marc's been gone all week. I have no idea where he went other than I saw him wheeling a suitcase out to his car one afternoon when I couldn't sleep and noticed he hasn't been back since. Yeah, sleep's been hard to come by lately.

"They've been checking in but this week is crazy," I say around a yawn, stretching my arm above my head to pick at my pillion. While it's true the boys have called to talk to me, none of them have made the effort to visit Mom which still frustrates me.

"I bet it is with those two hot roommates to keep you busy."

I snort, grateful nobody's around. I already scanned the lot, twice, for Beckett's bike, knowing he took it in place of his Tahoe today, and finding it strangely absent. It'll make this awkward lunch date with Cruz easier without him here. That's what I tell myself as I check the lot for the third time.

"I wouldn't put it that way."

"Are you telling me they're not? I saw them for myself, Paige."

Spotting a pizza delivery car pull in, I sit up and meet the busted ass Honda in front of my own busted ass Honda. At least mine is faster though. And thanks to Beckett, not quite as busted anymore. Although she still isn't special to most, she's precious to me. I pay the awkward teen with an extra tip for his excellent taste in rides when I catch him eyeing my baby. Too bad I'm on the phone or I'd let him rev the engine. That always gets the kids excited.

"I didn't say that." And I never would. Hot describes my roommates perfectly even if they're like night and day. Where Marc is an opaque depth warning you away from impending peril, Beckett is a sparkly surface just above a murky unknown coaxing you to come a little closer. "Sunbrook's just been insane, that's all. It hasn't left much time for anything else."

I would've assumed the garage was slammed, too, based off Cruz not being able to even break away for a quick bite but this place seems pretty tame compared to how he made it sound this morning. He apologized profusely but still wanted to go out. As he started hinting toward my cherished weekend, I quickly volunteered to bring lunch to him instead. It'd cross this stupid date off the list and leave my weekend open. Not that I have any plans but spending my only night off with Cruz sounds like a supreme waste of time. Time I could spend at home. Or something. I don't know. Going out just doesn't hold the same appeal anymore.

I haven't seen Beckett since the morning after our shower when I slipped from his bed unnoticed. When he begged me to stay the night with him, I assumed it was to play Red Rover, Red Rover, Send Beckett's Monster Cock Right Over again and I was right. The man is like a tree I want to climb.

Wanted. I *wanted* to climb. But that's done and over with now. *We* are done and over with. This date today proves that.

But, that was four days ago and the only reminder of the hours we spent together under his sheets are the hickeys littering my body. Beckett left marks everywhere. On every fucking part of me, even places I swore I'd never let him, or anyone else, reach.

Seeing his bike missing from Pop The Hood's lot fills me with more jitters than if it were here, front and center. *I think.*

I tune back in to Cynthia carrying on about her new coworkers.

"So, do you miss me already? How's the newest nurse? Please tell me Rosie hired someone with actual experience this time."

Rosie hired another nurse for nights but I'm not sure exactly why yet. I'm hoping it doesn't mean my time at Sunbrook is up. I still need time. I always need time.

"Oh, she's green. Like romaine."

Rosie's notorious for hiring girls fresh out of nursing school, thankfully, or else I would've never had the opportunity I have now.

"Hey, I gotta go," I tell her when I spot Cruz heading toward me. With a promise to hang out this weekend, I end the call and stand to meet him. He's covered in grease and gives me an awkward side hug.

"Thanks for bringing me food. I knew you were a keeper."

I hide my grimace as I follow him to the back of his pickup.

"I don't know about that." I do know. I'm not. "It doesn't look that busy. Did I just miss the rush?" I make a show of looking over the empty bays.

"Marc's M.I.A. right now and Beck's been taking off during lunch all week so we're short staffed at the moment." His hand reaches for my cheek but I pretend to shoo a fly away. "Beck asked me to take over the Gixxer he was working on before he left for lunch, but I'm happy to sneak away for you."

My eyes narrow while we eat on his open tailgate. "Do you usually work on bikes?" I don't remember seeing him working on any motorcycles when I came in with Beckett.

Cruz steals a pepperoni off my slice.

"Not really. That's Beck's thing but I can find my way around most undercarriages fairly well." He nudges my shoulder in what I'm guessing is flirtation but my eyes are still glued to the gaping hole of bare cheese on my pizza.

Gross. On both counts.

What I'd like to say is, "Well, don't let me keep you from sticking your fingers where they don't belong. I'll just be off now, staring at my ceiling until my shift starts."

What I actually say is, "Cool."

And I don't know which response is worse. Or why I'm still here.

What am I doing?

I scan the lot again, careful to add in a "hmm" every few words out of Cruz's mouth to keep the conversation flowing. Fortunately, the guy doesn't need much encouragement to run like Niagara Falls and soon I spot Angela coming out of one of the office doors just inside, giving me an excuse to wrap this date up tighter than a professional athlete's used condom—no room for negotiations here. None.

After cleaning up, we make our way over to Angela and chat while Cruz begins taking out parts that even I know shouldn't be removed. What was Beckett thinking?

My eyes flick to the open office door.

"Heard you guys are slammed. Did everyone take off and leave you to fend for yourself?" I ask Angela as she folds some towels for the wash. She's wearing a dark polo shirt half tucked into some khakis with her usual Aviators on the top of her head of long caramel hair. She somehow even manages to bring a beachy vibe to her work attire.

"It's not too bad. Marc goes wherever Marc goes often enough that we know how to pick up the slack while he's gone. Coty's good about not biting off more than he can chew." I raise my eyebrows looking back at her. "Well, not in business anyway." We both laugh. "And Beckett, I'm not sure what's going on there. I figured you would know."

"Me? Why would I know?"

"He's been leaving to go home for lunch every day this week. I thought you-" Confusion lines her face before her eyes catch on something over my shoulder then she looks between Cruz and the bike he's dissecting. Louder than any of our other conversation, she asks, "Did you two enjoy your date?"

Umm. What?

"Cruz!" Beckett barks from behind me making me jump. I didn't even hear his bike pull in. How long has he been here? "Put the fork down! It came in for new spark plugs, shitbird, you don't need to take off the fucking tires."

Cruz holds up both his hands to approach me with a rueful grin. "Okay. Maybe not all undercarriages are alike."

A loud scoff sounds behind me, closer than before, and I finally chance a look over my shoulder. My neck cranes up because damn, he's still so tall. Beckett's narrowed eyes soften slightly as they meet mine and my breath catches in my throat. My body yearns to go to his, to touch him in some way. Any way.

"Don't hold this against my skill set."

Huh? Oh, Cruz is still talking to me.

I face forward again, breaking the spell that had fallen over us. Or was it just me?

A peek over at a smiling Angela proves it wasn't.

"I think a second date is the only way to redeem yourself, Cruz," Angela says through a twinkling laugh.

"Don't you have to go on a first date to get a second?"

Cruz looks above me, answering his boss, "We just did. Paige brought the date to me. Isn't that sweet?"

"Sickeningly."

Cruz reaches for my…I don't even know, but I sidestep him, taking a sudden interest in the dismantled GX-R in Beckett's otherwise immaculate workspace.

"Where were you that you made Cruz take over a job he had no business doing?" I ask Beckett, feeling him at my side before I see him.

"Hey, I'm not that bad."

We both ignore Cruz's protest.

"Something came up," is all he says though.

I finally peel my eyes away from the wreckage spread at our feet and look at Beckett, finding him already watching me. Waiting.

"At the apartment?" I push.

"Maybe." He shrugs, holding my gaze and putting his hands in his front pockets. The muscles in his biceps flex, revealing some imprints of my nails. I left marks, too. I did climb that tree. Many times. And I didn't do it nicely.

Before I can question him further, Angela speaks up, saying, "I know. Why don't you come with us this weekend to the Gorge? We're all going to a huge music festival. We got a bunch of tents for glamping. You should join us." Beckett's eyes grow almost hopeful and I drop mine. "You too, Cruz. You guys can get to know each other better."

I swear there's something in Angela's voice that has me doubting her sincerity. What's she up to?

"Angie! The fuck? You can't invite everyone," Beckett shifts his gaze to Cruz, "and their dog. We didn't reserve that many tents."

"I have a tent I can bring," Cruz offers, his face lighting up like a Christmas tree.

I shake my head. "I have to work."

"Is Saturday still your day off?" Beckett asks and I nod. "We can ride together Saturday morning...after you get off."

I cock an eyebrow at his choice of words. He knows what he said and he's not backing off. Not with that guilty grin plastered to his face.

"You can crash with me," Cruz offers. "I'm sure I can make enough room for both of us."

Does anyone have a mute button? Holy shit, Cruz doesn't stop talking. Beckett looks like he's about to make one himself if I don't say something soon.

"But we need your SUV, Beckett. It's called glamping for a reason. All the shit we need won't fit in Coty's Camaro and it'll just blow out of my Jeep. And I'm not risking scuffing Marc's precious interior," Angela adds.

Beckett rolls his eyes. "You worked at a coffee stand for like five minutes. Why do you have to take your fancy espresso machine everywhere now?"

"You helped buy it for me! And you like my coffee," she shoots back, a grin tugging at her mouth.

Throwing up my hands, I start to back out of the bay. "I'll have my friend, Cynthia, take me." It's no rave—I don't think—but she loves to dance and we could both use the change in scenery.

"I bet three can fit fine in my tent," Cruz chirps unhelpfully, earning a death glare sent down from Beckett.

"Thanks for the invite," I say to Angela. "I'll see you all on Saturday."

Spinning on my booted heels, I dash across the lot for a quick exit before I have to deal with Cruz a second longer. I did not agree to another date with him. He's in for a rude awakening when I show up with one of Jesse's tents. I'll even buy one before I sleep in the same tent as that guy. If he's that grabby with pizza toppings that aren't his, I can't even imagine what else he'll try to touch without asking.

Just as I reach my bike, I hear Cruz call out a goodbye followed by an arrogant-as-shit Beckett asking me something.

What'd he say?

"Where's my shirt by the way? You didn't leave it somewhere in my room before you left, did you? I've been looking for it but can't find it anywhere."

Oh. My. God.

His self-satisfied smirk is on full display as I shift on my feet. Every set of eyes in the garage is glued to me as I mount my white and gray bike and lower one of the passenger foot rests, buying time. But why would he do that in front of everyone?

Unless he's purposely rubbing it in Cruz's face that we slept together. On the plus side, he probably won't be wanting that second date now.

Angela stands off to the side with wide eyes taking in the scene. Cruz said Beckett had been taking lunch off every day this week and Angela revealed he was going to the apartment but if that's true, why hasn't he said anything when he's there? Better yet, why haven't I noticed?

"I thought it looked better on me," I say with a shrug while affixing my helmet, leaving the visor open. "You want it back?" I jerk my chin at him and watch his smile grow. "Come find it."

Engine roaring to life, I shift into first and fly out of the lot but not before pulling up into a wheelie, using the back footrest to kneel on just to show the onlookers exactly how unruffled my feathers are.

So what if I slept in his shirt? And who cares if I've been wearing it to bed ever since? His sweet earthy smell still clings to the soft material and it helps clear my head after a long shift full of sadness and futility. It's the only reason I've been able to get the little bit of sleep so far this week that I have, and I'm not giving that up.

And fuck Beckett if he thinks he's getting it back anytime soon. Like I said, if he wants it, he can damn well come and try to take it from me.

CHAPTER 23

Beckett

DAYUM.

Pretty sure I'll never get tired of messing with Paige. Chick is just too damn fun to rile up, plus she never backs down. Ever. Most girls would've been embarrassed or pissed about what I just said and how I said it. Yeah, I know it was a dick move insinuating we fucked publicly, at my place of business no less, but I couldn't help it. I wanted every guy here to know that something is going on between me and Paige. Plus, teasing her gets my blood pumping like no other.

I should go after her.

Dumbfuck McGee shuffles on his feet next to me as we both gawk after Paige.

Fuck me, can she ride. And not just her bike either. Remembering how well she maneuvers whatever she's straddling has my dick growing hard.

I'm going after her.

Just as I move to follow though, Cruz stumbles beside me, "Hey, man, I didn't know it was like that between you two."

Well, that does the trick. My dick now fully scared off by this shit-for-brains talking about my…Paige, I turn to press down on him.

"It doesn't matter what it's like." Or not. Just 'cause we hooked up doesn't mean we're still hooking up, but Cruz doesn't need to know all that. He still can't have her.

"Yo, B! That chick hit up your bed? She ride like that out of the streets, too?" another one of my guys jokes and my spine stiffens with my fists tightening at my sides. *Motherfucker.*

"Listen up!" I call out to every idiot in the joint. Angela stays quiet off to the side, holding in a laugh and I resist flipping her off. Little shit set me up with that date talk and she knows it. "Paige, hot ass biker chick, my roommate, whatever you want to call her," someone mutters "fuck buddy" and I growl, silencing any more wannabe hecklers, "she's off-fucking-limits to all of you assholes."

A chorus of complaints fill the shop but I don't stick around to listen. I laid down the law and that's that.

Arriving to Creekwood earlier to find the apartment empty scared the shit out of me. I've been going home every day, knowing Paige was there. I don't know why exactly but I liked knowing she was home, safe. I never bothered her. Just knowing she was there was enough. Since she snuck out of my bed like a thief in the night, I haven't caught sight of her once and my afternoon visits to the apartment were the only thing keeping me from convincing the guys switching my shift to nights was a good idea. It's not completely unheard of for people to have car troubles in the middle of the night too, okay?

The worry lessened the second I saw her here before turning sour in my stomach when I realized she wasn't here for me. I'd hoped for a brief moment that she was being pulled toward me like I've been drawn to her. But no, she was on a *date* with Cruz—soon to be known as Numb Nuts if he mentions sharing a tent with her again.

Over my dead body.

"Here." I hand off the bag of doughnuts I picked up as Angela and I enter the main office, the cool air blasting my face a welcome relief.

Peeking inside, she scowls. "You don't need to buy me food all the time."

"Yeah, well, old habits die hard. And so do people that don't eat, so chomp chomp. Coty's orders." Not really, but I know he still worries about her previous eating patterns resurfacing just like the rest of us, so she can deal with it, whether she likes it or not.

"You're in so much trouble."

I ignore Angela, choosing to dive into the paperwork Coty left behind while he's out scouting location options for a second shop.

"You do know that, right? Beckett?"

"Angie, I love you, I really do, but if you try to set Paige up with another one of my employees, you'll be out back using the hose to wash cars by hand."

"Ha!" she barks out while I struggle to find the humor in that statement. I'll go hook that shit up right now. I'll even scribble out a little sign that says *FREE CAR WASH, DONATIONS ACCEPTED* for her. See if she's still laughing then. I think not. "What about someone that's not on your payroll then?"

I drop the paper to the desk, leveling her with my best authoritative look I can muster.

"You're fired."

Chick just snorts. "Lucky for you, you can't fire me."

"You mean lucky for *you*."

She takes in the office like she's a fucking tourist even though it's as much hers as it is ours. The three of us may have bought and built the place from the ground up, but Angela is the blood flowing through the veins making it a living, breathing force that none of us could've predicted.

"No, I mean you. If you fire me then Coty will kick your ass," now I'm the one snorting, "and hire me back anyway." She cheeses one of her best smiles at me and I melt a little. Like a tiny bit. The rest of me is still bitter as fuck about her trying to play matchmaker with Paige and, well, anybody. No, I don't like that one bit.

"Alright, fine. You can stay. Don't get your panties in a twist."

"Don't talk about my panties." She waits a beat then adds, "It's unprofessional."

"Why can't I talk about your panties? I used to see the fucking things every time I went to do laundry." Her jaw drops. "Yeah, the whole building saw your dental floss with fringe," I say, working to keep my laugh in.

Our building at Creekwood shares a laundry room and while there were many times I had to switch over her clothes when she lived next door to us, I don't remember the exact details of her underwear. As a general rule, I don't creep on my boys' women.

Eyes closed, breath held, I'd grab them with another article of clothing used as a glove then just sort of toss them in the direction of the dryer. If they made it in, sweet. If not, well, Gary from down the hall probably stole them for spank bank material. The old bastard needs it. I've never seen him host a single visitor since we moved onto the same floor as him years ago.

Now if he stole Paige's panties, that'd be a different situation. I'd have to…

"Why didn't you ever pick them up then?" Angie screeches, bringing me back to the conversation at hand. "That's so embarrassing," she whines, making me finally let out the laughter blocking my throat. "Whatever, crotch-mouth."

I cock an eyebrow at her. *Who's unprofessional now?*

"And FYI mine *never* had fringe. What kind of old ass women have you been with lately to know what fringe is anyway?"

I shrug my shoulders. "I haven't been with anyone actually. Not since…"

Wait. Have I really not smashed anyone since she moved in? There were a couple stragglers I thought about trying with but just couldn't make myself go through with it.

Angela plants her ass on the desk, looking me in the eye. "What are you doing?" At my silence, she continues, "With Paige. Are you two friends? Dating? Playing hide the drive shaft?"

My head shakes automatically. "What the hell kind of kinky shit do you and Coty get up to after hours?"

"Who says it's after hours?" she deadpans, making us both crack up. "I tried asking her but she's just as stubborn as you are. Maybe worse."

My ears perk up. "You guys talk about me?"

"Define talk."

"You know, where you gush about how hot I am and brag about all the charity work I do."

"Mmm," Angie pretends to think it over, "no, there was no gushing. And you don't do any charity work."

"I'm friends with your ass. What would you call that?"

She waves me away, not taking any of my shit. "Quit changing the subject. There's something different about you now. You care about her."

I'm not sure what she's getting at.

"She's my roommate," I say like that clears up any confusion. I mean, yeah, we live under the same roof but my feelings for her have nothing to do with where we lay our heads. I'd be attracted to her whether we lived together or not. It just so happens her close proximity makes things easier.

I almost laugh out loud. Nothing about Paige is easy.

Angela's hazel eyes squint at me. "Does she sleep in Marc's bed, too?"

I stand so suddenly my thighs knock into the desk and she has to steady herself so she doesn't fall off. She doesn't cower though. There's no reason to. I'd never hurt her or any female. She's pushing my buttons on purpose. She wants a rise out of me and talking about Paige in another guy's bed does just that.

"No, she doesn't. Fuck. You. Very. Much," I enunciate each word, louder for the people in the back. "And she never will if I have anything to say about it," I promise, deadass serious.

"And why do you think you have a say? Who are you to her?"

"I-" Well, damn if Angela didn't just hand me my own ass.

Who am I to Paige?

We had sex, amazing sex, but she hasn't even reached out to me. Not even with a cheesy-ass text like "hey." Or to tell me we're out of milk. Or to buy a new shower curtain. I can afford a thousand new shower curtains but I can't bring myself to replace the only physical evidence of what happened between us. That and the scratches decorating my back and arms right now.

That girl is under my skin in more ways than one.

I slump back in the seat. "Fuck, I don't know. I don't know what I'm doing, Angie. She's fucking everywhere. She's all I think about, all I see. She's a fucking mess and I'm a fucking wreck. We do not go together. We shouldn't. But-"

"But?" she urges patiently.

"But I literally can't stop myself from wanting her. It's like a sickness I never want the cure for."

"How deep are you?"

"Deep? Like love?" The idea of falling in love right now makes my skin prickle. "No, I think you misunderstood what I meant. I don't love her. I just like to-"

"Fuck her?" Angie stands, straightening her shirt. She always fidgets, not knowing what to do with her hands if they aren't busy with something. Let's just say Pop The Hood never runs out of freshly laundered and folded towels.

I frown at her directness. Fucking Paige then moving on doesn't sound as appealing as I made it sound in my head. As I made it sound when I was convincing her back into my bed.

"That's what I thought. You're different from before and you know it. You're just fucking around, wasting time. Grow a pair and figure out what you want, then let her know. She deserves that, especially with all the shit she's going through. In the meantime, stop acting like the spoiled brat you are," I finally give in and flip her off, "by marking territory that isn't even yours."

Snickering, I stand as well, wrapping her in a hug.

"Did you not hear me the first time? Chick rode my tongue like she was in a fucking rodeo." She rode something else just as good, too.

Angie smacks me away with a grimace and I tell her, "That territory is definitely mine."

"Then you better get your ass back in the ring or she might find someone else to ride."

Uh, no. I like that idea even less.

Before we leave the office—I don't know what the fuck I was thinking with this paperwork bullshit, plus I've got a project I need to finish before our new hire shows up—Angela stops, instantly serious and asks, "What if she meets someone at the festival?"

"Then I better bring two shovels." Her eyebrows nearly collide. "One for each of us so we can bury the fucker together. We both know Coty wouldn't last one night in jail and Marc fits the profile of a murderer a little too easily, he'd be caught immediately. You're my only hope, neighbor girl."

I'm promptly shoved out the door—only because I let her push me—and we return to work with a pair of matching smirks that may or may not lean on the evil side.

She knows I'm right.

CHAPTER 24

Beckett

"I LOVE THIS PLACE," COTY SAYS WHILE STRETCHING, taking in the morning light over the river, the song "Tired Of You" by Foo Fighters is playing from the Bluetooth speaker I brought along.

We arrived last night and slept like shit, or maybe that's just me. Whatever. These glamorous tents are an oxymoron if I've ever heard one and they're definitely not all they're cracked up to be. Glamping is exactly like camping but with more space, not amenities, save for the one outlet each tent gets. *Yip-fucking-ee.*

Thankfully we had the foresight to reserve theses tents though because they have actual beds instead of the cots provided down the hill from our site. I'd rather sleep in my Tahoe than on a fucking cot. The thick canvas walls are not soundproof by any means and Coty and Angie proved that last night. Multiple times. Goddamn, I don't miss that part of having him as a roommate.

It didn't help that my tent was as dead as an abandoned cemetery all night. There are plenty of chicks around this place, it's almost too easy, but none that have caught my eye. Not that they could anyway with Paige on her way today.

"Dude, she'll be here. Looking at your watch isn't gonna make her appear any faster."

"Oh, would you look at that? It's half past fuck you." I flip Coty the bird then quickly dodge the roll of paper towels he throws at me. I'm not picking that shit up either. Let one of these earth-loving freaks chew his ass out for littering, see how well that goes over.

Yeah, okay, I was checking the time—again. But I can't text Paige to see when she'll get here or she'll end up taking a detour just to spite me. Chick lives to stick it to me. And if I'm being honest, I wouldn't mind sticking it to her again, too.

I groan, sick of thinking dirty thoughts about the girl I already had in my arms less than a week ago. Why wasn't it enough to perform all those naughty things on Paige once and for all?

Because, like Angie so snarkily pointed out, Paige is different. No, not just Paige. Me. I'm different. Sleeping with her that night should've ended this...infatuation, but it hasn't. Not in the slightest. If anything, it's intensified—tenfold.

Maybe, just maybe, we can find some time this weekend to explore our options. Like which days of the week I can sneak home for a quickie. That's always an option, right?

Fuck, I'm not good with this shit. I'm not cut out for the domestic life either. And that's not to say Paige would even want that. Would she?

Coty doesn't make it look half bad but he's got a *life* partner in all this. Angela's his equal, even if she doesn't believe it yet. Her mom cast her away like Tom Hanks in that movie. But what Angie fails to realize is Coty's not that pathetic volleyball placating her loneliness until the next flimsy wave whisks him away for good, he's the fucking island built to withstand the fiercest of storms. His love will outlast the harshest conditions in the support he provides her.

I'm not that. I don't think I could ever be that. Not for Paige. Not for anyone.

I'm the palm tree that provides temporary relief when things get unbearable. But when the clouds come rolling in, what good am I? What can I really offer anyone when I'm weathering storms of my own?

Fuck.

Sitting here isn't doing me any good and if I don't find something to eat now, I'll pounce on Paige as soon as she shows—whenever the fuck that is—because ever since that little face-off at the shop, I've been hankering for more of what I feasted on just last weekend.

◆ ◆ ◆

A few hours later, I'm trashed out of my mind and ready to fuck or fight, both if I can find Paige—hopefully.

Marc sees me coming from across our glampsite—seriously, that's what it's called—and smirks. Dude's just sitting in front of a nice little spread of dirt like it's a roaring campfire. Open flames aren't allowed with how dry it gets out here so a dirt pit it is. But why is he here by himself when everybody else is out mingling, having fun? And why is he looking at me like he knows something I don't?

Oh, shit.

"Is she here?" I slur.

With a nod of his head he gestures to my tent. My hands immediately start rubbing together in anticipation. *Hell yeah.* She knew where she was sleeping tonight and I didn't even have to fight to get her there.

Unfortunately, as soon as I move for the tent, *my* fucking tent, Marc holds up his hand to stop me.

What now?

"She's sleeping."

"Thanks for the heads up," I mock. Like I give a shit. I wasn't gonna wake her. I mean, I wasn't gonna *try* to wake her.

"No man, she's..." He chances a look around, fully freaking me the fuck out. "She's not alone."

Oh hell no.

Dropping my head back, I look up to the sky, praying for a single iota of restraint because now is not the fucking time.

Coming back to reality, I scan our site, noticing Cruz's truck.

"If Cruz is in there, you should just call my dad now and tell him to meet me at county. Imma kill this motherfucker."

Marc meets my stare and...laughs? Like doubles over, holding his stomach, guffaws. Meanwhile, my jaw ticks out a nice little countdown. Not like a common timer either, like a bomb.

3, 2, 1.

I shove past his shaking form to rip open the pathetic excuse of a door and there in my bed is what fantasies are made of. Well, if the two hot chicks weren't passed out, drooling all over my fucking pillow. I *always* bring my own pillow. I like the amount of stuffing it has. It also makes for easier clean up if I wake up bloody, which has started back up again this week.

Paige's friend beside her flips to her side revealing it is, in fact, Cynthia. She is cute—if you're into mouth breathers. I'm more interested in the beautiful woman next to her though. Damn if she isn't just as captivating sleeping as she is when she's fired up, calling my ass out.

My chest releases some of the tension that's been there since she left me cold and alone in my bed back home. I missed her.

I miss her.

Looking back to her slumbering friend, I frown. She's in my spot. My alcohol fueled mentality tempts me with a chance at a fight if I wake them now. Paige would never let that shit fly.

I smile as my dick twitches at the hint of confrontation but before I can test my drunken theory, Marc grips my shoulder, pulling me back outside.

"They both got off graveyard shifts and drove straight here. Don't be a dick. Let them sleep. You can have my tent to sleep off your own shit," his hands wave at all of me, "and see her when you're sober."

"Who do you think you are? The voice of treason?"

With a roll of his eyes, dude just pushes me toward his uber glammed out tent. *Not.* Shit's just like mine. I go willingly though since I need the privacy anyway and with my phone already in hand, I place the call I've been waiting all day to make now that the coast is clear. A little liquid courage helps and the plan gets set in motion just before I drift off on a pillow that's not mine.

Man, I want my pillow back—with the girl currently occupying it still attached.

That's the last thought I have as I pass out.

CHAPTER 25

Paige

MILLIONS OF FLOATING BUBBLES FILL THE SKY AS THE sun begins to set for the day, bringing a whimsical feel to the already dream-like festival.

Cynthia grabs my hand along with Angela's and together we spin in circles enjoying the surreal moment. Arms spread wide, we whirl around faster and faster, only stopping to dance to the beat of the indie band on stage.

Cynthia's hair is pulled tight into two buns with glitter caked on her middle part while Angela's is braided down both sides with purple and pink strips mixed in to create an ombre effect. Mine hangs in loose waves around my confetti-covered cheekbones and hairline. We certainly look the part of carefree partiers even if we're not. Today though, after using Beckett's spacious tent to get ready in, we made a pact to shed all our worries, only if just for one night.

Cynthia fist pumps in the air Jersey-style making us lose it laughing amid the sea of other gyrating concert goers.

"I can't wait until Beckett sees you!" Angela yells over the thumping bass and I smile. It should be interesting, that's for sure.

Upon waking up—Cynthia also pulled an all-nighter at her new job—we hit up the carnival rides before returning to the designated campsite to get ready for the night festivities.

With Beckett still sleeping off his own good time apparently, we left the boys behind.

I tried talking Marc up to Cynthia the entire ride here but as soon as she caught sight of Cruz she forgot all about my reserved roommate. Then, as I introduced the two, Cruz treated me like he'd never met me, let alone stolen coveted toppings from my pizza just days prior. I'd been planning on pulling him aside anyway to tell him things weren't going to go any further than our pitiful parking lot lunch but he saved me the trouble by redirecting his heart eyes to Cynthia. The guy moves fast—onward and upward, I guess. I just hope Cynthia can catch him if that's what she wants. Or have a fun little fling for the night.

And I do mean little. His tent is *so* much smaller than he let on. It kind of makes me wonder if he has a habit of overcompensating when it comes to size.

Jesse's tent had a hole in it so I wasn't able to borrow his but Angela assured us there would be room for everyone. It should be funny to see Marc and Beckett flip a coin to see who gets to be the big spoon tonight. I can't imagine Marc losing that one. Beckett may be bigger, but Marc a little spoon? No way.

"I'm starving. Let's check out the food trucks."

Cynthia nods like an overzealous bobblehead as Angela agrees easily and together we hop from truck-to-truck, trying out the different offerings, joking with each other the entire time. Angela's witty sense of humor has Cynthia and me rolling in hysterics at a nearby picnic table when one of the bigger names takes the stage.

The guys still haven't shown up—not that I've been keeping an eye out or anything—so we debate whether we should wait for them or do our own thing. We decide to take our desserts to-go and make our way back to the lawn overlooking the amphitheater that's nestled just above the river. They can find us. That I don't doubt for a second.

We meander around for a while, taking in the breathtaking views and snapping silly pics along the way. The three of us finally claim a space in the grass that'll fit us and the guys, whenever they show up.

I lose myself to the music and the views, just moving to a beat only my heart can feel. One my body doesn't need to hear to know the lyrics. Having so many people around all the time during my childhood, I began to crave alone time. That's why my own apartment meant so much to me. I took great pleasure in being by myself there. Even in my new shared apartment, I reveled in my solitude my roommates' opposite schedules provided. But since growing closer to Beckett, and his friends, the seclusion doesn't feel as enjoyable as it once did. It's grown cold and unpleasant, like a day-old steak that never tastes as good as the first time around. There's a difference between being alone and being lonely, and this week I've been lonely as all hell. Maybe even more so than when my brothers were giving me their stubborn ass cold shoulders because as lonesome as I was before, it was never like this. Never had me itching in my own skin to reach out to another. To *one* other.

I shake the thought away. Roommates by circumstance, friends by accident, Beckett and I are not meant to have a happily-ever-after. At this point I'd settle for a content-ever-after by myself, but even that's a stretch without adding the 6'6" player to the mix.

I spot Coty, Marc, and Cruz in a group of what looks like a pack of salivating she-wolves, if she-wolves were half naked and so shimmery they could double as disco balls.

Tapping Angela's shoulder, I point over to them. To my surprise, she just laughs and continues dancing unconcerned. Coty, the ultimate man candy dressed in a dark deep V-neck and jeans that hug his slim hips just right, is surrounded by ravenous girls and she laughs? Maybe this is her part of no worries tonight? We never said your dignity though. She needs to get in there and claim her man.

When I don't so much as move, Angela stops, shaking her head. "They're not after him. It's been like that since we got here. It's Beckett they're after." She watches me closely. "He's been getting mobbed everywhere he goes."

Hold on.

Why the hell would they be after Beckett? I mean, aside from how good looking he is. And how sweet he can be. And how well he washes hair.

Okay, I get it, but I don't want to have to watch that. Especially when I'm trying to let loose and have my own good time tonight. That…doesn't sound fun. At all. For me.

Marc's eyes catch mine and his lips tip up as he scans my outfit then nudges Coty next to him, nodding my way. Coty's face splits into a grin as he takes in my dress, too. I'm glad they think it's funny. I'm still not sure how the big guy will take it.

"He seems to enjoy it though," Angela adds, side-eyeing me. "Don't you think?"

Just then the sea of bodies parts and there in the middle of the estrogen-fueled surf is my tsunami-sized roommate getting his picture taken from every angle, including selfies from a steady line of females ranging from tweens to cougars.

Something about seeing the snap-happy line bothers me. The smile stretching his face bothers me. The fact he's using it for them bothers me more.

When my gaze finally leaves his face, I see exactly why they're all gathered around him. The festival is named after Bigfoot himself so naturally all the 'grammers want to snap a pic with the tallest guy at the venue, especially when he's wearing a shirt that says *Ask Me About My Bigfoot*. And yes, he does seem to be enjoying himself. A little too much. Like way too much.

The more flashes go off, the more people join the throng of picture takers. They all think they're so clever, but if everyone has the same idea, that doesn't make you unique, it just makes you a part of the herd.

Two girls in matching thongs and bras with butterfly wings attached to the backs step up on both sides of Beckett to kiss each of his cheeks. His smile between the pair grows while vomit fills my throat.

His eyes meet mine for a split second before dropping, lingering for a beat, then snapping back to my face. The smile disappears right off his face and imagine that, I can swallow easier.

This should definitely be interesting.

I harden my stare, aiming my optic daggers at the semi-nude butterflies beside him before throwing him an unimpressed look. Turning around, I get back into the music. Whatever he chooses to do—or who—I'll still be here, doing my thing, having the best time because I need it. God, do I need it. And I'm not going to let him, or anyone else, ruin that.

I just wish he'd take his sideshow somewhere else. Somewhere I can't see it.

Several songs later though and I'm back to being alone. Alone in a crowd of thousands. This time I don't let the loneliness creep back in. Instead I welcome the freedom to move without limitations, to speak a language nobody else can decipher using only my mind and body. The two work in perfect harmony until everything else is blocked out and it's just me and the music and the music and me.

An up-and-coming rapper named, Julez, takes the stage along with the well-known pop singer, Collette. He's playing a guitar and belting lyrics while she croons into their shared mic. Their chemistry is palpable even from here and if they're not sleeping together already, they should be. I can't take my eyes off them and neither can Cynthia and Angela. Not until an arm snakes around Angela's exposed midriff. She's rocking a strappy halter top, a cut off skirt, and Continentals—the girl has a different pair of shoes every time I see her—but my eyebrows nosedive when the guy's face comes into view.

Soon Angela realizes it's not her man dancing so intimately with her and tries to throw the unfamiliar arm off but to no avail as it only tightens that much more.

With my arms in the air, winding above my head, I start to lower them when they're suddenly captured by two unrecognizable hands and held in place as I'm yanked back into an unyielding chest.

Hot breath trickles out like air in a deflating balloon on my neck. "Chill, babe. They'll be gentle."

Cynthia, in high-waisted pants, a short tube top, and Converse, tries to move closer to help out but is stopped when a guy steps in front of her. Her wide eyes fly to mine as she's guided backward, away from our trio.

What's happening? Divide and conquer? Survival of the fittest? Is that really a method for getting girls? We're not cattle.

Cracked lips that make my skin crawl touch my ear, whispering, "I can't say the same for me though."

Yeah, we're done here.

"Neither can I."

Just as teeth clamp down on the shell of my ear, I shove my ass as hard as I can into the disgusting groin plastered to my backside, freeing my hands in the same instant but nicking my ear in the process.

Worth it.

Swinging around, my elbow lances the side of his face making him sink to the ground.

"Rough enough for you?" I taunt as he tries to cradle his cheek and balls at the same time.

Angela, eyes locked on mine, jerks her head back, nailing the guy behind her square in the nose.

With a howl and some colorful words, he releases her, dropping to his knees all while blood rushes down his face. She winces briefly but it's hard to tell if it's from the headbutt or if his hold was that painful.

What assholes.

Luckily, she's able to shake it off and we turn together to see the tips of Cynthia's nails digging into the broad shoulders blocking the rest of her from view. As one, we surge forward only to be cut off by three menacing figures, one taller than the rest.

Only using one hand, Marc grips Cynthia's aggressor by the throat, tearing him away and tossing him like he weighs nothing. All three shout obscenities from the ground but what do they have to complain about? We're the ones being felt up without consent.

Yeah, my body's a wonderland but for who I choose to give a ride to. And when. That's the clause some people skip over in their haste to get past the gates. One ticket doesn't equal an entire wristband. Each one is earned. Every single time. Nobody gets unlimited free rides.

Cynthia manages to keep her shit together long enough to stand alongside us in a unified front and looking both girls over, I know we're all thinking the same thing.

Knocking Angela's attacker to his back, Coty mashes the toe of his boot against the guy's throat while his friends squirm in abrupt silence beside him. Marc hovers like a drone with a low battery, just waiting to fucking drop, and the hulk formerly known as Beckett towers over the guy still cradling his nuts.

Nobody says a word as the music plays on, the tempo building like the sexual tension coming from the stage. Other concert goers look over, trying to catch a piece of the action but none dare to interrupt.

The three men standing over the three pieces of shit currently contaminating the grass are fuming with barely contained rage but honestly, it's getting kind of ridiculous. This isn't the 1800s and we're not damsels in distress. We handled it. Well, we would've if it weren't for Coty and my roommates stepping in like superheroes straight out of boot camp—all pomp and no follow-through.

Cruz appears out of nowhere to join us and Cynthia turns into his shoulder, accepting the support he's offering in his own way. Not the other shitheads though. Nope. They'd rather plunder ahead in their testosterone-soaked mission than check to see if we're actually okay. As much as I appreciate their protection, this whole thing appears to be more about them than us.

"Thanks for your help but we got it." I nod at Angela rubbing the back of her head as she watches the scene unfold through narrowed eyes. Cynthia lifts hers in agreement and even though I know all she wants to do is collapse into herself right now, I respect her for trying, for putting on a tough air when it's taking everything out of her. She deserves better than being preyed on by someone with no concept of boundaries. We all do.

Beckett snaps out of his untamed fury, meeting my death stare with one of his own. "The fuck does that mean? These assholes were all over you. You're bleeding for fuck's sake!"

Instinctively, I reach for my earlobe and, sure enough, pull away a lone bloodied fingertip. *Fantastic.* Just as one injury heals, another pops up right behind it.

"No shit! But in case you hadn't noticed, we took care of it. We didn't need you riding in like some kind of fucking mod squad. If we needed help, we would've asked for it."

Beckett rocks side to side, adjusting his hat while Coty and Marc give nearly identical reactions—no remorse whatsoever.

Angela gives her man a flat look with a hint of a promise to it. Marc's off the hook since he didn't technically have a reason to step in. If anything, I would've expected Cruz to come to Cynthia's rescue. And Beckett, he can kiss my ass.

Wasn't he just getting his ass kissed? By *lots* of willing participants. It's a miracle he even noticed anything other than the bright flashes being thrust in his face every few minutes.

I cock an eyebrow, watching him shift from one foot to the other like he's got somewhere to be. And maybe he does. Maybe he already secured another tent to stay in tonight.

That would be just phenomenal. Spectacular even. The very reason I came here—to see Beckett with someone else.

Why did I come here?

With everyone distracted, one of the guys on the ground tries for a quick escape and the matter gets forgotten along with the self-control the boys were practicing because fists start flying while threats start sounding.

"You fucked up touching my girl."

Coty.

"All you pieces of shit are the same."

Marc?

"Bitch likes it rough, man. Look at her!"

When exactly has the "she was asking for it" excuse ever applied? Is *never* definitive enough of an answer? Unfortunately not, apparently.

"Motherfucker, I'm gonna kill you."

Beckett.

A bone-splintering crunch causes a gasp somewhere from my left but I can't tear my eyes off Beckett as he lays into the writhing mess below him. His anger is palpable, his intent clear. He will end him.

At some point I stop viewing the fight as an interested spectator and start watching as an invested member of the group. Beckett maintains most of my concentration but the others aren't far behind in my worry for their well-being. I may have something to lose here, too.

Or do I?

"Cruz, get them before someone gets killed," I order with a quiver in my voice.

Beckett's doing something to me.

I look over the others, one by one, landing on Angela last.

They all are.

Cruz works to separate the two groups but only one trio is left standing—mine.

Where did that come from?

I do a quick scan of each of them, checking for injuries, but they appear minimal, allowing me to finally take a full breath.

So, the pretty boys can fight after all. My brothers were scrappers, too. I think Jesse's first step was taken as he was landing his first punch actually. My dad was the one to show us how to take care of ourselves and each other. He knew that having four older brothers could make me soft, always relying on my siblings to stick up for me, but he didn't want that for his only girl. I was never Daddy's little princess. I was brought up just like the boys, learning to fight my way out of any situation that called for it, even against said brothers on certain occasions. And in a family with five kids, there was no shortage of scrapes. Ever.

His tutelage may have stopped when he died but my rebellious streak never did. I was taught not to cower to anyone, least of all some prick with grab hands, and that's not about to change because of one eye-opening concert.

Beckett catches my eye again but I don't break the spell, staring right back as his chest rises and falls with purpose and mine swells with...gratitude? I don't know what else to call it but it's warm and strong and threatens to consume me. All of me.

Just like Beckett.

Leaving the heaps of sad excuses of men on the ground, Cynthia, Angela, and I start walking before security can bust us. Our guys will catch up—if they know what's good for them.

CHAPTER 26

Paige

We make it back to the outdoor food court without incident and immediately start seeking out an open misting station. We're all hot and sticky, but more importantly fired up. The girls from the altercation, the boys from their fights, and everyone from the hormones provoked by that last one. It could just be me, but the hungry gazes being tossed around like smoke bombs during battle say otherwise.

Shots fired.

And now we wait for the chaos to ensue.

The high temps aren't showing any signs of dropping even without the sun's notorious presence and every one of the misters is crowded. Some are packed with actual overheated faces while others are full of influencer-types looking for a noteworthy shot. There are lots of those circle lights and people lying on the ground to get the best angle to make the overhead sprinkler look trendy. Or sexy or whatever. I just want to cool off.

Once a group finally leaves, we gather under the mist, getting just wet enough to feel relief but not enough to ruin our makeup. Our faces are caked in makeup and glitter, mainly because none of us are very good at applying either.

The boys, hot on our heels, join but forgo the same reservations about getting wet. All four stand in the middle of the fine mist, making me wish there was a higher setting option.

Holy. Hotness.

It's like watching four ripped—okay, three and one mildly average—firemen get drenched by the spray-back from putting out a nearby fire, except they're not extinguishing anything. Not really. Judging from the needy looks from other females around the edges, they're igniting much more than they realize. If they so much as lose their shirts, we won't even be able to stop the masses from swarming. It'll be apocalyptic—every woman, and probably some men, for themselves.

My eyes travel over Beckett, his damp shirt glued to his tense body like a second skin and I know without a shadow of a doubt I'd join the horde. I've not only seen what all of Beckett's rippled, glistening muscles look like up close, but I've *felt* them, so I understand what the others circling our personal watering hole are thirsting for. And Beckett's body, it goes on for miles.

Clenching my thighs together, I squeeze my eyes shut, inhaling deeply.

Shit.

When I reopen them, Beckett's watching me with something unidentifiable prowling in his gaze. Something primal. Something urgent and not open for debate. Whatever it is, I'm almost positive my eyes are its mirror image right now.

Coty hooks an arm around Angela's neck, keeping her secure in the crook of his elbow as he whispers in her ear. With a shaky exhale, he kisses her with a need so bright it forces some to look away. Angela relaxes into his chest, swaying seamlessly to the song in the distance and, noticing the way her face lights up when she closes her eyes, breathing in his nearly visible love for her, I can't help but wonder what that must feel like. To trust someone with your heart that's not even pumping the same blood in theirs?

I know from experience family betrayal can cause the worst pain imaginable but Angela's somehow found the one makeshift family that won't break hers.

They talk in hushed tones while Cruz busies himself checking over Cynthia like she couldn't out-nurse his ass if she wanted to. Some, if not all, healthcare professionals have a nasty habit of putting their own needs last and Cynthia's one of them. She could use someone fawning over her for a while.

It helps. Helps remind us of our own humanity. Helps remind us we matter, too.

It definitely helps.

"I'm out." Marc backs out from underneath the water, droplets falling from his furrowed brow, and says, "Hit me up if any more shit goes down. I'll be around."

I consider my secretive roommate as his lithe body saunters toward a Cuban food truck, hands in his pockets, probably digging for a cigarette. If anyone needs to let loose, it's him. I'm not sure what he actually does for fun aside from disappearing to unknown locations whenever the mood strikes but I imagine it involves scaring small children or winning staring contests with pit bulls. Although, he didn't scare off those kids at the park last weekend. Not in the slightest.

"I couldn't get there in time."

Beckett gives up his pseudo shower to press into my back, getting me wet, too. *Wouldn't be the first time.*

Probably won't be the last either.

I shake my head at myself and Beckett. Mostly Beckett.

"I told you we had it covered, so just stop already. I don't buy the prince act and you're not charming." Maybe a little. Sometimes.

"I don't give a baker's fuck if you had it covered," he growls, his voice skating over my skin like a wintry morning draft.

Slowly, oh so slowly, I turn to peek at him over my shoulder bringing our mouths inches apart.

"I didn't like his hands on you. I *hated* him touching you."

Finally, Beckett and I agree on something.

"You do know we didn't want that, right? I didn't want him."

Beckett's large hand spread wide on my stomach, he yanks me back into his toned middle, dropping his lips to the shell of my ear.

The tips of colorful wings dancing closer to our mister catch my eye.

"You're wanted though," I tell him with a nod that he ignores, grazing his lips along the sensitive skin that was just mistreated by another's. Shots are in order after this. Medical, alcohol, I'll take one of each.

"So are you," he whispers.

The poke to my backside proves he's telling the truth, but so was I. Splashes of color fill my peripheral as I turn in Beckett's arms coming face-to-face with him and essentially killing the sarcastic response on my tongue. It's been almost a week since he was wrapped around me like this and I forgot how imperfectly perfect he is.

I take a moment to run my gaze along his achingly beautiful face. How can someone that looks the exact same from only a short while ago appear so different all of a sudden?

His eyebrows almost meet in the middle. "I wasn't sure I'd get to you in time. I thought he was going to try to take you."

Away. He thought I was going to be taken away.

I study his eyes, dropping my voice for his ears only. "I'm not like your mom. I'm not going anywhere." And surprisingly, I mean it.

"Why's that? Who am I to you for you not to leave?" He frowns at the words, watching them stumble around between us, looking for somewhere safe to land.

"You're just-"

"Don't say just your roommate."

"You're...Beckett."

How am I supposed to label him? How am I supposed to label this? I don't even know. But he's right, he's not just my roommate. I don't know if he's ever been just my roommate. No matter how hard I tried to act like he was, the title never really fit.

"Hey, see you guys back at the site. We're out of here. Make sure you ditch the stringers first." Coty gestures to the pesky insects infringing on all of my personal space—even from ten feet away.

Without breaking our connection, Beckett nods easily at his friends as they pass.

When they're gone, I openly wave at the butterflies, saying, "They're waiting for you."

Neither of us blink for a minute then Beckett finally tears his tightened gaze from mine, lingering on the fluttering duo a little too long. His mouth once again sours every last bit of my mood by sucking his bottom lip between his teeth as his eyes roam the half-naked pair.

A snarl rips from my throat before I can swallow it fully.

Beckett bows his head, his grip seizing the middle of my back to bring me in as close as our bodies will allow. Still focused on the dancing girls, he says, "if something's bothering you, all you gotta do is say it," repeating what he told me the last time I was upset.

My response building—snowballing, really—into an epic spat dies in its tracks when Beckett brings his gaze back to mine making everything else fade away. Harmonic convergence, I think it's called when all the planets are aligned. There is nothing else in front or behind or even beside me. Nothing but him. He's all I see.

He's all I want.

Lips parting, his eyes bore into mine. "Just tell me."

Tell him what exactly? Tell him I don't want him to disappear either? That the mere thought of him slinking off with anyone else literally makes my stomach cramp?

Or does he want me to admit I'm falling for him? Because I could. I could say it all and mean it with every cell in my body.

But I won't. I can't. He's not ready for that. *I'm* not ready for that.

"What do you say, dream?"

Dream?

That ever-present glimmer of mischief only intensifies with his challenging tone. A challenge he's tossing at my feet while smiling in my face.

My heart pounds in my fucking throat like the clock in Hook's alligator's, the thrumming vein in my neck counting out the seconds. *Tick, tock. Tick, tock.*

What *do* I say? And why can't I make myself drop my hands from his confident arms?

Just as he begins to turn his head, my hand shoots up, grabbing his chin and holding his face in place with his triumphant stare locked on mine.

Time stops as we wait—him to see what I'll do next, me to also see what I'll do next.

I swallow some of my heart back down to where it belongs, safe in its home, surrounded by strong ribs protecting the susceptible organ from any harm—even from me—and without breaking eye contact with Beckett, I say, "find someone else to explore with tonight," to the pests.

When they make no move to leave, I meet the girls' disbelieving glares with one of my own, shooing them off, "Run along now. This one's busy." For tonight anyway.

A low growl in Beckett's throat builds, reverberating off my own vocal cords.

"There she is." A lazy smile curves his lips. "That possessive streak must run deep in your family."

"You don't even know my family."

Beckett flinches but shakes it off before I ask why. They met at Coty and Angela's briefly but there wasn't any real bonding. Or talking really. Or general friendliness whatsoever. They just kind of co-existed in the same airspace, like planets in a solar system except without the chance of ever aligning.

"Whatever," we hear as they finally turn away but not before muttering, "nice dress by the way," in a pissy tone I recognize all too well.

Their jealousy coming for my jealousy is the final straw and I tip my head back, laughing a mocking sort of sound.

What am I doing?

"Do you want to stay with me tonight?" Cruz asks Cynthia with too much desperation for his own good.

I'm about to argue on her behalf, even though I don't

technically know where else she could sleep, but when I look over to see them involved in a game of serious tonsil hockey, I drop the issue. They only break to wave goodbye then take off together for that pillow fort he calls a tent.

Beckett rumbles his own amused laugh before he presses his lips to the side of my throat eliciting an embarrassing shiver. He pulls back to smile down at me like I've just given him a gift.

"She's right, you know? That dress-"

"Is a shirt," I finish, then clarify, saying, "your shirt." Tilting my head, I ask innocently, "Still want it back?"

I didn't get a good look at the shirt I pulled from Beckett's dresser last weekend until the next morning when I wore it back to my room. I should've known it'd be one of his infamous riding innuendo shirts, this one saying *Put The Fun Between Your Legs*. Once I saw it though, I found the irony too great to return it. His scent embedded in the dark material was an added incentive to keep the shirt that much longer. Then when he made my harmless thievery common knowledge in front of everybody at his shop, I figured a little payback was in order. I cut the sleeves off, distressed the shit out of it, threw some sexy panties on underneath, and a dress was born. A short dress. He's tall but so am I. It covers all the important bits but barely.

He eyes the short hem, admitting, "More now than ever."

"The offer still stands." The one where he has to take it back. I'd prefer him use only his teeth but that's just me.

Beckett's arms coast down mine, along my sides and down to the bottom of my heavily altered dress, fingering the fabric.

"I can just get it off my floor in the morning."

"Your floor, huh?" I ask and he smirks. "Just because I chased off a couple of groupies doesn't mean I'm rooming with you. Marc-"

"Can go fuck himself," he finishes calmly. "But I doubt he'll need to. Dude has no problems finding chicks to warm his bed for the night. Which won't be you 'cause you'll be in mine. With me.

You're in my clothes." Fingertips snake beneath the fabric, rubbing the top of my thigh and goose bumps break out across my skin despite it still being in the eighties outside. "You're alone." Wandering inward, the pads of his fingers graze the lace edge of my panties, making my breath catch in my throat. "You better believe you're in my fucking bed tonight."

One of Beckett's nails catches on the front of the damp material covering my pussy.

Suppressing a needy moan, I counter, "Why are you so concerned with where I'll be sleeping tonight? Wouldn't you rather know who I'll be fucking?"

He's now frothing at the mouth, for blood...or something else. The feral look in his eye blazes as his entire body turns rigid and ripping his hand out from under my dress, he uses it to goad my backbone into submission to make my chest rise to his.

"You got a sharp tongue yourself. Ever use it for anything else?"

"Like this?" With a sweetness that could cause cavities, I raise my middle finger to my mouth and bite the tip, never backing down from Beckett's crazed eyes.

Deathly silent, he tracks the movement before gently pulling my finger away and nibbling the same tip I just had in my mouth, swirling his tongue down to my knuckle, making as much noise as a lion on the hunt—none.

Damn...

Hissing like his lioness, I clutch the top of my dress, surreptitiously waving air down the neckline.

"But the shirt you've got on is so popular."

I'm grasping at straws at this point and they're weak. So very weak.

Without hesitation, Beckett reaches up, gripping his Bigfoot shirt at the top of his back and rips it over his head in one smooth motion.

I love when guys do that.

I love when Beckett does it more.

What? No.

He tosses the shirt down, raising an eyebrow.

His hips begin to move with mine until we find a rhythm that doesn't exactly match the music but fits our mood perfectly—teasing, with a promise of more…soon.

Our friends long gone, it's just us as my palms rest on his bare chest, feeling his increased heartbeat calling to me like a lighthouse to the wayward ship. *Time to navigate to safer waters.*

Time to come home.

"God, I missed you."

Beckett lowers his mouth to mine, kissing the shit right out of me. I'm breathless, legless, and over-fucking-heated by the time he's done.

"Your mouth is the thing that I think about most. I want to shut you up and make you scream all at once. Fuck, that mouth," he groans deeply, pressing his erection into my stomach. "Do you feel what you do to me?" Swallowing thickly, I nod. "Say you'll stay with me tonight. Put me out of my misery. I'm dying here, girl."

Our bodies continue to stay in sync while our minds are slowly getting on the same page. We're playing this dangerous game that neither of us is ready for but both desperately want.

"One night," he pleads, searching my eyes.

"You said that last time," I challenge, feeling major déjà vu.

"That wasn't a full night! You snuck out halfway through."

We come to a stop, watching each other closely. Waiting. Hoping.

"So, you want a half-night then? What could you even do with half a night?" I snicker mockingly, knowing damn well what he did with the last *half-night* I gave him. Beckett doesn't need time to fuck everything up, he needs access. Access I have to deny him any way I can.

With a mocking smirk of his own, he says, "Let me show you."

CHAPTER 27

Paige

TOGETHER, WE BEGIN THE TREK BACK TO THE CAMPING portion of the venue. There's a long walkway between the amphitheater and the campgrounds that makes for an easy commute for concert goers who are also camping on-site.

Hand in gigantic hand, we stroll past other campers drunkenly making their own way back and it's not long before the tall canvas peaks of tents come into view.

Beckett brings me closer, tucking me under his arm. Thankfully, he doesn't smell bad. That's something I noticed about him, that even after working his ass off all day in a sweaty garage in excruciating heat, he still smells good—like really good. If anything, the hard work smell on top of his usual musk only amplifies his attractiveness.

He catches me eyeballing him and smiles knowingly.

"Half a night," I remind him, nerves scattering across my body like bats in an attic.

This will work, right? We can do this, have sex again and still walk away as friends afterward? The last person I tried this with was Dean and he couldn't. He couldn't accept that I didn't want anything other than sex with zero strings attached.

But this doesn't feel like it did with Dean. I don't feel the same way I did with Dean. When I'm with Beckett I don't want to fuck to forget. I want to be cherished, like I'm worthy. And he makes me feel that way. He's as tempting as the devil himself but caring enough to rival any saint. He rides, he's stable with a promising future within his grasp, and he goes down on me like I'm his favorite dessert.

He also happens to be my roommate. Someone I cannot escape even if that option no longer feels like an option at all.

I'm a disaster though. Disasters can't be contained. They're feared, not trusted. Tracked, not predicted. They aren't going to suddenly quell their chaos because of some strong-as-oak man with crystal blue eyes and a gifted tongue.

"Half a night, all night, whatever. Let's not limit ourselves."

Stopping dead in my tracks forces Beckett to come to a halt as well and I turn a glare on him. A glare I should be directing at myself.

His right hand comes up to cup my face but I flinch right, too.

The look in his eyes freezes me to the spot and when he tries again, I let him.

"I'm kidding."

I frown.

"Fine." He laughs. "Kind of. I'm kind of kidding. But I need-" His fingers tighten on my jaw. "I want you. If I only get you for half a night or two hours or twenty minutes, I swear someone'll have to pry my fingers off you one by fucking one before that time is up. Give me the chance to show you why, okay?"

My eyes search his.

Why?

I already know my reasons why. But despite my best efforts I really want to know his, too.

"Ok-" His lips crash against mine, silencing my verbal answer but igniting my body's response.

One hand in my hair—grappling, claiming—Beckett lifts me off my feet then walks us the rest of the way with only one hand on my ass to hold me up. It helps that I'm glued to him like a spider monkey and soon we're almost to the crew's tents. I try to pull back so he can see better but Beckett's not having it. Instead, he sculpts his hand to the back of my head, keeping me in place while maintaining a punishing pace of lip service. Without so much as breaking for breath, we make it back to his tent all in one piece.

The man is a multitasker, I'll give him that.

"What the fuck is all this?"

My eyes fly open to find him scowling inside and following his gaze, I cringe. *Shit.*

"It looks like a unicorn puked all over the place."

"We needed somewhere to get ready."

To keep Angela away from Coty, we avoided their tent altogether. Beckett was occupying Marc's, so his was the only logical place for us to get dressed. I don't think any of us could've predicted how messy the glitter would be though. It could pass for a mythical crime scene in here. *Unicorns, fairies, and sprites, oh my.*

"Were you naked?" he asks as I'm dropped onto the bed with Beckett following, positioning his body overtop of mine.

"Yes. In fact, we all stood naked in a circle throwing handfuls of glitter at each other just hoping some of it would stick. The more crevices the better." I'm actually not that far off. Aside from the naked crevices part. *Ew.*

We stare at one another for a beat until my lips quirk making us both laugh out loud.

"Why didn't you say so?"

Beckett lowers his mouth to mine again, placing a tender kiss to the corner of my lips.

"All this for a shirt?" I tsk.

I chase his lips with mine when he pulls away to look down at me, all traces of humor gone.

"It was never about the shirt. It was always about the girl in it." He guides the shirt over my head slowly, taking his time admiring every inch of my skin as it's revealed. "And now out of it. Were you like this all week?" he asks, scanning my thighs and stomach.

There are still some faint hickeys here and there that haven't healed completely. Luckily, the darker ones were easily hidden under my work uniform while I had to use foundation to cover the lighter ones on my neck.

"Yes," I sigh, acting put out. I hated the extra effort toward hair and makeup this week but not the markings covering my body. I didn't hate those at all.

He leans down to swipe his lips across a yellowish one by my hip, and says, "I like that. I like that a lot." The last part comes out jagged, like the glass in my throat.

A choked sound breaks the silence as he makes his way to my bare chest.

"Fuck, dream." *There's that name again.* "You were walking around without a bra on? Had I known that I would've dragged your ass back here sooner."

Just as I open my mouth to ask him about his little pet name, he drags his palm down my neck between my tits all the way to my belly button and another hiss comes out instead. His fingers hover at the top of my panties with the same gleam in his eye I've seen a time, or two, before.

My knees raise on their own accord but he looks back up at me, hunger leaking out of his every pore.

Oh, goddamn.

The rip of fabric is all I hear before my panties are tossed to the side like the trash they now are.

"Beckett!" I scold, just as he drops to his knees at the end of the bed, tugging my ankles to bring me to him.

"Just like that," he demands. "Keep my name on the tip of your tongue just like that while I fuck you with the tip of mine."

And he does. Beckett lowers himself, fucking me with his tongue until I follow through on my end of the deal and scream his name so loud the band onstage can probably hear it over their adoring crowd.

Grabbing a condom out of his shorts' pocket while trying to undress one-handed, he quickly rolls it down his straining cock once it's freed.

Catching me studying every detail, he says, "I like you watching me. Everywhere. At work. At home. In the shower. Now. I want your eyes on me always."

There he goes again with the eternal talk.

I drop my stare to the pastel quilt, my fingers plucking at a stray thread.

"Fuck it. Let's go for another one."

"What?" I ask but Beckett doesn't answer as he sits beside me, keeping his heavy-lidded gaze locked on mine.

I break first to watch between my bent knees, mesmerized as he glides two fingers along my sensitive slit. When he presses both fingers inside, I clamp around him, moaning from the delicious intrusion. He rewards me by pumping in and out but in a slow rhythm that I swear will be the death of me. He may have asked me to put him out of his misery but I can promise I'll be the one dying a slow, torturous death if he continues like this.

To help him out, I press my hand over his, arching my back clear off the bed and moving with our combined hands in a faster, harder pace. Unable to resist, he matches me pump for pump, his eyes eventually dropping to watch us bring me over the same wall of ecstasy I just climbed only moments ago.

I release his hand, letting my own fall limply beside me.

"That was hot," he says before snapping, "eyes on me now."

"Give me something to look at then."

"God, I love that mouth."

He removes his hand from between my thighs then proceeds to crawl up my body licking both fingers like he can't help himself.

"I might love your pussy more though."

Recovered and ready for more, I pull him to me, making sure every bit of his front is touching every bit of my front as my knees fall open to the sides. I *crave* his skin. I *yearn* for his touch. I *need* him.

It's like he said, I'll *never* get enough.

No.

This wasn't supposed to happen. None of this.

But here I am, scrambling to get him closer. To let him in further.

Leaning on one elbow, he looks down at us, his long body fitted to mine, and grips the inside of my thigh to push my leg open even wider. Lining us up, he plunges inside, fusing us together and continues to watch himself roll his hips then slowly pull his cock out only to plunge back inside all while using my thigh like a handle.

A wobbly gasp flutters across his cheek and his eyes squeeze shut.

"Careful. I could blow right now and I still got a point to prove."

"What point is that?" I breathe out.

Slowly, he drags his gaze up to my face and says, "You'll see."

Too many emotions bubbling to the surface, I close my own eyes, trying to keep them in. Keep them from him.

I don't need to see though, my body's willing to blindly go wherever the hell his takes it. My mind, however, is working overtime to keep my heart where I need it. Where I can control it. My ribs have proven just how useless they are and now it's up to my brain to protect my most valuable defense.

He slides my left leg over his back giving him better access and his back muscles constrict beneath my fingernails as he lures me out of the self-imposed mental refuge I'm stuck in.

A growl from his throat, from his very core, stirs me though and I open my eyes again. "Stay here. With me."

Something about the way he says it, it's like he's confessing. Revealing a truth he's not used to facing.

"I want to see all of you."

You already do, I want to tell him but ultimately don't.

I keep my lips tightly sealed as he flips our positions so I'm on top, straddling his narrow hips. I feel his thighs touch my back and when he nods over my shoulder, I see his feet flat on the bed with his knees bent right behind me. I lean back against them with my shoulders supported by his knees, looking down my nose at him.

One large hand where my hip meets my waist and another at the base of my throat, he says, "Hold on."

"You first."

His plump lips shimmer with a light layer of sweat as they spread into a wicked smile a second before his hips thrust into me from below, his fingers biting into my flesh.

He is not patient, he is not quiet, but goddamn is he skilled in everything he does.

Beckett looks up through those long eyelashes of his while I grind myself against the base of his cock each time we meet in the middle with hard thrusts from different directions.

"That's it, dream. Ride me."

Shudders set in and the vibration affects us both as our moves grow erratic. Our bodies don't need much guidance though; they always know what to do even when we don't.

"Come here."

Still holding my throat, he pulls me to him and he captures my lips in a bruising kiss. From the new angle, my sensitive clit gets more of that incredible friction and my frantic moans threaten to end our kiss but Beckett keeps his mouth plastered to mine, continuing the give and take dance we're locked in.

It's messy and chaotic and sloppy as all hell but it's real and raw and I'm losing my grasp on that small piece of my heart I've been working to keep out of Beckett's reach.

"Beckett," I moan against his lips when it all becomes too much.

His hand glides from my collarbone to my breastbone, preparing to steal the whole organ right out of my chest.

"Take it all," he tells me softly. "Take what you need. I'm already yours."

And there it goes, my heart, into Beckett's open palm.

Our shared release hits hard and fast and we both curse and moan, our bodies still riding out the aftershocks together.

With his cock still buried inside me, his hands glide down

over my ass, spreading my cheeks, and jerking me firmly against him. My mouth drops open from the insane stimulation on my swollen nub, then he thrusts upward, rasping, "Again."

And fuck if I don't give him exactly what he wants one last time by coming on command with a high-pitched scream that I've never heard in my life.

Absolutely boneless, I drop into a wilted heap on top of Beckett's sweaty middle, making him huff out a laugh. He positions us so I'm tucked tightly against his side with my head resting on his chest and I can't remember anything in my life ever feeling so right. This moment, us sharing so much more than either of us were prepared for, changes into something I've been trying to deny myself and before I know it sneaky tears flow out of the corners of my eyes.

Beckett wipes them away, stroking his fingers into my hair.

"You feel it, too?"

I don't speak. I just nod against his chest.

I feel *everything*.

He takes care of the condom without jostling me and I take the time to glance around the tent. The thick canvas probably allowed our neighbors to hear more than they wanted to tonight. Tomorrow morning will be hard. Tonight will be harder.

After that we're quiet for a while, his hands rubbing up and down my side, giving me goose bumps that his warmth promptly chases away.

"This changes everything," he says barely above a whisper just before his arms go limp around my back.

Like always, that bitch Hope ignores my silent request that Beckett's wrong somehow and this didn't just change everything.

CHAPTER 28

Paige

The tawny sky is just waking up as I stare out over the gorge in the heart of this beautiful state. The rolling hills are mostly brown with some green sprinkled throughout closest to the river and the shadows they cast have an almost eerie feel to them as foggy clouds loiter menacingly along the crevices.

From my spot just past the now deserted amphitheater, I can see a few early risers making their way to the bathrooms in the distance and figure I better head back in case Cynthia is among them.

Waking this morning, more comfortable than I expected I'd be in a rented outdoor bed with a brick wall of pure heat at my back, I slipped from Beckett's warm embrace to find my phone completely dead. As soon as I stepped out of the tent, a frantic Angela informed me her coffee machine had taken out the power to all the other glamping sites. Each individual tent gets an outlet for phones and whatnot but with one flick of her espresso maker, she singlehandedly sabotaged my plan to slip out unnoticed.

Unable to help, I went back inside immediately realizing I had no underwear—thanks, Beckett—so I borrowed a pair of Beckett's sweatpants to wear under my shirt dress. I had to roll up each pants leg and flip the waist band down a few times but it worked out okay especially since it's actually chilly this early.

Since I couldn't reach Cynthia by phone, I decided to walk around down by the do-it-yourself campers, but with no clue which tiny tent Cruz's was in a huge mess of other tiny tents, I gave up and went to watch the sunrise instead.

Back at their site, Marc and Coty are sitting under a canopy at a folding table. Squinting, I see they're eating sausage and eggs which is impressive considering Angela killed the only possible source of heat before I left.

When they notice me approaching, they exchange glances with each other, then continue eating while taking me in curiously.

They know.

They know what happened between me and Beckett last night but they don't know what *happened* between me and Beckett last night.

And maybe, just maybe Beckett doesn't either.

Just then I hear two heavy thumps and a short exhale. Looking over I see Beckett coming out of his tent, shirtless with a pair of gray sweatpants that I swear were made just to torture me, and hair sticking out at all angles like he's been yanking his hands through it. He pins me to my spot with a wide-eyed stare and a tight line to his lips.

Unsure what to do, or say, or even think, I wave. A stupid flimsy little wave compared to the momentous actions that just took place between the two of us but it's my wave and I'm sticking with it.

As I consider tossing in a nice fake smile, Beckett storms across the dirt lined site, putting him toe-to-toe with me in just a few long strides and then his lips are crashing into mine. His hand grasps the back of my head keeping me to him as he deepens the kiss, pushing his tongue just past my shocked lips and, even in my brain fogged state, I silently thank myself for stopping to brush my teeth during my walk. Beckett's kissing me with so much emotion it's clear this is more than a simple morning after mind-blowing, life-altering sex kiss.

This kiss is a punishment.

Whatever my offense, I'm ready to surrender and atone for the wrong I've committed because this kiss is more than I've ever been given, ever been shown.

But, more importantly, it's a claiming. It's a lasting promise, a foreboding threat, a sentence I'll happily spend the rest of my life serving if there's more where this came from.

I was ready to run, willing to break my promise to Beckett that I wouldn't. But this. This is why I said I'd stay to begin with. This connection between us that neither of us can deny anymore. It's here. We're here. I'm still fucking here.

Before my greedy hands do some claiming of their own, Beckett pulls away, leaving me breathless and feverish. With his hand still cupped to the back of my head, he says, "I thought you left."

How did I ever look at him and see a selfish screw-off that doesn't take anything seriously?

Because he wanted me to.

Because he wants everyone to.

I nod a bit, glancing toward Angela's tent. "You can thank your accomplice over there for making me your hostage."

"Nah, dream, I'm the one being held captive."

The intensity both in and around that sentence threatens to set the wilderness around us ablaze.

"Why do you keep calling me dream?"

Beckett licks his lips, dropping his gaze to mine and then back up to my eyes again before answering vaguely, saying, "You'll see."

The last time he said that he followed through. So much more than I could've ever prepared for.

With a smack on my ass, he tells me, "Now go sit and eat something. And don't take off yet. I want you to go home with me."

"We live together, Beckett," I deadpan.

"Yeah, but I want to drive you back, not Cynthia." He drops his voice for my ears only. "Just, give me this one, okay?"

He's acting a little nervous and a lot suspicious. What is he up to now?

Beckett disappears into the tent, hopefully to put a shirt on so I can function normally again, and with a shake of my head, I move to join the guys who aren't even pretending to eat, they're full on gaping.

Coty recovers first once I have a plate of food, saying brightly, "good morning," while Marc jerks his chin up in greeting, watching through dark eyes.

"It appears that way," I draw out.

After a beat of awkward silence, we all let out our forced laughs just as Angela emerges from her and Coty's tent, carrying a steaming mug.

"Oh, perfect timing. Here's your chai. Beckett thought you coyote-uglied his ass but I knew you'd be back."

My eyes grow wide as she places the milky cup of tea in front of me.

She chuckles, explaining, "As soon as he saw his phone was dead, he lost his shit and helped get the power up and running again." Stopping to give the guys a private look, she then nods toward my drink. "He searched two stores on the way up just to find the right brand for you."

I smile warmly, thanking her and tucking all of that away.

"It's perfect." And it is. Spicy yet sweet, creamy but thin, and piping hot. Exactly the way I like it.

Beckett reappears, wearing a shirt that says *I like it hard, fast, and loud,* and I know from experience this shirt is actually true. Beside me, he flips a chair around backward before sitting down and slinging his long arms over the back casually, saying, "For the record, I've never been coyote-uglied in my life."

Angela's response is immediate, "Only because no one's ever lasted until morning to see your face in the light of day."

The table falls silent and I swear I can feel four sets of eyes land on me simultaneously. My food becomes very interesting though as I keep my gaze glued to the plate.

"Are we all going to beat around the bush about this?" My eyes widen a fraction, hearing Beckett. "Fine, I'm just gonna come out and say it: who invited neighbor girl? She's a total party pooper."

Coty sobers from laughing at the two friends going back and forth to warn, "Hey."

Angela shushes him saying, "I'm more fun than you three losers put together." With a mumbled "sorry" to Coty she continues, saying to me, "Paige, would you please tell him?"

I glance up, rushing to say, "Oh, I'm not… This isn't…"

Beckett turns my face to his, seeing straight through me. "You are. And this most definitely is."

Our staring contest continues until Coty coughs, asking, "What time are you guys heading out? We can help load everything up as soon as we're all properly caffeinated."

"Speak for yourself," Marc mutters. "I didn't even want to bring all this shit."

"How you liking that hazelnut latte, Marc?" Angela snaps and Marc just sips his coffee in silence, fighting a smirk over the rim.

Beckett steals a sausage link from my plate but instead of getting offended like I did when Cruz did the same thing, I lean over, snatching his hand with mine then bite the end off. Better he learns it now—what's yours is mine, but what's mine is still mine until I say otherwise.

He pauses then tosses the rest of the link into his mouth like it's a mint.

"Unless Paige needs more sausage after this," his perverted wink earns a heavy eye roll from me, "we'll get ready after breakfast."

I murmur "half a pound" under my breath, making Beckett full-on howl with laughter.

"I'm happy to prove you wrong, girl." Using one arm on the table and one on the back of my chair to cage me in, he whispers against my ear, saying, "Again."

My head shakes his obnoxious snicker away but not the pulsing between my thighs.

Cynthia and Cruz stroll over then, their movements planned and agitated, with guilt written over every inch of the both of them. Something tells me that whatever happened between them last night doesn't hold the same shine to it now that we're in the light of day and that it won't be happening again.

The now familiar hand stroking my thigh under the table rubs away the uncertainty I've been wrestling with all morning and I know our story doesn't hold the same fate. I don't know what will happen tonight or tomorrow or a month from now but we already tried the avoidance path. It was painstakingly long and tedious and took a lot more energy than I have to spare.

Unfortunately, a relationship of any kind with me will be chockfull of scarce interactions laced with even less communication. A guy like Beckett, the life of every party, will not remain patient for a girl that isn't even around, let alone attempt the faithful route for her.

Looking at him now though, completely at ease with his affections for me on full display, he makes a pretty convincing argument for what could be.

Someday.

* * *

The drive home should've been an hour and a half tops. Beckett stretched it to an even three hours. He insisted on stopping at every rest stop, fruit stand, and general tourist trap along the way. It was when he pulled over at a little free library for a selfie that I figured Beckett was stalling. I just don't know why.

Finally back at the apartment, before I even have a chance to drop my bag, Beckett grabs my hand excitedly to tug me along behind him.

"Come on. I got something I want to show you."

"Was this all really just so you could show me your dick again?"

Beckett's laugh echoes off the walls as I trail after him down the hall and at my room he stops to peer in before dragging me through the door I know I left closed but is now wide open.

Complete darkness meets us.

"No, but I'd like to revisit that offer."

I blindly shove his arm since I can't see a thing.

"It wasn't an offer."

"Agree to disagree." I can practically hear his smile. "Seriously though, this isn't about me." The light flicks on, illuminating my room—or at least I think it's mine—and he says, "This is all for you."

My gasp cuts the silence before my hand can cover my mouth.

"Did you do this?" I look to Beckett, whose hands are twisting in front of his torso and he nods shyly.

So, this is why he was acting so different.

"How? When? It wasn't like this yesterday."

He walks further into my new and improved room and spins to face me with his hands spread wide.

"I've been working on getting some stuff put together all week but had to call in some reinforcements to get it just right. Thanks to your brothers, everything came together last night."

I blink at him before scanning the wall over his head. It's covered in pictures. Photos of me with my brothers, old family photos with my parents, and even one of me…sleeping? Right in the middle of the collage is a large black and white close-up of me in what looks like Beckett's bed.

My eyes fly to his.

"I took that one while you were asleep last weekend." His voice is velvety smooth with a snag at the end. "You looked-"

"Happy," I finish. And it's true. Snuggled between his soft sheets on his massive bed surrounded by his sweet woodsy scent, I do look happy, peaceful, like there's nowhere else I'd rather be.

He asked me recently if I was happy living here. In this one photograph, he was able to capture what I wouldn't voice. What I couldn't even allow myself to recognize. Until now.

"And the others? How did you get those?"

"I asked Tysen and he gave me what he could find. Thank God for the cloud." His chuckle fills the room and I lean into it. Into him.

"Wait, what do you mean you asked him? Since when do you talk to my brother?"

"I asked him not to tell you yet, but Tysen works at Pop The Hood now. Dude started a few days ago. When I told him what I wanted to do, he was happy to help and thankfully he got the rest of your brothers on board, too, because I wouldn't have been able to pull this off without them. After all that shit came out," my eyes drop to the floor, "I think they just wanted to make you feel comfortable. Cared for." His tone drops a few decibels. "They wanted you to know you're loved. To feel it no matter what."

I glance back to him and after several attempts at swallowing down the new emotions clogging my airway, I say, "Thank you. For doing that. With this and Ty. You have no idea what you've done for him. He's…"

"A great mechanic," he cuts me off adamantly. "We're lucky we found him. We're gonna need him if we want to open a second location."

He doesn't leave any room for argument with that but I know. I know what Beckett did even if he won't admit it.

Nodding, I take in the rest of the room. It's decorated in my favorite colors: white and gray. Different sized pillows of all textures spruce up the perfectly made bed with a black throw blanket draped across the bottom. Running my fingers over the luxurious fabric, I notice something shiny hanging above the head board next to an artistic print of a curved road.

Beckett explains, saying huskily, "It's a dream catcher."

"Is that a sprocket? And chain links?"

He nods, shrugging a little too nonchalantly. "I used some old parts I had lying around from my first dirt bike."

I can't hide the disbelief from my voice. "You made that?"

When he nods again, I say, "It's beautiful. Do you always make these or something?"

His eyebrows crease and he shakes his head softly. "I, uh, no, this is the only one. I made it for you."

I step into his space making him lean his head back to meet my stare.

"Why?"

Eyes searching mine, he says, "You're my dream catcher and I thought you should have your own."

My breath catches in my throat. I didn't think he knew.

"If you don't like it, I can take it-"

"No," I gasp out, catching his arm. "I love it. I love it all," I tell him honestly, gesturing around the room that I'm just now realizing has a black-out shade that wasn't there before on the window along with a noise machine in the corner. I've always hated wearing ear plugs and an eye mask just to sleep but never even thought about an alternative.

Beckett did though. He put in a lot of thought for not only my comfort but my overall well-being. Like I matter.

My old apartment was decorated in similar tones but I like what he did here better. He took the smallest details from my personality while adding in his own twists to make a perfect blend for stylish simplicity.

Standing silently, I give him a once-over through new eyes. It's like seeing him for the first time all over again but instead of the ever-pouting brat I once saw, I see a man with more depth than I could've ever anticipated.

Afraid of falling, of drowning in my own helplessness, I was so worried about where I'd land, I never thought to look around on the way down. Had I stopped to check my surroundings, I would've noticed Beckett treading his own waters, fighting against another current. And through the pain and hurt he's been living with, he still managed to think of me and my comfort. He put my needs first when I know his haven't been met in years, if ever. If a shattered child can grow into a complete man like Beckett, full of unconditional love and persistent kindness, then maybe a fractured woman like me can draw strength from her last reserve to give him the same. Together, we can sift through the wreckage of the remaining fragments like a jigsaw puzzle and fill in each other's lost pieces that would otherwise never be found.

"Actually," stepping closer, I bring my hands up to grasp his jaw, running my fingers over the day old stubble, "I think you're right."

Firm hands grab ahold of my hips, pulling me against his sculpted front.

"I usually am." He clears his throat, finishing hoarsely, "But, just so I know we're on the same page, what exactly am I right about this time?"

Locking eyes, I repeat his words back to him, saying, "This changes everything." Then, giving him everything I fucking have, I kiss him. I kiss him for him, for everything he's done to earn not only my affection but my respect as well. I kiss him for me, for all the things I wish I could've given him from the beginning but am just getting to now. I kiss him for us, for the chance that we both deserve. The opportunity we've deprived ourselves of just long enough for us to find each other.

We didn't sink to the bottom, letting life's harsh realities win out. We both kicked our way back to the surface, giving it our all without ever knowing the other would be waiting to start the journey back to shore, together.

CHAPTER 29

Beckett

"Yo, I'm out for the day. I gotta get my girl."

Wow. Words I thought I'd never say and yet they flow out of my mouth like it's the most natural thing in the world. But that's just it, with Paige it is that natural. With her everything just feels...right. Normal. No, better than normal. Fucking fantastic. Perfection personified. Alright so maybe that's overkill but seriously, I never thought having a girlfriend would be so easy.

Not that my girl's easy. She's the definition of tough as shit, pain in the ass, fight me at every turn, beautiful fucking goddess, and I wouldn't have it any other way.

I turn the key on my bike after knocking knuckles with a few of the hourlies we just hired. I wasn't lying when I told Paige we needed her brother. Fuck, we could use five more Tysens. Our second location of Pop The Hood is on track to open in just a few months and we're busier than ever building up our clientele.

That doesn't stop me from cutting out early to meet my girl though. She should be getting out of class right about now, and if I'm lucky she'll wait for me so we can ride home together. Luck hasn't been on my side lately though as she's been leaving my ass in the dust before I can even reach her. Not that I'm complaining about the view when she does. I could watch Paige ride her bike all day. She's as assertive on her bike as she is in the bedroom. That's one thing I've always admired about her both on the streets and off—her confidence. She knows who she is, faults and all, and still stands with her head held high and a come-hither smile on her face daring anyone to fuck with her.

Silly me, I did. A lot.

And if I catch her tonight, I'll be doing it again. And maybe again for her troubles. I'm generous like that.

On the walk to their car, one of her classmates sees me but before I can ask about Paige, they point out the white and gray Honda across the lot. At the exit.

Oh, yeah, she'll pay for this alright.

My dick starts to swell but I'm not riding home with a fucking chubby so forcing thoughts of Paige naked and at my mercy out of my head, I speed after her, dipping through the lot like I'm in a video game or some shit and come within close enough range for our speakers to work. Quickly reaching up to hit the power button on the device attached to the side of my helmet, I use voice command to select a song and hope Paige turned her Bluetooth speaker on before she left so she can hear the music, too. The second the song drops her spine stiffens as she throws a glance over her shoulder seeing me approach. An updated rendition of a classic, "Pony" is exactly the kind of punishment she has to look forward to when we get home.

I only have a small window from now until the time she leaves for work in a bit but it's enough. It has to be. I'll make it be, goddamn it.

Just like the last several weeks, I've been making it a point to spend as much time together as our crazy schedules allow. The constant need for her hasn't lessened like I thought it would once we became exclusive. Instead, it's changed. Evolved. What started out as a physical craving is now a soul deep fucking ache. An absolute need for her, all of her, all the time. Our opposite shifts make things a little complicated without adding in her new classes she's taken up gunning for that twat-face Vernon. I hear his hours were reduced thanks to his incompetence but I won't be happy until the fucker is gone entirely. He continues to mutter stupid shit to Paige even though I've done my fair share of unannounced drop-ins. What can I say? They serve good food there.

Regardless, dude needs to go.

Paige's boss offered to cover the additional schooling for the position, and my girl took it head-on just like I knew she would and has been killing it in her new courses. It doesn't leave a lot of time for us but that's why I'm here. To sneak in that little something extra. Paige likes to be pushed, she fights for everything she has, so some competition here and there keeps her spark from going out and it gets me hard like nothing else. So it's a win-win.

Out of the corner of my eye, I catch Paige as she leans down and takes off like the hellion she truly is. *That's it, dream. Show me what you got.*

Sometimes she wakes up early just so she can stop over for my lunch break before her class and on those days, I eat twice. While Tysen is out of earshot obviously. Can't go fighting my girl's family just because I have an insatiable appetite for her.

Fuck it, I still would. She's that good. Hell, I probably would even if she wasn't. Her love, even though we haven't actually said the words yet—which I plan on remedying tonight—is like warm apple pie, and not that perverted shit from that cheesy teen movie Angie made me watch when neither of us could sleep one night. No, it's like that classic comfort feeling you can't find anywhere else but know you'll always connect it back to that sweet fulfilling dessert. Sure, everyone can eat a slice of apple pie but not everybody associates it the same way. Apple pie was the last thing my mom made the day before she took off and I can still remember basking in the warmth it brought. Not only the flavor of the flaky, gooey pie but just walking into the kitchen and smelling the sweet aroma with just the right amount of spicy tang to wake up your senses and the way we sat around the table, looking each other in the eye, believing everything was alright. That day will forever be burned in my brain as one of the best up until that point. The day after, of course, is a different story but that pie will always hold a special place in my heart. And I'll always think of Paige the same way I associate apple pie—home. Safe.

She said something similar to me once and I finally get it. I understand how a person who has nothing to do with your past can bring up the fondest memories with just a smile.

I told her she was my dream catcher, which she is, but she's more than that. She keeps the nightmares away while bringing my best dreams to life. She makes the impossible feel possible. Paige taught me how to influence an outcome not by changing the events, or even the players, but by switching the vantage point—like changing lanes. By looking at things from a different angle you can take your future into your own hands and mold it to a more tolerable result.

I'm not saying I've forgiven my mom for what she did, but I've released the obligation I'd been holding her to. Letting go of some of that blinding resentment changed my outlook on not only the past, but also the present and hopefully the future. A future I couldn't even see because of the monumental baggage my mom left in her wake. A future I can now fully envision Paige in.

That knowledge has me laying on the gas that much more. Shit, I'm seconds away from pulling her off to the side of the road, I'm so hopped up, but Creekwood comes into view sooner than I thought since I was more focused on Paige's ass fanned out on her seat.

I stumble through the natural routine of removing my helmet while dismounting my Ninja when the next thing I know my helmet is knocked clear out of my hands, skidding to a halt across the chipped blacktop.

Swinging around, I bark, "what-" but am quickly silenced when Paige smashes her mouth against mine. I release a growl, rounding my hands over her ass, directing her back to where she belongs—level with me. Not below, not above. Equals in everything we do.

She's just flexing right now, proving she has just as much control over this as I do.

As if I'd have a problem with that.

Thanks to Angie's heavy-handed influence, I'm basically a feminist now so Paige can steer all she wants. Hopefully to the bedroom first but hey, I'm down for whatever.

"You chose that song on purpose," she accuses once she breaks for air, teasing my lips with her teeth, driving me absolutely mad.

"You're damn right I did. You knew I was on my way but you left anyway. The way I see it, you still owe me a full ride. Time to pony up, dream."

She groans, tilting her head back, trusting I won't drop her. That I'll *never* drop her. I see my opening though and go for the kill before she realizes her mistake, taking her neck between my lips and sucking so hard she'll have a mark for days. Hell, she's marked me for life, ruined me for all others, claimed me as hers alone, so the least I could do is return the favor, even if it's only temporary.

Stealthy as fuck, we make it upstairs and into my room. I like her room well enough, especially since the makeover her brothers and I gave it, but my bed is bigger and we'll need the extra room. Time may not be on our side tonight but size is never a question where I'm involved. Bigger is better, I don't care what anybody says.

Paige is naked and writhing against my sheets in record time, just taunting me with her flawless body. I hold back though, standing above her, just wanting to get a good look at her first.

That lasts all of three seconds until a needy moan makes its way up her exposed throat causing me to throw my good, romantic, unhurried intentions right out the goddamn window. Maybe they'll land next to my forgotten helmet out on the asphalt so I can pick them all up at once in the morning 'cause nothing's taking me away from my girl right now.

Dipping my head between her legs—I always need a taste—I lick her slit like a fucking lollipop, swirling my tongue the way I know she likes, then lavish her stomach with sloppy nibbles as I make the climb to her stiff peaks awaiting me with perfectly pebbled nipples.

When Paige's back arches like a fucking bow, I know she's ready. Our lips clash in an epic battle to see who wants it more but I'm pretty sure it's me. With Paige, it's always gonna be me.

She flips over so suddenly, I almost roll off the side of the bed but manage to play it off by grabbing a condom from the nightstand instead. Propped on my side, I reach an arm around her middle and bring her to me, plastering her back to my front with her top leg bent over my thighs.

As we line ourselves up for what might be the hundredth time already, it still feels like the first time all over again. When you love someone, sex is no longer just a physical act, it's a total experience fusing your minds, bodies, and souls together as one. I knew it at the festival, probably before that if I'm being over-the-top, confessional-type honest instead of my usual understated self. I'd thought, hoped, maybe even prayed a little, but I wasn't sure until that moment when we came together that she was what I would spend the rest of my life trying to replicate if she denied her true feelings for me. Fuck, even during our quickies—not because *I'm* quick, just because we've had to rush a few times thanks to our time restrictions—the connection is just as strong.

There's something that happens, something inexplicable but no less bone deep that lets you know that this, this is what you'll never find again. No matter how hard or long you look, you'll never be with another person that sets off that emotion in you so you better grab hold while you can and never let go.

My hand fists her hair, and using my elbow for leverage, I draw her head back before sinking into her fully from behind. The angle is incredible and since I have damn near every part of Paige's toned body on display, I take a minute to simply look at her as she adjusts to the snug fit. Only when she starts cursing me out for having more patience than her—which is laughable in itself—do I move. Not at the rate she wants but the pace I need. I got one shot at this and I'm not blowing it along with my load in the first thirty seconds.

"Dream?"

Low-key ignoring me, her hand drifts up the back of my neck, searching for leverage of her own and I lean forward to bite her collarbone, basically blocking her chance to speed things up. Breaths become strained, stomachs begin shaking and I know, I know she's dying for the release I'm quickly approaching myself.

Not yet though.

With a rougher tone, I try again. "Dream?"

Gasps fall from her open mouth in time with my chaotic rhythm, as I pump into her from behind with long, shaky strokes, hitting her core with every thrust. My other hand slides around to her neglected clit and I'm rewarded with a frantic cry as I squeeze the swollen nub between two fingers.

"You love me, dream?"

After a slight hesitation, a jolted nod is all I get in response but damn, that's not enough. I need more. The first woman in my life never even bothered to earn the pedestal I built for her. I'm not making that mistake again. Now the spot at my side is cleared and ready to be claimed by the only woman that's proved she deserves it. Hell, she'll be the last woman in my life as far as I'm concerned unless she gives me that curly haired daughter I've found myself imagining lately.

Paige just needs to show me she wants it as much as I do. I need the words like I need the actions to prove them. Call me jaded but reassurance never hurt anybody. Deception sure the fuck did though.

Paige's nails dig into my wrist, nodding harder and pleading with me so I slam into her unchecked, pulling her hair taut and whispering in her ear, "Damn, you feel so good."

"I missed you today. I miss you every day."

"I want you, always."

And, finally, "I love you, Paige."

That last confession sends us both spiraling into a sea of stars so bright I have to close my eyes briefly.

While I wait for Paige to catch her breath, I kiss her shoulder, loving the way her skin breaks into goose bumps.

"Shit, Beckett. Do you *ever* shut up?"

My mouth splits into a grin at the crook of her neck. She knows damn well I don't but her sarcasm never ceases to amuse me.

"Yes, I love you," she says. "Of course I love you. You're the shining nightlight that brought me out of an abyss of darkness. You're everything I didn't know to look for."

I feel her ribs stiffen against mine.

Smile dropping, I reposition us so we're on our sides face-to-face, gazing into each other's eyes where I can see my own sentiment looking back at me. She means it. At least I hope she does. There's still that little flicker of doubt I'm not sure I'll ever fully rid myself of.

Her finger traces the band on my arm making me freeze.

Squinting at the barely noticeable letters, she asks a little breathless still, "What does that say anyway?"

Most people think my tattoo is a solid band and for good reason. I designed it like that. I wanted the quote to be for me and me alone but Paige isn't most people and if I want this to work, I can't hide any part of me from her. I just didn't think it'd be this soon. I haven't had to think about it at all with my dream catcher always around now.

With a husky lilt, I say, "The cure for pain is in the pain." I'd already realized how much the pain from another wound distracted me from the pain of my mother's abandonment and figured a tattoo was just one more form of redirection.

The Rumi quote's directly above one of my many scars. I got it done after a particularly bad accident, landing a jump I had no business being on to begin with. I nailed it actually, but ultimately had to bail when my tire came loose. I'd just checked it that morning but must've missed something. At least that's what I told everyone. Now, I'm not so sure. Maybe I never was.

"Like your nightmares."

My chest constricts. "What do you mean?"

Paige maneuvers to her back, avoiding my stare completely.

"Just how you bleed after a bad nightmare. When you hit yourself?" Her eyes come back to mine. "It landed me in your bed a couple times, don't you remember? I caught you doing it and tried to help." She points at the door that I just replaced and I feel all the blood drain from my face.

Well, isn't this just fucking peachy. The girl of my dreams—literally—who also moonlights as my personal dream catcher—also literally—was only in my room to watch me bust up my own goddamn nose, not because she felt drawn to me like I thought, how I'd hoped for, but out of pure pity. Because of some crazy need for pain I can't control.

I've been pitied my entire life as the boy whose own mother didn't want him, I don't need it from her.

Just when I thought we were in the same place, seated at the same table, and now, now I find out she's just getting through the restaurant door while I've already eaten all the fucking apps.

Eyeballing the time on my open laptop, I say, "Shouldn't you be leaving?"

I watch the hurt as it mars her face but I'm too wrapped up in my own head to care. Here I thought I was going to have to reveal one of my darkest secrets to my girlfriend only to find out she was keeping one of her own. She never said a word, just kept her judgment to herself and let me think I was secure in my anonymity of being a basket case with Mommy issues.

Fucking deception, man, it's a son of a bitch and I'm the son of the biggest bitch there is so that's saying something.

Angie likes to think she has the worst mom but the truth is I'd pick aversion over indifference any day. At least with hatred there's emotion motivating it, letting you know where you stand. With indifference, there's just cold, empty space with disillusionment running absolutely rampant.

Without another word, I get up and slip on some shorts.

Fuck this.

Laughter echoing off the walls stops me in my tracks though.

"You inconceivable prick. I tell you I love you. You basically fuck it out of me."

Spinning around, I find Paige rising from the bed in her birthday suit that I like to call *my* birthday suit any other time and I have to clench my fists, still, to keep from touching her.

"Then you have the *audacity* to get pissy because I saw you with a few bloody noses?" She steps up, putting her exposed chest just under mine. "Oh, I see. You only like the spotlight on you when it's your doing." My jaw flexes on instinct. "I never said anything because I thought you knew. Now that we've established you didn't, think about it. I stopped you from hurting yourself because I cared. Because I care. Because I *love* you. And whether you like it or not, I'd do it again. In a heartbeat. And even if you won't admit it right now because you're scared, we both know you'd do the same for me."

My shoulders relax a fraction seeing the honesty in her eyes. I want to believe her, I really do, but my entire life has been one letdown after another and I've become conditioned for disappointment. It's damn near my natural habitat at this point. Paige was the one person, other than my chosen brothers, that I didn't anticipate breaching those boundaries.

"I-"

What? I hate thinking that one more person saw the broken little boy I'm trying desperately not to be anymore?

It's bad enough Marc and Coty know what they do but they're family.

Then again, the bond I have with Paige feels just as strong, if not stronger, and all within a much shorter time frame. Definitely in a more intimate way.

What if I rushed into all this with only her issues in mind? When was I going to take care of my own shit? A shift in perspective and, *poof*, I'm healed? If only it were that easy.

But getting upset with Paige about my own closet full of dusty skeletons doesn't feel right either. The only one that can face them before packing their ancient asses up for good is me. Regardless of Paige knowing about them or not, they're still there, waiting to haunt me for eternity unless I get rid of them once and for all. Can I do that with her holding my hand or should I take on my demons alone, the way I always have?

"I need some time."

Her emerald eyes barely visible through slits, she hums, "Hmm... do you know how long it should take you to pull your head out of your ass?"

Before I can get a quip of my own out, she raises to her toes and locks lips with me, stealing my breath for what might just be the last time. I don't know.

With a gentle push, she's gone, walking out my door and maybe, just maybe out of my life, too.

She's not going out of this room like that though, is she? *I think the fuck not.*

My hand meets air as she saunters across the hall and into her room, still very much naked and still very much testing every last bit of my patience. Framing the doorjamb with my hands, I watch Paige through heavy lids, fighting every molecule in my body to snatch her ass back here. I pray Marc isn't home. If he is...

"Four seconds." Paige's words bring me back to the topic at hand, or better yet ass, mine more specifically, with my head apparently lodged deep inside. "Four seconds, one kiss, and you should fucking know, Beckett. I didn't do anything other than help protect you from your biggest enemy which is you. And I'd knock down a thousand more doors to get to you again. Don't let this be the one that keeps me from making it in. If you want to run because shit got real, then run. Do what you think you need to do. But know this, Beckett Meyers," a gravity I usually give into, but am battling like hell now spills from her eyes as she says, "I'm fast, too." Just before she slams her door shut, she calls out, "maybe even faster," making my fingers dig into the wood trim.

First off—hell.

And secondly—no.

Paige may have missed the mark about being faster than me—*puhlease*—but she was right about one thing, shit did just get real. Really real. Too fucking real. No woman has ever reached into my empty chest to fill the cavity. It's always been to take.

I need to get out of here.

Finding the apartment empty, I breathe a sigh of relief. No matter what happens between Paige and me, she can't walk around naked again. That's a hard line I'm drawing in the sand right fucking now. Girlfriend or not, her body is a temple that should be worshipped, not paraded around for any idiot to accidentally peep.

And now I'm picturing paying my respects all over again even though I just asked her for space.

Fresh air. I need fresh air, away from the reason my head is twisted up to begin with.

Immediately, my dirt bike springs to mind. Riding has always been the quickest way to clear my thoughts and tonight I need more than paved roads, timed lights, and safety precautions.

I scribble out a quick note that basically says all common areas are officially banned to people not wearing proper clothing and slip it under Paige's door.

After a moment's hesitation, I put one under Marc's, too.

If there's one thing I learned from our old neighbor it's that feminism is exhausting.

But necessary.

Dude should cover up anyway. *Nobody wants to see that eight pack, bro.*

With that, I'm out the door and on my way to his dad's farm.

◆ ◆ ◆

My eyelids fluttering like a butterfly in a wind tunnel, I can't make out a single thing. Just bright. Very bright.

Jesus fuck. I was just riding my dirt bike and now…

"What is this?" I try to say but only garbled nonsense comes out. *What the hell?*

A sharp inhale somewhere nearby has me straining to see against the constant flurry of lashes until a form finally comes into view.

Who is...

Blonde. *Long* blonde hair. With what appears to be a motherfucking halo on top. But no, that can't be. She'd have horns.

I pause, letting my eyes rest for a bit, then try again, squinting with my heart beating out of my chest.

She's younger than I thought she'd be. Like a lot younger. Like my age maybe. And she doesn't look anything like I remember her.

Is this for real? Is she?

Am I? What's going on?

Am I dreaming?

My throat croaks again and she takes a hesitant step forward, the shine on her head dimming to show a much darker shade of blonde than I thought she'd have.

"Hey, it's okay. It'll be alright." The voice is all wrong though. Unfamiliar.

And just like the last time I heard that, I bristle. *Worst famous last words ever.*

Another feminine voice from close by that sounds slightly more familiar says, "Oh, she'll make sure of it. I just called and she's on her way."

What?

But...she's already here. Isn't she?

And why don't I feel relieved by that fact? Not like I thought I'd be. Not at all.

Where's the happiness? The gratitude? The filling of the deep void I've had for far too long? There's just...nothing.

I don't even *want* her here. Not anymore. She can't roll in now, after missing out on most of my life, just to catch the ending credits. Fuck that. And fuck her.

The edges around her starting to blur, I struggle to raise my suddenly heavy hand, breathing shallower and shallower just to lift it, but she doesn't rush forward like a concerned mother—what a joke—only widens her eyes when I stick my middle finger up but that's when I see them. Her eyes. And they're nothing like mine.

Who is she?

I don't get to ask because everything goes black.

◆ ◆ ◆

Why is it so cold? And what's that smell? It smells like disinfectant.

I'm met with damn near blinding white lights as soon as I crack my eyes open enough to see my surroundings.

Oh, shit. Not again.

The hospital. Or the emergency room to be exact. A place I'm all too familiar with, unfortunately.

"I thought you'd be out of this phase by now."

I stiffen at the hoarse voice at my side and looking over, I find my father perched on the edge of the seat next to my uncomfortable hospital bed. His hair, same shade as mine but cut much shorter, is ruffled like he's been holding his head in his hands. A tailored suit in dark tones matches his newly polished dress shoes proving he's very much the lawyer whether he's in the courtroom or not.

If only he could've fought for our family like he fights for all his cases.

I blink a few more times, looking around the room but not seeing her anymore.

Was it a dream?

"And what phase is that?"

"Don't give me that. How many times do we have to go through this for you to finally get it? The constant *accidents* that always result in you hurting yourself. You've been pushing boundaries further and further since the day she left, trying to see how far you can go before she comes to your rescue."

I flinch involuntarily. "Jesus, Dad. That's not what this was about."

He meets my stare with a raised eyebrow, a cocked head, and a *don't try me* attitude, saying, "Wasn't it?"

"No," I say with a boldness I try not to use with my only parent. Even if he was a disappointment, he stuck around. He was there when she wasn't.

A lawyer juggling a single father gig—it couldn't have been easy for him, especially during my more rebellious teen years. And he tried in his own detached sort of way so for that I cut him some slack. But today, that patience is all used up. I wasn't trying to get hurt. I know some of the previous injuries were made during sketchy situations but today was far from that. My mom wasn't even on my mind when I went sailing over that weird ass flat spot. The hill I scaled had a hidden lookout at the top, that probably holds one helluva view of Vega Farms. As soon as my tires touched down though I knew it was going to hurt. I didn't anticipate ending up in the hospital and now that I think about it, nothing even hurts. Why am I here? The last thing I remember was going ass over head over the top of my handlebars, then I woke up to him.

Or was it her?

I cast another look around the tight room, frowning.

She wasn't really here, was she?

"Then what happened this time, son?"

Fuck, why is he hounding me with the questions? It's not like I'm concussed. *Am I?*

"An accident, Dad! Can't it just be that simple?"

Also, how *did* I get here? Someone must've found me somehow but who goes all the way out there? It's nothing but open land, I thought. I went out there just before sunset, using the last bit of daylight to weave between trees stock full of apples almost ready to be picked, but ventured out past the orchard parameters, exploring some of the craggier outskirts. I had no idea someone might be out there at the same time.

But didn't I see something in the distance like a factory or a barn or something when I crested that sandy knoll?

"Was it?"

He's still on about this? The accident was just that, an accident. A stupid err of judgment. I shouldn't have been flying over unfamiliar terrain without at least a vague rundown of the area. Sailing up unknown inclines without knowing what was on the other side was dumb as fuck but it happens.

It happened.

I didn't go looking for a place to wipe out but I wasn't not looking either. I was taking things a few seconds at a time. Four seconds, actually.

Shit.

I shut my eyes, rubbing a hand over them and finding it strangely heavy, then replay everything from back at the apartment in my mind. The sex, the confessions, the subsequent fight.

That's what Paige had said to me—four seconds—and that's what was running through my head the entire time I was riding. I wasn't thinking about where I was going because I was worried about where I'd just been. With Paige.

And then without.

Because of my bullshit hang-ups.

Maybe my dad's right. Maybe it was about her after all. Maybe it was always about her. Maybe she still has a hold over me despite her letting go years ago.

But it *was* different this time. I didn't do it hoping she'd come back.

Maybe I did it hoping the one last time of her not showing up would be what sets me free for good. The final nail in the coffin to her plaguing presence.

A distraught female voice down the hall slices through the strained silence of my small room like a guillotine and my eyes fly open. Swinging them over to Dad, his entire body stiffens. Dude's gripping the chair's armrest so hard I wouldn't be surprised if it buckled from the pressure. Even though he's a lawyer, he still works out daily to keep his shit tight. I know he never had any issue finding dates after my mom took off but he never brought them around and I think the irony in that speaks for itself.

I wasn't the only one holding out for her.

As we hear my name said in a panicked tone, we both make a move but my dad pushes me back down. I stay frozen, not knowing the extent of my injury, but really, if she came to see me, if she loves me, she won't let him or anything else get in her way. I've seen news articles about moms lifting cars to get to their kids.

"Excuse me, ma'am, are you family?" a nurse, I assume, asks as I strain to hear how she'll answer.

Family doesn't desert each other. They don't fall off the face of the planet without a word for years. They stick it out. They give each other the benefit of the doubt, however many times it's needed. Like I should've with Paige, damn it, instead of accusing her without listening like she deserved. I treated her with the one thing I've spent my life trying to shake—indifference.

Fuck. I need to call her after this.

With my dad's back to me, I study his brawny frame as he takes a huge breath, readying himself to face whoever's on the other side of the privacy curtain.

At the same time I hear a confident "yes" in answer, a voice that sounds a lot like my girl's best friend speaks up, saying, "I called her. Let her in."

Didn't I hear that already? Was that Cynthia in here before? Then who else was with her? And who's outside?

My dad cautiously peels back the curtain to reveal a very different face than the one we were expecting as Paige comes barreling through the thick fabric, pushing my dad out of the way in her haste to get in. To get to me.

Our eyes collide and hold.

One.

A single tear brimming her eye falls, making my heart pinch.

Two.

Strong legs I know like the back of my hand bring her closer but not close enough.

Three.

"I love you," the sentiment spilling from her mouth as serious as the expression on her face. Simple words to some, powerful words to others, everything to me.

Four.

Equally anxious hands, both mine and hers, reach at the same time as we welcome each other back. Back into each other's embrace, back into each other's lives, back into each other's hearts.

Four fucking seconds for everything to become crystal clear. All of it.

I always thought that my mom would be the one to come to my rescue. That she'd swoop in and save the day, put me back together again. But now I realize I'd been waiting for the wrong person all along. It wasn't my mom at all. It was a foul-mouthed, sarcastic as all hell, sexy as sin biker chick with wild hair, hypnotizing eyes, and a hell of an insulated heart worth chipping away at.

Turns out the savior I'd been eagerly awaiting was the love of my life.

Four seconds, one kiss, and you should fucking know.

I raise my mouth to meet hers and I finally let her in. All the way in. For good.

EPILOGUE

Paige

THE SMILE ON MY FACE WOBBLES AS I TAKE IN THE scene around me. The four men surrounding me at the group of tables we're seated at are so busy in their banter with each other that they don't notice my emotions running on high. They've been that way all week but kicked up a notch seeing my brothers finally sitting all together for a meal again. And with our mom nearby.

Sunbrook's kitchen staff pushed a few tables together for our gathering on my day off. I thought it'd be good for everybody if we all visited Mom at the same time instead of individually. It might blow up in our faces or we might find our balance fully restored while leaning against each other like we used to. Either way, it's time. After watching each of my siblings come in for solo visits only to leave complete wrecks, I suggested trying it as a whole. Not just as pieces of our jumbled puzzle of a family, but as a united front. An unbreakable force that Mom will feel even if she can't show it. It's like Beckett said, I have to believe in my love for her but also her love for us. We know it's there even if we can't see it and that's what matters. She is what matters, to all of us.

She isn't getting any better though sadly. Her bouts of lucidity are less frequent these days even though I've had her meds adjusted and fully returned to her prescribed dosages. I'm getting ready to take over Vernon's position in a matter of months and I can't wait. I'll be on days, too, so I'll get more time with my mom—however long that may be—and more time with Beckett. Well, more nights with him. He does a pretty good job already with making our nearly opposite schedules work. He's in here so much, he's even got his own favorites. And surprise, surprise, he's *everybody's* favorite as well.

Deciding it's time to reintroduce ourselves, I walk over to invite our mom to join us, relaxing when she agrees.

Even though I know she's not the same person she was from my childhood and never will be again, the pain from that knowledge doesn't stop from piercing a hole in my heart just the same. I miss my mother with every molecule in my body. We all do.

An hour later the hurt I feel down to my marrow is mirrored back on each of my brothers' faces but it's not as debilitating. It's manageable. There's comfort in collective suffering. To know you're hurting is one thing, to see you're not the only one is another.

Tysen stands out of nowhere, pulling my attention away from my mother's untouched plate of food. She still isn't eating as much as she should be.

"What's up, boss?"

My gaze swings over my shoulder to see Beckett strolling across the cafeteria with a broad smile stretching his face and a...

Is that a baby?

Upon closer inspection, I realize it's a baby doll. A girl baby doll to be exact. With a mess of dark waves covering the face.

Ignoring my questioning stare, he leans down to peck my lips before shaking hands with Ty and nodding to my other brothers. Tysen now manages the second location of Pop The Hood. Him and Angela. Apparently, Coty worked out some kind of deal that made her a partner as well. One that she only agreed to under the condition that none of the guys had a say over her decisions anymore. They even held a family meeting and everything where Beckett threw every argument he could think of at her, all with a teasing smile plastered to his face. He's such a shithead.

And I love him so much.

They all figured it out and she now spends her time between both locations as does my boyfriend. He's in high demand.

I let my gaze fall over him, seeing he's not wearing one of his typical biker shirts but a crisp white tee pulled tight over those muscles I never get tired of exploring and jeans hung low on his tapered waist.

Very high demand.

A chill runs through the room, or just me maybe, and I pull my cardigan a little tighter against my front.

He must've dropped his coat off upfront on his way in. It's one of those cold April days today where the wind absolutely whips but that doesn't stop him from riding still.

Did he ride his Ninja here with that doll? How? And why?

He's freshly showered, too, even though I know he had work today. He was planning on only working a half day since he knew I'd be busy with my family for a few hours, otherwise he would've taken the day off, too. His busiest day and he takes it off regularly just to be with me. I try to go in with him from time to time but homework has been kicking my ass every which way lately. Especially this week it seems. I'm just so exhausted the second I even look at an assignment.

Eyes tracking him, he positions himself in the seat next to my mom, giving her a view of what's in his hands then he...plays with it. Legit plays with the baby doll. Like coos at it and tickles its plastic belly.

The boys all look to me with identical expressions but all I can do is nod. *Yes, my boyfriend has lost his mind.* What other possible explanation could there be for him pretending a fake baby is real and next to our mother of all places?

Despite Beckett blowing raspberries at a dolly and making me genuinely concerned for his mental health, my family feels complete in this moment. More than it has in years. Even with how happy I was to get all of us Christensens together, it still felt like a piece was missing. A piece of me.

But he's here now and that feeling is gone.

I glance around the table, at each face occupying it, and grin as my chest fills with solid warmth.

"Hey, Beckett? What are you doing?" I ask around a smirk.

My overly tall, yet boyishly handsome boyfriend just winks over at me before turning to my mom, telling her, "I came to eat lunch with my girl over there." Motioning his chin at me, I can only smile warmly when my mother meets my gaze. "Do you mind helping me out by taking over for a little bit?"

Before she can even fully answer, he places the baby doll in her arms, sits back down, and looks at her with a hopefulness I'm all too familiar with.

Shit.

Getting to my feet, Jesse puts his hand up to stop me and I drop back down.

Every single one of my brothers and I are fully captivated, rooted in our spots, witnessing our mother break into the first smile she's given all day. And it's directed at the tiny bundle she's now cuddling.

Helplessly mesmerized, we all watch on as she pushes the baby's crazy locks away from the face and beams down at the doll with pure delight.

"She is beautiful, isn't she?" Her glistening gaze lands back on Beckett before quickly returning to the baby.

Gently, Beckett says, "It's her eyes. They get me every time."

When I turn to him though, he's not looking anywhere near my mother, he's staring right at me.

A few blinks and a giggle, an actual fucking giggle, and my mom replies, "I can see why. She reminds me of my little girl. Not my boys though. Oh, they were good-looking, too, but nothing like her. She could quiet a room with those eyes."

My hand flies to my mouth as I hear one of the boys suck in their breath but I'm not sure which one because I can't tear my eyes away from our mother as she bounces the wad of blankets that harbors a memory none of us could evoke in our hour together.

Beckett encourages her to continue, his comforting voice

blending with hers to glaze over the cracks in our family, sealing them from the outside in, while helping us to latch onto the smallest of details from our past.

Other residents join in the excitement and soon there's a whole melee of long forgotten memories being shared. Whether they're real or not I'm not completely sure but it feels like actual progress. More than I've encountered since working at Sunbrook.

I glimpse several wet eyelashes around the room and know I'm not the only one thinking the same thing. Could this be a new form of therapy? Could it help long term?

Sneaky Hope creeps back in, wanting a spot at the table, too, and this time I let her for a change, instead of cursing her stubborn existence in my life.

"Why don't you hang on to that one for me?"

Too focused on the scene in front of me, I miss Beckett standing at my side until his hand falls on my shoulder, turning me to face him.

Keeping his eyes on mine, he says to my mother, "I've got my own to look forward to anyway."

He can't know. Not yet. I barely know.

Much quieter, he rasps out, "I read this article online about the happiness babies bring to Alzheimer's patients and how sometimes they can spark recognition when everything else fails. I thought it was worth a try today with all of you here." Gesturing to my brothers who have now tuned into our conversation as well, he continues, "I figured even if it didn't work, it'd still be good practice for me. For us."

Guiding me out of my seat, Beckett wraps his impossibly long arms around my back, gazing down at me through shimmery pools of his own.

New tears meet up with my earlier ones and they all fall down my face freely as his Adam's apple bobs a couple times.

"Funny thing is you can find a lot online if you know what to search for. Like symptoms your girlfriend is experiencing who just so happened to miss her period." A hiccup escapes my trembling lips. "You made my dreams come true the day you walked into my life and you've been chasing out the bad ever since, but I'd gladly live through nightmares for the rest of my life if you'll grant me another wish."

Somehow, through another round of sobs, I manage an incredulous laugh, asking, "What's that?"

Beckett drops to his knees, both knees, and clasps my hips tenderly, bringing his face in line with my newly occupied belly. "That our daughter will look just like you. Your hair, your eyes. I want a baby Dream running around our new home."

A hand in his hair, I tilt his head back, locked onto his blue eyes, misty like ocean spray on a sunny day.

As soon as the ground thawed enough to start construction on the property Beckett purchased near Coty and Angela, he got a crew out there to start work on the design Coty helped us sketch up for the house we'll be moving into later this year. I didn't think we'd be filling one of those spare rooms we spoke about this soon though. We've been careful. *Except when we weren't.*

"And if it's a boy?" I ask, my voice shaking as bad as my hands.

Yesterday, I snuck off to the doctor to confirm what the at-home test had already showed—that I was, in fact, pregnant. I was planning to tell him tonight but he beat me to it by doing what he always does, by paying attention. Only a few weeks along, there's no way for either of us to know what the gender is yet but that won't stop Beckett from trying to bend the situation to his every whim with his sheer determination alone.

"Even better." His lips pull into a smile and he stands, cupping the back of my head with a hand to plant a kiss to both corners of my mouth. "Then when his sister does come along he'll get to look out for her the way your brothers did for you," he nods over to my four brothers, "and he'll love her the same way my brothers chose to care about me." He nods over my shoulder and I turn my head to see Coty, Marc, and Angela standing in the doorway to the lunchroom and release a watery laugh. With smiles on their faces, they watch on just like the rest of my family. Our family.

Harmonic convergence.

Want more of the Creekwood Crew? Find bonus material along with links for playlists and inspiration boards on my website amarieauthor.com.

ACKNOWLEDGEMENTS

First of all, a huge thank you to you for taking a chance on me and reading Changing Lanes. As a reader myself, I know how many books there are to choose from and I'm truly grateful that you chose to spend some time with these characters that are so dear to my heart.

Next up, my three beautiful kids. (They're banned from reading this or any of my other romance novels until they're over thirty years old but I let them read this one and only paragraph.) You three are the epitome of what I wish I could be in life. You're supportive, you're understanding, and your unwavering courage inspires me to be brave enough to go after what I want every day. You never, ever make me feel bad for spending countless hours in fictional worlds with fictional characters that do not adhere to a 9-5 schedule. Thank you for letting me be me with only encouragement and positivity. I love you more than I could ever write in a paragraph. You know this. You hav my heart, forever and always.

To my hubby, thank you for loving this girl. The one that used to only bleed punchlines and smile the bandages to cover them but now has more to laugh for, more to love for, more to live for. Thank you for sticking it out with me while I figured that out and loving me through it all.

To my main girl Shanna C., you already know. But in case you don't, I love ya. Oh, how much I value you and your infinite help. You are a true gem and I'm so grateful we crossed paths. Forever and ever and ever, let's do this.

To Sarah P., my editor, you are a light. Really. I appreciate how you go about your business and how much you truly love what you do. It shows. Thank you for your endless help and insight.

Julie D., your eagle eye will be missed, truly. If I could have your attention to detail on all my books for all of eternity, I would, but for now, I'm incredibly grateful I got you on two. You've helped me grow so much in just that short amount of time and I'm so happy I experienced your expertise, even if for a moment. Thanks from the bottom of my heart.

Murphy Rae, I'm still pinching myself that I got you to design my covers. Your work is phenomenal and I'm honored to have the chance to showcase some of it on my books. Thank you!

Stacey B., thanks for making my books look a million times better than I ever could! Seriously, thank you.

Stephanie Rinaldi, dang girl, I should list what you don't help me with, that might be quicker. You are such an amazing person and I'm so glad I get to call you my friend. I appreciate every single bit of your support. Thank you for constantly being willing to give it to me.

Self-publishing a romance novel felt a little like showing up to the lunchroom on the first day of high school. You don't know where to sit but the empty spots suddenly being filled with backpacks as you walk by speak volumes. But so do the genuine authors that go out of their way to make room for you next to them. Thank you to the authors that have always made a spot for me at their tables. I really appreciate it and you.

To all of my insta-fam, the ones that have stuck it out with me and buckled in for the long haul—wherever I go, whatever I choose to do, you're down to go alongside me, support fully in place, and I love you for it. Thank you.

For all the bloggers, 'grammers, and readers that helped spread the word for this release—thank you so much! I continue to be blown away by the support you all have given an unknown like me.

To my Nantucket ladies, thank you. Always.

Huge thanks to Tara K for your nursing insights.

And lastly, thank you to Jo and Give Me Books Promotions.

Made in the USA
Middletown, DE
27 September 2023

39424990R10210